Praise for David M...

'Morrell expertly captures in prose th... ...cal divisions of Victorian society, bu... ...his social commentary with moments of high adventure.' *Kirkus*

'A feat of brilliant storytelling.' *Huffington Post*

'*Murder as a Fine Art* was fantastic, and *Inspector of the Dead* is even better . . . Morrell is darkly inventive with the murders and cleverly mines very real history . . . The author brings each character back to life, and they spring fully formed from the page . . . I dare you to put this down once you've picked it up!' *My Bookish Ways*

'A literary thriller that pushes the envelope of fear . . . Morrell's thorough and erudite research of the people and cultures of the British Empire's heyday informs every page.' *Associated Press*

'A riveting novel packed with edifying historical minutiae seamlessly inserted into a story narrated in part by De Quincey's daughter and partly in revealing, dialogue-rich prose.' *Booklist*

'The finest thriller writer living today, bar none.' Steve Berry

'An absolute master of the thriller, plays by his own rules and leaves you dazzled.' Dean Koontz

'Morrell's use of De Quincey's life is absolutely amazing. I literally couldn't put it down: I felt as though I was in Dickens as he described London's fog and in Collins when we entered Emily's diary . . . a triumph.' Robert Morrison, author of *The English Opium Eater*

'A masterpiece – I don't use that word lightly – a fantastic historical thriller, beautifully written, intricately plotted, and populated wit... ...n, a...

Also by David Morrell

Novels

Short Fiction

Illustrated Fiction

Nonfiction

Edited By

Inspector of the Dead

DAVID MORRELL

MULHOLLAND
BOOKS

HODDER

First published in Great Britain in 2015 by Mulholland Books
An imprint of Hodder & Stoughton
An Hachette UK company

First published in paperback in 2016

A CIP catalogue record for this title is available from the British Library

Paperback ISBN 978 1 444 78138 0
eBook ISBN 978 1 444 78136 6

Typeset by Hewer Text UK Ltd, Edinburgh
Printed and bound by Clays Ltd, St Ives plc

Hodder & Stoughton policy is to use papers that are natural, renewable
and recyclable products and made from wood grown in sustainable
forests. The logging and manufacturing processes are expected to
conform to the environmental regulations of the country of origin.

Hodder & Stoughton Ltd
Carmelite House
50 Victoria Embankment
London EC4Y 0DZ

www.hodder.co.uk

*To Grevel Lindop and Robert Morrison
for guiding my journey into all things Thomas De Quincey
and to historian Judith Flanders
for leading me along dark Victorian streets*

Contents

Contents

Introduction

We take strict laws controlling the sale of narcotics so much for granted that it comes as a surprise to learn that opium, from which heroin and morphine are derived, was legally available in the British Empire and the United States for much of the 1800s. Chemists, butchers, grocers, and even paper boys sold it. The liquid form was called laudanum, a mixture of powdered opium and alcohol (usually brandy). Almost every household owned a bottle in the same way that aspirin is common in medicine cabinets today. The only pain remedy available (apart from alcohol), opium was dispensed for headaches, menstrual cramps, upset stomach, hay fever, earaches, back spasms, baby colic, cancer, just about anything that could ail anybody.

Thomas De Quincey, one of the most notorious and brilliant authors of the nineteenth century, first experienced the drug when he was a young man suffering from a toothache. He described the euphoria he felt as an "abyss of divine enjoyment . . . a panacea for all human woes . . . the secret of happiness." For eight years, he used the substance occasionally, but by the time he was twenty-eight, he lapsed into lifelong dependency. The concept of physical and mental addiction was unknown in the 1800s. People considered opium abuse simply a habit that could be broken by anyone with character and discipline. Because De Quincey couldn't stop, he was condemned for his lack of self-control, even though the pains of attempted withdrawal left him "agitated, writhing, throbbing, palpitating, and shattered."

In 1821, when De Quincey was thirty-six, he released *Confessions of an English Opium-Eater* and sent a shock wave through England. The first book about drug dependency, it made him infamous for his candour at a time when many people shared his affliction but would never confess it because they feared the shame of exposing their private lives to public view. By then, the elixir effects of the drug had subsided, and De Quincey needed huge amounts merely to function. A tablespoon of laudanum might kill someone not accustomed to it, but at the height of his need, just to feel normal, De Quincey swallowed sixteen ounces a day while "munching opium pills out of a snuff box as another man might munch filberts," a friend said.

The drug caused De Quincey to endure epic nightmares that seemed to last a hundred years every night. Ghosts of loved ones visited him. Every hurt and loss of his life surfaced to haunt him, and because of these nightmares, De Quincey discovered a bottomless inner world, "chasms and sunless abysses, depths below depths." Seventy years before Freud, he developed theories about the subconscious that were similar to the future great psychoanalyst's *Interpretation of Dreams*. Indeed De Quincey invented the term "subconscious" and described deep chambers of the mind in which a "horrid alien nature" might conceal itself, unknown to outsiders and even to oneself.

De Quincey demonstrated yet another remarkable ability. He was an expert in murder.

In the murderer worthy to be called an artist, there rages some great storm of passion—jealousy, ambition, vengeance, hatred—which creates a hell within him.

—Thomas De Quincey
"On the Knocking at the Gate in *Macbeth*"

The Killing Zone

London, 1855

Except for excursions to a theatre or a gentlemen's club, most respectable inhabitants of the largest city on earth took care to be at home before the sun finished setting, which on this cold Saturday evening, the third of February, occurred at six minutes to five.

That time—synchronized with the clock at the Royal Greenwich Observatory—was displayed on a silver pocket watch that an expensively dressed, obviously distinguished gentleman examined beneath a hissing gas lamp. As harsh experiences had taught him, appearance meant everything. The vilest thoughts might lurk within someone, but the external semblance of respectability was all that mattered. For fifteen years now, he couldn't recall a time when rage had not consumed him, but he had never allowed anyone to suspect, enjoying the surprise of those upon whom he unleashed his fury.

Tonight, he stood at Constitution Hill and stared across the street toward the murky walls of Buckingham Palace. Lights glowed faintly behind curtains there. Given that the British government had collapsed four days earlier because of its shocking mismanagement of the Crimean War, Queen Victoria was no doubt engaged in urgent meetings with her Privy Council. A shadow passing at one of the windows might belong to her or perhaps to her husband, Prince

Albert. The gentleman wasn't certain which of them he hated more.

Approaching footsteps made him turn. A constable appeared, his helmet silhouetted against the fog. As the officer focused his lantern on the quality of clothing before him, the gentleman made himself look calm. His top hat, overcoat, and trousers were the finest. His beard—a disguise—would have attracted notice years earlier but was now fashionable. Even his black walking stick with its polished silver knob was the height of fashion.

"Good evening, sir. If you don't mind me saying, don't linger," the constable warned. "It doesn't do to be out alone in the dark, even in this neighborhood."

"Thank you, constable. I'll hurry along."

From his hiding place, the young man at last heard a target approaching. He'd almost given up, knowing that there was little chance that someone of means would venture alone onto this fog-bound street but knowing also that the fog was his only protection from the constable who passed here every twenty minutes.

Deciding that the footsteps didn't have the heavy, menacing impact that the constable's did, the young man prepared for the most desperate act of his life. He'd endured typhoons and fevers on three voyages back and forth from England to the Orient on a British East India Company ship, but they were nothing compared to what he now risked, the penalty for which was hanging. As his stomach growled from hunger, he prayed that its sound wouldn't betray him.

The footsteps came closer, a top hat coming into view. Despite his weakness, the young man stepped from behind a tree in Green Park. He gripped the wrought-iron fence, vaulted it, and landed in front of a gentleman whose dark beard was visible in the shrouded glow from a nearby street lamp.

The young man gestured with a club. "No need to draw you a picture, I presume, mate. Give me your purse, or it'll go nasty for you."

The gentleman studied his dirty, torn sailor's clothes.

"I said, your purse, mate," the young man ordered, listening for the sounds of the returning constable. "Be quick. I won't warn you again."

"The light isn't the best, but perhaps you can see my eyes. Look at them carefully."

"What I'll do is close them for you if you don't give me your purse."

"Do you see fear in them?"

"I will after *this*."

The young man lunged, swinging his club.

With astonishing speed, the gentleman pivoted sideways and struck with his cane, jolting the young man's wrist, knocking the club from it. With a second blow, he whacked the side of the young man's head, dropping him to the ground.

"Stay down unless you wish more of the same," the gentleman advised.

Suppressing a groan, the young man clutched his throbbing head.

"Before confronting someone, always look in his eyes. Determine if his resolve is greater than yours. Your age, please."

The polite tone so surprised the young man that he found himself answering, "Eighteen."

"What is your name?"

The young man hesitated, shivering from the cold.

"Say it. Your first name will be sufficient. It won't incriminate you."

"Ronnie."

"You mean 'Ronald.' If you wish to improve yourself, always use your formal name. Say it."

"Ronald."

"Despite the pain of my blows, you had the character not to cry out and alert the constable. Character deserves a reward. How long has it been since you've eaten, Ronald?"

"Two days."

"Your fast has now ended."

The gentleman dropped five coins onto the path. The faint glow from the nearby street lamp made it difficult for Ronald to identify them. Expecting pennies, he felt astonished when he discovered not pennies or even shillings but gold sovereigns. He stared at them in shock. One gold sovereign was more than most people earned in a week of hard labour, and here were *five* of them.

"Would you like to receive even more sovereigns, Ronald?"

He clawed at the coins. *"Yes."*

"Twenty-five Garner Street in Wapping." The address was in the blighted East End, as far from the majesty of Green Park as could be imagined. "Repeat it."

"Twenty-five Garner Street in Wapping."

"Be there at four tomorrow afternoon. Buy warm clothes. Nothing extravagant, nothing to draw attention. You are about to join a great cause, Ronald. But if you tell anyone about Twenty-five Garner Street, to use your expression it'll go nasty for you. Let's see if you do indeed have character or if you throw away the greatest opportunity you will ever receive."

Heavy footsteps approached.

"The constable. Go," the bearded gentleman warned. "Don't disappoint me, Ronald."

His stomach growling more painfully, astonished by his luck, Ronald clutched his five precious sovereigns and raced into the fog.

As the gentleman continued up Constitution Hill, his watch now showed eight minutes past five. The watches of his associates—also synchronized with the Greenwich Royal Observatory—would display the same time. Everything remained on schedule.

At Piccadilly, he turned right towards one of London's most respectable districts: Mayfair. He had waited what seemed an eternity for what he was about to enjoy. He had suffered unimaginably to prepare for it. Despite his fierce emotions, he kept a measured pace, determined not to blunt his satisfaction by hurrying.

Even in the fog, he had no trouble finding his way. This was a route that he had followed many times in his memory. It was the same route that he had taken fifteen years earlier when, as a desperate boy, he had raced to the right along Piccadilly, then to the left along Half Moon Street, then left again onto Curzon Street, this way and that, begging.

"Please, sir, I need your help!"

"Get away from me, you filthy vermin!"

The echoes of that hateful time reverberated in his memory as he came to the street known as Chesterfield Hill. He paused where a gas lamp showed an iron railing beyond which five stone steps led up to an oak door. The knocker had the shape of a heraldic lion's head.

The steps were freshly scrubbed. Noting a boot scraper built into the railing, he applied his soles to it so that he wouldn't leave evidence. He clutched his walking stick, opened the gate, and climbed the steps. The impact of the knocker echoed within the house.

He heard someone on the opposite side of the door. For a moment, his anticipation made it seem that the world outside the fog no longer existed, that he was in a closet of the universe, that time had stopped. As a hand freed a bolt and the door opened, he readied his cane with its silver knob.

A butler looked puzzled. "His Lordship isn't expecting visitors."

The gentleman struck with all his might, impacting the man's head, knocking him onto a marbled floor. Heartbeat thundering with satisfaction, he entered and shut the door. A few quick steps took him into a spacious hall.

A maid paused at the bottom of an ornate staircase, frowning, obviously puzzled about why the butler hadn't accompanied the visitor. In a rage, the gentleman swung the cane, feeling its knob crack the maid's skull. With a dying moan, she collapsed to the floor.

Without the disguise of his beard, the gentleman had been to this house on several occasions. He knew its layout and would need little time to eliminate the remaining servants. Then his satisfaction could begin as he devoted his attention to their masters. Clutching his cane, he proceeded with his great work.

Memories needed to be prodded.

Punishment needed to be inflicted.

2

The Curtained Pew

St. James's Church looked almost too humble to occupy the south-eastern boundary of wealthy Mayfair. Designed by Sir Christopher Wren, it gave no indication that the great architect was also responsible for the magnificence of St. Paul's Cathedral, so strong was the contrast. Narrow, only three storeys tall, St. James's was constructed of simple red brick. Its steeple had a clock, a brass ball, and a weather vane. That was the extent of its ornamentation.

As the bells announced the 11 a.m. Sunday service, a stream of carriages delivered the district's powerful worshippers. Because a special visitor was expected to relieve the war-gloom, St. James's filled rapidly. The morning's sunlight gleamed through numerous tall windows and radiated off white walls, illuminating the church's interior with glory. It was a dazzling effect for which St. James's was famous.

Among those entering the church, a group of four attracted attention. Not only were they strangers, but two men in the group were exceptionally tall, nearly six feet, noteworthy at a time when most men measured only about five feet seven inches. In contrast, the third man was unusually short: under five feet.

The group's clothes attracted attention also. The tall men wore shapeless everyday street garments, hardly what one expected among the frock coats in St. James's. The short man—much older than the other two—had at least made an attempt to dress for the occasion, but his frayed cuffs and shiny elbows indicated that he belonged in another district.

The fourth member of the group, an attractive young woman of perhaps twenty-one . . . what was the congregation to make of *her?* Instead of a fashionable, elaborate hooped dress with voluminous satin ruffles, she wore a loosely hanging skirt with female trousers under it, a style that newspapers derisively termed "bloomers." The outline and movement of her legs were plainly visible, causing heads to turn and whispers to spread throughout the church.

The whispers increased when one of the tall men removed what seemed to be a newsboy's cap and revealed bright red hair.

"Irish," several people murmured.

The other tall man had a scar on his chin, suggesting that his background wasn't much better.

Everyone expected the motley group to remain in the standing area at the back, where servants and other commoners worshipped. Instead, the attractive young woman in the bloomer skirt—her eyes a startling blue, her lustrous, light brown hair hanging in ringlets behind her bonnet—surprised everyone by approaching the chief pew-opener, Agnes Barrett.

Agnes was sixty years old, white-haired and spectacled. Over the decades, she had risen through the ranks of pew-openers until she was now the custodian of the most important keys. It was rumoured that the gratuities she received from pew renters had over the years amounted to an impressive three thousand pounds, well deserved because a good pew-opener knew how to be of service, polishing the pew's oak, dusting its benches, plumping its pillows, and so forth.

Puzzled, Agnes waited for the young woman in the disgraceful bloomer skirt to state her intention. Perhaps the poor thing was lost. Perhaps she intended to ask directions to a more appropriate church.

"Please show us to Lord Palmerston's pew," the young woman requested.

Agnes's mouth hung open. Had this strange creature said "Lord Palmerston's pew"? Agnes must have misheard. Lord Palmerston was one of the most influential politicians in the land.

"Pardon me?"

"Lord Palmerston's pew, if you please." The troubling visitor gave Agnes a note.

Agnes read it with increasing perplexity. Beyond doubt, the familiar handwriting was indeed Lord Palmerston's, and the message unquestionably gave these four odd-looking strangers permission to use his pew. But why on earth would His Lordship lower himself to do that?

Agnes tried not to seem flustered. She moved her troubled gaze towards the unusually short man whose eyes were as strikingly blue as the young woman's and whose hair was the same light brown. *Father and daughter,* Agnes concluded. The tiny man clutched his hands tensely and shifted his balance from one foot to the other, walking in place. On this cold February morning, his forehead glistened with sweat. Could he be sick?

"Follow me," Agnes reluctantly replied.

She walked along the central aisle, past pews in a configuration known as "boxed." Instead of rows that stretched from one aisle to another, these pews were divided into square compartments, eight feet by eight feet, with waist-high sides, backs, and fronts. They contained benches sufficient to accommodate a gentleman and his family. Many box pews resembled sitting areas in homes, with cushions on the benches and carpeting on the floor. Some even had tables on which to set top hats, gloves, and folded coats.

Lord Palmerston's pew was at the front, to the right of the centre aisle. For Agnes, the distance to it had never seemed so long. Although she kept her gaze straight ahead, she couldn't help sensing the attention that she and the astonishing group with her received. Approaching the white marble altar rail, she turned to face the congregation. Conscious of every gaze upon her, she selected a key from a ring she carried and unlocked the entrance to Lord Palmerston's pew.

"If His Lordship had notified me that he intended to have guests use his pew, I could have prepared it for you," Agnes explained. "The charcoal brazier hasn't been lit."

"Thank you," the young woman assured her, "but there's no need to give us heat. This is far more comfortable than we're accustomed to at our home church in Edinburgh. We can't afford to rent a pew there. We stand in the back."

So she's from Scotland, Agnes thought. *And one of the men is Irish. That explains a great deal.*

Lord Palmerston's box had three rows of benches with backs. The two tall men sat on the middle bench while the woman and her father occupied the front one. Even when he was seated, the little man's feet moved up and down.

With a forced nod of politeness, Agnes jangled her keys and proceeded to the back of the church, where a churchwarden shifted towards her, looking as puzzled as Agnes felt.

"You know who that little man is, don't you?" the churchwarden whispered, trying to contain his astonishment.

"I haven't the faintest. All I know is, his clothes need mending," Agnes replied.

"The Opium-Eater."

Again, Agnes was certain that she hadn't heard correctly. "The Opium-Eater? *Thomas De Quincey?*"

"In December, when all the murders happened, I saw a picture of him in the *Illustrated London News.* I was so curious that I went to one of the bookshops where the newspaper said he would sign books for anyone who bought them. An undignified way to earn a living, if you ask me."

"Don't tell me he was signing *the* book." Agnes lowered her voice, referring to the infamous *Confessions of an English Opium-Eater*.

"If his name was on it and someone was willing to buy it, he was ready to sign it. That scandalously dressed woman is his daughter. At the bookshop, whenever he tried to pull a bottle from his coat, she brought him a cup of tea to distract him."

"Mercy," Agnes said. "Do you suppose the bottle contained laudanum?"

"What else? He must have drunk five cups of tea while I watched him. Imagine how much laudanum he would have consumed if his daughter hadn't been there. I hope I don't need to emphasize that I didn't buy any of his books."

"No need at all. Who would want to read his wretched scribblings, let alone buy them? Thomas De Quincey, the Opium-Eater, in St. James's Church? Heaven help us."

"That's not the whole of it."

Agnes listened with greater shock.

"Those two men with the Opium-Eater. One of them is a Scotland Yard detective."

"Surely not."

"I recognize him from the constitutional I take every morning along Piccadilly. My route leads me past Lord Palmerston's mansion, where the younger man over there visits each day at nine. I heard a porter refer to him as 'detective sergeant.' "

"A detective sergeant? My word."

"I also heard the porter and the detective talk about another detective, who apparently was wounded during the murders in December. That other detective has been convalescing in Lord Palmerston's mansion. The Opium-Eater and his daughter stay there, also."

Agnes felt her cheeks turn pale. "What is this world coming to?"

But Agnes couldn't permit herself to be distracted. The

special visitor would soon arrive. Meanwhile, gentlemen gave her impatient looks, waiting for their pews to be unlocked. She clutched her ring of keys and approached the nearest frowning group, but as if the morning hadn't brought enough surprises, she suddenly saw Death walk through the front door.

The mid-Victorian way of death was severe. A grieving widow, children, and close relatives were expected to seclude themselves at home and wear mourning clothes for months—in the widow's case for at least a year and a day.

Thus Agnes gaped at what she now encountered. Astonished churchgoers stepped away from a stern, pinch-faced man whose frock coat, waistcoat, and trousers were as black as black could be. Because Queen Victoria and Prince Albert disapproved of men who wore other than black, gray, or dark blue clothing, it was difficult to look more sombre than the male attendees at St. James's, but the stranger made the glumly dressed men in the church look festive by comparison. In addition, he wore the blackest of gloves while he held a top hat with a mourning band and a black cloth hanging down the back.

A man whose clothing announced that extremity of grief was almost never seen in public, except at the funeral for the loved one he so keenly mourned. Dressed that way at a Sunday service, he attracted everyone's attention.

But he wasn't alone. He supported a frail woman whose stooped posture suggested that she was elderly. She wore garments intended to show the deepest of sorrow. Her dress was midnight crepe, the wrinkled surface of which could not reflect light. A black veil hung from the woman's black bonnet. With a black-gloved hand, she dabbed a black handkerchief under the veil.

"Please unlock Lady Cosgrove's pew," the solemn man told Agnes.

"Lady Cosgrove?" Agnes suddenly realized who this woman was. "My goodness, what happened?"

"Please," the man repeated.

"But Lady Cosgrove sent word that she wouldn't attend this morning's service. I haven't readied her pew."

"Lady Cosgrove has more grievous concerns than whether her pew has been dusted."

Without waiting for a reply, the man escorted the unsteady woman along the centre aisle. Again Agnes heard whispers and sensed that every pair of eyes was focused on her. She reached the front of the church and turned towards the right, passing the Opium-Eater and his strangely dressed companions in Lord Palmerston's pew. The little man continued to move his feet up and down.

The next pew at the front was Lady Cosgrove's. Situated along the right wall, it was the most elaborate in the church. Over the centuries, it had acquired a post at each corner and a canopy above them. Curtains were tied to the posts so that in the event of cold draughts, Lady Cosgrove's family could draw the curtains and be sheltered on three sides while facing the altar. Even on a warm day, the occupants had been known to draw the curtains, supposedly so that they could worship without feeling observed by the other parishioners when in actuality they were probably napping.

As Agnes unlocked the pew, Lady Cosgrove lowered her black handkerchief from beneath her black veil.

"Thank you," she told the pinch-featured man.

"Anything to be of assistance, Lady Cosgrove. I'm deeply sorry."

He gave her a black envelope.

Lady Cosgrove nodded gravely, entered the pew, and sank onto the first of three benches.

Hearing a discreet cough, Agnes noticed that the vicar stood in a doorway near the altar, ready to begin the service.

At once the church's organ began playing "The Son of God Goes Forth to War," the choir's voices reverberating off the arched ceiling. With a rumble, everyone stood. Followed by the funereal attendant, Agnes made her way to the back of the church, where she turned to ask about Lady Cosgrove's distress, but to her surprise, whichever way she looked, the sombre man was no longer visible.

Where on earth could he possibly have gone? Agnes wondered. What she did see, however, was the scarlet coat of the special visitor who waited in the vestibule, and with so much excitement, Agnes had difficulty calming the rush of her heart.

"The Son of God goes forth to war / A kingly crown to gain."

Amid the rising chords of the majestic hymn, the Reverend Samuel Hardesty made his way to the altar, bowed to it, and turned towards his congregation.

Proudly, he scanned his domain: the servants and commoners standing at the back, the wealthy and the noble seated in their pews. Any moment, the special visitor would appear. With a smile that he hoped hid his confusion, the vicar noticed four poorly dressed people, obviously not residents of Mayfair, who inexplicably occupied Lord Palmerston's pew.

To his farther left was Lady Cosgrove's pew. The vicar was shocked to see her wearing the blackest of bereavement garments. She unsealed a black envelope and read its contents through her veil. In despair, she rose, untied the curtain at the back of her pew, and pulled it across. She drew the other curtains forward.

Her grief now hidden from everyone except the vicar, she knelt at the front of her pew and rested her brow on its partition.

A glimpse of scarlet made the vicar swing his attention towards the back of the church.

The scarlet became larger, brighter. A fair-haired,

handsome man emerged from the crowd. He wore an army officer's uniform, its brass buttons gleaming. While his erect posture conveyed discipline and resolve, his elegant features were pensive, his intelligent eyes pained, suggesting that his resolve came at a price, the most obvious sign of which was his wounded right arm, which he supported in a sling. A beautiful young woman and her parents accompanied him.

This special visitor was Colonel Anthony Trask. All of London was abuzz about his bravery in the Crimean War—how he had single-handedly dispatched thirty of the enemy at the siege of Sevastopol. After emptying his musket, he had used his bayonet to lead a victorious charge up a blood-drenched slope. He had rallied weary troops and repelled a half-dozen enemy attacks, and if that wasn't extraordinary enough, he had saved the life of the queen's cousin, the Duke of Cambridge, when the enemy surrounded the duke's unit.

Upon his return to London, Queen Victoria had knighted Trask. *The Times* reported that when she addressed him with his new title as "Sir," the colonel had asked the queen to keep calling him by his military rank "in honour of all the valiant soldiers I fought with and especially those who died in this blasted war." When the queen blanched at so vulgar a word as "blasted," Trask had quickly added, "Forgive my language, Your Majesty. It's a habit from the years I spent building railways." Trask hadn't only physically built railways, but he and his father also owned them and made a fortune from them. Rich, handsome, a hero—privately, it was said, young noblemen hated his perfection.

As the hymn reverberated, the group reached the front of the church. After Agnes hurried to unlock the pew, Colonel Trask followed his beautiful companion and her parents inside.

The organ extended the hymn's final chord. St. James's fell into a noble silence.

The Reverend Samuel Hardesty smiled broadly. "My deepest welcome to everyone, with a more-than-special welcome to Colonel Trask. His heroism inspires us all."

Some parishioners raised their hands as if to applaud but then remembered where they were.

The vicar shifted his gaze to the left, towards Lady Cosgrove. "Whenever our burdens become too great, consider the hardships that our brave soldiers endure. If they can be strong, we can also."

Flanked by curtains, Lady Cosgrove remained kneeling with her forehead against the front of her pew.

"There is no calamity with which God tests us that we cannot bear. When we have the Lord on our side . . ."

A glimpse of scarlet made the vicar pause. But this time it wasn't the scarlet of Colonel Trask's uniform. Instead it was liquid on the floor in front of Lady Cosgrove's pew.

The vicar's hesitation caused a few puzzled whispers.

"Indeed, with the Lord on our side . . ."

The scarlet liquid was spreading. Its source was the bottom of the entrance to Lady Cosgrove's pew. *Had Her Ladyship spilled something?* the vicar wondered. *Might she have brought a container of medicine that she had accidentally dropped?*

Lady Cosgrove shifted, inexplicably moving in two directions.

Her black-veiled face tilted upward while the remainder of her body slid downward.

"My God!" the vicar exclaimed.

Up and back went Lady Cosgrove's head, and now the vicar saw her mouth, but the mouth became wider and deeper—and great heaven, that wasn't Lady Cosgrove's mouth. No mouth was ever that wide and red.

Her throat was gashed from ear to ear, and her veiled face was now angled so far back that it stared impossibly towards the ceiling while the rest of her kept sinking.

"No!"

The vicar lurched from the altar. Pointing in a frenzy, he saw that the scarlet pool was spreading even wider.

The gaping slit in Lady Cosgrove's throat grew wider also, deepening as her head tilted farther back, threatening to fall from her body.

The Reverend Samuel Hardesty screamed.

From the Journal of Emily De Quincey

After last night's fog, a strong breeze cleared this morning's sky. The only thing brighter than the sun was Lord Palmerston's eager smile as he greeted us for what he clearly hoped would be the last time.

Glad to be rid of us, one of the most powerful politicians in England shook our hands heartily as we reached the ground floor of his mansion. Despite the war crisis that had caused the government to collapse, Lord Palmerston's voice was enthusiastic.

"Pressing national matters prevent me from being here when you return from church." His aged eyes were bright next to his brown-dyed sideburns. "But be assured that your bags will be waiting for you, and my coach will most certainly be ready to transport you to the railway station."

Following the murders in December, it had been Lord Palmerston's idea for Father and me to stay in the top-floor servants' quarters of his mansion while we recovered. He had also insisted that Inspector Ryan stay there while his wounds healed. None of us was deluded into believing that His Lordship's motive was selfless. A former war secretary and foreign secretary, he was now home secretary, the supervisor of almost everything that took place in England, particularly matters of national security and the police. I sensed his worry that, during our investigation, we might have learned secrets that could compromise him. He found frequent opportunities to ask seemingly innocent questions, the answers to which might reveal whether we knew things we shouldn't.

But the answers failed to enlighten him, and after seven weeks, I cannot blame him for urging us, in the politest way, to leave. Indeed I'm surprised that he tolerated us as long as he did, or rather that he tolerated Father, whose incessant pacing as a way of controlling his laudanum intake clearly aggravated His Lordship's nerves.

A few nights ago, as St. James's bell tolled three, I went down to the ballroom to collect Father where he marched back and forth, his footsteps echoing throughout the dark mansion.

Pausing just outside the ballroom's entrance, I saw Lord Palmerston—in a robe, with a three-flamed candelabrum in one hand—confronting Father.

"Good God, man, doesn't the opium make you sleepy?"

"On the contrary. According to Brunonian medicine—"

"Brunonian medicine? What the devil is that?"

"John Brown developed his Brunonian system at Edinburgh University. When you studied there, My Lord, perhaps you heard of his *Elementa Medicinae*."

"I heard nothing about Brunonianism whatsoever."

"It maintains that physicians invent ways to make medicine seem complicated in order to delude ordinary people into believing that physicians are more learned than they truly are."

"Not only physicians but also lawyers and politicians inflate themselves. Finally you make sense," Lord Palmerston said.

Observing from the dark hallway outside the ballroom, I flinched when I felt someone next to me. Turning quickly, I discovered that Lady Palmerston had joined me. The light from Lord Palmerston's candelabrum reached just far enough for me to see her wrinkled, troubled features under her nightcap. I expected her to scowl at me for eavesdropping. But in fact, her look indicated that she worried about His Lordship's pensive late hours as much as I worried about Father's.

We exchanged nods and turned towards the conversation in the ballroom.

"My Lord, the Brunonian system concludes that illness comes from a lack of stimulation or else too much of it. When these polarities are in balance, good health is the consequence," Father said.

"At the moment . . ." Lord Palmerston sounded exhausted as he set the candelabrum on a table, then continued, "I suffer from too much stimulation."

"Because of the war and the collapse of the government, My Lord? Your responsibilities must be considerable."

"Talking about the war gives me a headache. Please answer me. Some people die from a spoonful of laudanum, but you drink ounces of it, and you're not only walking around—you never stop walking. Why doesn't the opium make you tired?"

"The Brunonian system considers opium to be a stimulant, My Lord. It's the most powerful of all the agents that support life and restore health."

"Ha."

"That is the truth, My Lord. When I was a university student and first swallowed laudanum to remedy illness, the increase in my energy was palpable. I suddenly had the strength to wander the city for miles on end. In markets and on crowded streets, I heard the details of countless conversations all around me. When I went to concerts, I heard notes between notes and soared with unimagined crests in the melodies. The reason I pace is to reduce opium's stimulation to a beneficial level."

"What I'd like to reduce is this confounding headache."

In the shadows outside the ballroom, Lady Palmerston clutched my arm.

"If I may suggest . . ." Father pulled his laudanum bottle from his coat pocket. "This will relieve your headache."

"The queen dislikes me so much, she'd be only too happy if she learned that I drank opium with you."

"One sip will not create a habit, My Lord. But if you won't accept the benefit of laudanum, I recommend that you walk with me. At best, the activity will balance your nervous congestion. At worst, it will make you sleepy."

"That would be a blessing."

In the shadows outside the ballroom, Lady Palmerston and I watched the two elderly men pace. They started at the same time, but despite Father's short legs, he soon outdistanced the home secretary. They looked incongruous, Father's diminutive figure as opposed to Lord Palmerston's tall bearing and powerful chest.

"You're speedy for an old man," Lord Palmerston said grudgingly.

"Thank you, My Lord." Father didn't point out that, at seventy, Lord Palmerston was one year older than Father. "I try to walk at least twenty miles each day. Last summer, I managed sixteen hundred miles."

"Sixteen hundred miles." Lord Palmerston sounded exhausted just repeating the number.

Father was the first to reach the opposite side of the ballroom and turn.

"*The Times* has invented a new creature of the press: a war correspondent," Lord Palmerston murmured.

"Yes, I'm familiar with William Russell's dispatches from the Crimea," Father said.

"Russell does not tell the truth about the war."

"It isn't going as badly as he describes? Expose his lies, My Lord."

"I wish they were lies. Because of incompetence, the war is going even worse than Russell claims. More soldiers are dying from disease and starvation than from enemy bullets. Who could have imagined? A journalist with the power to create such a clamour that he toppled the government. Oh, dear. My head."

The next morning, Lord Palmerston behaved as if the conversation, with its suggestion of a budding friendship, had not occurred. In fact, he spoke more gruffly than usual, perhaps embarrassed at having revealed weakness. It became obvious that Father and I needed to leave, even if that meant confronting our numerous debt collectors in Edinburgh.

Meanwhile, Inspector Ryan (whom I call Sean in private) had recovered from his wounds sufficiently to accompany us to church. Newly promoted Detective Sergeant Becker (I call him Joseph) joined us also. When I had first met them seven weeks earlier, their suspicion that Father was a murderer naturally made me hostile to them. But after the four of us joined forces against the danger facing not only us but London itself, I discovered a growing fondness for both of them, although in a different way for each.

At twenty-five, Joseph is only four years older than I. Our youth naturally creates a bond between us, and I confess that his features are appealing. In contrast, Sean—at forty—is almost two decades older than I. Normally, that might have created a distance, but there is something about Sean's confidence and experience that appeals to me. I sensed a subtle competition between them, but none of us felt at liberty to speak about any of this and weren't ever likely to, given that this was to be the last Sunday morning that we spent together, appropriately at church services, where we intended to give thanks for our lives and our friendship.

*　　*　　*

The Reverend Samuel Hardesty kept screaming. Among the congregation, whispers became murmurs. Had the vicar taken leave of his senses? Why in heaven was he pointing towards Lady Cosgrove's pew?

Adding to the shock, one of the shabbily dressed men in Lord Palmerston's pew vaulted from it and rushed towards where the vicar pointed.

A woman's screams joined those of the vicar. So did another's. At the front, Colonel Trask opened his pew. With his left hand supporting the sling on his right arm, he stepped out to determine the source of the commotion. The sight of the hero's scarlet uniform prompted other gentlemen to decide that they too could investigate.

"God save us!" one of them shouted.

"Blood! There's blood all over the floor!" another exclaimed.

Amid further outcries, the congregation hurried in two directions, towards the front to discover what was happening or else towards the escape of the rear doors. Nobleman crashed against nobleman, lady against lady. Agnes, the pew-opener, was nearly trampled until a churchwarden pulled her to the side.

"Blood!"

"Get out of my way!"

As the vicar lurched towards Lady Cosgrove, his vestment caught under one of his boots, toppling him. The shabbily dressed man who'd leaped from Lord Palmerston's pew grabbed him just in time, pulling him upright before he would have fallen into the crimson liquid spreading across the floor.

Now the second shabbily dressed man unlatched the entrance to Lord Palmerston's pew and blocked some of those charging forward. He held up a badge, shouting, "I'm a Scotland Yard detective inspector! Calm yourselves! Return to your seats!"

A Scotland Yard detective? The congregation reacted with greater shock. *Here in our midst? In Mayfair? In St. James's?*

The panic intensified.

"You're blocking my path!" a gentleman warned another, threatening with his cane.

"Stop!" the inspector yelled, holding his badge higher. "Go back to your pews! Restrain yourselves before someone gets hurt!"

"Before someone *else* gets hurt!" a lord insisted, telling another lord, "Step out of my way!"

Colonel Trask returned to his pew and climbed onto a bench. Tall to begin with, he now towered above the congregation.

"Listen to me!" he shouted with the commanding tone that only a man who built railways and an officer who'd just returned from the hell of the Crimea could project. "You! And that also means *you*, sir! All of you! Do what the inspector requests and return to your pews!"

The commotion persisted.

"Blast it all!" Colonel Trask yelled.

That caught their attention. It was as close to an obscenity as anyone had ever heard in St. James's.

"Bloody hell, do what you're told!"

The shock of *those* words struck everyone motionless. Some noble ladies had perhaps never heard those words in their lives. Mouths opened. Eyes widened. A woman collapsed.

"The sooner we establish order, the sooner we'll have answers! Don't you wish to know what happened here?"

The appeal to their curiosity, along with the impact of Colonel Trask's language, persuaded them to ease into their pews.

As tall as the colonel, the inspector followed his example and stepped onto a bench. His Irish red hair attracted as much attention as his badge.

"My name is Inspector Ryan! The man talking to the vicar is Detective Sergeant Becker!"

Another detective!

Ryan's raised voice betrayed a hint of pain. His left hand pressed against his abdomen, appearing to subdue an injury. "Stay where you are! We need to speak to each of you, in case you noticed anything that will help us!"

Becker steadied the vicar, then pivoted towards the pool of crimson in front of the curtained pew. Its source was the bottom of the pew's gate. Avoiding the blood, Becker returned to Lord Palmerston's pew and again vaulted the partition. Iron rings scraped against a rail as he pulled the curtain aside and peered into the next compartment.

With so many people staring at him, Becker strained not to show a reaction. After the events of seven weeks earlier, he'd assumed that he wasn't capable of further shock.

The black-clad woman he'd seen enter the pew was sprawled on the floor. Or rather, the woman had once been clad in black. Now her garments were soaked with the crimson that pooled around them. Her right hand clutched a black-bordered note. It and a black envelope were stained with blood also. Her head was tilted so far back that her veiled face peered almost behind her. Her throat had been slit so deeply that Becker could see the bones at the back of her neck.

After five years as a uniformed policeman, he almost reached for the clacker that would normally have hung on his equipment belt. He was prepared to unfold its wooden blade, run from the church, and swing it. The base of the rotating blade would repeatedly hit a flap in the handle, causing a noise loud enough that constables would hear it from as far away as a quarter mile.

But of course, he no longer had a clacker or an equipment belt. He was a detective sergeant now, wearing street clothes, and it was his duty to take charge as much as to summon help.

Feeling a presence next to him, he turned towards the vicar, who had entered Lord Palmerston's pew and whose cheeks lost their colour when he saw what lay beyond the partition.

The vicar's knees bent. Becker grabbed him, easing him onto one of the benches.

Someone else stood next to Becker: De Quincey. The little man rose on his tiptoes to peer over the partition. The grotesquely sprawled corpse, the quantity of blood—these horrors seemed to have no effect on him, except to intensify his gaze.

"Are you all right?" Becker asked.

The Opium-Eater's blue eyes were so focused on the body that he didn't reply. For the first time that morning, he wasn't fidgeting.

"I don't know why I asked. When it comes to something like this, of course you're all right," Becker concluded.

He turned towards Emily, who remained seated, watching her father. "And *you*, Emily? Are *you* all right?"

"What's over there?"

"The woman in black."

"Dead?" Emily asked.

"Yes."

"Did she perhaps fall and strike her head? Perhaps an accident?"

"I expect it's more than that."

Someone other than Emily would have blurted further questions—*She was murdered? How? Why is there so much blood? Are we all going to be killed?*—but Emily merely absorbed the implications of Becker's statement and nodded resolutely.

"Do what your responsibilities require, Joseph. There's no need to concern yourself with Father and me."

"Yes, seven weeks ago you more than proved that you're steady," Becker said.

At that moment, Inspector Ryan came along the front of the pew and stopped before the blood.

Colonel Trask followed. Seeing Emily, he frowned as if

something about her troubled him. Emily couldn't help being puzzled. The colonel's expression suggested that he had seen her somewhere before, but she had no idea when that could possibly have happened.

Immediately Trask turned towards the woman's pew. He was tall enough to look inside without stepping in the pool, and what he saw made his cheek muscles tighten, presumably with surprise but not with shock. In the war, he had no doubt seen too many examples of violent death to be shocked.

He stood straighter. "Inspector, how can I help?"

"We need to keep people away from this area," Ryan told him. "If they come near, someone will inevitably step in the blood. We won't be able to tell which marks were caused by the crowd and which by the killer."

"I guarantee that won't happen."

The colonel assumed a protective stance in front of the blood.

"Becker." Ryan turned.

"I don't understand," the younger man said. "How did the killer get into the pew without being seen? How did he escape?"

Ryan sounded equally baffled. "Yes, there's so much blood, the killer would have been spattered with it. Even in the commotion, he couldn't possibly have left the church without being noticed." A sudden thought made Ryan pause. "Unless he didn't escape."

"You think the killer's still in the church, hiding somewhere?" Becker looked around sharply.

"Bring constables," Ryan told him. "As many as possible."

As Becker hurried along the centre aisle, he saw a blur of terrified faces. He told a churchwarden, "Make a list of everyone who left! Lock the doors behind me! Don't let anyone else go out!"

★   ★   ★

Hearing Becker race from the church, Ryan focused on the vicar.

The man was seated in Lord Palmerston's pew, bent forward, his head between his knees.

Emily sat next to him, a comforting hand on his shoulder. "That's right. Keep your head down. Take slow, deep breaths."

"Vicar, are you able to answer a few questions?" Ryan asked. "The woman in the pew next to us—I heard the gentleman who escorted her refer to her as Lady Cosgrove."

"Yes, that is her name."

"I know a *Lord* Cosgrove. He directs the committee that oversees the prison system."

"That's her husband," the vicar said.

"Why is she dressed in mourning? Did Lord Cosgrove die?"

"I saw him only yesterday—in the best of health." The vicar's voice sounded muffled from keeping his head down. "I was extremely confused when I saw Lady Cosgrove dressed this way this morning."

"Did you see her attacker?" Ryan asked.

"I saw no one else in the pew." The vicar shuddered. "She was kneeling with her forehead on the front partition. Then I noticed the blood spreading across the floor. Then her body slid down. Her head tilted backward. God save us. How could it possibly have happened?"

"Take another slow, deep breath," Emily advised.

Ryan walked to the partition between Lord Palmerston's pew and Lady Cosgrove's.

De Quincey remained there, continuing to stare over the partition towards the corpse.

"Did you hear what he said?" Ryan asked.

The little man nodded thoughtfully.

"The attacker must have been hiding beneath a bench at

the rear of the pew," Ryan said. "Then the vicar was distracted by the procession."

"Perhaps," De Quincey told him.

"There's no other way." Ryan kept his voice low to prevent being overheard. "The killer would have attracted attention if he'd parted the curtains to enter the pew from the back or the sides. Our vantage point was such that we ourselves would have seen him climb over the front. In any of those cases, Lady Cosgrove couldn't have helped noticing him. She'd have cried out in alarm. The only way the killer could have done this is if he crept towards her after he'd hidden beneath a bench at the back of her pew. While he struck, the procession and the music distracted everyone."

"Perhaps," De Quincey repeated.

"Why do you keep talking like that? Do you see a flaw in my logic?"

"Lady Cosgrove's veil is intact."

"Of course. To guarantee a fatal blow, the killer needed to pull her chin up in order to raise the veil and expose her throat," Ryan explained.

"But those several motions might have given Lady Cosgrove time to struggle and scream," De Quincey concluded. "Also, the violence of those several motions might have attracted the vicar's attention in spite of the other distractions."

"In fact, they did not, however," Ryan emphasized.

"It was a puzzling risk for someone who otherwise planned carefully. In addition, we're making a great assumption," De Quincey said.

"Assumption?"

"Please remember Immanuel Kant, Inspector."

"Immanuel . . .? Don't tell me you're going to talk about *him* again."

"The great philosopher's question proved of immeasurable help seven weeks ago. Does reality exist outside us—"

"—or only in our minds? That question will drive *me* out of *my* mind."

"We heard this woman's escort address her as Lady Cosgrove," De Quincey noted.

"Yes."

"We saw her admitted to Lady Cosgrove's pew. The vicar referred to her as Lady Cosgrove," De Quincey added.

"Yes, yes," Ryan said impatiently.

"But as we discussed, she's wearing a veil."

When Ryan understood, he muttered an indistinct word that might have been an expression seldom heard in church.

"How do we know that this woman is in fact Lady Cosgrove?" De Quincey asked.

Ryan turned. "Vicar, how often do you see Lady Cosgrove?"

"Frequently. Yesterday she invited me for tea."

"Thank you. Colonel Trask, may I request a favour?"

Ryan left the pew and approached the colonel. He spoke softly. "I need you to do something that only a hero can accomplish."

"The men who died in combat next to me are the heroes," Trask said.

"I understand, but as Mr. De Quincey often reminds me, reality is different for different people."

"I miss your point."

"For the moment, would you allow the vicar to see you as a hero?"

Puzzled, the colonel replied, "What do you need me to do?"

When Ryan explained, Trask's features became solemn. "Yes, and that will require *the vicar* to be a hero."

They returned to Lord Palmerston's pew.

"Vicar," Colonel Trask said, "please look at me."

The vicar raised his head from his knees. His face was grey.

"I'm going to tell you something that I never revealed to anyone," Colonel Trask said.

The wrinkles in the vicar's forehead deepened.

"During the war, when the enemy charged, I was so terrified that my legs shook. I almost dropped to the mud and hid beneath corpses."

The vicar blinked. "It's difficult to believe that a man such as you could be afraid."

"We want to hide. Even so, we need to do what's required. Can *you* do what's required, Vicar?"

"I'm not sure what you mean."

"In a few moments, I'm going to ask you to look over that partition."

"But Lady Cosgrove is there," the vicar objected.

"Indeed. You'll soon know what I need from you," Colonel Trask said. "Can *you* do what's necessary? Will you be a hero for me?"

The vicar hesitated, then nodded.

"No matter the effort, for every monster, men such as the vicar and the colonel must strike the balance," De Quincey murmured.

"Especially the vicar," Colonel Trask said. He turned towards Ryan. "Whenever you're ready, Inspector."

Ryan drew a breath and lifted his right trouser cuff. The congregation inhaled audibly when he removed a knife from a scabbard that was buckled against his leg. Sunlight through the windows glistened off the blade.

Ryan whispered to Colonel Trask, "The killer might be hiding under one of the benches in Lady Cosgrove's pew."

"If he is, I promise you, Inspector—despite my injured arm, he won't get far should he try to run."

"It's good to have you here, Colonel."

Under other circumstances, Ryan might have hesitated, but with the colonel watching, he mustered his resolve and climbed onto a bench. Stretching his long legs over the partition, he stepped onto the first bench in Lady Cosgrove's pew.

The bench had a back that prevented him from seeing under the second and third benches. Even crouching, all he saw were shadows. Breathing rapidly, ready with his knife, he lowered his barely healed stomach to the first bench. He tried not to think about what might confront him as he leaned his head down and peered under the first bench, seeing beneath the other two benches.

No one was under there. Feeling the thump of his heart against the bench, he looked up towards Colonel Trask and De Quincey, shaking his head from side to side, indicating that the area was clear.

"Vicar, please stand," the colonel requested.

Determined not to interfere with the murder area by stepping into the blood, Ryan remained flat on the bench and extended his arm. The blood's coppery odour almost overwhelmed him as he reached the tip of his knife towards the veil that covered the dead woman's face. Feeling his scars stretch, he strained his arm to its limit, snagged the bottom of the veil, and tugged it away, exposing the corpse's features.

"Vicar, is that Lady Cosgrove?" Colonel Trask enquired.

"God preserve her soul, yes."

Ryan heard a thump and assumed that the vicar had collapsed.

"Lean against me," Emily was saying.

Forced to keep his head down near the blood, Ryan shifted his knife towards the note in the corpse's fingers and managed to free it. After transferring the note to his other hand, he speared the envelope on the floor, much of its paper now soaked with blood.

He rose from the bench and studied the envelope. Not only was its original colour black—so was the wax that had sealed it. The note had a one-inch black border that was used to express only the severest grief.

Wondering what dreadful news Lady Cosgrove had

received before she was murdered, Ryan opened the crum-
pled note.

He discovered only two words.

In shock, he focused on them, recognizing their terrifying
significance. Furious memories rushed through him.

Of fifteen years earlier.

Of shouts and panic and gunfire.

Of chaos and the unthinkable.

He jerked his head up, startled by fierce pounding on the
church's main door.

3

The House of Death

In 1855, the concept of preserving a crime scene had existed for only a few decades. Disciplined investigation of a crime depends on organization, but not until 1829 had London's police force been created, the first citywide unit of its kind in all of England. Its principles were formulated by two commissioners, one of whom was a retired military commander, Colonel Charles Rowan, while the other was a barrister experienced in criminal law, Richard Mayne. Rowan's military background was essential in the short term, modelling the police force on the regulations and ranks of the army. But over the years Mayne's legal expertise made the difference.

Mayne understood that it was one thing to arrest someone for supposedly having committed a crime. It was quite another to prove guilt in a court of law. He taught officers that evidence was as important as an arrest. A thorough search of a crime scene, interviews with everyone in the area, the collection and cataloguing of possibly incriminating objects—these methods were revolutionary.

Mayne insisted on detailed records for anybody who was arrested: height, weight, colour of hair and eyes, scars, aliases, a handwriting sample if that person could write, anything that might be useful in linking someone to a crime and proving it in court. He established a system of what he called "route papers," in which the details of unsolved crimes in one district were communicated each morning to every other police district in the city.

"Evidence," Mayne insisted. "That's how you capture criminals and put them in prison. Every criminal leaves a trail. Look for it. Follow it. I want details."

The pounding on the church's door persisted.

"It's Detective Sergeant Becker!" a voice yelled from outside. "Open up!"

"Let him in!" Ryan shouted.

He returned his knife to its scabbard under his trouser leg. He shoved the envelope and its dismaying two-word note into a coat pocket, then hurried over the partition into Lord Palmerston's pew.

Colonel Trask stepped towards him. "Your face . . . What did you read in the note?"

Ryan pretended not to hear him. Ignoring the pain in his recently healed abdomen, he veered around De Quincey and the others. As he rushed along the aisle, he saw a church-warden unlocking the door.

When Becker hurried inside, his face glistened from the effort with which he'd summoned the dozen constables behind him.

"More men are on the way."

"Good. We need all of them and plenty of others," Ryan said.

A dozen constables were indeed not sufficient. Nor were a second dozen—and a further dozen after that. Everyone in the church—not to mention those who'd fled amid the cries of "Blood!"—needed to be questioned. Each area of St. James's needed to be searched: its vestry, its offices, its bell tower, under every bench, behind the organ in the choir loft, *everywhere*. All the worshippers needed to be identified to make certain that they belonged there. Each garment needed to be checked for blood.

Ryan sought out Agnes, the chief pew-opener. "The man who escorted Lady Cosgrove, do you know his name?"

"I never saw him before."

Ryan asked the churchwardens and the other pew-openers, "Did you recognize the man who was with Lady Cosgrove?"

"A face that sour—I'd remember it," one of them said.

"He was never in *this* church before, I can tell you," someone else added.

Constables went from box pew to box pew, interviewing the congregation. The waist-high compartments provided the illusion of privacy, even though the conversations rumbled throughout the church.

"I'm expected at my uncle's home in Belgravia for two o'clock dinner. Surely you don't expect me to stay here while you . . ."

"Part my coat? Unbutton my waistcoat? Constable, if I didn't know better, I'd say you intended to search me. I belong to the same club that Police Commissioner Mayne does, and if you wish to continue being a . . ."

"What did I notice? That unspeakably dressed woman with trousers under her skirt, and those two poorly dressed men whom I now discover are police detectives, and that little man over there with the frayed cuffs who, I've been told, is the Opium-Eater. Here in St. James's! *That's* what I noticed! The Opium-Eater is the one you should question!"

As Ryan walked up and down the aisles, listening to the conversations, similar details were repeated again and again with the same impatience about being questioned and the same indignation about being detained.

The reaction to being questioned was by no means a sign of callousness. The rich and powerful inhabitants of Mayfair were indeed shocked by Lady Cosgrove's murder, which was even more alarming because it had happened in St. James's. But London's upper class felt an intense suspicion about intrusion into their personal affairs. Respectable people didn't commit violent crimes. That was a lower-class phenomenon. If commoners attacked one another in taverns or lurked in alleyways to stab passers-by for their purses, how did that concern the inhabitants of Mayfair? Surely these labourers who called themselves constables—for the police were members of the working class—didn't actually believe that anyone who belonged to St. James's could have been responsible for Lady Cosgrove's murder. A rapid search of the streets would soon reveal someone who didn't belong in Mayfair. That's how the police should be spending their time, not preventing decent people from travelling to their country houses or visiting family members at Sunday dinners that had been scheduled weeks earlier.

Ignoring these complaints, Ryan glanced towards the church's entrance, where an unshaven man in rumpled clothes appeared, carrying a satchel.

The man nodded to Ryan and approached through all the activity.

"Perhaps you're up and about too soon," the man said, a trace of alcohol wafting from his breath. "The way your hand's pressed against your stomach."

"Just a stitch in my side," Ryan told him.

"Literally several stitches to hold you together. Maybe you should sit down."

"In a while."

"I know I ought to attend Sunday church more often, but I never expected to go to church for *this* reason." The man held up his satchel. "The constable you sent told me some of the details. I assume you want plenty of sketches, just like the last time."

"Not exactly like the last time," Ryan informed him.

"What do you mean?"

Another man joined them. His overcoat hung open, revealing that he didn't wear a waistcoat, a condition of semi-dress hardly ever seen in Mayfair. Pale, he carried a tripod under one arm and a large equipment case in each hand, burdens that seemed almost too much for his thin frame.

"Thanks for coming," Ryan told him.

"Where do you want me?"

"At the front. I need photographs from several angles. Don't step in the blood."

"Blood?"

"This'll be harsh to look at, but at least you won't need to worry that the person you're photographing will move and blur the result," Ryan explained.

"I've photographed dead people before. Families of the deceased hire me."

"Then half of this won't be unusual for you. If this succeeds, I guarantee steady employment."

"I can use it."

As the man carried his equipment up the aisle, the sketch artist objected. "You're putting me out of business by hiring a blasted *photographer*."

"I need to keep up with the times."

"Then why did you send for me?"

"To make drawings of a man who isn't here."

"What?"

Ryan escorted him to where Agnes, the other pew-openers, and the churchwardens were gathered.

"This is a gentleman from the *Illustrated London News*," Ryan told them. "Please describe Lady Cosgrove's escort to him. He'll draw a picture, and you can help him make it appear exactly as you remember the man. When everyone is satisfied," Ryan told the artist, "put it in the newspaper. I'm hoping someone will identify him. After that, go to the front and make sketches of the body."

"But you already have someone taking photographs of it."

"Which might not be adequate." Still absorbing the shock

of the two-word note in his pocket, Ryan said, "I need to have everything done twice."

"*Ryan.*"

The authoritative voice made Ryan turn. Commissioner Mayne took quick, troubled steps towards him.

Mayne was fifty-eight. His thin features looked shrunken beneath thick, grey sideburns. This was his twenty-sixth year as a commissioner, and the effort showed on his face. No one knew more about London's Metropolitan Police, or indeed about law enforcement anywhere in the world, than he did.

"I passed several journalists outside," Mayne said.

"A team of constables is keeping them at a distance, sir. I know you had an emergency meeting with the home secretary. I wouldn't have interrupted if this didn't need your immediate attention."

Ryan suddenly wondered if there *was* a home secretary. Given the government's collapse, did Lord Palmerston still hold that position? The political chaos made everything uncertain.

"The murder of someone as distinguished as Lady Cosgrove—in St. James's." Mayne sounded outraged. "I came at once."

"I'm afraid it's even worse than you think, sir."

"I don't see how that's possible."

"Lady Cosgrove was holding these." Ryan removed the envelope and the note from his pocket.

Mayne stared at the bloodstains on them. Taking the note from Ryan, he studied the two stark words.

His face became gaunter.

"Heaven help us. Who else knows about this?"

"Only you and I, sir."

For one of the few times in the fifteen years that Ryan had known him, the commissioner looked shaken.

"We're without a prime minister and a cabinet," Ryan said.

"Because this concerns Her Majesty's safety, shouldn't the queen be told at once?"

Accompanied by a constable, Becker hurried along Piccadilly, hoping to avoid attention but attracting stares nonetheless. Twenty-six years earlier, the public had been slow to accept helmeted policemen on seemingly every corner. But in 1842, an even more alarming development had occurred: a plain-clothed detective unit. The radical notion of a constable out of uniform was greeted with great suspicion. The middle and upper classes granted that there was merit to disguised policemen infiltrating taverns, gambling dens, and other places of low repute where criminals plotted their outrages. But at what point would these detectives become spies? How would respectable citizens know whether the seemingly ordinary person they spoke to wasn't actually a detective prying into their personal affairs?

Clothing that appeared inconspicuous on ordinary streets didn't have that advantage in wealthy Mayfair. It was difficult to say which attracted more attention: Becker's shapeless garments or the uniformed man who accompanied him. He felt eyes peering from behind closed curtains. A group of servants leaving their places of employment for their half-Sunday of liberty regarded him nervously, evidently assuming that Becker was a criminal whom the constable had arrested. The scar on Becker's chin indicated a rough background. But if that were the case, why was the constable escorting the criminal into the heart of Mayfair instead of to the nearest police station?

Following the directions Becker had received at the church, he turned right onto Half Moon Street, then left onto Curzon Street, navigating his way to the side-by-side houses on Chesterfield Hill.

"Go to Lady Cosgrove's house," Ryan had told him. *"Inform the occupants about what happened. God willing, you'll get there before the reporters tell them. Learn what you can."*

White stone buildings stretched before him, one adjoining the other—imposingly different from the cramped, squalid hovels that Becker had patrolled in the East End. These expensive, four-storey houses looked so much alike that, if not for discreet brass numbers near each door, it would have been impossible to distinguish them.

The air felt colder. A growing breeze swept dark clouds over the sun. When Becker reached the address he'd been given, he paused at an iron gate and peered up the steps towards the entrance. All the curtains were closed, but in wealthy neighbourhoods curtains were always closed, so that was no indication of whether anyone was at home.

Becker pointed at two reporters who followed him. "Constable, make certain those men don't come closer. No one passes this gate without permission."

So recently promoted that he felt awkward giving orders, Becker opened the gate and approached the house.

How can I deliver the news about Lady Cosgrove? he thought. He recalled rushing to his mother in their leased farmhouse, frantically telling her that his father had fallen from a ladder in the barn and that his neck was twisted at a terrible angle. The devastated look on his mother's face was something that Becker had never banished from his nightmares.

After a deep breath, he climbed the steps. There were only five, but they seemed like more. At the top, he used the lion's-head door knocker, its solid impact reverberating.

Ten seconds passed. No one responded. Feeling like an intruder, Becker knocked again, this time louder. Again, no one answered.

He looked down, braced himself to knock once more, and noticed a stain from a liquid that had trickled under the door. The liquid had dried. The colour had dulled to brown. But after the events of the morning, there was no mistaking the nature of the stain—it was blood.

Aware of the reporters watching from the street, Becker managed not to show a reaction. Testing the latch, he felt his pulse lurch when the door moved.

He opened the door a few inches and shouted, "Hello?" People inside might have chosen not to respond to a knock on the door, but surely they would react to a voice.

"Can anyone hear me? My name is Detective Sergeant Becker! I need to speak to you!"

His voice echoed back to him.

He pushed the door a few inches farther, trying to see as much as he could. But now the door encountered resistance, an object blocking the way.

"Hello?" Becker called.

He glanced over his shoulder. The two newspaper writers were stepping closer to the gate.

"Constable, make certain they keep their distance!"

Becker leaned harder against the door, felt the object on the other side move, and created enough space to step through.

He smelled death before his eyes adjusted to the shadows.

The object on the other side was the corpse of a butler. His head had been bashed in. Blood had gushed from it, forming a pool, now dried, that had trickled under the door.

Again Becker reached for the truncheon that had been on his equipment belt when he was a constable. Of course it wasn't there. But he had a knife that Ryan had taught him to wear in a scabbard under his trouser leg. ("Use the blunt end before you use the blade," Ryan had warned, "or there'll be questions.")

Drawing it, feeling cold fear spread through his chest, Becker steadied himself against a possible attack and scanned the area. A murky vestibule led to a hall in which there were two doors on each side—both shut—and an ornate staircase that ascended towards the upper floors.

Until now, Lord Palmerston's mansion had provided Becker's only experience with wealth. Although he'd been there on numerous occasions, he still had not adjusted to the contrast with the leaky shacks in which he had lived while working sixty hours a week in a brick factory. He found it amazing that Lord Palmerston referred to his residence as a house. Perhaps he was so accustomed to wealth that to him it was indeed no more than a house, in which case what would Lord Palmerston envision a mansion to be?

Normally, Becker would have been distracted by the black-and-white squares of the marble floor or by the intricate design on the bronze of the staircase's balustrade—a word with which Becker had only recently become familiar. But this was hardly a normal occasion. Becker's concentration quickly focused on a heap of clothes at the bottom of the stairs. Wary, he took three steps forward, just far enough to determine that the heap of clothes was the body of a female servant, whose head had been similarly shattered and who lay in the dried remnants of her blood.

His chest cramping, he walked cautiously backward. At the front door, he returned his knife to its scabbard to avoid alarming anyone when he stepped outside. When he squeezed through the gap he had made, the cold breeze outside couldn't compare to the chill of the house. The clouds were darker.

The two newspaper writers were trying to persuade the constable to let them through.

"What did you find?" one of them shouted.

"Constable, use your clacker!" Becker yelled.

Thinking that Becker wanted the constable to hit them, the reporters scurried backward.

The constable gripped the clacker's handle and swung its blade, the fierce noise gaining volume from the confines of the narrow street.

Alarmed faces peered from behind curtains across the way. Servants hurried from doorways. What had been deserted thirty seconds earlier suddenly came to life.

A constable ran along the street. The system of patrol areas was such that policemen were never out of hearing range of one another. Seeming to prove the point, an additional constable ran from the opposite direction.

Becker told the first one, "I'm Detective Sergeant Becker. Stay here to help keep order." He instructed the other newcomer, "Run to St. James's Church. Tell Inspector Ryan that Lady Cosgrove isn't alone."

"She isn't alone?"

"The inspector will understand what it means. Tell him to come at once. Bring more constables. As many as possible."

As the policeman raced away, two more arrived.

"What's 'appened?" a woman in an apron yelled from the crowd.

"My master wants to know what's all the commotion," a footman in livery demanded.

"Tell him everything's under control. All of you, return to your places," Becker ordered. "There's nothing to see here."

"Bobbies can't tell us what to do in Mayfair," the aproned woman shouted.

Becker was tempted to ask her how she'd enjoy talking about it behind bars at the police station. But how would *Ryan* handle this? he wondered.

"Come here," Becker told her.

The woman suddenly didn't look so confident. "Me?"

"You're the one I'm pointing at. Come here."

She hesitantly obeyed.

"Do you want to help? This'll give you something to tell in the kitchen."

The idea of bringing gossip back to where she worked made the servant smile.

"Are there back entrances to these houses?" Becker asked.

"There's a mews behind 'em. That's where they lets *us* enter—where the groceries and the coal comes."

"Show this handsome constable where the back entrance is."

"He don't look 'andsome to me."

"Now you hurt his feelings. Show him the back entrance. Constable, nobody goes in. And watch yourself, because somebody with nasty intentions might come rushing out."

"Understood, Sergeant."

Becker wasn't used to being called by his new title. For a moment, it seemed that the constable was talking to someone else.

As the servant led the constable away, three other policeman ran from one end of Chesterfield Hill while two more hurried from the other.

Showing his badge, Becker motioned for them to gather close. He kept his voice down so the reporters couldn't hear. "At least two people inside have been killed. I haven't searched the entire house."

Violence in this district was so unusual that their features tightened.

"First St. James's and now *this*," one of them murmured, news about the earlier murder having travelled fast.

"It looks like it happened several hours ago. Two of you stay here and watch the gate. The rest of you talk to these people. Find out if they saw or heard anything unusual."

When the constables separated, one of the reporters called, "Hey, let *us* know, too!"

Becker told the constable at the gate, "No one comes through, except Detective Inspector Ryan."

He turned to the constable who'd accompanied him from the church. "Follow me."

They mounted the steps and squeezed through the opening.

*   *   *

"This is the first one," Becker said.

The smell of death seemed stronger. Even in the shadows, Becker could see that the constable's eyes narrowed when he stared down at the corpse's cratered head.

"Step around. Don't disturb anything," Becker said. "I need your help in case the man who did this is still inside."

The constable drew his truncheon from his belt. As he entered the hall, he gaped at the statues on marble pedestals, the gilded moulding, and the frescoed panels.

"Blimey, people actually live like this," the constable said in wonder.

"They're also murdered in it," Becker reminded him. "Pay attention to why we're here."

Becker approached the body of the female servant at the base of the stairs. Again asking himself what Ryan would do, he knelt and studied the circular wound on her head, which seemed to have been made by the same object that had killed the butler at the entrance.

He opened the nearest door, one on the right. Closed curtains made it difficult to see the upholstered furnishings of a formal sitting room. Tassels hung from table covers, every surface decorated. The amply padded chairs and sofa had a multitude of tapestried cushions. As Becker crossed the thick Oriental carpet, he couldn't recall having been in a more muffled room.

He parted the curtains and looked warily around, but nothing seemed amiss. He crossed the hallway, opened an opposite door, and again the smell of death greeted him.

"Constable, be ready in case I need you."

Becker pushed the door farther open, revealing a library. The curtains were closed here also. Scanning the shadows, he saw a man in a red leather chair. The man appeared to be reading a book.

"Lord Cosgrove?" Becker asked. He didn't know why he'd

spoken. The sour odour in the room made clear that the man could never reply.

Prepared to defend himself, Becker walked to the left and opened the curtains. Light fell on the man in the chair. Agony twisted the corpse's wrinkled face.

A voice spoke so unexpectedly that Becker flinched.

"Where's Detective Sergeant Becker?" The voice belonged to Ryan. It came from the hallway.

"He's in there, Inspector," the constable replied.

Ryan appeared in the library's doorway. " 'Lady Cosgrove isn't alone'? Your message certainly made me curious."

"How does De Quincey put it? Several people in this house have joined the majority." Becker referred to De Quincey's observation that over the millennia, more people had died than were currently alive.

Ryan crossed the library, focusing on the man in the leather chair.

"Have you ever met Lord Cosgrove?" Becker asked.

"Once. Commissioner Mayne sent me to make some comments to the prison committee. As the director, Lord Cosgrove had a few questions for me afterward."

"Is *this* Lord Cosgrove?"

"I doubt that even his wife, if she still had breath, would recognize him," Ryan answered.

The man was tied to the chair. A rope encircled his neck and was secured to the top of a ladder directly behind him. The ladder was anchored to rails on the wall and provided access to the upper shelves of books.

One of those books was open in the man's hands. His head drooped as if he were reading it.

"His eyes," Becker said. Appalled, he gestured towards what was in them. "Have you ever seen anything like this?"

"No," Ryan answered.

A tapered silver pen projected from each eye. Dried dark streaks descended from the ruptured orbs, making it seem that the figure had wept blood. Becker repressed a shudder as he imagined the agony of the steel nibs being rammed into the eyeballs.

"It's hard to know what finally killed him," Becker said. "Did he bleed to death or was he choked?"

"The pens in his eyes were torture. The rope is what did it," Ryan answered.

"But how can you be certain?"

"What colour are his lips and tongue?"

Knowing that Ryan was testing him, Becker overcame his revulsion and stepped closer, staring at the pain-contorted mouth and the tongue protruding from it.

"Blue."

"Have you ever been to a hanging?" Ryan asked.

"Once. From a distance. That was enough."

"Blue lips indicate that the body struggled for air. Loss of blood weakened him. His head drooped towards the book. The killer arranged things so that the victim hanged himself. What's the book he's supposed to be reading?"

Aware of how much he needed to learn, Becker steadied himself and raised the book from the corpse's hands, noting the title on the spine. "It's about the law."

A piece of paper projected from the pages. Becker pulled it out. The note had the same kind of black border that was on the message Lady Cosgrove had clutched when she was killed.

"What does the note say?" Ryan asked.

"It's a name, but it isn't familiar to me. Edward Oxford."

"*Edward Oxford?* Are you sure?"

"You recognize that name?"

"God help all of us, yes."

Continuing the Journal of Emily De Quincey

While the questioning persisted in St. James's, Father sat on the altar rail. His legs too short to reach the floor, he moved his boots up and down as if walking on air. When he wasn't staring at the pool of blood, he studied Lady Cosgrove's pew, where a photographer arranged a camera. Father's need made his face sickly pale. Seeing him reach beneath his coat for his laudanum bottle, I hurried to restrain him lest he further outrage the church members.

Meanwhile, Colonel Trask continued to assist the police in keeping order while the beautiful woman whom he'd escorted into the church gazed in admiration at the respect he received. I couldn't help noticing that the colonel occasionally glanced at me with the same puzzlement that he'd shown when he first saw me, seeming to recognize me but unable to recall the occasion. That increased my own puzzlement. I waited for a moment when the colonel wouldn't be occupied so that I could approach him and provide an opportunity for him to explain, should he be inclined to do so.

But before I could manage that, Sean (I refer to Inspector Ryan) led Father and me outside, guiding us to the edge of a growing crowd.

"Lord Palmerston's coach is here. His driver and footman have firm orders to take you to Euston Station."

"I should stay," Father said.

"You were of help seven weeks ago," Sean granted. "But Lord Palmerston made clear how displeased he would feel if you missed your train. He controls the police force more than Commissioner Mayne does, so I don't have a choice. You answered all my questions. If I have others, I can telegraph them to you in Edinburgh. Fortunately Sergeant Becker and I saw the same things that you did."

"Did you in fact see the same things that I did?" Father asked.

"I promise to remember your theory about many realities."

Shaking hands with us, Sean held mine longer than simple friendship required. Despite the cold weather, I felt warmth rise in my cheeks.

"Emily, I shall miss our conversations," he said.

I don't normally lack words, but I confess that my sorrow about leaving made it difficult for me to speak.

"I shall miss our conversations, also," I managed to say.

Remembering the proprieties, Sean turned towards Father. "And of course I shall miss my unusual conversations with you, sir."

"It's been a long time since anyone addressed me as 'sir,'" Father admitted. "Not many weeks ago, you referred to me in other ways."

Sean glanced down, embarrassed. "We have all come a long way. I wish we could have gone farther."

He looked in my direction. "Thank you for helping to nurse my wounds, Emily. Godspeed in your travels."

As he continued to hold my hand, my cheeks felt warmer. "Be safe," I whispered, leaning close, trying to lend privacy to our farewell. "I shall write when we arrive in Edinburgh."

A constable suddenly ran towards us, forestalling the many other things that I wanted to say. "Sergeant Becker needs you at Lady Cosgrove's home, Inspector. He said to tell you to come at once—that she isn't alone."

"Not alone?"

"Those are his words. He said that you'd understand what it meant—and that it was urgent."

The look in Sean's eyes did indeed show understanding. He told Father and me, "I'm afraid I must go."

"Yes, please do your work," I told him. In truth, I wished that he would stay, but when I reached to touch his arm, he was already hurrying through the crowd.

Abruptly Lord Palmerston's footman rushed towards us through the mass of newspaper writers and onlookers.

"Quickly. We should have departed for the station a long time ago." The footman sounded distraught. "Lord Palmerston's orders are emphatic. He doesn't want you to miss your train."

While the footman urged us towards the coach, one newspaper writer told another, "There goes the Opium-Eater. Did you hear what he said about the great nebula in Orion?"

"Is that the new public house on the Strand?"

"In the night sky. The Opium-Eater said that the nebula looks like a man's skull with a gap in it and celestial matter streaming from his brain. That's what opium'll do to you."

When I saw our meagre bags strapped to the top of the coach, the reality of our unhappy departure weighed on me. No sooner had the footman shut the door on us and clambered onto the back than the coach bolted forward, its driver determined to obey Lord Palmerston's orders.

Sitting across from me, Father trembled.

"It's all right now," I told him.

He instantly withdrew his laudanum bottle and drank its ruby liquid. He closed his eyes, paused, opened his eyes, and drank again. Their blue acquired a misty glitter. The dull sweat on his face seemed to be absorbed back into his skin. Gradually, he stopped moving his feet up and down.

If we had been travelling directly back to Edinburgh, our schedule would have been impossible, for trains to that distant area depart early in the morning in order to disembark their passengers on the night of the same day. But during our final weeks in London, Father had lapsed into a melancholy that was deeper than usual. I attributed his mood to his ever-increasing dependence on opium and his fears that if he didn't soon make a final heroic effort to free himself of its bondage, it would destroy him.

His melancholy made him want to visit the graves of his two sisters at his boyhood home in Manchester. The newspaper reporter couldn't have known that Father's obsession with skulls and matter pouring from them came from the post-mortem surgery performed on one of his sisters to see whether her unusually large head had been the consequence of a fatally misshapen brain. Father had nightmares about the deep cleft that a surgeon had made in her skull.

One of my brothers, William, had died from ravaging headaches that reduced him to blindness and deafness. After my brother's ordeal had finally ended, an autopsy disclosed a large section of green matter in his brain. Father suffered nightmares about that opened skull, too.

As the coach turned north, rattling from Piccadilly onto Regent Street, Father leaned out of the window, calling to the footman on his perch at the back, "What is your route to Euston Station?"

"From Regent Street to Portland Place! Then right onto the New Road!"

"Please turn right onto Oxford Street instead."

"We know the way to the station."

"My route will take you there as quickly. I wish to look at something."

Despite the noise of the coach's wheels, I heard the footman mutter before calling to the driver, "Turn east at Oxford Street!"

"What for?"

"A request from our passengers!"

"Ha! The last one we need to oblige!" the driver said, perhaps unaware that we could hear.

After the coach veered right onto Oxford Street, Father called to the footman, "Stop!"

"But we need to get to Euston Station!"

"Stop!" Father shouted. For a small man, his voice was so loud that it startled me.

The sound of the horses' hooves didn't hide the driver's curse as he halted at what I saw was the bottom of Great Titchfield Street.

Father opened the door and stepped down.

I followed.

"No, don't get out!" the footman exclaimed. "You said you only wished to look at something! We need to go to the station!"

Early on Sunday afternoon, the shops on Oxford Street were closed. Traffic was sparse, only a few hansom cabs and carriages clattering past. Low clouds darkened the sky. Chimney smoke obscured the tops of buildings.

Father mournfully surveyed his surroundings. When he was seventeen, it was on this street that he had spent four starving months among prostitutes and beggars, trying to survive by his wits in the cruelty of a London winter. One of them, Ann—swallowed by the pitiless city long ago—had been the love of Father's life before he met my mother.

"Even near death, I was more alive then," Father murmured.

"Please don't talk about death, Father."

"Hurry!" the footman shouted. "If you miss the train, Lord Palmerston will blame us!"

"Tell His Lordship that the fault was mine," Father said. "Tell him I refused to climb back into the coach."

"What are you talking about?" the footman blurted.

"My deepest apologies. Kindly return our bags to Lord Palmerston's house. I shall decide what to do with them later."

"No!" the driver protested.

Father marched along Oxford Street, heading west now instead of east.

"Father," I insisted, hurrying after him. "Did you consume too much laudanum in the coach? Tell me what you're doing."

We passed Regent Street, continuing west. Even with Father's short legs, his determined pace was such that many people could not have matched him. Only the freedom of my bloomer skirt enabled me to keep up with him.

"Death," Father said.

"You frighten me, Father."

"Until seven weeks ago, I wakened at noon after opium nightmares of regret. If we hadn't come to London, I would probably now have been waking at sunset instead of noon. Or perhaps an excess of opium would have prevented me from ever waking at all. Then I too would have joined the majority. At last I'd have been able to forget the pain that I caused you and your brothers and sisters and above all your mother ... the debt collectors that I forced all of you to flee ... the poverty that I made you endure."

"Father, truly you are frightening me."

"Edward Oxford?" Becker stared at the note he'd found in the book the corpse held. "What do you mean, 'God help all of us'?"

"Fifteen years ago—how old would you have been?" Ryan asked.

"Only ten."

"You told me that you were raised on a tenant farm in a remote part of Lincolnshire. Did your father read newspapers?"

"He couldn't read at all. He was ashamed of not being able to," Becker said. "When I wasn't doing chores, he made me go to school."

"Then maybe you couldn't have known about it."

"Known about what? Is this related to the message you found at the church and you wouldn't tell me about?"

"There's no time," Ryan told him. "We need to search the rest of the house."

"Stop being evasive. What does the name Edward Oxford mean? Tell me what was in the note at the church," Becker demanded.

"I can't."

"It's that difficult to talk about?"

"I'm not allowed to. Only Commissioner Mayne has the authority to do that."

"The look on your face. Is this going to get worse?"

"It did fifteen years ago. Please stop asking questions that I can't answer. We need to search the house. Where are the other servants?"

The odour of spoiling food—and worse—directed them downstairs towards the kitchen.

Becker paused on the stairs.

"Are you all right?" Ryan asked.

"How long will it take before I can be like you?"

"Like *me?*"

"This doesn't bother you," Becker said.

"It *always* bothers me," Ryan told him.

"But you don't show any emotion."

"Because I distract myself. Concentrate on the details. Commissioner Mayne taught me that. Focus on finding evidence and on making certain that the killer never has a chance to do it again."

Becker nodded and forced himself to descend.

At the bottom, he concealed his reaction when he saw the corpses of a cook and a scullery maid on the kitchen floor. Like the servants upstairs, each had been killed by a blow to the head. Dried blood stained their aprons.

Struggling to follow Ryan's advice, Becker mastered his emotions by noting details. The ashes in the stove were cold. Soup congealed in bowls. Meat pies sagged in baking dishes, next to flat meringue desserts.

They mounted the gloomy servants' staircase, passed the

entrance level, and reached a higher floor that was dominated by an immense dining area capable of seating forty people.

"When I patrolled the East End, I never dreamed that people could enjoy such luxury," Becker said.

They climbed to the third level, where they found three open doors and one that was closed.

An odour seeped from beneath the closed one.

Ryan shoved it all the way open with such force that it banged loudly.

"Any trouble up there, Inspector?" the constable yelled from downstairs.

"We'll let you know!" Ryan answered.

Ready with their knives, he and Becker entered. The room was dark. They made their way towards curtains, pulling them open.

When Becker saw what was under his boots and all over the bed and in fact everywhere, he stumbled back.

The walls, the dressing table, the curtains, the rug, everything was covered with dried blood.

"What in the name of hell happened here?"

The revenger never forgot the last happy moment in his life. He and his sisters, Emma and Ruth, were boiling potatoes in a pot hanging over the fireplace. The potatoes were all that their family could afford for supper. The wood that they burned would have been hard to come by also, if it hadn't consisted of worthless scraps their father salvaged from his carpentry work. They had little, but they loved one another. They laughed often.

Not that day, however. Near sunset, when their father returned home, he set down his tool belt and looked puzzled.

"Colin, where's your mother?" he asked. Sawdust flecked his canvas apron.

Emma answered for him. "Mama didn't come back from

her errand yet." Emma was thirteen. Her eyes were blue, and each day since then, Colin had never failed to recall how they illuminated a room.

"But she's been gone all day." Rubbing a calloused hand against the back of his sunburned neck, their father crossed the kitchen to the front door of their tiny cottage.

Colin, Emma, and Ruth followed. Ruth was the little one. Somehow, the gap where one of her front teeth had fallen out brightened her smile. They watched their father step outside and peer down the dusty lane in the direction that their mother had taken in the morning. Their village had existed for only a short time. Most of the cottages were still being built, stacks of bricks and lumber standing next to skeletal frames. The village's owner, a property developer, had bought this parcel of land four miles from St. John's Wood, the north-western extremity of London, in anticipation of London's expansion.

"Maybe she stopped at a neighbour's," their father said.

He walked to a nearby cottage.

Colin and Emma held Ruth's hand while they watched their father knock on a door and speak to someone. As the crimson sun touched the horizon, he walked farther along, reached another door, and spoke to someone else. They had lived in the village for only ten days and didn't know anyone, but all the people were labourers the same as their father, and even though Colin's family was Irish, they hadn't encountered any hostility.

Frowning harder, their father returned and hugged them, saying, "Let's put supper on the table. She'll be along any time now."

But Colin couldn't help noticing that his father's hands were unsteady when he picked at his few potatoes, then divided them among the children.

"Colin, watch your sisters." In the chill of evening, he put on a coat. "I'll soon be back."

In fact, it was long after dark when he returned. But their

mother wasn't with him, and their father now looked afraid as he tucked them into the stacked cots that he had made for them, next to the narrow bed that he and their mother shared.

"What do you think happened to her?" Emma asked.

"I don't know," their father answered. "It got so dark that I had to stop looking. In the morning, I'll try again."

"Let's say a prayer for Mama," little Ruth said.

Their mother had set out for St. John's Wood with a basket of her knitting. What she was able to accomplish with needles and yarn was amazingly intricate, colourful patterns that created wonder. If not for their mother's skills, Colin and his sisters wouldn't have had warm gloves, caps, and scarves in winter. She had gone to St. John's Wood to sell three jumpers. Someone had told her that there was a merchant who would buy them, and with the coins she was paid, she had hoped to purchase meat for several meals.

But St. John's Wood was only an hour's walk away.

In the morning, after their father made certain that Colin and his sisters had bread and cheese on the table, he opened the door to continue his search.

He paused in surprise at what was before him.

Colin, who followed, saw a constable approaching.

"Are you Ross O'Brien?" the constable asked.

"I am."

The Irish accent made the constable study him harder. "Is Caitlin O'Brien your wife?"

"She is." Colin's father stepped forward. "Why? Has something happened to her?"

"You could say that."

"I don't understand."

"She's been arrested."

4

The Crystal Palace

The cold breeze was welcome, clearing the odour of death from Ryan's nostrils as he and Becker stepped from the house. They faced the clamour of what seemed a hundred people pushing against each other, jostling to get as close as they could, complaining when someone shoved ahead of them. Most of the crowd consisted of footmen in breeches and knee-length coats or else maids and kitchen staff in aprons. They couldn't have left their places of employment without permission, so their lords and ladies had presumably sent them to determine the nature of the commotion. With so much of interest happening, and with the responsibility of reporting every detail, the onlookers seemed indifferent to the increasingly cold weather.

Surveying them, Ryan felt a shock of recognition. "Can that be Emily?"

"And good God, that's her father!" Becker said.

Somehow De Quincey had managed to squirm through the mass in front of the house. The force of so many people pressed the little man against the iron railing. Emily struggled next to him. Jostled, she begged a constable to allow them past the gate. The constable kept waving her away.

"Go home!" another constable yelled to everyone. "There's nothing to see!"

"Then why are coppers goin' around, askin' if we noticed anythin' strange?" a servant wanted to know.

"Well, *did* you notice anything strange?" a constable demanded.

Emily called to Ryan, but the din of the crowd absorbed her words.

Ryan and Becker hurried down the steps.

"Those two are with us!" Ryan told the constables.

As Becker opened the gate, Ryan tugged at Emily, who tugged at her father.

"Make room!" a constable ordered the crowd.

"Tell us what's going on!" a reporter yelled.

"Emily, we'll need to find a place to take you," Ryan said, pleased to see her but fervently wishing it were under other circumstances. "Bad things happened inside."

"Worse than in the church?" De Quincey asked. His overcoat was askew. A button had been torn from it.

"That depends on how you look at the matter."

"Immanuel Kant couldn't have phrased it better."

The breeze intensified. Clouds lowered and darkened. Snow flurried, finally prompting some members of the crowd to hug themselves and disperse.

"Sean, when we go inside, warn me when to look away," Emily said.

"When we go inside? But I just explained . . ." Ryan exhaled with resignation. "Yes, when we go inside."

"Emily, peer up at the ceiling. I'll guide you," Becker said.

More snow blew past.

They settled her into a plush chair in the sitting room.

"I can't start a fire to warm you," Ryan told her, pointing towards the shadowy hearth. "There might be evidence in those ashes."

"I understand."

"What happened? You're supposed to be on a train."

"Father refused to obey Lord Palmerston."

"Refused?" Becker asked in amazement.

"At the church we overheard the vicar saying Lord Cosgrove's address. Father insisted on coming here."

"I had no difficulty finding it," the little man said proudly. Just outside the room, he crouched at the base of the staircase and peered at the injury to the dead servant's skull. His right index finger almost touched the crater. "Fifty-three winters ago, I begged in Mayfair many times. I know it almost as well as I know Oxford Street and Soho."

"Lord Palmerston—" Ryan started to say.

"Will be furious. I'm aware." De Quincey drank from his laudanum bottle. "At the church you said that you and Sergeant Becker saw the same things that Emily and I did. Surely our many conversations seven weeks ago make you realize that wasn't the case."

"A police investigation involves *more* than invoking the name of Immanuel Kant," Ryan said, barely controlling his frustration. "Does reality exist outside us or only in our minds? I can tell you very definitely that reality exists at the front door and at the base of those stairs. Further reality exists in the kitchen beneath us, and reality very definitely exists tied to a chair in the library."

"Tied to a chair in the library?" De Quincey straightened with interest. He saw the open door on the opposite side of the hall and walked towards it.

"Hey, you can't go in there!" the constable on duty objected.

"It's all right," Becker said. "I'll go with him."

Ryan redirected his attention to Emily. "But how will you manage without Lord Palmerston's support? You don't have any money. Where will you sleep? How will you feed yourselves?"

"Father says that he can survive on the streets just as he did when he was seventeen."

"But now he is sixty-nine. And what about *you?* How will *you* survive?"

"Father says that he will teach me how to do it."

"I fear that opium has finally unhinged his mind."

"Death," Emily said.

"What?"

"Father talks frequently about it."

"Inspector?" De Quincey's voice interrupted from across the hall.

Emily touched Ryan's arm. "I think the reason Father came here is that helping you might give him a purpose and make him want to live."

Ryan crossed to the library, where he found De Quincey shifting from one perspective to another, studying the grotesquely positioned victim.

"You look impressed," Ryan said.

"The noose, the blinded eyes, and the law book amount to a masterpiece."

"I suppose I shouldn't expect anything else from the man who wrote 'On Murder Considered as One of the Fine Arts.' "

"The victim's position suggests that the motive was revenge for an injustice."

"It doesn't appear to have been robbery," Ryan agreed. "The pens in his eyes are silver. A gold watch-chain dangles from his waistcoat. There are many other items of value in this room, but it seems that nothing was taken."

"You mentioned the kitchen. Are there other victims?" De Quincey asked.

"A cook and a scullery maid," Ryan answered. "Lady Cosgrove must have been away from home when the murders occurred."

Becker stepped forward, confused. "But when she returned and discovered the bodies, why didn't she alert the police? Instead of raising an alarm, why did Lady Cosgrove put on a mourning gown and go to St. James's? It doesn't make sense."

"At least one of the victims hasn't been found," Ryan said. "A bedroom upstairs was covered with dried blood."

De Quincey peered over the corpse's shoulder and studied

the black-rimmed piece of paper that Becker had returned to the open book.

"There's a name here. *Edward Oxford?*"

"That means something to you?" Ryan asked.

"How could it possibly not?"

"I don't understand, Father. Who is Edward Oxford?"

Emily's voice surprised them. Turning, they saw her at the library's entrance, where she averted her eyes from the horror in the chair and looked up at the corniced ceiling.

"Emily, it might be better if you stayed in the other room," Becker suggested.

"I'd rather be here with everyone than alone elsewhere in this house."

"I wouldn't want to be alone in this house, either," Ryan agreed.

"Father, given the astonishment with which you say Edward Oxford's name, I feel foolish not to recognize it."

"You were only six when it happened," De Quincey explained. "Inspector, Edward Oxford is still in Bedlam, am I correct?"

De Quincey referred to England's only institution for the criminally insane—Bethlem Royal Hospital, commonly known as Bedlam.

"Yes," Ryan answered. "I would definitely have been told if Oxford had been released."

"But *who* is Edward Oxford?" Emily insisted. "What outrage did he commit? Sean, your tone suggests that it must have been something truly terrible. Is this related to the note that Lady Cosgrove received at the church? You refused to tell us what you read."

"I'm afraid you'll need to ask Commissioner Mayne about that."

"Perhaps not," De Quincey concluded.

"What do you mean?" Ryan asked with suspicion.

"At St. James's Church, before you shoved the note in your pocket, I saw enough to determine that it consisted of only two words. If those words were 'Edward Oxford,' the same as in *this* note, the secret would be out—you wouldn't need to conceal it any longer. That means the two words were something else. Under the circumstances, they could only be . . . Inspector, please tell Emily about Edward Oxford."

Wednesday, 10 June 1840

Queen Victoria insisted on releasing her daily schedule to the newspapers. Having ascended the throne only three years earlier, the young monarch wanted to show how different she was from her recent predecessors, who had almost never been seen by commoners. Determined to establish a connection with her subjects, she took frequent carriage rides through London's streets and wanted the populace to know exactly when she planned to do so, giving people ample opportunity to view and cheer their queen.

Her most frequent exposure occurred almost every day at 6 p.m. when she and Prince Albert, her husband of a few months, left Buckingham Palace in an open carriage. Their route always took them left onto Constitution Hill and past Green Park, from where they proceeded to Hyde Park, circled, and returned to the palace. Two horsemen accompanied the carriage.

The queen had reason to seek the affection of her subjects. Her husband was a foreigner from a poor German state. Although he spoke English, he preferred to use German. The queen's mother, a foreigner from the same poor German state, also preferred to speak German. Newspapers predicted that soon all of England would be forced to speak German and empty the national treasury to pay German debts. People feared that it wouldn't be long before England became a German state.

Thus, the thousands of spectators who had cheered Queen Victoria prior to her marriage now were reduced to mere hundreds during her appearances with Prince Albert. A few people on the street were known to hiss as she rode past. If her carriage happened to be empty, some even threw stones.

On that balmy Wednesday evening, one member of the crowd made a stronger display of disapproval. As the royal carriage passed Green Park, a man emerged from the onlookers.

He raised a pistol.

He fired from fifteen feet away.

"I was only a constable then," Ryan said, "assigned to the area near the palace."

Past the library's parted curtains, snow gusted. The crowd was no longer audible, the harsh weather presumably having driven the onlookers back to their places of employment.

"The government buildings, St. James's Park, and Green Park—those are some of the areas I patrolled. I always made a point of watching the path next to Green Park when Her Majesty went on her customary carriage ride. Even though the crowd was small compared to earlier ones, it still attracted dippers. The evening was rare when I didn't catch a man with his hand in someone else's pocket. At the sound of the gunshot, the crowd became paralyzed."

Ryan looked at Emily, who continued to stare at the ceiling, avoiding the horror in the chair.

"The sitting room is a better place for this," he decided.

He guided her across the hall, followed by De Quincey and Becker.

As Emily eased onto a sofa, Ryan took a place across from her, grateful to relieve the strain on his healing wounds.

"When the pistol was discharged, the queen's drivers stopped in confusion," he continued. "No one could believe it was a gunshot. I tried to determine the direction of the sound. Then I saw the smoke rising near the carriage and realized what had happened. A man lowered a duelling pistol. His other hand raised a second one. I struggled through the crowd, but before I could reach him, he fired again. All these years later, I still recall the pain in my ears. More smoke rose, but now the queen's drivers were finally in motion again, speeding the carriage away.

" 'The queen!' someone yelled. 'He tried to shoot the queen!' Someone else shouted, 'Kill him!' Then everyone was shouting it. 'Kill him! Kill him!' By the time I reached the struggle, I found *two* men with pistols. The crowd was tearing at both of them. '*I* didn't do it!' one of them insisted. 'I grabbed this pistol from *him!*' 'They're *both* in it!' someone yelled. 'Kill them both!'

"Several constables arrived. Using our truncheons, we separated the crowd. It was clear to me which man had carried the pistols. The first wore a suit too tight to have concealed the weapons. The second wore cheap linen trousers with big pockets. But the mob didn't care. 'Kill both of them!' people kept shouting.

"The other constables and I managed to drag the two men away from the mob. 'Take them to the station!' I yelled. Even though I knew the innocent man from the guilty one, there wasn't time to explain. 'We'll sort it out there!' I shouted.

"Carriages and cabs stopped to learn what was happening. Even more people gathered, perhaps a thousand now. Grabbing for the two men we had in custody, they followed us angrily towards the station in Whitehall. The mob clawed at each man's coat. Hands yanked at their collars, almost strangling them. As more constables arrived, we managed to get the men inside, where it became obvious that the man in the loose trousers was the only assailant. The other man, the one in the suit, had a card identifying him as a spectacles maker.

He had a companion who confirmed that he'd wrestled one of the pistols from the attacker. In future days, the newspapers hailed him as a hero."

De Quincey lowered his laudanum bottle from his lips. "The man in the loose trousers was Edward Oxford."

Ryan nodded. "He readily identified himself. In fact, he was furious at the spectacles maker for drawing attention away from him. 'I'm the man who fired! It was me!' he kept insisting. Since the shots didn't seem to have injured the queen or Prince Albert, I asked him whether the pistols were loaded with more than just powder. He answered angrily, 'If the ball had come in contact with your head, you would have known it!'"

"And the queen truly wasn't injured?" Emily asked.

"Neither she nor Prince Albert. To my amazement, I soon heard that instead of ordering her drivers to hurry back to the safety of the palace, she told them to continue up Constitution Hill to her Hyde Park destination, as if nothing had happened. According to reports, their pace through Hyde Park was almost stately. Thousands cheered their survival and their bravery.

"By the time they finally returned to the palace a half hour later, the news had become even more dramatic. Prince Albert, it was now believed, had been nicked by a bullet as he threw his body protectively over Her Majesty. That wasn't the case, but as the rumours magnified, the heroism of the queen and the prince were universally admired. The prime minister, the cabinet, the Privy Council, all rushed to Buckingham Palace to express their outrage at what Oxford had done and to thank God that the attempt had been unsuccessful."

"All this in the course of an evening," Emily marvelled. "But you said that Her Majesty was disliked at the time. Why did the crowd suddenly show allegiance to her?"

"What initially shocked them was that to attempt to kill a

monarch was unthinkable—a crime against nature," Ryan answered. "But they soon had another reason to cheer her survival."

"The queen's condition," De Quincey noted. Peering down, he studied his laudanum bottle.

"Condition? Are you referring to . . .?" Emily started to ask.

Embarrassed, Ryan answered, "The palace had kept the information private. Now it revealed that Her Majesty was with child. The news about the possibility of an heir spread like fire throughout London. King George IV and William IV had an abundance of"—Ryan looked delicately away from Emily—"mistresses and illegitimate children, but now Her Majesty offered a legal heir to the throne. Prince Albert's German origins, his preference for speaking German—all fears about him were forgotten as the population praised him for siring a potential monarch. That night, all the theatres interrupted their performances to announce that the queen had survived an assassination attempt. Everyone sang 'God Save the Queen.' Concert halls, eateries, all public gathering places, everywhere high and low, events were interrupted for toasts and songs in honour of Her Majesty."

"What happened to Edward Oxford?" Becker asked.

"The Metropolitan Police didn't have a detective division in 1840. Commissioner Mayne instructed two of my superiors and me to proceed across the river to where Oxford had a room in a Southwark lodging house. Among other pressing matters, we wanted to learn if he had accomplices. We searched his room and discovered a locked container. When I broke it open, I found bullets, gunpowder, a sword, and a puzzling black cap with two red bows. I also found documents and a notebook."

As the snow increased beyond the window, Emily hugged herself. She turned towards a creaking sound in the hallway.

"The documents referred to an organization called Young England," De Quincey said.

"That is correct," Ryan acknowledged.

"And those are the two words that you found in the note at the church," De Quincey added.

Ryan looked surprised. "You should be stupefied by all the laudanum you drink, and yet you're almost able to read minds. Yes, the two words on the note at the church were 'Young England.'"

"I don't understand," Emily said. "Young England? It sounds innocuous: a group of young people in support of their nation. Or historians devoted to England in its youth—Magna Carta and so forth."

"The purpose of Young England was the overthrow of the government and the abolishment of the monarchy," Ryan told her.

She and Becker stared.

"There were four hundred members," Ryan continued. "Each was required to have a pistol, a musket, and a dagger. Each had a false name and a fictitious background. Working as carriage drivers, carpenters, and so forth, many were trusted by noble families. Some had even managed to pretend to be gentlemen and join fashionable clubs. The black cap— which every member was required to have—could be pulled down to conceal features when the time came for the revolt. The two red bows on the cap in Oxford's locked container indicated that he had the rank of captain.

"There were more alarming items," Ryan added. "Letters referred to the group's secret meetings in which they were prepared to fight to the death if the police stormed in. The letters also referred to Young England's mysterious commander, who lived in the German state of Hanover."

"Hanover?" Emily asked. "But isn't that where . . .?"

"Indeed," Ryan answered. "The queen's oldest uncle had assumed the throne in that German state after Her Majesty became queen of England. Many believed that the uncle harboured fierce resentment that he hadn't been made king and that he would do anything to take the queen's place. He seemed to be the power behind Young England and its plot to overthrow the government and Her Majesty. Fears that England might become a German state appeared to be justified."

"Since the overthrow didn't occur, the police must have arrested all the members of the conspiracy," Becker said.

"No."

"They escaped?"

"They were all Edward Oxford's delusions," Ryan answered.

"What?"

"My superiors later informed me that all the documents were in Oxford's handwriting and that Young England and the rest of it were his inventions," Ryan said. "At his trial, the Attorney General himself acted as prosecutor, insisting that Oxford was insane. He pointed out that Oxford's father had beaten his mother before she gave birth, thus damaging his brain. Phrenologists measured his skull and determined that its bulges and indentations argued for an unusually shaped brain and consequent insanity. This insanity could also have been inherited from his father, who had once ridden a horse inside a house and had twice tried to commit suicide with an excess of laudanum."

Ryan gave De Quincey a significant look as he mentioned death and laudanum.

De Quincey shrugged. "It's perhaps a pleasant way to join the majority."

"Father, I beg you not to think this way," Emily said.

"Do you realize how often you've drunk from that opium bottle since you entered this house?" Ryan asked.

"I confess I failed to keep count."

"Six times."

"You see, Emily—only six. I'm improving. Please continue, Inspector. I believe that Oxford was known to break out in giddy laughter that frightened those around him."

"Yes, while at other times he stared at walls for hours on end. His behaviour was so strange that he couldn't hold jobs for more than a few months. He was mostly employed as a potboy, serving beer in taverns. 'Don't believe a word of what this lunatic says,' the Attorney General told the jury at his trial. 'Put him in a madhouse, where he belongs.' "

"Which is where he now resides for the rest of his life," De Quincey said. "But let's return to a previous topic. Did Oxford's pistols actually contain ammunition?"

For a long moment, Ryan didn't answer. "You can indeed read minds. You sense that it troubled me."

"How many people do you estimate were in the crowd at the time the shots were fired?" De Quincey asked.

"Perhaps two hundred."

"Among that many people, fifteen paces from the queen and Prince Albert, Oxford fired twice, and not only failed to hit his supposed target but also failed to hit anyone else or even several horses and the queen's carriage. That is a remarkably poor aim. The bullets were never found, am I correct?"

Ryan nodded. "The palace wall is on the opposite side of Constitution Hill. The pathway there was searched. After that, it was raked, every pebble studied. No bullets were discovered. The wall itself was examined in case the bullets had become embedded there. On the opposite side of the wall, the palace gardens were searched in case the bullets had flown over. But they were never found."

"So Oxford's only proven crime was that he frightened the queen," De Quincey said.

"Without evidence to the contrary, yes."

"Plenty of Londoners break out in giddy laughter and stare at walls. People say that they're lunatics, but those poor souls aren't sentenced to a lifetime in a madhouse."

"They don't shoot at the queen," Ryan noted.

"With pistols that no one can say for certain had ammunition," De Quincey countered.

"Remember what Oxford told me—that if the ball had come in contact with my head, I would have known it," Ryan said.

"But the conditional clause is not persuasive. As you admitted, this part of the event troubled you," De Quincey parried.

"The only way you could know so much about this is by reading everything you could possibly find about it," Ryan said. "You could have described that evening as well as I did, even though you weren't there."

"I could have described different versions of that evening, but not the vivid version that *you* provided, Inspector. The many newspaper accounts disagreed with one another, again proving that there are many realities. Some witnesses claimed that they heard the balls whistle over their heads. If true, Oxford's aim was so high that he couldn't have pointed his pistols at the queen, and therefore he didn't try to kill her. As for the whistle of the balls, can we give credence to those statements, when no bullets were found after several days of looking for them? Without any evidence to prove that Edward Oxford did in fact try to kill Her Majesty as opposed to merely startling her, why was the queen's Attorney General so determined to ensure that Oxford was sequestered in a madhouse for the rest of his life?"

"Do you have answers?" Ryan asked.

"Several."

"Tell me. They might explain why someone wants us to connect these murders with what happened fifteen years ago."

"I can't speak the answers."

"You can't speak? My God, the laudanum has finally impaired your faculties."

"In this case, I *dare* not speak the answers," De Quincey told him. "They border on treason."

Again, something creaked outside the room.

As a shadow grew in the doorway, Emily gasped.

Ryan and Becker stood protectively.

"Treason?" a voice asked.

Startling them, Lord Palmerston entered, followed by Commissioner Mayne. They brought the cold with them, their overcoats dotted with melting snow.

"What are you saying about treason?" Lord Palmerston asked.

"We were discussing Edward Oxford and Young England, My Lord," Ryan answered.

Lord Palmerston kept his gaze on De Quincey and Emily. "What are *you two* doing here? Why are you in London at all? Imagine my surprise when I returned to my house and found your bags being unloaded from my coach."

"Given the emergency, My Lord, I felt that it would be better to stay and offer any observations that might seem helpful," De Quincey explained.

"Perhaps your observations will become more acute when you find yourself sleeping in a snowdrift."

Commissioner Mayne kept his gaze on Ryan and Becker. "Why are you discussing Young England with outsiders? At the church we agreed that the note was to remain confidential to avoid panic."

"Mr. De Quincey guessed the note's contents."

"He did what?"

"After he read Edward Oxford's name on a second note."

The commissioner's surprise increased. *"A second note?"*

"With another victim." Ryan gestured across the hall towards the library.

Lord Palmerston and Commissioner Mayne hurried in that direction.

"Thank you for changing the topic from treason," De Quincey told Ryan.

"You'll tell us about it later, I hope," Becker said.

"Definitely," Emily promised. "It's a rare thought that Father will not express. Anything that makes him hesitate is something I intend to hear."

Commissioner Mayne and Lord Palmerston returned, looking shaken.

"Is it Lord Cosgrove?" Ryan asked.

Lord Palmerston nodded. Normally he exuded a sense of power. But now the pinched skin at the corners of his aged eyes communicated his shock. His usually powerful-looking chest seemed deflated.

Commissioner Mayne drew a sorrowful breath. "What kind of monster would have done that to him?"

"The noose, the law book, and the blinded eyes suggest that whoever did it believed *Lord Cosgrove* to be the monster," De Quincey replied.

"You insult him," Lord Palmerston said.

"That wasn't my intention, My Lord. But the elaborate staging suggests that the killer did this because of what he felt was a justified rage."

"Rage about *what*? Lord Cosgrove was one of the most admired members of the peerage. His efforts towards prison reform were exemplary. Who could have hated a man of such virtue?"

"Or hated *Lady* Cosgrove enough to kill her as well?" Commissioner Mayne asked. "I don't understand why she put on a mourning gown and went to the church instead of alerting the police? She might still be alive if she had."

"Perhaps she didn't go to the church," De Quincey suggested, and drank from his laudanum bottle.

"For heaven's sake, she's lying in her blood there right now," Lord Palmerston said. "Will someone put this man on a train to Scotland and rid me of him? The opium makes him unable to know what is real and what isn't."

"Father, don't say it," Emily warned.

"No, I want to hear," Lord Palmerston insisted. "Maybe one day your father will say enough to merit being put in the madhouse."

"I was merely going to note that what appears to be one thing can turn out to be the opposite." De Quincey pointed towards the corpse in the hallway. "The impression in the maid's skull—and in that of the servant at the front door—was made by a weapon that had a round object at one end. The angle of the blows is such that they could have been inflicted only on a downward trajectory. Such as this."

De Quincey raised his right arm and struck downward violently, startling Lord Palmerston. "The knob on a gentleman's walking stick matches these conditions. The question is, did a gentleman carry it, or was he disguised as a gentleman in order to gain admittance to the house?"

"No one of breeding could possibly have committed so grotesque a crime," Lord Palmerston declared. "We don't have time for your musings. Young England. Edward Oxford. When the commissioner told me about the note at the church, I immediately petitioned Her Majesty for an audience. Ryan, since you investigated Oxford's attempt against her life, you're coming with us."

"If I may suggest," Ryan said, "Sergeant Becker ought to accompany us. It's the quickest way for him to learn the background."

"All right, Becker, come along. Hurry. We can't keep Her Majesty waiting," Commissioner Mayne urged.

"And . . ." Ryan hesitated.

"What *is* it? We don't have time."

"Mr. De Quincey should come also."

"You're not serious."

"My conversation with him convinces me that he knows as much as I do—and possibly more—about Edward Oxford's attempt against the queen."

"The Opium-Eater meeting the queen?" Lord Palmerston asked. "Have you been drinking his laudanum?"

"Her Majesty would want us to use every means, no matter how unusual, to protect her, don't you agree, My Lord?"

Lord Palmerston groaned.

The revenger could be very specific about the day, date, and time when he realized how he could vent his long-suppressed rage. Thursday. The first of May, 1851. Three minutes past eleven in the morning.

That was the first day of the first world's fair, the Great Exhibition, although everyone called it by the name of the magnificent building in which it was housed: the Crystal Palace. On paper, the "palace" was only a gigantic green-house. Many people of influence had laughed when Prince Albert endorsed the idea.

But who could have imagined the glorious result, one of the most remarkable structures anyone had ever seen? As vast as it was resplendent, the Crystal Palace consisted of nearly one million square feet of glass. One million! It occupied a massive fifty-eight acres of Hyde Park and stretched twelve storeys high, so tall that the full-grown elm trees left in place as inte-rior landscaping couldn't reach the ceiling. Immense foun-tains received water pressure from gigantic towers outside. Music from two huge organs as well as two hundred other instruments and six hundred voices could barely be heard within it.

The revenger could vouch for the latter because he had stood among the powerful guests that day. Despite the more than eight hundred performers, the music had seemed to vaporize. When the royal procession entered, the immense structure fell into respectful silence. Even the fountains were made to go quiet as ten thousand people watched what they regarded as deities walking past them.

Queen Victoria: short, weak-chinned, tending towards plumpness.

Prince Albert: tall, soft-featured despite his moustache, his thin shoulders stooped.

The queen wore jewels of unimagined value and an ornate bonnet that resembled a tiara.

Although the prince had never been in combat, he wore an army uniform with numerous medals.

The revenger hated both of them with a force that he thought might break the bones in the fists that he clenched at his sides. He scanned the towering galleries, floor after floor of exhibits from countries all around the world. Prince Albert had been the impetus behind all of this, and the revenger had hoped with the passion of his hatred that the enterprise would fail. When he read mocking items in the newspapers, he had inwardly cheered.

The crowned heads of Europe had refused to accept the prince's invitation for fear of mixing with commoners and possible assassins. Those crowned heads had reason to be fearful. Only a few years earlier, in 1848, some 150,000 protesters had marched on London, demanding yearly elections and voting privileges for every man, not only those with property. The army had managed to disperse them. But who knew when another mob would threaten London?

Despite these worries, the Crystal Palace had been a colossal triumph. The admiration of the ten thousand privileged first-day guests had made the revenger direct his hatred towards them as well. Despite the pretence that the Great Exhibition celebrated the brotherhood of nations, he had no doubt that Albert's purpose was to emphasize the power of Great Britain. How the revenger seethed when people spoke glowingly about the Victorian age, a term that Albert had championed. The revenger fantasized about using the cover of night to sneak gunpowder into the Crystal Palace and blow it apart. But what point was there in destroying a building? It was people that he wanted to destroy: Victoria, Albert, and many others.

The queen, the prince, and two of their many children had joined the prime minister and other dignitaries on a red dais with a lush blue canopy above them. Barely controlling the expression on his face so that his hate didn't show through the mask of his apparent admiration, the revenger had listened with contempt to the uninspired speech that Albert gave.

The prince's German-accented voice could barely be heard. The rich and powerful listened with feigned awe, even though most of them probably couldn't understand a word he said. He droned on and on, addressing his remarks to the queen. When he mercifully concluded his speech, the queen rose from her throne and said something in acknowledgement of whatever wondrous words she felt he had said. Abruptly a choir sang the "Hallelujah Chorus" from Handel's *Messiah*. No one except the revenger appeared to consider the choice of music blasphemous as it equated the queen and the prince to Jesus Christ.

Then an amazing thing happened—a life-changing event for the revenger. A brightly dressed man stepped from the crowd. He was Chinese. He wore an elaborately coloured Oriental robe. While everyone in the audience seemed paralyzed, the Chinese man approached the queen's throne and offered deep, profound bows. The queen's children gaped. Her Majesty, not knowing what else to do, gave the Oriental stranger a respectful nod.

Murmurs spread through the crowd. *Who was this man?* everyone wondered. *The Chinese ambassador,* some suggested. Others claimed to have seen him talking with dignitaries as esteemed as the Duke of Wellington. Politicians whispered to each other. The prime minister and the lord chamberlain consulted with Victoria and Albert.

They all agreed: without question, this was the Chinese ambassador.

When the queen and the prince led their children towards the thousands of exhibits, politicians and dignitaries followed. The stranger joined them, among the first to appreciate the scope and splendour of the Great Exhibition.

The mystery about his identity occupied the public's imagination until a newspaper reporter revealed that he was merely a Chinaman who owned a business on a junk on the Thames. His name was He-Sing, and he had put on his native costume, approaching the queen in order to draw attention to his Museum of Curiosities.

For one of the few times in his life, the revenger had smiled honestly, enjoying the Chinaman's mockery of the queen, the prince, and the Great Exhibition. But the revenger's smile took nothing away from the fierce resolve that had come to him on that Thursday morning when, at three minutes past eleven on the first of May, 1851, he had understood how to achieve his destiny.

In the falling snow, Ronald struggled to find his way through the labyrinth of narrow streets in London's notorious East End.

He was afraid.

The previous evening, the bearded gentleman had given him five gold sovereigns.

"Would you like to receive even more sovereigns, Ronald? Twenty-five Garner Street in Wapping. Be there at four tomorrow afternoon. You are about to join a great cause."

Now, as Ronald strained to see through the falling snow, he still had three of the five sovereigns, the others having been used to buy the warm clothes that the bearded gentleman had instructed him to obtain—waterproof boots and woollen socks, not to mention a warm coat and hat to replace the ragged sailor's coat and cap he'd been wearing. And warm gloves. And a surfeit of kidney pies and beer, his first full meal in three days.

Few people were on the streets, most having taken refuge in whatever warren they called home. With little opportunity to ask for directions, Ronald felt more panicked. He had started searching at two, using clocks in various shops to measure his progress. But the farther he moved into the decay of Wapping, the fewer places had clocks, and in the falling snow, many windows were shuttered. Now Ronald had no idea how close it was to four o'clock. Eager to receive more sovereigns, he had a dark suspicion that the bearded gentleman would not be pleased if he was late.

Coughing from the chimney smoke that the snow pressed onto the streets, Ronald reached a partially covered sign on a wall. Brushing snow from it, he felt his blood rush when he saw the words garner street. He took longer steps through the snow and studied the numbers on walls. Nine. Seventeen.

Twenty-five!

A dark corridor beckoned.

Ronald peered nervously into it. Without lights or any sign of habitation, could this be the address that the gentleman had meant? Had Ronald failed to remember correctly? If he didn't find where he was supposed to go, if he didn't reach there in time, he wouldn't receive more sovereigns.

Frozen boards creaked as he inched inside and strained to see through the darkness. Dangling plaster touched his head.

A shadow suddenly appeared before him, raising the shield

on a lantern, shining the light into his face. "What's your name?"

"Ronnie," he answered in surprise, then remembered the bearded man's insistence that he should always use his formal name. "No. I mean Ronald."

"What were you given?"

"Five sovereigns."

"Follow me."

The shadow stepped across what Ronald now saw was a hole in the floor, an ominous blackness beneath it. The man opened a door and motioned Ronald into a small courtyard that was occupied by a half-collapsed shed.

At another dark corridor, another shadow stepped into view.

"If he brought company, they won't have trouble following his tracks," the first man said.

"I didn't tell anyone," Ronald protested. "I swear it."

"We'll soon find out. No one will get past me," the second man promised the first.

Ronald continued to follow his guide. At the end of the corridor, stairs lacked a banister. The lantern revealed occasional missing steps. At the top, they reached a gaping window, where a board stretched across an alley towards another gaping window.

"Go," the guide ordered, closing the shield on the lantern.

Ronald's confidence returned. Accustomed to climbing masts on a British East India Company ship, he had no difficulty advancing over a slippery, snow-covered board in near darkness. It was nothing compared to securing sails on a vessel pitching in a storm.

Four paces took him to the opposite side and a murky room that seemed to be filled with crates. His guide stepped down after him and pulled the board inside, then opened the shield on the lantern and led Ronald to a stairway, down which they descended to a cold, musty basement filled with more crates.

A murmur attracted Ronald's attention. The murmur grew louder as they approached a door.

A shadow emerged from behind a crate. "Are you Ronald?"

"Yes."

"Excellent." The man put a friendly hand on Ronald's shoulder. "Everyone's been waiting for you."

The man opened the door. The three of them entered a room filled with the glow of lanterns, the aroma of ale and tobacco, and the smiles of several men, who rose in greeting.

At the centre stood the bearded gentleman with the silver-tipped cane.

"Welcome to Young England, Ronald!"

5

The Throne Room

Lord Palmerston's coach hurtled along Piccadilly, snow muffling the sound of horseshoes and metal-rimmed wheels. Despite the body heat of six people squeezed into a vehicle intended to hold four, the enclosed area felt cold, the silence outside unnatural.

Ryan pointed towards the two gates and the curved driveway in front of Lord Palmerston's mansion, telling Emily, "Five years ago, someone tried to kill Her Majesty there."

"*Another* attempt against her?" Emily asked in surprise. She was seated between Ryan and Becker. Once more, she was grateful for her bloomer skirt. A woman in a hooped dress could never have fitted into the crowded coach.

"All told, there have been *six* attempts," Ryan answered. "I intend to make certain there isn't a seventh."

"*Six* attempts?" Emily sounded even more taken aback. "And one of them was outside your house, Lord Palmerston?"

"It wasn't mine then. The queen's favourite uncle lived there. When Her Majesty went to visit him, a curious crowd gathered around her carriage and prevented it from moving. A man suddenly stepped forward and struck his cane across Her Majesty's head. The blow was so strong that it drew blood."

"Good heavens!"

"Indeed," Lord Palmerston said. "Royalty is not supposed to be capable of bleeding."

"Was *he* a member of an imaginary secret organization also, Your Lordship?" Emily asked. "Did *he* too write documents plotting to overthrow the government and the crown?"

"No. His name was Pate. He was a strange man who paid the same cab driver every day for months on end to drive him to various parks, where he charged into thickets and returned with his clothes soaking wet, covered with brambles. On the street, he marched with a goose step while he flailed his cane as if it were a sword in combat."

De Quincey stared pensively towards the snow streaming past his window. "Pate wasn't always that way. At one time he was a cavalry officer with three horses that he treasured above everything. All three were bitten by a rabid dog and had to be shot. After that, Pate acted strangely."

"So, a mad dog was responsible for turning him into a mad man," Becker offered.

"Except that, according to the law, Pate *wasn't* mad," De Quincey said as the coach jolted to the left from Piccadilly onto Constitution Hill.

"But his behaviour . . ." Becker said.

". . . was bizarre in other respects as well," De Quincey added. "He sang raucously at all hours, annoying everyone around him. He refused to bathe in anything except whisky and camphor. People describe such a man as a lunatic, but eccentric behaviour isn't proof of madness. According to the law, insanity is a disease of the mind that prevents someone from being aware of what he does and whether his actions are wrong."

"You know the law?" Commissioner Mayne asked in surprise.

"After my studies at Oxford, I considered a career in it," De Quincey answered, "but a year of legal training made me decide that it wasn't for me."

"To the benefit of the legal profession," Lord Palmerston murmured. "Murder as a fine art indeed. You're the one who's insane."

"But not according to the law," De Quincey noted. "At Pate's trial, the jury concluded that, even though his behaviour—goose-stepping down streets, flailing with his cane, and so on—was unnatural, he knew that he was doing wrong when he struck the queen. The jury declared him guilty. As the judge said when sentencing him, 'You're as insane as it's possible for a person to be who is sane.' "

"My headache worsens," Lord Palmerston said.

"As is proper when considering matters of the mind," De Quincey told him. "Determining madness isn't simple. How interesting that Pate's name is synonymous with the head."

"We're here," Commissioner Mayne said tensely.

The coach stopped before the awe of Buckingham Palace.

Less than a hundred years earlier, Buckingham Palace had been nothing more than a house. In 1761, King George III purchased the building for his wife to use and began improving it. In 1820, when George IV became king, he lived elsewhere while continuing the apparently eternal process of renovation, at the expense of more than half a million pounds, until the house had finally been expanded into a palace. When Queen Victoria assumed the throne in 1837, she was the first monarch to use it as a primary residence, but as the number of her children increased, it needed to be enlarged yet again.

Surveying the vast, three-storey edifice, De Quincey marvelled, "So much has changed. When I last saw London decades ago, the Marble Arch stood here as an entrance. In place of this wing, there was only a wall."

Commissioner Mayne nodded. "To make room for the east wing, the arch was dismantled eight years ago and eventually rebuilt in Hyde Park."

"It celebrated our victory over Napoleon," De Quincey said, "and yet it occupied its original place of honour for only fourteen years before Her Majesty and His Highness took it down. How glory fades."

"For God's sake, don't speak that way inside," Lord Palmerston warned.

The home secretary walked through the snow and approached a gate. Announcing himself, he told a guard, "Her Majesty expects us."

The guard snapped to attention and led them to another guard, who took them to a third. Finally they were escorted into a tunnel-like entrance, where an attendant conducted them through a bewildering sequence of corridors.

As if in a laudanum dream, De Quincey peered up at the stunningly high ceilings and their ornate chandeliers. He walked along the soft carpet in a daze, prompting Lord Palmerston to urge him to walk faster. The walls were papered and wainscoted and stuccoed and pillared in a French neoclassical style with pink, blue, and gold high-lighting everywhere. There were Chinese patterns also, the strange contrast making De Quincey feel that he was hallucinating.

Lord Palmerston's urgent request for an audience with Her Majesty must have included the caution that the matter needed to be discussed in utmost confidence, for their escort took them away from the palace's public areas, guiding them through deserted sections and up a narrow staircase perhaps used only by servants. The deeper they penetrated into the palace, the colder it became.

More stairs, twists, and turns brought them to the largest room that De Quincey had ever seen. It was three times the size of the ballroom in Lord Palmerston's residence.

De Quincey wasn't the only person who was amazed.

"The Throne Room?" Lord Palmerston asked the attendant. Confused, he indicated the vast pink-and-gold magnificence. "Are you certain there hasn't been a mistake? Surely this isn't Her Majesty's idea of a place for a confidential meeting."

"My Lord, the queen was explicit. She said that she and Prince Albert would meet you in the Throne Room. Please be seated."

As the attendant departed, De Quincey reached to open a curtain.

"Don't touch anything," Lord Palmerston warned. "Get over here and sit down." He pointed towards a line of chairs between French doors. Like almost everything else in the palace, the chairs were neoclassical in style.

Everyone sat.

"I wish my mother and father were still alive so I could describe this to them," Becker said, awestruck.

At the far end of the massive room, a throne dominated an ornate dais. Pink curtains hung in the background, creating the impression of a theatre's stage.

Emily kept her coat on and pressed her arms to her chest.

"It used to be even colder before the fireplaces were repaired," Ryan said.

Emily looked confused. "You sound as if you've been here before."

"Often," Ryan answered. "The first time was in eighteen forty—because of Edward Oxford. The palace had an odour then."

"Quiet," Lord Palmerston said. "The queen might hear you."

"But it's a compliment to Prince Albert that the odour was removed," Ryan noted. "Mostly it was caused by the smoke from the poorly designed fireplaces. The maids spent most of their time wiping soot from the furniture. The ventilation was so poor that when gas fixtures were installed, we worried that everyone might die from asphyxiation. Prince Albert took charge and put the palace in order."

"I met King George the Third once," De Quincey said.

"Be still," Lord Palmerston repeated. "I hear footsteps."

"When I was fifteen, through a friend whose family had a title, I was invited to a royal event at Windsor," De Quincey recalled, reaching for his laudanum bottle.

"No, Father," Emily said.

De Quincey sighed and returned the bottle to his coat. "I was playing next to a stream when the king and his escorts strolled along it. 'And how are you, young man?' the king asked. 'Fine, Your Majesty,' I answered. 'What is your name?' the king wanted to know. 'Thomas De Quincey, Your Majesty,' I answered. 'De Quincey,' the king said. 'That sounds aristocratic. Were your ancestors French?' 'They came to England from Normandy with William the Conqueror, Your Majesty,' I replied. The king indicated that he was impressed and walked on."

"You come from noble ancestry?" Lord Palmerston asked with new regard for him.

"No, My Lord."

"But you told the king . . ."

"I needed to tell him *something* that sounded of consequence. I couldn't just say that one day my mother decided to add 'De' to the family name to give it more dignity."

Commissioner Mayne gasped. "You lied to the king? Thomas De Quincey isn't your real name?"

"What magazine editor would buy essays from someone whose name was as plain as Thomas Quincey?"

"I wish I had never met you," Lord Palmerston said.

Footsteps again sounded in a corridor.

"Stand when the queen and the prince enter," Lord Palmerston told the group. "The men will bow their heads. Miss De Quincey will curtsey."

Lord Palmerston looked at Emily's bloomer skirt. His expression suggested that he'd become so accustomed to seeing trousers beneath it that only now did he realize how unorthodox her garments might appear to the queen.

"Commissioner Mayne and I will approach the queen and the prince when they indicate that is what they wish," he explained quickly. "Inspector Ryan, stay here until we summon you. Sergeant Becker, Miss De Quincey, and Mister De Quincey"—Lord Palmerston sounded sarcastic when he used "Mister" and "De"—"remain standing. Under no circumstances say anything. How I wish you were on a train bound for Scotland."

"Mister De Quincey will be useful, My Lord," Ryan said. "I have no doubt."

As footsteps entered the vast room, the group hurriedly stood, facing the most powerful monarch in the world and her closest adviser, her husband, Prince Albert.

In 1855, Queen Victoria and Prince Albert had been married for fifteen years. Initially the adjustment had been difficult. A husband normally exerted unquestioned dominance, to the point that his wife had no legal rights for herself or her children and no share of the property that she brought to a marriage or that the husband subsequently acquired. But in this extraordinary situation, the queen enjoyed centuries-long legal rights and owned massive amounts of property over which Albert had no control. Indeed Parliament insisted that Albert occupy a lower rank than his wife, making their marriage the most unusual alliance in the empire.

There were many other ways in which the marriage was unusual. Middle- and upper-class wives took pride in not having an occupation, but the business of being the queen was the most prominent anyone could imagine. Wives were normally satellites of their husbands, but Albert was the satellite of his wife.

When the excitement of the wedding passed, he had little to do except blot the ink on documents that Victoria signed. She excluded him from her meetings with her prime minister and her Privy Council. She didn't allow him to read the parliamentary reports that occupied hours of her time.

Albert took to pacing the palace corridors. In a fit of boredom, he became the equivalent of a nineteenth-century wife and organized the royal household, which absolutely needed to be organized. Servants responsible for the interior of the palace could wash the inside of windows but weren't allowed to go outside and finish the job, a task reserved for other servants. Those responsible for placing wood in a fireplace weren't allowed to light the fire, a chore assigned to others. The inefficiency was such that the palace, only recently renovated, was dirty and already showed signs of disrepair. Burdened by far more servants than were necessary, the household budget—grudgingly awarded by Parliament—needed to be increased each year. But after Albert released superfluous staff members and coordinated the work of the remainder, the improved conditions in the palace—not to mention the money he saved—prompted politicians who had initially disliked him to become his supporters.

Meanwhile, Victoria gave birth to a succession of children, four boys and four girls by 1855. Frequently unable to attend public functions, she assigned Albert to take her place. In time, she asked him for advice and gave him a desk next to hers. After she read confidential documents, she passed them to him. He added his notes to hers. He attended her meetings with the prime minister and her other advisers, offering his opinion. In all but name, he became a co-monarch.

But only four years after Albert's triumphant Crystal Palace Exhibition, England declared war against Russia. The mismanagement of the Crimean War, the needless deaths of thousands of English soldiers, and the real possibility that Russia would be the victor turned the populace against the government and the monarchy.

Albert, in particular, experienced a spectacular fall from public admiration. Despite all his efforts to make England forget his origins, by February of 1855 people on the street had reverted to their initial dislike of him as a foreigner from a poor German state. They again believed that he would plunge the country into debt and make it the vassal of another nation. Germany. Russia. What was the difference? They decided that Albert was probably a spy.

Standing in a doorway with a shadowy corridor behind them, Queen Victoria and Prince Albert seemed to have materialized rather than entered the Throne Room. If they'd been members of the working class, they would have attracted no attention. Victoria's slender nose emphasized how round her face was. Albert's moustache and long sideburns did nothing to broaden his narrow, soft features.

But when it came to royalty, the shape of a face didn't matter. These were Queen Victoria and Prince Albert, after all. Their elevated status led observers to endow the couple with an almost religious aura.

Victoria's hooped dress—made from yards and yards of ruffled satin and brocaded silk—was a green so dark that no one could have called it festive, an example of her determination to appear reserved in contrast with the extravagance of her predecessors. The only decorations on Albert's black suit were brass buttons and a gold-coloured epaulette on one shoulder.

The queen's light brown hair was combed close to her head and parted in the middle. A bonnet covered the back of her head, concealing where the ends of her hair were gathered. Although the bonnet was made of ornate cloth, it somehow resembled a small crown.

Prince Albert slouched slightly, but Queen Victoria stood perfectly straight. When she was a child, her mother had placed spiked holly leaves beneath the back of her dress. Thus at an early age, Victoria had learned to walk with flawless posture to prevent the holly leaves from pricking her skin.

"Your Majesty and Your Highness." As Lord Palmerston bowed, the others imitated him, Emily curtseying.

The queen gestured for Lord Palmerston to approach.

"When you asked for a confidential meeting of utmost urgency, I did not expect that you would bring others." Victoria's voice was high-pitched in a way that newspaper reporters kindly described as silvery. "Who are these other people? That red hair. Constable Ryan, is it you?"

"Yes, Your Majesty." Ryan again bowed.

"Why aren't you in uniform?"

"I'm not a constable any longer, Your Majesty."

"You left the police force? How will London get along without you? No one will be safe."

"I was promoted, Your Majesty. I'm now a detective inspector."

"Coming up in the world? Excellent. Prince Albert and I remain grateful to you for protecting us."

"It was my privilege, Your Majesty."

"And who is that tall man next to you?"

"His name is Detective Sergeant Becker, Your Majesty."

Becker bowed again.

"My goodness, we're awash in detectives." Prince Albert joined the conversation, his German accent strong. "And Commissioner Mayne is here also. The little man next to you, is *he* a detective as well?"

"No, Your Highness," Ryan answered.

"Thomas De Quincey, Your Highness." Having been instructed not to speak, he received a sour look from Lord Palmerston.

"I know that name from somewhere," the prince said. "It sounds distinguished."

"One of my ancestors came from Normandy with William the Conqueror, Your Highness."

Lord Palmerston coughed.

"Is something wrong, Lord Palmerston?" the queen asked. "Commissioner Mayne, perhaps *you* can resolve our confusion."

"Your Majesty, a member of the peerage was murdered this morning in St. James's Church."

Queen Victoria's mother had also trained her to conceal her emotions. A monarch—especially a female monarch—needed to appear strong. A public show of feeling was an admission of weakness.

"Murdered?" the queen asked in a forced, neutral tone.

As delicately as possible, Commissioner Mayne told them what had happened at the church.

"Were you familiar with Lord Cosgrove?" the commissioner asked. "I regret to say that he too was killed. At his home in Mayfair."

The queen and prince continued to hide their reactions, except that now the corners of their eyes tightened.

"Your Majesty, we would not normally trouble you with news of this sort," Lord Palmerston continued, "but Lady Cosgrove was holding a note that read 'Young England.' "

"Young England?" Now Queen Victoria's voice betrayed her concern.

"And Lord Cosgrove was holding a note also."

"What was in it?" Prince Albert asked sharply.

"The name of Edward Oxford, Your Highness."

The queen and Prince Albert quickly looked at each other.

"*Edward Oxford?* Has he escaped from Bedlam?" Queen Victoria asked.

"No, Your Majesty. We don't yet know who wrote the notes or committed the crimes."

In a rare public gesture, the queen touched the prince's arm.

"It's happening again," she said.

"We came to tell you that everything is being done to ensure your safety," Lord Palmerston promised them.

"And what could that be?" Queen Victoria objected, her round features straining with concern. "Without a government, no cabinet official has authority. You no longer act as home secretary, with the full power of your former office. What's more, there's no longer a war secretary to give orders to the army and increase the guards who patrol the palace."

"With direct instructions from you, Your Majesty, we can bypass the lack of government," Lord Palmerston tried to assure her.

"But the newspapers would object that I exceeded my power."

"Would the newspapers prefer that you were harmed?"

"By giving orders to the army, I could survive but lose something more precious than my life: the monarchy."

"Your Majesty, my own authority is still in effect," Police Commissioner Mayne said. "The newspapers can't object if I arrange for more constables to patrol the palace. A few unofficial words from me will prompt the army guards to increase their numbers as well, without any suggestion that you were responsible. Your schedule—if I may take the liberty—needs to be restricted, especially your public appearances. I recommend that you avoid contact with anyone whom you don't know."

"Such as that young woman over there." Queen Victoria pointed with suspicion.

"She is Mr. De Quincey's daughter, Your Majesty."

"Why do I know that name?" Prince Albert wondered.

"He . . ." Commissioner Mayne was at a loss for words. ". . . consults with the police force, Your Highness."

Queen Victoria kept staring at Emily. "What is that strange costume she's wearing?"

"A bloomer skirt, Your Majesty," Emily volunteered.

"Step forward, young woman. Anyone who walks around in that sort of costume could be suspected of being an anarchist. Are those *trousers* under your dress?"

"Yes, Your Majesty. Along with the absence of a hoop, the dress gives me freedom of movement. An American woman named Amelia Bloomer championed the style. She believes in rights for women."

"Rights for women?" Even though the queen herself enjoyed unusual rights, she looked mystified.

"Your Majesty, the dark green of your costume is beautiful, if I may say. But danger can come from many sources."

"I don't understand."

"The dye on your dress is almost certainly embedded with arsenic."

Colour drained from Queen Victoria's cheeks. "Rat poison?"

"Clothing manufacturers use it to strengthen the green colour in their material. May I demonstrate, Your Majesty?"

Emily opened her handbag and withdrew a vial.

Commissioner Mayne grabbed it. "What on earth are you doing? Don't tell me that's arsenic."

"Liquid ammonia," Emily explained. "Your Majesty, if you would trust someone to put a drop of this liquid on your sleeve, you can determine whether you are wearing arsenic."

Victoria directed another confused gaze towards Emily's bloomer skirt.

"Albert," she said.

The prince took the vial from Emily.

"Your Highness, please choose a spot that can't be seen," Emily instructed. "Merely touch the wet stopper to the material."

"If this kills me, there are plenty of witnesses," Queen Victoria warned.

"Your Majesty, honestly, I—"

"It is a joke," the queen told her.

Albert bent Victoria's left cuff outward and touched the wet stopper to the inside.

Instantly the spot turned from green to blue.

"The ammonia reacted with arsenic, Your Majesty," Emily said.

"Rat poison on my clothes?"

"I'm afraid so. I've saved many women and children from illness by showing them this method of detection. I'd be honoured if you kept the vial, Your Majesty. Perhaps you can help others."

Queen Victoria regarded Emily for several seconds. A slight smile formed. "Prince Albert and I are hosting a dinner at eight this evening. We would be amused if you attended. You can't come without an escort, of course. Your father is invited also."

One of Lord Palmerston's eyelids twitched.

"Commissioner Mayne, arrange for the increase in constables at the palace," the queen ordered. "Inspector Ryan, I know you'll do everything in your power to ensure my safety."

"I swear it, Your Majesty."

"Lord Palmerston," Queen Victoria said with distaste.

"Yes, Your Majesty?"

"We wish to speak to you alone," she told him, as if it were in fact the last thing she wished to do.

The queen's distaste reached all the way back to 1839. In the second year of her reign, she had invited Lord Palmerston to a weekend gathering at Windsor Castle. There, he had recognized a female guest who'd been one of his lovers. Indeed, in his youth his fondness for female companionship had prompted the newspapers to nickname him "Lord Cupid." After dinner, he tried to follow the woman but lost his way in the labyrinth of the castle's corridors. Believing that he'd found her room, he stealthily opened the door, closed it behind him, and discovered that instead of his former paramour, he was face-to-face with someone he didn't know, a married woman who was one of the queen's ladies-in-waiting. The woman whose privacy he had accidentally invaded was so attractive that he adjusted to the situation and made an effort to persuade the woman to accept his amorous advances. When she screamed, he tried to calm her, but servants were already pounding on the door. With profuse apologies, explaining that he had become lost, he asked directions to his room.

Victoria and Albert had detested him ever since, an intense dislike that increased when, as foreign secretary, Lord Palmerston acted on his own authority, issuing edicts to foreign governments and even dispatching military units. Most notably, he had ordered the Royal Navy to blockade the port of Athens, threatening to punish the Greek government if it didn't reimburse a British citizen for damage to his property during a riot. Repeatedly, the queen had summoned him to Buckingham Palace, where she and the prime minister angrily ordered him to stop behaving like an absolute ruler. Again and again, he had offered his profound regrets, promising to abide by their wishes, only to break those promises and continue to behave as if he controlled Great Britain.

While the queen and the prince led him to the end of the enormous room, their distaste looked more pronounced. They mounted the dais, where Queen Victoria sat on her throne while Prince Albert stood to her left.

"When your message informed us that you had a matter of utmost urgency to discuss, we assumed that it related to the lack of a government," Queen Victoria said.

"No. My purpose for coming here was to keep you from harm, Your Majesty."

"We thank you for your concern." The expression on the queen's face said otherwise, communicating her doubt that Lord Palmerston could ever wish her well. "With Lord Aberdeen unable to continue as prime minister because of the war's misconduct, we consulted with various other lords in the hope that one of them could form a new majority. None, it appears, is popular enough to unite all the factions."

The queen and the prince studied Lord Palmerston with graver dislike.

"We imagined that you intended to make suggestions about how to solve the political crisis," Prince Albert said grimly.

"I regret that I do not have *any* suggestions, Your Highness. The war has thrown everyone into disarray and uncertainty."

Queen Victoria and Prince Albert seemed to wish fervently that they didn't need to continue the conversation.

"Under certain conditions, would *you* be willing to accept the position of prime minister?" the queen asked, sounding forlorn.

"*I*, Your Majesty?" Lord Palmerston hid his immense surprise. Hundreds of years earlier, such royal disfavour would have prompted his beheading. "Become prime minister?"

"We said *under certain conditions*," the queen emphasized.

"Kindly tell me what they are, Your Majesty."

"You must swear to consult with the cabinet and Parliament, and above all with *us*, before you make policy."

"Your Majesty, I have always tried to be at your service. On former occasions, an excess of zeal prompted me to act before consulting with you. But I have learned with age. I shall do my utmost to be your loyal prime minister."

The queen and the prince continued to regard him sourly.

East of Buckingham Palace stretched St. James's Park. Bordered by the Whitehall government buildings and the newly built Houses of Parliament, the park was surrounded by Britain's sites of power. All Sunday afternoon, people hurried to its frozen lake, bringing skates or else renting them. This was a rare occasion when high and low, rich and poor, ignored social barriers.

Sweepers cleared the accumulating snow, hoping for a penny in return. A central drift formed the focus around which skaters glided, pirouetted, stumbled, or fell. A few even managed to skate backward, looking over their shoulders in a way that reminded some spectators of crabs. If a skater needed a respite, for twopence a vendor provided a chair and restrapped loosened skates. Brandy-ball men held trays of refreshments, their round confections laced with peppermint, ginger, or red pepper rather than the promised brandy.

A corner of the lake remained unfrozen, accommodating geese, ducks, and swans. Dark ripples warned that if too many skaters swarmed across the ice or jumped in acrobatic manoeuvres, the ice might break. Along the bank, signs warned danger. A large tent contained stimulants, hot-water bottles, dry clothes, and blankets heated by hot bricks to resuscitate people who fell through the ice—an increasing possibility as more people slid across it.

The ice began to tremble. Hearing a crack, the horde sped towards the banks, causing the ice to heave more severely. Amid screams, a large section made an explosive sound and broke away, dark water erupting as skaters plunged into it.

"Help!"

Rescuers grabbed ropes and ran towards the bodies thrashing in the icy water.

"Can't feel my legs!"

As the crowd watched in horror from the safety of the banks, a man tried to pull his friend from the dark water but couldn't quite reach him. He took off one of his skates, lay on the ice, squirmed as close as he dared, and swung the skate towards his struggling companion. The drenched, freezing man stretched out his dripping arm and managed to grab the blade when suddenly the ice broke again, plunging the would-be rescuer into the water with his friend.

So many flailing hands reached for the proffered ropes that

the rescuers were nearly yanked into the water. Dripping, the victims hugged themselves and shivered, staggering towards the medical tent. The finest overcoats became as stiff with cold as the most ragged jackets. The most expensive boots became as waterlogged as those with gaps in their soles.

"There's blood on the ice!"

"Look! Somebody's floatin' in the water!"

Even though wet, the quality of the gentleman's clothes was readily apparent. He bobbed face down among chunks of ice. Blood tinted the water.

"Must've banged 'is 'ead! Quick! Get a pole!"

A half-dozen earnest souls sped to the task, dragging the fashionably dressed man from the water and turning him over.

"Can you hear me?" a rescuer yelled.

But it was obvious that the gentleman would never hear anything again, just as it was obvious that he had not struck his head on the ice—because the blood did not come from the gentleman's head. The source of the copious crimson was his throat, which had been slashed from ear to ear. Sickened, one of the rescuers spun towards the snowbanks, where countless faces stared back at him.

"Murder!"

"What's that he said? It sounded like—"

"Murder! Police! Someone get the police!"

A few rushed to obey. Most stayed to see what would happen next.

"I recognize 'im! That's Sir Richard Hawkins! He's a judge!"

"A judge? *Are you certain?*"

"Oh, that's 'im all right. I was in court when he sent my brother to prison last month."

"Blimey, look at 'is throat! It's cut to the back of 'is neck!"

6

The Warehouse of Grief

"Why are so many people yelling?" Commissioner Mayne asked.

Panicked shouts made the group pause as they left the immensity of Buckingham Palace. It was after five o'clock, and night was upon them. In the falling snow, nothing was visible beyond Lord Palmerston's coach waiting at a shrouded street lamp beyond the palace gates.

The commotion intensified, coming from the gloom across the road.

"Something must have happened in St. James's Park," Ryan said.

Police clackers penetrated the shouts, sounding the alarm.

"Sergeant Becker, find out what's wrong," Commissioner Mayne ordered.

"Yes, sir." Becker hurried away, disappearing into the darkness.

"Inspector, kindly take us back to the church," De Quincey said. "Emily and I have something to show you there. But first we need to stop at Jay's Mourning Warehouse."

"Jay's Mourning Warehouse?" Lord Palmerston objected. "Why on earth do you need to go *there*? You barely have time to prepare for the queen's dinner."

"Prepare what?" Emily asked in confusion.

"Your dinner clothes," Lord Palmerston explained.

"But we don't have any."

"A bloomer skirt isn't suitable for a royal event. Your father's sleeves are threadbare. A button is missing."

"Do you have a coat that might fit him?" Emily asked, comparing her father's short, thin frame to Lord Palmerston's towering stature and powerful chest.

"None." Lord Palmerston groaned. "The two of you are associated with me. If you ruin the queen's dinner, she will blame me."

Using the shouts to guide him, Becker rushed through the darkness. He tugged gloves from his coat and pulled his cap down over his ears, but neither they nor his exertion dispelled the cold.

A shadow loomed; a man ran past.

"What happened?" Becker demanded.

"No tellin' who'll be killed next!"

Another figure suddenly appeared, jolting Becker and charging on.

"Hey!" Becker yelled, but the figure was gone.

The railings that enclosed St. James's Park came into view a moment before he would have struck them. Beyond, faint lights bobbed from what Becker guessed were police lanterns. He ran along the fence, found people rushing through an open gate, and ignored the shoulders that bumped against him as he squeezed past. Taking long strides through the snow, he reached a constable, who aimed his lantern at a panicked crowd.

"I'm Detective Sergeant Becker. What happened?"

"A judge had his throat slit!"

"A judge?"

"Sir Richard Hawkins," the constable answered.

"But I saw him only a week ago. I gave evidence in his court."

"He won't be in court again, I can tell you."

Becker hurried to where other constables strained to establish order. Abruptly he felt movement beneath his feet. The ice rippled, seemingly alive. Dizzy, he spread his arms to keep his balance. The crowd hurried towards the shore. As the ice slowly stopped heaving, Becker took a long breath to calm his speeding heart and shifted cautiously towards the body before him.

A constable stood next to it, his lantern revealing the corpse's unusually broad chin, a distinctive feature of Judge Hawkins. Falling snow speckled the crimson gash in his throat.

Feeling an emotion colder than the snow, Becker remembered Ryan's warning: *Distract yourself. Concentrate on the details.*

"Any witnesses?" Becker asked.

"Hundreds," the constable answered. "But I doubt any of them knew it. The murderer probably bumped into him when he was skating, slit his throat while he was down, then moved on before anybody noticed."

"Skating?"

The constable shifted the lantern, revealing skates on the corpse's expensive boots. Somehow the skates seemed more grotesque than the snow on the red throat.

"He still has his purse and his watch, so it doesn't look like a thief killed him. *This* was wedged into his coat." The constable handed Becker an oilskin-covered pouch.

Cold seeped through Becker's gloves as he broke the ice that had started to form on the pouch. Inside, he found a piece of paper that the oilskin had kept dry. The paper had a one-inch black border identical to the one he'd seen at Lord Cosgrove's residence.

"Aim your lantern," Becker said.

The light revealed handwriting that appeared to be the same as on the earlier note.

The message contained only two words.

"*Young England?*" the constable asked. "Do you know what that means?"

"I'm afraid I do." Becker's chill sank deeper into his chest. "Do you know where the judge lived? I need to go there at once."

The coach stopped on fashionable Regent Street. De Quincey, Emily, and Ryan stepped down into the snow and faced a three-storey building that seemed to be weeping. Its wood trim was black and resembled teardrops. Every window was draped in black. Lamps in the windows revealed that, all the way to the rear, every display and counter was also draped in black.

A sign indicated that this was jay's mourning warehouse, one of the most prosperous businesses in all of London. After a family member died, relatives were immediately required to put on mourning clothes. If such garments weren't available, a servant or a neighbour was quickly dispatched to Jay's, where a vast array of funereal raiment was available. If the bereaved family had means, Jay would even send them fitters in a hearse-like carriage with black horses and a black-clad driver, lest the neighbours be scandalized by an insufficient show of grief.

"I still don't understand why you brought us here," Ryan said.

Instead of answering, De Quincey proceeded towards the front door. Lord Palmerston and Commissioner Mayne were no longer with them, attending to urgent duties related to the queen's protection.

"Please wait," Ryan said as they reached a protective canopy.

De Quincey looked at him questioningly.

"This has been bothering me since we were at Lord Cosgrove's house," Ryan said. "I need to ask what you meant when you said that you had doubts about what happened fifteen years ago and Edward Oxford's intentions to kill the queen."

"His pistols were almost certainly not loaded," De Quincey said. "His only crime was to startle Her Majesty, and yet the Attorney General ensured that Oxford was sequestered in a madhouse for the rest of his life."

"You said something about treason," Ryan persisted. "Before I could ask for an explanation, Lord Palmerston and Commissioner Mayne arrived. We were forced to interrupt the conversation. What did you intend to tell me?"

"Not until I'm certain."

As snow gusted under the canopy, De Quincey turned towards the front door.

Death didn't maintain a predictable schedule. Day or night, the warehouse of grief was always unlocked. When the three of them entered, the impression of sorrow and gloom was even stronger than it had seemed through the window. The floor was covered with a thick black carpet that deadened sounds. Black mourning garments hung from spectre-like mannequins. Coffin palls and bereavement veils were arranged on shelves. One counter had stacks of black envelopes with black-bordered notepaper next to them—the same death-announcement stationery they had found at the church and at the Cosgrove mansion.

A gaunt, sombre man in a black suit with an armband emerged from the gloom. His voice was soft. "I'm sorry that circumstances require you to come here, and on such a terrible night."

The man paused, doubtfully assessing Emily's bloomer skirt, De Quincey's frayed coat, and Ryan's newsboy's cap, which he took off, revealing his Irish red hair.

The clerk gathered himself and continued, "Jay's Mourning Warehouse will assist you in every way possible. May I ask which of your loved ones has departed?"

"We are fortunate that our loved ones remain with us," De Quincey replied, glancing towards Emily.

"Then it's a friend who has died?" the clerk asked. "A true friend is a treasure. To lose a trusted companion—"

"We haven't lost a friend, either."

"Then I fail to understand."

"You're not the only one," Ryan murmured.

"Have you perhaps lost a distant relative or the friend of someone close to you?" the clerk asked.

"None of those, either," De Quincey answered. "Do you have a frock coat that would fit me and that I could wear to a formal dinner?"

The clerk looked baffled. Assessing De Quincey's diminutive height, he answered, "I might have a youth's coat that would fit you. But I never heard of anyone wearing funereal garments to a formal dinner."

"Do your clients sometimes need medication to help them endure intense grief?"

"Medication?" the clerk asked.

"To soothe the nerves."

"I believe he's talking about laudanum," Ryan said unhappily.

"Well, yes, we have what you refer to as medication, in case a client succumbs to extreme emotions."

"Would you be so good as to refill this?" De Quincey gave the clerk his laudanum bottle.

"You came here for a coat and laudanum?" The clerk began to lose his sympathetic tone.

"And funereal garments for a woman."

"Why for a woman?" Ryan interrupted, puzzled.

"Of the deepest gloom," De Quincey specified.

"If I may enquire," the clerk said, "under these unusual circumstances, considering that none of you has lost a loved one or a friend or even a friend of a friend . . ."

The clerk paused delicately.

"You want to know who's going to pay for this?" Ryan asked.

"In a word," the clerk answered.

"As much as I hate to say it—the Metropolitan Police." Ryan showed his badge.

For a moment the clerk looked doubtful that the badge was authentic. Then he nodded. "We always wish to be on good terms with the police." He turned towards De Quincey. "Follow me, sir."

"Inspector, would you be patient enough to wait here while Emily and I attend to something?" De Quincey asked. "It would be better if you didn't know my intentions."

"It usually is," Ryan said.

Becker ran towards Mayfair, a half mile north of St. James's Park. The sharp rush of cold air into his mouth froze his throat.

The address he'd been given was on Curzon Street, which he'd hurried along five hours earlier. His urgent strides sent snow flying as he rounded a corner and studied what he could see of the narrow street.

Like the other areas in Mayfair, the buildings here were attached. Their Portland stone and uniform four levels, with matching wrought-iron railings, made each house identical to its neighbour. The snow clinging to them reinforced the illusion that they were interchangeable.

The number he'd been given was fifty-three.

He raced along, counting off the brass numbers that lamps over entrances revealed. But at one entrance, the lamp wasn't illuminated. Nor did any lights glow behind any of the curtained windows. If any tracks had preceded him, they had been buried by the snow.

Becker hurried up the steps and banged the brass door knocker repeatedly. The impact resounded inside but received no response. He reached for the latch and wasn't surprised to find it unlocked, just as he wasn't surprised that no one answered when he opened the door and shouted into the darkness.

"This is Detective Sergeant Becker! Can anyone hear me? I'm coming in!"

De Quincey had once talked to him about an opium dream in which he experienced the same grotesque event again and again, trapped in a hellish circle of time. That was how Becker now felt as the door jolted against something on the floor. He found a table and touched a box of matches lying next to a candle. His hands shook as he lit the taper.

A male servant lay on the floor. His head was cratered. Congealing blood indicated that the attack had been recent.

Holding the candle with his left hand, Becker drew his knife from under his right trouser leg, then cautiously entered a front hall. Hothouse flowers filled Oriental vases. The scent was cloying. A portrait of a man in a military uniform gazed sternly down at him. As the echo of Becker's footsteps faded into silence, he listened for any sound of movement, but all he heard was the ticking of a clock.

Closed doors confronted him on the right and left. The candle wavered as he opened the one on the right. Beyond it he found a sitting room like the one at Lord Cosgrove's house. There, the sitting room had been deserted. Here, a silhouette sat in one of the many plush chairs.

"I'm a detective sergeant. Can you hear me?" Becker asked.

As he warily approached, the candle revealed that the silhouette belonged to a woman. She was tied to the chair. Her head was tilted back. An object of some sort projected from her mouth.

Feeling sick, Becker realized that the object was a bladder made from animal skin. The room had a distinctive odour, not of death (too soon) or of blood (there wasn't any). No, the odour was something that he recognized from years of having lived on a farm. What he smelled was sour milk. The woman's hair and clothes were drenched with it. The white liquid seeped from the bladder stuffed between her lips. Someone had forced milk down her throat, pouring relentlessly until she drowned.

Her right hand gripped a piece of paper. With a terrible premonition, Becker pulled it from her fingers and recognized the one-inch black border. Two words were written in the strong, clear script that was becoming all too familiar.

John Francis.

Becker couldn't identify the name, but feeling an even deeper chill, he had no doubt that it belonged to another of the men who had tried to kill Queen Victoria.

When De Quincey entered St. James's Church and took off his overcoat, Commissioner Mayne stared at the bleak suit he revealed.

"You look like you're going to a funeral instead of a palace dinner," Mayne said.

"Since the police force paid for the suit, I was grateful for what I could find," De Quincey told him.

"The police force paid for that suit?" Commissioner Mayne directed a disapproving look at Ryan.

"He claims he has a demonstration to make," Ryan answered uncomfortably, changing the subject.

"Demonstration?"

"Of Immanuel Kant's great question," De Quincey replied. "Whether reality exists outside us or in our minds."

"This kind of speculation is irrelevant to the law," the commissioner said. "A jury needs solid, factual, verifiable evidence. Whatever you intend to demonstrate, there isn't much time. The queen expects you in an hour."

The zigzag of lanterns revealed constables hurrying to complete their investigation. The congregation had been dismissed; only a few churchwardens and pew-openers lingered.

Mayne looked startled as a woman in mourning approached

him from the shadows. The black crepe of her dress absorbed the rays from the lanterns. A thick black veil hung from her black bonnet.

Like the commissioner, the constables looked unnerved by her arrival.

"Inspector, this is how Lady Cosgrove looked when she arrived at the church this morning—do you agree?" De Quincey asked.

Ryan nodded. "Are these the woman's garments that you obtained at Jay's Mourning Warehouse? Are they what you kept hidden in the packages you brought here? Emily, now I understand why you stepped into the room off the vestibule when we entered the church. You changed clothes."

"What is this intended to prove?" Commissioner Mayne asked. "Don't tell me that the police force paid for *these* clothes, also."

Ryan looked away, more uncomfortable.

"Lady Cosgrove had an escort," De Quincey said. "Emily, allow me to serve in that capacity."

Pretending to support a bereaved woman, he accompanied her along the aisle. The group followed.

At the front, De Quincey paused before the altar rail, its marble eerily white in the beams from the lanterns. He pointed towards Lady Cosgrove's pew on the right.

"Has Her Ladyship's body been removed?"

"Not yet," Commissioner Mayne said.

"Then we'll need to use the church's other curtained pew." De Quincey pointed towards the far left. "Come, Emily."

Situated in front of a pillar, the box pew was identical to Lady Cosgrove's. It had posts at all four corners, with curtains tied to the posts. There were three rows of benches in it, the same as in Lady Cosgrove's pew.

"May I borrow some lanterns?" De Quincey asked the constables.

He placed several in front of the pew. "To try to create the effect of daylight," he explained. "This morning, Lady Cosgrove's pew was locked. Would someone please unlock *this* one?"

A pew-opener stepped from the group and did so.

De Quincey turned towards the woman in black. "Emily, I'm deeply sorry."

"Sorry? About what?" Commissioner Mayne asked in confusion.

"That's what Lady Cosgrove's escort said to her this morning," De Quincey answered. "Except that of course the man addressed the woman as Lady Cosgrove and not Emily. He said, 'Lady Cosgrove, I'm deeply sorry.' Inspector Ryan, is that correct?"

"Yes," Ryan answered. "That is what I heard."

"Emily, please raise your veil."

When she complied, Commissioner Mayne stepped back in surprise.

"But . . ."

The woman behind the veil wasn't Emily.

She was a white-haired woman of around sixty, whose height approximated that of Emily.

"What on earth?" the commissioner exclaimed.

"When Inspector Ryan referred to her as Emily, this woman nodded," De Quincey said. "When I frequently referred to her as Emily, everyone assumed that they were indeed seeing Emily. That is what happened this morning. The woman who entered the church was *not* Lady Cosgrove. Her escort addressed her as such, however, and convinced everyone that she was indeed so. The reality in our minds differed from what actually stood before us."

"But Lady Cosgrove's body lies on the floor of her pew," Ryan objected.

"Without question." De Quincey turned towards the

woman in the funereal dress. "May I introduce Agnes, a pew-opener who greeted us this morning? When we arrived a while ago, she was in the vestibule and agreed to assist us. Thank you, Agnes. Please lower your veil and resume being Lady Cosgrove—or should I say Emily? So many names. Commissioner, are you well? Your brow is pinched as if you suffer a constriction."

De Quincey reached into his new suit and removed a black envelope that had a black seal, giving it to Agnes.

"I obtained this from Jay's Mourning Warehouse. It resembles what Lady Cosgrove's impersonator was given this morning in plain sight of the congregation. Emily, or rather Agnes, no, I mean Lady Cosgrove, you may continue to re-enact what happened this morning."

The veiled figure entered the pew, shut it, and sat on the first bench.

De Quincey turned towards the constables. "Now will all of you kindly select various pews and pretend that you're at a church service?"

"Whatever's going on, I intend to be near it," Commissioner Mayne said, choosing the adjacent pew.

"I have a better vantage point for you," De Quincey told him. "Please follow me."

De Quincey led him towards the altar railing.

"What are you doing?" the commissioner demanded.

De Quincey drank from his laudanum bottle. "You're going to pretend to be the vicar. A little closer to the railing, please."

"I'm very uncomfortable," Mayne said.

"Now face the congregation."

"Very uncomfortable indeed."

"Because only the vicar was on this spot, I shall leave and give you instructions from the aisle," De Quincey said.

With his back to the altar, Commissioner Mayne watched in bewilderment as De Quincey proceeded past the constables and churchwardens in various pews. The little man diminished into the shadows.

"Commissioner, in your youth, did you ever perform in plays?" De Quincey's voice echoed from the darkness at the rear of the church. "I have some lines for you to recite."

"Really, this is—"

"The service began with a hymn. 'The Son of God Goes Forth to War.' How many of the constables know it?" De Quincey enquired.

Some raised their hands.

"Then join me."

De Quincey's voice rose towards the vaulted ceiling, surprisingly sonorous. *"The Son of God goes forth to war / A kingly crown to gain."*

The constables began singing.

As the commissioner listened in confusion, his attention was directed towards the pew on the right, where the severe figure—what was her name?—tore open the black envelope, unfolded a black-rimmed piece of paper, and read it through her black veil.

The figure moved towards the posts at the corners of her pew. She untied the curtains and closed them at the back and the sides. Hidden from everyone except the commissioner, the woman knelt at the pew's front and placed her brow on the partition.

"Is that what Lady Cosgrove did this morning?" Commissioner Mayne called to De Quincey in the back.

"Yes." The Opium-Eater's voice echoed from the shadows. "The vicar welcomed the congregation, saying something like, 'Whenever our burdens become too great, consider the hardships that our brave soldiers endure.' Can you repeat that, Commissioner? 'Whenever our burdens become too great . . .'"

" 'Whenever our burdens . . .' "

The commissioner frowned as De Quincey emerged from the darkness. Proceeding along the aisle, he held a stack of hymnals. "Please say the rest, Commissioner, about the hardships that our brave soldiers endure."

"I—"

De Quincey suddenly lurched. The books flew out of his hand, scattering along the stone floor. The noise rebounded through the almost-empty church.

"Oh, my goodness!" De Quincey cried.

He scrambled to retrieve them, dropping several more in the process. Two constables opened their pews and stooped to help him.

"What are you doing?" the commissioner demanded.

"My apologies. How clumsy of me." The little man picked up more of the hymnals, delicately balancing the stack. More of them threatened to fall. "Please continue the service."

"*What* service?"

Commissioner Mayne looked towards where the grieving woman—Agnes! *that* was her name—knelt with her forehead on the front of the pew.

But now Agnes was sliding down. At the same time, her head tilted back, revealing . . .

"No!" Mayne cried.

Agnes's veil and dress were covered with crimson.

"My God!" the commissioner shouted. "Her throat's been slit!"

Agnes collapsed out of sight.

Mayne rushed from the altar, joined by Ryan, who hurried from the next pew.

"It's happened again!" Mayne shouted.

De Quincey approached the pew and peered down at the unmoving figure on the floor. The black-rimmed note was clutched in her hand.

"Inspector Ryan, would you please determine if Agnes can

be helped? I recall that you lifted Lady Cosgrove's veil with the tip of your knife, but that won't be necessary in this case."

Confused, Ryan entered the pew. "At least the floor isn't covered with blood."

"Only the front of her dress and a portion of her veil. It's actually red ink from a bottle that I took from the desk in Lord Cosgrove's study. I have a better idea. Commissioner Mayne, would *you* make certain that Agnes hasn't been harmed?"

Frowning, Mayne entered the pew, knelt, and pulled Agnes's veil away.

He jerked back in shock. The face that smiled at him didn't belong to the pew-opener.

The face was Emily's.

"I'm sorry to startle you, Commissioner," she said.

Clutching the black-rimmed note, she rose from the floor.

"What you saw just now is what happened this morning in front of the congregation," De Quincey explained. "Agnes, where are you?"

The white-haired pew-opener stepped from the rear of the group, where she had joined them while they were distracted. She no longer wore mourning clothes.

"Thank you for your help, my dear," De Quincey said.

Agnes couldn't help looking pleased.

"But . . ." Ryan said.

"At Lord Cosgrove's home, you mentioned a bedroom that was splattered with blood. You indicated that you were looking for another victim. Actually, the victim had already been found. She was Lady Cosgrove, who was killed at her home last night. For certain, she did not walk into this church. As you yourself said earlier, it made no sense for her to come home, find the corpses of her brutally murdered husband and household, and then go to church in mourning rather than alert the police. The only way this could have happened is that she was killed at her home. Then her body was dressed in bereavement garments and brought here in the middle of the night. There are so many keys that I doubt it would have been difficult to acquire one of them." De Quincey turned towards the group. "Is any of you missing a key to the entrance?"

"I am," a churchwarden said. "I couldn't remember where I mislaid it. I've been looking everywhere for it."

"In the night, Lady Cosgrove's body was brought here and hidden beneath the rear bench of her pew. Agnes, did you by chance receive a message from Lord and Lady Cosgrove, indicating that they wouldn't attend the church service this morning and that it wasn't necessary to dust their pew or light the charcoal heater?"

"As a matter of fact, I did."

"Thus the killer and his accomplices ensured that the body wouldn't be found by someone unlocking Lady Cosgrove's pew and chancing to find the body beneath the third bench. During the distraction of the hymn, the woman pretending to be Lady Cosgrove closed the curtains in the pew. The only person who could see her was the vicar, but he was preoccupied by the sight of the esteemed war hero, Colonel Trask, proceeding along the aisle in his scarlet uniform, accompanied by an uncommonly beautiful woman. Every eye, including the vicar's, was upon that glowing pair. It was an easy matter for the impostor to slip down out of sight below the pew's partition. Unseen, she pulled Lady Cosgrove's body to the front and propped her into view before the vicar was no longer distracted by the procession. My meagre distraction of dropping the hymnals and scurrying to retrieve them was sufficient in this case. The note that the impostor was given and the identical note in the victim's hand reinforced the impression that the two figures were the same."

"But what about the blood on the floor?" Ryan asked.

"A bladder of it—probably blood from an animal—was hidden with the corpse. After propping up Lady Cosgrove's body, the impostor emptied the bladder so that it drained under the pew's gate. Before the sight of the blood alarmed the vicar, the impostor returned to her hiding place beneath the rear bench, removed her disguise, and put it in a bag. During the commotion, she slipped out the back of the pew, using the curtain and the pillar behind the pew to conceal her. A woman would not have attracted attention as she mingled with the alarmed congregation, just as Agnes didn't attract attention when she rejoined us."

"People saw what they had been told to see," Commissioner Mayne said.

"Indeed. The question of whether reality exists outside us or in our minds is not an idle one, Commissioner. Worshippers were deluded into thinking that a brutal murder occurred in their midst, in St. James's Church of all places, and that the killer was capable of vanishing mysteriously. Tomorrow morning, London's fifty-two newspapers will spread that conviction. People will believe that if they aren't safe in church on a Sunday morning, surely they aren't safe in their beds or anywhere else. The purpose isn't only to achieve revenge but also to create panic. You can be certain there'll be other murders that involve public places."

A sudden noise made De Quincey turn.

A door banged open at the back of the church. Becker rushed in, snow falling from his hat and coat. He struggled to catch his breath. "A judge . . . Sir Richard Hawkins . . . throat slit . . . St. James's Park!"

"*What?*" Commissioner Mayne exclaimed.

"His wife . . . a tube down her throat . . . drowned her with . . ."

The revenger never forgot his father's shock when the constable approached their meagre cottage, asking, "Is Caitlin O'Brien your wife?"

"She is. Why? Has something happened to her?"

The Irish accent made the constable look him up and down. "You could say that."

"I don't understand."

"She's been arrested."

"Arrest . . ." Colin's father couldn't finish the word. It was the first time Colin had ever heard him sound afraid. "My God, for what?"

"Shoplifting."

"No!"

"From Burbridge's linens."

"There has to be a mistake. That's the shop where Caitlin went to sell her knitting."

"I don't know anything about knitting, but I know when your wife left Burbridge's shop, she had more in her basket than when she went in."

"No! Caitlin would never—"

"Be careful who you raise your voice to. Maybe you can get away with yelling at constables where you came from, but over here, people show respect for authority."

"I'm not trying to . . . I didn't mean . . . Where *is* she? At the police station in St. John's Wood?"

"If you want to help her, you'd better find a lawyer."

The constable turned to walk towards the wicker seat of a two-wheeled pony cart that he'd driven from the city.

"Can you take me with you?" Colin's father begged.

"You can see there's space for only one man in the cart."

"At least wait for me so that you can show me to the police station! Please! I need to see her!"

The constable let out an irritated sigh. "I can give you five minutes."

Colin's father hurried back to the cottage.

"Emma, you're the oldest. Stay here and watch Ruth. This is all the money I have." It amounted to just a few coins. "I'll take Colin with me. He can bring back messages if I don't return right away."

The constable flicked the reins on the cart's pony and started to drive away.

"Colin, grab your coat and a chunk of bread for each of us," his father said quickly.

Breathless, trembling with fear, Colin did what he was told, then raced to catch up with his father, who hurried to catch up with the constable.

All along the half-built street, women and children stood at open doors, watching.

The lane of their village merged with a broader one and then a main road, the mass of traffic increasing along with the clamour of hooves and wheels.

"Police! Out of the way!" the constable shouted.

When carriages and animals wouldn't part for him, the constable swerved his cart into the ditch and hurried through the rising dust.

Colin tripped and fell, scraping his arm on gravel. He scrambled to his feet and stretched his short legs to rush after his father. Dust caked his lips.

At last they reached the sign St. John's Wood, but the narrow streets increased the congestion, the cobblestones adding to the din of hooves and wheels.

The constable turned his cart onto a lane and stopped the horse at a building that resembled a shop, although its sign announced police.

"I don't know what use it did you to follow me here. You'll spend your time better if you look for a lawyer."

"But I need to talk to my wife!"

A sergeant stepped from the police station. "What's all this shouting?"

"My wife's here! Caitlin O'Brien!"

"The Irish shoplifter? No, you're wrong. She *isn't* here."

"You mean you released her?"

"I mean we no longer had space. An hour ago your wife was carted to London with two other thieves."

"London?"

"To Newgate Prison. Yell at somebody *there* and see what happens."

"God help us. Newgate." For a moment, Colin's father was paralyzed with dismay. Recovering, he asked, "Where's Burbridge's?"

"Make trouble with a witness, and you'll join your wife in Newgate."

Colin's father ran into the street, begging directions from passers-by.

"Where's Burbridge's linen shop? Can you tell me where to find . . .?"

People backed away.

"Two lanes up. On the right," a man finally said, to be rid of him.

Colin's legs ached from the effort of so much running. Somehow, he managed to keep his father in view as they hurried through the crowd. His father rushed into a shop where shirts, handkerchiefs, and tablecloths were displayed in a window.

When Colin entered, he heard his father saying to a man behind a counter, "My wife came here yesterday to sell three jumpers that she knitted."

"I didn't need them." Burbridge was heavyset, round-faced with thick dark eyebrows.

"We live in Helmsey Field, four miles north of here," Colin's father said. "A woman there told us she's your sister."

"I don't know what *that* has to do with anything."

"Your sister told my wife to come here. She said that the jumpers my wife knitted were the kind of special item you like to sell."

"My sister might have thought the jumpers were special, but they weren't up to my standards. I told your wife I couldn't use them, and the next thing I knew, I saw her putting a shirt under the knitting in the basket she carried."

"No! Caitlin wouldn't do that!"

"Well, she *did*. I know what I saw."

"There's got to be a mistake."

The door opened. The constable they'd followed to St. John's Wood stepped inside and put a hand on his truncheon.

"Trouble?" the policeman asked.

"This Irishman's calling me a liar."

"No! I didn't say that! All I'm saying is there's been a mistake!"

"In your place, I wouldn't be bothering the man your wife stole from," the constable advised.

"He's scaring off my customers," Burbridge complained.

"You can go to Newgate Prison and try to help your wife," the constable warned, "or else I can arrange for you to go to Newgate a different way."

Colin's father looked at both men in desperation. Then he ran from the shop.

Colin chased after him. They reached the main road and joined the relentless roar of vehicles and livestock surging onto it from various lanes. The accumulating noise and dust became overwhelming, carrying them along with such force that even if they'd wanted to return to their village, they couldn't have broken free. The boy had the feeling of being trapped in the relentless rush of a swollen river, hurtling towards a waterfall, but instead of spray hovering over the waterfall, a thick brown pall hung above London.

As Becker finished his breathless message, the group listened in shock at the back of the church. The fidgeting of police lanterns illuminated the group's stark expressions.

"Drowned the judge's wife in ...?" The commissioner turned towards De Quincey. "*Milk?* That doesn't make sense. No one in his right mind ..."

"It makes perfect sense," De Quincey said. "The killer knows exactly what he's doing and is definitely in his right mind, at least as the law defines sanity."

"But only a monster would do this."

"Or someone who feels that his victims are monsters," De Quincey said. "It's clear that the killer believes his horrid actions are perfectly justified. When I say 'milk,' what's the first thought that comes to you, Commissioner?"

Mayne's quick mind responded, "Because we're in church: a biblical passage. 'A land flowing with milk and honey.' "

"And *you*, Inspector Ryan? *Your* first thought?"

"The purity of a mother's milk. But I don't see how either of those expressions helps us."

"Emily?" De Quincey requested. "What comes to *your* mind when I say the word 'milk'?"

"*Macbeth*, of course."

"Excellent, my dear."

Commissioner Mayne looked baffled. "Miss De Quincey, do you indulge in laudanum also? I fail to see what milk has to do with—"

"Have you seen *Macbeth* lately, Commissioner?" De Quincey asked. "Or perhaps you read my essay about it: 'On the Knocking at the Gate in *Macbeth*.'"

"The drug makes you jump around in your mind."

"Lady Macbeth scorns her husband for lacking the resolve to kill the king and take his place. She ridicules Macbeth for what, Emily?"

"For being too full of the milk of human kindness."

Commissioner Mayne reacted to the reference. "Milk? Human kindness?"

"That's what Sergeant Becker smelled when he found Lady

Hawkins. Her body was filled with it. The milk of human kindness gone sour. Again, the killer indicates that he seeks revenge for a great injustice."

"But the connection seems so arbitrary," Mayne said.

"Not if you consider the plot of *Macbeth*. It's about assassinating a monarch."

The commissioner's sudden pallor showed that he now understood.

"The name on the note in Lord Cosgrove's hand was Edward Oxford, who shot at the queen," De Quincey said. "The name on the note that Sergeant Becker found in the hand of the latest victim was John Francis."

"Who also attacked the queen," the commissioner said.

Sunday, 29 May 1842

Among a crowd near St. James's Park, a dusky-skinned man watched Queen Victoria and Prince Albert ride past in an open carriage, returning from church services. With so much attention directed towards the queen and the prince, only a few people saw the man pull out a pistol.

One of the few who noticed was a boy who happened to look in the man's direction as he aimed and pulled the trigger.

The result was merely a clicking sound. When the hammer fell, the pistol failed to discharge. The man hurried away.

Another witness was Prince Albert, who glanced towards the crowd and turned to Victoria, saying, "I may be mistaken, but I'm sure I saw someone take aim at us."

The boy who had seen the attempt was afflicted with a stutter. When he tried to tell people about the pistol, his halting speech made them so impatient that they walked away. But when the boy returned home and managed to tell his family, they decided that someone needed to be informed about the incident.

For the next twenty-four hours, they sought out various officials, persuading them to listen as the boy stammered his account. Meanwhile, Prince Albert's own report brought Commissioner Mayne to Buckingham Palace.

"As His Highness indicated, there was a chance that he might have been mistaken," Mayne told the group at the church. They had retreated to a room off the vestibule, where they couldn't be overheard. "Then word reached us of a boy who had seen what Prince Albert reported. We no longer had any doubts and cautioned the queen and the prince to remain in the palace while we increased the number of constables in the area.

"Imagine our surprise when, without informing us, the queen decided that cowering in the palace was a bad example. Her subjects expected her to appear when her schedule in the newspapers indicated that she would. She was determined to honour what she considered a promise. So, on the next day, at six in the evening, she and Prince Albert went on their customary carriage ride from the palace, up Constitution Hill, towards Hyde Park. We knew nothing about this. Thousands watched the carriage go past. It was an astonishing act of heroism."

As the commissioner paused, Ryan added to his account. "I was still a constable patrolling in that area. Because I'd captured Edward Oxford and because I'd been helpful in finding a thief who sneaked into the palace and stole items of the queen's wardrobe, I was being used for special assignments. In this case, I wore plain clothes, blending with the crowd. The detective division hadn't yet been created, but you could say that unofficially I was already a detective.

"I established a position close to where Oxford had fired at

the queen two years earlier—at the edge of Green Park. I'd
been told that, because of the danger, the queen had refused
to appear in public that day. Of course, her potential assailant
couldn't have known that. There was a chance he would
return, and I hoped to recognize him based on the description
I'd been given.

"To my shock, the queen and the prince actually drove
past. I don't know which of my emotions was stronger—my
relief when Her Majesty went by unharmed or my sudden
worry that she would be in danger when she returned from
Hyde Park.

"The crowd stayed in place, waiting for a further glimpse
of the queen and the prince. More people accumulated, shouting, 'Here she comes!' as the carriage reappeared twenty
minutes later. Watching for anything out of the ordinary, I
noticed someone on the opposite side of Constitution Hill. A
constable was looking intently at a young man who stood next
to a water pump. The young man had a dark complexion,
matching the description of the person I'd been warned about.

"Ahead of the returning royal carriage, I started across the
road," Ryan continued. "The crowd's noise became louder. I
heard the clatter of horseshoes and carriage wheels as the
queen and the prince drew nearer. The young man had
retreated behind a tree. When I reached the crowd in that area,
the carriage came by. The constable astonished me by turning
from the young man and standing at attention as the carriage
passed. Apparently the constable had never been that close to
royalty, but I had seen Her Majesty many times, and my attention was solely on the young man, who suddenly raised a
pistol from behind the tree.

"I lunged for it. The roar of the shot made the crowd
scream. As gun smoke filled the area, the constable hurried
over, helping me struggle with the man who'd pulled the
trigger."

"John Francis," De Quincey said.

Ryan nodded. "Other constables then joined us. We took Francis to a guard station at the palace and from there to the police station at Whitehall."

"Were the queen and the prince injured?" Becker asked.

"Thankfully, no," Commissioner Mayne answered. "Francis kept claiming that the pistol contained only powder and wadding. His barrister argued that Francis's motive was to draw attention to a failed tobacco shop that he owned, hoping to attract customers and pay off his debts. Nonetheless the government charged him with high treason."

"High treason? Even if the pistol might not have been loaded?" Emily asked.

"A firearms expert testified that the wadding from the pistol would have been a serious projectile if it had struck the queen's face. The wadding—ignited by the gunpowder—might also have set fire to the queen's dress. Francis was found guilty."

"And sentenced to be hanged until he was dead," De Quincey said. "Because the offence was high treason, the further details of the punishment harkened back to the days of Henry VIII. Francis's head was ordered to be cut off and his body divided into four quarters."

"Emily, I'm sorry if this conversation upsets you," Ryan said.

"I've read worse in Father's writings, Sean, but thank you for your concern."

Commissioner Mayne seemed taken aback by the familiarity with which they addressed each other. Then he returned his attention to what was being said.

"There were some who believed that Francis felt in such despair over his debts that he hoped to be judged insane and confined to Bedlam," De Quincey told Emily. "After all, Edward Oxford was rumoured to have a comfortable existence there. Perhaps Francis wished for a life without the need to worry about lodging or his next meal. If that was indeed his motive, he was sorely disappointed."

"Was Francis executed?" Becker asked.

"No," De Quincey replied. "At the last moment his sentence was changed to a life of hard labour in Van Diemen's Land. When Francis heard where he was going, perhaps execution might have seemed a better fate."

"All because of poverty." Emily's voice dropped, her tone revealing how well she understood the desperation of being poor.

"For years I had championed the idea of a detective unit that would use plain clothes and have jurisdiction throughout all of London's police districts," Commissioner Mayne said. "This second attack on the queen hastened my resolve. Thirteen years earlier, it had taken twelve weeks to create the Metropolitan Police Service. Now the detective unit—with its two inspectors and six sergeants—was established in a mere six days."

"Just in time," Ryan said. "Two months later, someone else tried to shoot the queen."

"Where's Newgate Prison?" Colin's father begged as they struggled to find their way through London's chaos.

Carriages, coaches, carts, cabs, and overflowing omnibuses rattled past them, passengers perched on top of the buses, servants clinging to the backs of coaches. The din was overwhelming. Newsboys yelled about the latest crimes. Costermongers shouted the virtues of the fruits and vegetables in their carts. Beggars pleaded for pennies.

Some streets were so congested that Colin and his father were constantly bumped and jostled.

"Tell me how to get to Newgate Prison!" his father implored.

"Strike someone on the head and steal his purse," a man said and laughed.

"If I was you with that Irish accent," another man said, "I'd run in the opposite direction."

"Please! Tell me where Newgate Prison is!"

"In the City of London."

"But I'm already *in* London. *Where* in London?"

"I told you—in the City of London."

"Don't joke with me!"

"Raise your fist like that, and I'll call a constable. Then you'll find out for certain where Newgate is. You're in London, but you're not in the *City* of London."

"I don't have time for games!"

"The City of London is the business district. A city within the city. Newgate Prison is where one of the original gates used to be. It's across from the Old Bailey, where the criminal courts are."

Again Colin and his father raced through the streets, asking for more directions. "Where's the Old Bailey? Where's Newgate Prison?"

"Over there," someone finally said.

But all Colin noticed was a huge dome on what appeared to be a massive church, and *that* surely couldn't be the prison, which indeed it was not, for he soon learned that the dome belonged to St. Paul's Cathedral.

He turned a corner, and this time he had no doubt that what he saw was the prison. It stretched for ever along a street, brutal looking, made of huge, soot-covered stones that reeked of gloom and despair.

They ran to a guard at the studded iron door.

The guard grasped the truncheon on his equipment belt as if he feared he was being attacked.

"My wife was brought here," Colin's father said, trying to catch his breath.

"Too bad for her."

"She didn't do what they say she did."

"Of course not. Nobody in there ever did what the law says they did."

"They claim she stole, but I know she didn't. I need to get inside and talk to her!"

"Visiting hours were this morning. Come back tomorrow. Bring a lawyer."

"Where do I find a lawyer?"

"The Inns of Court. Do you want the Inner Temple or the Middle Temple?"

"Temple? You told me to go to the Inns of Court!"

"The Inner Temple and the Middle Temple are two Inns of Court near Temple Church."

"I shall go insane with these riddles. Where is Temple Church?"

"Between Fleet Street and the Thames." The guard tightened his grip on his truncheon. "I'd keep my voice down if I was you, or it'll go harsh for you."

It turned out that the Inns of Court near Temple Church weren't inns at all, but huge clusters of buildings with chapels, libraries, dining areas, and lodgings for lawyers as well as offices.

Colin and his father ran into office after office.

"I need a lawyer for my wife!" Colin's father blurted.

Clerks frowned at the pair's dusty, sweat-streaked faces.

"If it's a barrister you want, you need a solicitor," a clerk told them.

"What are you talking about? I need a *lawyer!*"

"You go to a solicitor first. He chooses a barrister, the only kind of lawyer who can speak in court."

"This is madness. My wife needs help. Where do I find a solicitor?"

The clerk reluctantly gave them directions.

Colin and his father raced into another office, where clerks sat on high stools, leaning dutifully over desks discoloured by age, dipping their pens into inkwells and writing furiously.

A clerk surveyed their rumpled, patched clothing and asked what they wanted.

"We need a solicitor!"

Obviously lying, the clerk said, "He went home."

In the next office, the solicitor couldn't be disturbed. The solicitor in the office after that was leaving and told them to come back the next morning.

"But that's when the prison allows visitors. I need to be there to see my wife."

"Come back with three pounds. I'll see what I can manage."

"Three pounds? I don't have any money."

"Better not come back at all."

Desperation dwindled into weariness. They ate the scraps of bread that Colin had been told to bring. They drank water from a neighbourhood pump. They watched shadows lengthen.

"Emma's a big girl," Colin's father said, trying to reassure himself. "She can take care of Ruth for one night. They have bread and leftover potatoes. They have the coins I gave them."

Colin's father was sturdy and broad shouldered, with solid, steady features. He'd seen his family through the poverty that had driven them from Ireland, and Colin had never doubted that his father would protect them in whatever other hardships came their way. But now he noticed that his father's chest seemed to be shrinking, that his shoulders seemed less broad, that his face looked sunken.

They slept in an alley. In the morning, they drank more water from the neighbourhood pump and did their best to wash their hands and faces. Using their fingers to comb back their wet hair, they hurried to Newgate, where hundreds of people waited in front of the ominous iron door.

"Old Harry's chilblains won't stand the cold walls," a woman told another woman. "I don't know how he'll bear bein' kept in there much longer."

"When's his trial?"

"Nobody can tell me."

The door opened. The crowd surged ahead.

"How do I visit my wife?" Colin's father asked a guard.

"Through there."

It took an hour for the hundreds of people to speak to the single clerk, who gave notes to guards who in turn summoned prisoners.

"Caitlin O'Brien. Yes, a shoplifter. Not good."

By the time Colin's mother arrived, a guard was announcing that only a half hour of visiting time remained. The dank, shadowy, stone-walled room was filled with the reverberating din of desperate conversations. Prisoners and visitors stood apart, forbidden to touch.

Colin's mother was pale. "I didn't steal anything. Burbridge looked at my knitting. He told me he didn't want the jumpers and put them back in my basket. When I stepped outside, he shouted that I'd stolen a shirt from him. A constable searched my basket. He found a shirt under the knitting. I don't know how it got there!"

"I'll find out," Colin's father said. "I'll get you out of here, I swear."

"The walls are cold. Four women and I share a cell. Three of them are sick. I try to stay away from them in a corner."

"Do the guards feed you?"

"Broth and stale bread. What about Emma and Ruth?"

"They—"

"Visiting hours are finished!" a guard announced.

7

The Palace Dinner

Of my many experiences with Father, I shall never forget our dinner with Queen Victoria and Prince Albert.

Father would have preferred to go to the judge's house and examine the corpses there, but I pointed out that it had been twelve hours since we'd eaten. Without the benefit of Lord Palmerston's hospitality, we needed to find our meals as luck handed them to us, and a dinner with the queen and the prince was lucky indeed. Not only would it be sumptuous, but also it would not cost us anything.

I settled his hesitation by telling him distinctly, "I'm hungry, Father."

As a police van transported us to the palace, he peered mournfully out towards the falling snow. He fingered his laudanum bottle as though it were a talisman, but the sadness of his expression made clear that the talisman had long ago lost its magic.

"Sergeant Becker said that the judge wore ice skates," Father said.

"Yes, making his death all the more disturbing," I replied. "To be cruelly killed unaware while enjoying himself as a child might."

Father turned from the window and stared down at the laudanum bottle, as if the skull-and-crossbones symbol on its label were a hieroglyphic to be deciphered, revealing a truth about the universe.

"The judge was not killed unaware. It isn't coincidental that his wife was murdered at the same time. The events were coordinated. The killer forced his way into the judge's home in the same way that he entered Lord Cosgrove's home. He then admitted his companions, for none of this could have been done without help from the Young England of the notes that were left with the victims."

Continuing to focus on his laudanum bottle, Father gave the impression of repeating a voice that only he could hear, the drug seeming to shift him into a half-world between the living and the dead.

"Perhaps they persuaded the judge to go with them by threatening to kill his wife if he didn't comply. His wife, of course, was doomed, but the judge desperately hoped that wasn't the case. When he was taken to the frozen lake at St. James's Park, he pretended to engage in the skating frolic, fearing that something would happen to his wife otherwise. His terror increased as the seeming pointlessness of the activity persisted. There were numerous people skating around him, their laughter contrasting with his panic, but for love of his wife, the judge didn't dare beg anyone for help."

Father paused, then nodded in sombre agreement with the voice he seemed to hear. "At an appropriate moment, he was made to fall onto the ice. Under the pretence of helping him, his abductors slit his throat and left their message in his pocket. They also left an unstated message that no one is safe in a crowded park any more than among a congregation at a Sunday church service."

"You make it sound as if you were there, Father."

"Tonight I shall dream that I'm the man who slit the judge's throat. How I wish that, fifty years ago, I had not succumbed to opium's charms."

*   *   *

The guards at the palace did not look favourably at us when Father and I stepped down from the police van. Seeing our common overcoats, perhaps they thought that we were clerks or else criminals inexplicably being set free at the palace.

I followed Lord Palmerston's earlier example and told the gatekeeper, "My name is Emily De Quincey. This is my father. The queen expects us for dinner."

The gatekeeper's dubious look immediately left him. Indeed the queen must have been expecting us, for the man snapped to attention. He briskly escorted us to a guardian of the main entrance, who in turn escorted us to someone else. This time, we weren't taken through lesser-used passages and remote staircases. On the contrary, our route went through the main part of the palace, along corridors that were even more extravagant than those we had seen earlier. Father gazed around with increasing wonder, seeming to marvel at an opium mirage.

Our escort led us from a corridor towards what he called the Grand Staircase. The adjective was no exaggeration. Beneath a gleaming chandelier in a brilliantly lit hall, I gazed in awe at two curving staircases that were separated by another luxurious corridor. The balustrades on each of the staircases were made of wondrously cast bronze, depicting intricate clusters of various kinds of leaves. Colourful friezes of the four seasons and portraits of royalty lined the magnificent walls. The rose-coloured carpeting on the Grand Staircase was the softest that I ever walked upon. Overwhelmed by the grandeur, I could only shiver when I remembered the numerous hovels in which Father and I had lived.

We followed our escort to a room from which several voices drifted out.

"May I have your coats?" an attendant asked. When we handed them over, he looked confused about why we'd worn bereavement clothes to a royal dinner. I imagined his greater confusion had we arrived in our usual threadbare garments, with Father's elbows shiny and a button missing.

The attendant took us into the room, where a group of splendidly dressed men and women stopped speaking and studied us with greater puzzlement than the attendant had displayed.

"Miss Emily De Quincey," he announced, "and her father, Mister Thomas De Quincey."

The "miss" and "mister" made clear that we had no claim to any titles whatsoever. In theory, since we were obviously commoners, we had no business being there. But titles were the last things that the group was concerned about, so fixated were they on Father's grim suit.

My own garment at least had the benefit of being less dour. I'd gone to the Mitigated Affliction department of Jay's Mourning Warehouse, in which clothes of various gradations of sorrow were available—from black, to dark grey, to light grey—depending on how many months had passed since a loved one's death.

I had chosen light gray, but on principle I refused to wear a fashionable hoop under the dress, preferring the freedom of my bloomer trousers. Fortunately I was so accustomed to judgemental reactions that I paid no attention. Even the queen and Prince Albert could not compel me to wear clothes that made me uncomfortable. Besides, I had the strong impression that one of the reasons Her Majesty had invited us was the novelty of displaying someone in a bloomer skirt.

The silence—I might even say the shock—of the group persisted until the most conspicuously dressed and most handsome of the men stepped forward to greet us. His scarlet uniform and immaculate white arm sling were familiar from the morning's horrors at St. James's Church.

"Mister and Miss De Quincey, I didn't expect to see you again," Colonel Trask said.

I remembered the troubled look he had given me at the church, as if we'd met before but he couldn't recall when. Now the warmth in his eyes replaced his earlier confusion. He kindly failed to direct even a casual glance towards our unusual clothing.

"What a delightful surprise. May I introduce you?"

Colonel Trask led us to the uncommonly beautiful woman whom he had escorted into the church that morning, an event that seemed days in the past, so much having happened in the meantime. Her hair was resplendently straw coloured.

"Allow me to present Miss Catherine Grantwood. These are her parents, Lord and Lady Grantwood."

Catherine made a pretence of smiling, but it was obvious that something untoward had happened in the past few hours. Even in the midst of the horror at the church, she had gazed with undisguised admiration at Colonel Trask as he helped the police maintain order. Now her admiration had been replaced by what I interpreted as grave disappointment or worse.

Her parents did not look happy, either, but they hadn't looked happy when they'd entered the church that morning, and I couldn't tell whether solemnity was their natural aspect. Some lords and ladies seem to allow themselves to smile only when among their own kind.

"And this is a friend of Lord and Lady Cosgrove," Colonel Trask added without enthusiasm. "Sir Walter Cumberland."

Sir Walter appeared to be the same age as Colonel Trask, around twenty-five. He was almost as handsome as the colonel, but in a dark way that contrasted with the colonel's fair-haired demeanour. While the colonel's eyes were appealingly warm, Sir Walter's had a dusky fire that suggested muted anger.

Sir Walter merely nodded, as did Lord and Lady Grantwood. It became even more obvious that prior to their arrival at the palace, something besides Lady Cosgrove's death had upset the group.

"And may I also present you to"—Colonel Trask was pleased to get away from Catherine's parents and Sir Walter—"the queen's cousin, with whom I had the honour of serving in the Crimea. The Duke of Cambridge."

Somewhat overweight, the duke seemed to be in his mid-thirties, but already he had lost most of his hair and compensated with a full dark beard. He turned his head aside and coughed, a deep sound that suggested he had been ill for some time.

"Forgive me. That's my souvenir from the war," the duke said. "It is I who feel honoured to have served with Colonel Trask. He saved my life on the heights above Sevastopol."

"I did what anyone else would have done, helping a fellow officer," Colonel Trask said.

"The enemy turned out to be uncomfortably close in the fog." The duke looked at Father and me. "This young man came out of nowhere, leading a group of soldiers who helped my Grenadiers repel a Russian attack. The gun smoke was thicker than the fog. He and I stood next to each other, striking with . . ."

Aware that the others in the room had become silent, Lord Cambridge told them, "My apologies. I was merely complimenting the colonel. I hope I didn't excite you." He nodded towards Colonel Trask's sling, his tone becoming confidential. "Is your wound healing?"

"It's been slow, but my physician assures me there's no need for concern."

"That's what my own physician says about my cough. Two invitations to the palace in less than a week, one of them to receive a knighthood. You're becoming a favourite."

"I doubt that I could ever get used to this magnificence.

The dining room is no doubt equally splendid." Colonel Trask pointed towards a closed door.

The duke chuckled. "That door leads to where the servants prepare to bring in the dishes. The entrance to the dining room is along that hall. It's easy to get lost here." The duke looked at Father. "De Quincey. I know that name."

Father gave a little bow. I worried that he was about to announce that he came from a noble lineage.

Blessedly, Colonel Trask changed the subject. "Mr. De Quincey, you seem to be looking for something."

Father's forehead was sweaty. "I thought that there would be wine or . . ."

At that point, everyone straightened as Her Majesty and Prince Albert arrived. I and the other women curtsied while the men bowed.

"Mister and Miss De Quincey, we are pleased to see you again." Queen Victoria turned towards the group. "Miss De Quincey introduced us to several new ideas this afternoon, including the freedom of her costume."

This gave permission to the women—all with hoops beneath their dresses—to study my bloomers without pretending not to. The men continued to look away, lest they seem fixated on the outline of my legs.

"You'll notice," the queen told the group, "that I'm not wearing any garment that is green. Until I'm assured that arsenic is not in their dyes, I ordered all green clothes to be removed from my wardrobe. Lady Wheeler, I see that you are wearing green, however."

"Your Majesty, I didn't realize that green was no longer . . ."

"If I may, Lady Wheeler," Prince Albert said.

He reached inside his uniform and withdrew the vial I had given him.

"Please unfurl your cuff," Prince Albert told her.

Lady Wheeler nervously did so.

He removed the stopper from the vial and pressed it against the inside of the cuff.

"Aha!"

At the touch of the stopper, the green turned blue.

"You're wearing a dye laced with rat poison. Lady Barrington, shall we determine if the green dye on your clothes is contaminated also?"

Five of the ladies in the room had green somewhere on their garments, and on all of them the stopper caused a spot of blue.

The women looked startled.

"Miss De Quincey drew our attention to a health crisis," Queen Victoria said. "There's no telling how many of us and our children have become sick because of poisonous adulterations in the dyes of our clothing."

"And also in our food, Your Majesty," I noted.

"Food?" the queen asked with a troubled expression.

"Yes, most prepared food that is green—pickles, for example—has arsenic in its dye, Your Majesty. A jar of brown ones might not look attractive, but the green ones—for all their better appearance—are harmful to you."

"Pickles? I can guarantee that no one here shall encounter pickles—green, brown, or any other colour—at our table tonight," Queen Victoria said. "Ah, Lord and Lady Palmerston have arrived at last. Just in time to go in."

"My apologies for being late, Your Majesty." Lord Palmerston gave her a significant look. "I was attending to the various matters we discussed earlier."

"We had begun to despair of your attendance," the queen said.

I now witnessed a strange ritual. The order in which the guests entered the dining room depended on the position they occupied in society: duke, marquess, earl, and so forth.

The order was so complex that I found it bewildering, but the dinner guests quickly made the intricate calculations to determine who stepped ahead of whom.

I mention this because something curious happened with regard to Sir Walter and Colonel Trask. Queen Victoria had knighted the colonel in gratitude for his having saved her cousin's life. Thus, like Sir Walter, he too could be called "Sir." But Sir Walter was emphatic in stepping forward to escort Catherine, as though his title outranked Colonel Trask's. Sir Walter's expression indicated that he considered this distinction to be significant. Catherine's parents dourly seemed to think that Sir Walter's "Sir" was more exalted also. For his part, Colonel Trask looked despondent. It became his duty to offer his arm to *me*.

And what of Father? There was no woman of lower status whom he could accompany. In a surprising show of good nature, Lady Palmerston broke ranks and paired with him. Clearly our status as commoners caused disorder in the ritual.

Additional surprises awaited me, for at one end of the long dining table, the place card with my name was next to that of Prince Albert, who was known for his curious mind.

Because all the women wore hooped dresses, they had difficulty settling into their chairs while I, of course, had no trouble whatsoever.

The multitude of bowls and the vast selection of offerings went beyond anything I had ever experienced. An elegantly handwritten copy of the menu lay before me and each of the other guests in case we failed to notice something. Truly, I had not seen this much food at one time ever in my life:

White Soup
Broth
Baked Salmon
Baked Mullets

Filet de Boeuf and Spanish Sauce
Sweetbreads
Shrimp Croquettes
Chicken Patties
Roast Fillet of Veal
Boiled Leg of Lamb
Roast Fowls with Watercress
Boiled Ham with Carrots and Mashed Turnips
Sea Kale, Spinach, and Broccoli
Ducklings
Guinea Fowl
Orange Jelly
Coffee Cream
Ice Pudding

Matching the abundance on the table were the place settings. The many types of forks, knives, spoons, and glasses totalled twenty-four for each guest. As the combined aroma of the various dishes drifted over me, I was embarrassed to hear my stomach growl.

Colonel Trask, who sat next to me, coughed several times. When I glanced his way, he gave me a conspiratorial smile that suggested he had kindly masked the noise that my stomach made. I raised my napkin and returned his smile, reminded of schoolchildren sharing a secret.

Servants brought white wine, which Father was happy to accept.

Lord Palmerston raised his glass. "To our gracious hosts, Queen Victoria and Prince Albert."

"Hear, hear!" the Duke of Cambridge said. "God save the queen."

Under the circumstances, the duke's comment was unfortunate. Evidently he hadn't been informed that the queen's life was in danger and that she did indeed need saving.

"And to the health of your children," the Duke of Cambridge continued. "Has Prince Leopold recovered from his injury?"

The duke referred to Her Majesty's most recent child, whose birth two years earlier had been celebrated in every newspaper throughout the empire.

"Thank you, yes," Queen Victoria replied. "The cut on his forehead finally stopped bleeding. Even Dr. Snow is at a loss to explain why the slightest of falls causes Leopold to bleed so profusely. It seemed that the injury would never seal itself."

A true monarch, Her Majesty did not allow her many concerns to spoil the occasion. "But enough of unhappy matters. Our original purpose for this dinner was to celebrate my cousin's safe return from the war and Colonel Trask's gallant service to him."

Neither Sir Walter nor Catherine's parents looked pleased about the glowing reference to the colonel.

"But now we have another reason to celebrate," the queen continued. "Lord Palmerston has agreed to act as prime minister and form a new government."

She said this as though her wine tasted bitter.

Catherine's father asked Lord Palmerston, "With your experience as secretary for war and foreign secretary, do you see an opportunity to dominate the Russians?"

"I believe that is why Her Majesty entrusted me with this honour," Lord Palmerston replied. "I shall pursue a victory with all of my strength."

"Hear, hear!" everyone said.

Father finished his wine and accepted more from a white-gloved servant who patrolled the table.

"I confess I was not always clear about the reasons for going to war," Lord Bell said.

"The Ottoman Empire has separated East from West for more than five centuries. But now it shows signs of crumbling," Lord Palmerston explained with the expertise of his years as foreign secretary. "Taking advantage of its weakness, Russia invaded its eastern border, an area known as the Crimea. In response, we joined forces with France, declaring war against Russia."

"I have not heard it put so simply and elegantly," Catherine's father said.

"But even put simply, it seems complicated," Lord Bell persisted. "The Ottoman Empire is halfway around the world. Why do we care what happens there?"

"If we allow Russia to invade a portion of that empire, where will the aggression stop?" Lord Palmerston replied.

"And don't forget the Suez canal," Father interjected.

It was the first time he had spoken. His short stature required some guests to lean forward to get a better look at him.

"The Suez canal? I don't believe I know of such a thing," Lord Bell said.

"Because it doesn't exist." Father removed a tin box from his coat and selected a pill from it. "For my digestion," he explained.

"But how can the Crimean War be caused by something that doesn't exist?" Sir Walter asked.

"England's wealth comes from trade with the Orient," Father answered, "but a ship requires six months to return from India, sailing around Africa. Perhaps the distance can be shortened."

The pill Father chewed was opium. Worried that the queen would realize, I hastily devoted myself to the soup in case I might not receive anything more to eat.

"Shorten the distance?" Sir Walter asked in confusion. "The world's circumference can't be changed."

"Suppose British ships didn't need to sail around Africa,"

Father suggested. "Suppose that instead our ships journeyed across the Indian Ocean to the Gulf of Suez, deep within Egypt. The overland distance from that gulf to the Mediterranean Sea is only eighty miles. A British company plans to build a railway there. The journey from India to England would be reduced to a previously undreamed of nine weeks. Three times more ships would make the journey, with vastly greater profits."

The group looked stunned.

"Is this true, Lord Palmerston?" Lord Wheeler asked.

"I'm not permitted to discuss it."

Colonel Trask spoke up. "But I can. I was asked to help finance that railway."

Catherine's parents and Sir Walter looked unhappy about the colonel's allusion to his wealth.

"And did you invest in that railway?" Lord Barrington asked.

"I did not. I considered it unwise."

"But the profits!"

"For a few years."

"Why only a few years?" Lord Wheeler asked in confusion.

"Because something more ambitious is being planned," Colonel Trask replied. "The French have negotiated with Egypt to build the canal that Mister De Quincey refers to. That canal will revolutionize international trade. But the French want the project to themselves. I was disappointed not to be invited to participate in the financing."

"Among magazine writers, it's common knowledge that the future canal is the cause of the war," Father said. "But we don't feel at liberty to express it in print. It comes down to this—Egypt is part of the Ottoman Empire. If Russia's invasion spreads to Egypt, Russia will control the Suez canal and world shipping."

"But . . ." Sir Walter was temporarily speechless. "In that case, England would lose its dominance!"

"Indeed," Father told him. "We allied with the French, hoping that if we both defeat Russia, the French will allow us access to the canal that they plan to build. Opium from India creates much of our trading profit. Imagine if our soldiers— dying from starvation, disease, and cold—suspected that they risked their lives not for England but for the opium trade. That's why this information has not appeared in the newspapers and magazines."

I have never seen so many jaws hang open in shock.

Clearly a distraction was needed.

I removed a vial from my purse and asked for a portion of red salmon. When I put a drop of the vial's liquid on the salmon, everyone looked perplexed, seeing a part of the salmon turn brown.

"What are you doing?" Queen Victoria asked.

"Arsenic is not the only toxin used in dye, Your Majesty. Lead is often added to red dye in food."

"Lead?" Prince Albert asked.

"This salmon was injected with red dye to improve its colour, Your Highness. As you see, the red dye has lead in it."

"Lead in the fish?" Queen Victoria set down her fork.

"It can be fatal, Ma'am. May I also test the lamb?"

I applied a drop of the liquid to an especially red part of the lamb, and that spot turned brown also.

"Lead in the lamb?" Queen Victoria murmured. "Mr. De Quincey, is that why you're not eating? Are you suspicious about the food?"

"I have a sensitive stomach, Your Majesty." Father munched another pill. "Perhaps I could have a bowl of warm milk in which to soak bread."

"De Quincey." Prince Albert searched his memory. "Now it comes to me. I read about you in connection with the murders in December. Your reference to opium triggered my recollection. Those pills ... Good heavens, don't tell me you're the Opium-Eater."

Certain that my moments at the dinner table were limited, I tested the beef and ate as much of it as I could.

"You're also the man who wrote 'On Murder Considered as One of the Fine Arts,'" Colonel Trask said. "We were together at St. James's Church this morning. Do you have a theory about the murder that was committed there?"

I never expected to be relieved by a reference to murder. The group suddenly became distracted from Father's opium.

"Not only that murder, but the ones at Lord Cosgrove's home," Father said.

"There have been several murders?" someone exclaimed.

"Including that of a judge, Sir Richard Hawkins, in St. James's Park, not to mention his wife and a servant in his house," Father said.

The faces of the men became red with alarm while those of the women drained of colour.

"Sir Richard Hawkins?" Lord Barrington asked. "But he belongs to my club."

"Lord Palmerston, why didn't you inform us of these further crimes?" Prince Albert asked unhappily.

"I ... I had no idea," Lord Palmerston replied in confusion. "Your Highness, they must have occurred after I saw you."

"Is no one safe?" Sir Walter demanded.

"That's exactly the impression the killers wish to create," Father said. "Tomorrow when London's newspapers spread word about these terrible crimes, people will believe that neither their homes nor public areas are immune from danger. But there is another way to achieve panic. Your Majesty and Your Highness, with your permission—the newspapers will almost certainly print rumours about it."

The queen and the prince stared at each other along the table. Her Majesty made a slight gesture, seeming to indicate that the choice belonged to her husband.

"It's better if our friends hear it personally rather than read it in the newspapers," Prince Albert decided.

"Notes were found at each murder," Father said, "indicating that the deaths are part of a plot against Her Majesty."

The men looked more outraged, the women paler.

"We feel confident in the ability of Scotland Yard to protect us," Queen Victoria said.

"But why would anyone have hostile intentions toward Her Majesty?" the Duke of Cambridge protested. "She hasn't harmed anyone. It's the reverse. She's the paragon of grace."

"The Russians might not feel that way," Colonel Trask said.

"Are you suggesting that the queen is not in fact a paragon of grace?" Sir Walter challenged.

"I suggest nothing of the sort," the colonel answered. "But we need to consider the possibility that the Russians wish to cause panic here in the hopes of weakening our war resolve. As Mr. De Quincey explained, the stakes are huge."

"The motive also seems to be personal," Father added. "Notes left with the victims suggest that the murders are the result of long-held hostility towards them and also towards Her Majesty."

"That is preposterous!" Sir Walter objected. "Her Majesty has never harmed anyone."

"Again, the blasted Russians might not feel that way," Colonel Trask said, exasperated with Sir Walter.

The vulgarity caused each woman, including the queen, to put a hand to her mouth.

"My apologies, Your Majesty," the colonel said.

This time it was Prince Albert who provided the

distraction. "But surely the killers won't be hard to identify. Anyone capable of these crimes must be unstable. Murder will out. Their viciousness will display itself in their everyday behaviour and give them away."

"In some cases, Your Highness, that is correct," Father agreed. "But I once enjoyed dinner with a murderer, pleasantly discussing every manner of topic, without once realizing the darkness in his soul. It came as a shock that I could not tell from someone's demeanour what evil deeds that person was capable of performing. I refer to Thomas Griffiths Wainewright, the distinguished painter and contributor to *London Magazine*, a friend to Hazlitt, Lamb, and Dickens as well as to me, although I don't wish to attempt to raise myself in your estimation by including my name among those worthies.

"Wainewright had an extravagant way of living that put him in debt. He and his wife were forced to move in with his uncle, who soon died and left Wainewright his house. Wainewright then persuaded his mother-in-law to prepare a will that favoured his wife. His mother-in-law died shortly afterward. Wainewright then insured his sister-in-law for twelve thousand pounds. Soon, that woman died also. Suspicious, the insurance company hired investigators, who believed that Wainewright had used strychnine to kill his victims. While no poison was ever located among his belongings, the investigators did find insurance documents with signatures that Wainewright had forged, so it was for embezzlement rather than murder that he was found guilty. In prison, someone asked him if he had really killed his sister-in-law. 'It was a dreadful thing to do,' Wainewright admitted, 'but she was easy to dislike—she had very thick ankles.' "

Queen Victoria, Prince Albert, and everyone else listened with open mouths. The topics of arsenic, lead, strychnine, and foul murder had caused all of them to stop eating, while

I devoured as much of the beef as I could, more certain with each passing moment that Father and I would soon be ejected.

"I enjoyed one of the most pleasant dinners of my life and never dreamed I sat across from a monster," Father said. "So you see, Your Highness, you can never tell."

Everyone remained speechless.

Prince Albert finally broke the awkward silence. "Mr. De Quincey, I have never heard anyone speak so rapidly and unusually."

"Thank you, Your Highness."

Catherine's father cleared his throat. "Perhaps I have a topic that will relieve the gloom. Her Majesty began our dinner with the announcement that Lord Palmerston had accepted the position of prime minister, hopefully to produce a victory in the war. May I conclude our dinner by announcing that my wife and I have the honour to inform you that our daughter, Catherine, will marry Sir Walter Cumberland. We welcome him into our family."

It's difficult to communicate my surprise. Catherine and Colonel Trask had seemed so splendid a pair when they entered the church that morning, her radiant gaze so adoring, that I assumed they were engaged or about to be.

Silent throughout the dinner, Catherine now peered despondently down at her hands.

Meanwhile, Sir Walter gave Colonel Trask a scornful look of triumph.

8

The Wheel of Fortune

The snow lessened as a police van transported Commissioner Mayne through midnight streets. Even at this late hour there was usually some traffic, but tonight, returning to his house from intense meetings at the various crime areas, Mayne didn't hear the hooves and wheels of even one other vehicle.

Because he lived in Chester Square in the exclusive Belgravia district, he would have preferred to arrive home in a coach or a cab. But surely none of the residents on his street would be awake and peering from a window to see him arrive in a vehicle normally used to transport criminals, he decided.

He'd been co-commissioner of police for more than a quarter of a century, and tonight he felt the weight of all those years. The stress had thinned his frame, lessened his hair, and added lines to his face. The day's savage crimes, following the bloodshed in December, made him suspect that London's many newspapers were to blame, inspiring diseased imaginations to imitate violence that no one would otherwise have thought of.

The van had a lantern inside it, which Mayne used to study the numerous reports he'd been given, but as the vehicle rolled through the muffling snow, his eyes felt heavy.

Suddenly the police driver was saying, "We're here, sir."

Mayne jerked his eyes open and realized that his head was slumped against the wall, that the reports were on the floor, and that, despite his best efforts, he had fallen asleep.

"Thank you, Constable."

He gathered the pages and stepped down to the snowy pavement.

"It's almost stopped, sir," the constable said. "The snow may be pleasant to look at now, but tomorrow the streets will be a mess."

"At least the crossing sweepers will be happy."

"Yes, sir." The constable chuckled. "As a lad, I worked as a crossing sweeper. Tomorrow, they'll earn more pennies than they normally do in a week. Shall I come back at the usual time in the morning?"

"Sooner. With so much to do . . . ."

"I'll see that it happens, sir."

The horses struggled to maintain their footing as the constable drove the van away, disappearing into the night.

Across from Mayne was a small garden, the principal feature of Chester Square. A gas lamp allowed him to see the snow-covered shrubs and the beds where flowers would bloom in the spring. In good weather, if his responsibilities allowed, he enjoyed sitting on a bench there and reading a morning newspaper while he waited for his carriage to arrive.

The peacefulness of the scene was refreshing. Even the pile of debris in front of a residence five doors away—the result of renovation for a new owner—no longer offended him, the snow obscuring the ugly mound. The labourers had promised to complete their work soon. Then Chester Square would return to its uniform vista of handsome adjoining residences, three and a half storeys high, all of them stuccoed white, the snow making them even whiter.

The only footprints belonged to Commissioner Mayne and his driver. He savoured the quiet, the feeling of being isolated from the troubles that awaited him the next morning.

But then a breeze chilled his face, and the odour of smoke from the many chimneys broke the spell. He approached the wrought-iron railing at his home, took out his key, and unlocked the door.

He'd sent a constable to inform his wife, Georgiana, that he'd be late and that she shouldn't wait up for him. Nonetheless he found her sitting in the front room.

He smiled.

"So late?" Georgiana asked.

"Many disturbing things happened today," he told her.

"Lady Cosgrove at St. James's? Lord Cosgrove at their home?" Georgiana asked.

"You heard?"

"The news spread quickly. When Becky"—Georgiana referred to their servant—"returned from her afternoon of leisure, she had much to report."

Because Georgiana didn't also mention the judge and his wife, Mayne decided that there was no point in alarming her with the additional news. The stress of his years as co-commissioner had greyed her hair and lined her face just as it had left its marks on him.

"To bed," she told him, gripping his hand. Using her other hand to carry an oil lamp, she walked with him up two flights of stairs.

They reached the level for their daughter's bedroom and their own room farther along.

As they passed the stairs that led up to the servants' area, something caused Mayne to frown, although the shadows made it difficult for him to be certain of what he saw.

"The lamp seems to need a new wick. Let me check it," he told Georgiana, taking the lamp from her.

Under the guise of inspecting it, Mayne lowered the light enough to dispel the gloom on the stairs that led to the top level.

There were moist areas on the carpeting where boot soles wet from snow appeared to have descended. They proceeded along this level and stopped at the door to a linen closet under the stairs.

"I'm mistaken," Mayne told Georgiana, quickly raising the lamp. "The wick is perfectly fine. My eyes must be tired."

"All the more reason to go to bed," she gently ordered, leading him along the shadowy corridor.

They passed the door to their daughter's room on the right and neared the door to the closet on the left. Mayne's chest tightened as he walked next to the wet marks on the carpet.

Someone had entered the house from the roof. The only access was the skylight that allowed chimney cleaners to climb up there. *But how could anyone have got onto the roof in the first place?* Mayne thought as he came abreast of the closet door.

At once he remembered the nearby building that was being renovated. Someone could have forced open a back door to the empty structure, gone up to the top floor, lifted its skylight, and proceeded along the roofs of the adjoining houses until he came to the skylight that provided access to here. The roof was relatively flat. Even in the snow, a man could have walked along it if he was careful.

Mayne thought about urging Georgiana to run down the stairs as fast as she could. But she would be puzzled. She would ask questions. Meanwhile, the intruder would burst from the closet and attack.

If we can get into our bedroom, we can barricade the door, Mayne thought. *But what about our daughter? The intruder will turn his attention towards her.* As for their servant upstairs, Mayne had every certainty that she was dead.

Mayne's legs trembled as he neared their bedroom. He hoped that his voice wouldn't tremble also.

"How is Judith?" he asked. "Did her cough improve?"

"Very much. We don't need to worry any more," Georgiana replied.

"But she's coughing now, and she doesn't sound any better. The opposite."

"I don't hear her coughing," Georgiana said, confused.

"Step back to her door and listen. She sounds as if she needs attention."

Backtracking, Mayne listened for any sound to indicate that the closet door was being opened. He gambled that the intruder's plan was to wait until the household was asleep and then kill everyone in their beds, reinforcing the growing conviction that no one in London was safe anywhere.

"You really don't hear Judith coughing?" Mayne asked. "I'll open the door an inch."

"You'll waken her," Georgiana cautioned.

"From the sound of it, she's already awake."

With the lamp in one hand, Mayne used the other hand to open the door.

As Georgiana peered in, saying "I don't hear—" Mayne pushed her into the room, hurried in behind her, and slammed the door. In a frenzy, he set the lamp on a table and strained to shove Judith's bureau in front of the door.

"What are you doing?" Georgiana demanded. "Have you lost your mind?"

"Quickly! Help! There's no time to explain!" Mayne yelled.

Startled by the loud intrusion, Judith bolted upright in bed. Thirteen years old, she screamed, "Who's there?"

"Help me!" Mayne shouted.

He heard the closet door in the corridor bang open. Heavy footsteps pounded along the carpet. Someone jolted angrily against the door. As it threatened to fly open, Mayne succeeded in shoving the bureau against it.

"Get chairs! Anything to help keep the door closed!"

Whoever was out there rammed a second time against the door. Mayne shoved his full weight against the bureau. With the third impact, Georgiana came to her senses and rushed to bring a chair, adding its weight to the bureau. The door had a lock, but it had never been used, and Mayne had no idea where the key was.

The fourth time the intruder crashed against the door, the bureau lurched back. Mayne, his wife, and his daughter pushed harder to keep the intruder from storming in.

"*Father, what's happening?*" Judith pleaded.

"God eternally damn it!" a man yelled from the opposite side of the door. He had an Irish accent.

The door jolted inward, again shoving the bureau away. Mayne renewed his efforts to keep it in place.

"The bed!" he shouted to the women. "Try to push the bed here!"

But as they struggled, unable to move it, the intruder struck the door with such strength that the bureau nearly toppled.

If he manages to get in, do the three of us have a chance to over-power him? Mayne desperately wondered. *Is there a weapon in here, anything I can use to protect us?* He couldn't think of one. All he could imagine was that the intruder would have a knife and that he would charge in, slashing repeatedly.

"Georgiana, help me keep pushing against the bureau! Judith, tie sheets together!" Mayne ordered.

"Sheets?" Judith asked in bewilderment.

"Like a rope! Do it! Make certain that the knots are tight! Georgiana, keep pushing at the bureau! Harder than you ever imagined!"

"Your daughter will suffer the way my sisters did!" the Irish voice yelled beyond the door.

The intruder charged with such force that part of the door cracked.

He charged again.

The crack sounded louder.

"Judith, hurry!" Mayne shouted.

"I'm *trying,* Father!"

Looking over his shoulder, Mayne saw his daughter knotting one end of a sheet to another.

"We'll need several!" he told her. "As tightly as you can! Do you understand what we need to do?"

Shoving against the bureau, Mayne directed his desperate gaze towards her window. In the dim glow from the lamp on the table, he saw Judith nod with comprehension.

"Your wife and you will suffer the way my mother and father did!" the attacker yelled.

The next time he charged, a piece of the door flew into the room.

"Father, it's ready!" Judith said.

"Tie one end to a bedpost! Make certain it's tight!" Mayne ordered, pressing his body against the bureau. Another piece of the door flew into the room.

"Put on a dressing gown, Judith! Put on shoes!"

Mayne was grateful that his wife was wearing a dressing gown, but when he looked down at her feet, he was dismayed to see that they were covered only with slippers.

Another chunk of wood flew from the door.

"Judith, open your window!" Mayne ordered.

She hurried to it, but when she tried to push up, it didn't move.

"It's frozen!" Judith exclaimed.

"Push harder!"

Abruptly, she managed to force the window up. A cold breeze rushed into the room. The man in the corridor was now kicking at the door, trying to shatter more of its wood.

"Throw the sheets out, Judith! Climb down!"

"But . . ."

The street was at least thirty feet below them. The thought of falling and perhaps landing on the spikes of the wrought-iron railing terrified Mayne, as it no doubt terrified his wife and his daughter. But what threatened them on the other side of the door was even more terrifying.

"I'll make you drink your blood!" the Irish voice shouted.

"Do it!" Mayne told his daughter. "Hurry! Go!"

As the door trembled on its hinges, Judith surprised Mayne by how quickly she moved. Her face was pale with fear as she squirmed out of the window into the darkness. Mayne and his wife continued to press against the bureau.

He counted to ten. *Was that long enough for Judith to slide down?*

"Now it's your turn, Georgiana!"

"I won't leave you!" she insisted.

"I'll come after you! Do it!"

Georgiana studied his features as if she didn't think she'd ever see them again.

"Go!" he urged.

One of the door's hinges threatened to break away.

Georgiana rushed towards the window and squirmed through it. A moment later her face descended into the darkness.

Without her help, Mayne couldn't muster the strength to keep the bureau from sliding back.

One, two, three . . .

Mayne dug his boots into the carpet and pressed all his weight against the bureau.

Six, seven, eight . . .

The bureau slid towards him.

Nine, ten.

Mayne couldn't wait any longer.

He released his weight from the bureau and raced towards the window. The sheet tied to the post was slack, showing him that Georgiana had reached the bottom. Without thinking he grabbed the sheet, backed out of the window, and slid.

The sheet felt cold from the winter air. At the same time,

friction burned his hands. Through the open window, he heard a crash as the bureau toppled. He imagined the man rushing into the bedroom.

Mayne reached the first knot and jerked to a stop, but he immediately grabbed lower and slid again. Above him, the intruder wailed with an intensity that Mayne could never have imagined.

Wincing from the pain in his hands, he reached the second knot and jerked to another stop. Desperate, he again grabbed lower and slid as quickly as he could, ignoring the blood that was now on his hands.

When he jolted to a final stop, his knees collapsed. His wife and his daughter hurried to raise him from the snow.

"Run!" Mayne shouted.

Looking up, he saw the dark outline of a man surging out of the window, starting to climb down.

They ran onto the snow-covered pavement.

"This way! East! Towards the palace!" Mayne yelled. It was a quarter mile away. Constables were there in force. *But can we outrun him?* Mayne desperately wondered. His wife wore only slippers. Could she and their thirteen-year-old daughter outdistance their attacker? If they pounded on a neighbour's door, how long would it take for someone to waken and reach the entrance?

"No!" Mayne shouted. "*This* way."

He dragged his wife and daughter back towards their front door.

The figure slid with alarming speed down the bedsheets.

Mayne fumbled in a trouser pocket for his key.

The figure released his grip and dropped.

With trembling hands, Mayne scraped the key against the door's lock.

The figure landed, bent his knees, and rolled.

"Father!" Judith screamed.

Mayne shoved the key into the lock, twisted it, and thrust the door open.

As the man sprang to his feet, Mayne briefly saw that he had a beard. The speed—indeed the frenzy—with which the man charged towards them was terrifying, his palpably savage emotion communicating a rage more extreme than anything Mayne had ever encountered.

Mayne felt paralyzed by the force racing towards him. Abruptly, with a desperate shout, he pushed Georgiana and Judith into the house, hurried inside behind them, and slammed the door.

The three of them pressed against the door as their attacker walloped against it. Mayne turned the key as the man outside struck the door again and screamed.

"He can smash through a window!" Judith warned.

"Up the stairs! The master bedroom!" Mayne urged them.

"But he'll have us trapped!" Georgiana said.

"Do what I ask!"

A window shattered in the sitting room.

They climbed hurriedly, hearing someone from a neighbouring house yell, "What's going on? You! What are you doing over there?"

Out of breath, they passed the shattered door to Judith's room and the open door to the closet where the intruder had hidden.

With a final rush they entered the master bedroom, slammed the door, and slid a bureau in front of it. While Georgiana and Judith leaned against it, Mayne opened the closet and took out a firearms case from a corner.

The case contained an Enfield rifle-musket, the improved weapon that English soldiers were using in the Crimea. The rifling in the barrel meant that bullets flew with greater accuracy. Some members of the gentry who lived in Chester Square had acquired Enfields for hunting boar and stags in

Scotland. A duke had invited Mayne to a shooting holiday on his estate there the previous autumn, but the pressures of work had prevented Mayne from going.

He tore a cartridge packet open and poured gunpowder down the barrel. After dropping a bullet down the barrel, he used the Enfield's ramrod to tap the load securely into place. Then he placed a percussion cap under the weapon's hammer.

All night long, sitting in a corner, with Judith and Georgiana next to him, he aimed towards the door.

Just west of the Tower of London sat a gin-house called the Wheel of Fortune. Convenient to the banks, insurance companies, and trading enterprises of the business district, the Wheel of Fortune was nestled on Shore Lane, near the Thames. Many clerks and even their supervisors made their way to it after their daily labours. They claimed to savour the quality of its pork pies, but the real attraction was the bargain price of the beer and the gin.

Noting the late hour, the tavern's owner herded his few remaining patrons out of the door.

"Closing time. Drink up. I'll see you tomorrow. Thanks for your patronage. On your way now. Be careful of the snow. Don't fall down and freeze to death."

The owner's name was Thaddeus Mitchell, and as he locked the door, he showed no surprise that one customer remained, hunching over his drink at the end of the bar.

Thaddeus shuttered the windows. "I don't believe we've met before," he said.

"Quentin Quassia, Doctor of Drink, at your service," the man replied. Turning with a smile, he offered his sizeable hand. He had a round, florid face and a mischievous look in his eyes.

"Where's Edward?" Thaddeus asked.

"In bed with a stomach ailment, but not because of anything

he drank." Quentin chuckled as if he'd made a grand joke. "Never fear—my brother and I are equally expert doctors of drink." This, too, he found humorous enough to merit a chuckle.

"But how do I know you can really do the job?" Thaddeus asked.

"If you're not satisfied, it won't cost you a penny. I can make that promise because I know you'll like the result."

"Show me."

Thaddeus went behind the bar and raised a trapdoor that revealed stairs down to the cellar. After lighting a lantern, he motioned for the stranger to follow him down.

The cellar had a damp odour that came from the nearby river. The place felt cold. Several rows of large barrels stretched before him.

The stranger carried a large sack. "I'll start with the beer," he said.

"That's what your brother always does. What's your name again?"

"Quentin Quassia."

"Your brother never gave his last name. Quassia. Unusual."

"It's a plant from South America. Tea from it helps the digestion."

Quentin unpacked various bottles and packages, putting them on a shelf.

Sitting on a stool, Thaddeus watched. He was thirty-two. He had owned the Wheel of Fortune for eight years and intended to sell it. With his profit from the sale and the £10,000 he'd saved over the years, he planned to retire on a country property. The return on his investment put to shame many of the financial schemes that he'd overheard clerks and their supervisors discussing over their pork pies and drinks.

Anyone could get a beer licence. The problem was how to

obtain a *gin* licence. In the early weeks of his business, Thaddeus had been happy to lose money, serving the best brew available, selling it for less than he paid, winning the goodwill of the neighbourhood. After a time, he let his enthusiastic customers know that he was thinking about acquiring a gin licence. When he asked them to support his petition to the necessary magistrates, they gladly did so, and after acquiring the gin licence, Thaddeus then consulted with a drink doctor, who gradually diluted the beer and the gin, adding ingredients to make the beverages taste the same as before. In this fashion, three casks of beer or gin could be multiplied into seven. Although Thaddeus kept the price of the drinks as low as he had earlier, his profit would have made the eyes of the financial experts widen.

Of course, Thaddeus could have diluted and adulterated the beverages on his own, but his father—a tavern owner also—had warned him to rely only on an expert, lest his customers sense the difference.

"Your brother never told me what he puts in the beer and the gin," Thaddeus told Quentin.

"Of course not. If you knew our secrets, we'd be out of business."

Quentin opened four empty barrels and distributed the beer from three full barrels so that each of the seven contained the same amount. He then measured and added various ingredients to each barrel.

One of the substances was in fact the powdered wood from quassia, the plant that provided Quentin's last name. Quassia stimulated appetite, which was why Thaddeus's customers devoured his pork pies and demanded more beer.

Next came liquorice, just enough to add a distinctive taste that allowed Thaddeus to brag to his customers that his brewer was a genius.

Then Quentin added powdered Indian berry, which had an

extreme intoxicating effect that compensated for the reduced alcohol in the mixture.

"Where are your casks of water?"

"There." Thaddeus pointed.

The two of them added the water to the seven barrels and tasted the result.

"You're right. This beer's as good as your brother makes," Thaddeus said.

"*Better* than what my brother makes."

"Perhaps, but I'm not paying you any more than I pay *him*."

Quentin laughed and proceeded to the gin. Again he distributed the contents of three barrels so that they were equally divided into seven.

"What do you call this when you serve it to customers?" Quentin asked.

"Cream of the Valley."

"Ha."

The only ingredient that Thaddeus was allowed to know about was the cakes of sugar that he'd been told to obtain.

Quentin added the necessary amount of sugar to each barrel, experience having shown that after customers acquired a fondness for sweetened gin, they wouldn't accept the gin supplied by honest distillers.

"Now a little flavour." Quentin added the powder of juniper berry.

"And a little bite." He poured in a measured amount of a substance known as vitriol, which chemists called sulphuric acid. Some customers learned to crave it.

"And water." Quentin filled the barrels and stirred. "You now have another delivery of Cream of the Valley."

Thaddeus tasted it. "Yes, better than your brother makes. Can you come back next time instead of him?"

"Edward wouldn't like me stealing his customers," Quentin said with another chuckle.

"You're the happiest man I met today."

"No point in being glum. But I'll be happier when you pay me."

Thaddeus counted out three sovereigns. After the two men had climbed the stairs, Quentin shouldered his bag of ingredients and walked across the sand-covered floor towards the exit.

"Tell your brother I hope he feels better," Thaddeus said.

"Thank you. He'll be grateful for your concern."

As the man who called himself Quentin stepped outside into the cold, he thought, *Feel better? Hell, Edward Quassia won't feel anything again. He's frozen stiff under a snowdrift with his head bashed in.*

The member of Young England had taken care only to seem to taste the beer and gin that he'd diluted and adulterated. Although the tavern's owner hadn't consumed enough to be affected, tomorrow the thirst-creating beverages would show unforgettable results. Young England and the bearded man who led them would be pleased.

"In the morning, I heard distant pounding on my front door," Commissioner Mayne told the shocked group in his Scotland Yard office.

Ryan and Becker listened intently. De Quincey and Emily sat on wooden chairs next to them, having spent the night at Lord Palmerston's house. His Lordship had reluctantly invited them to resume living there after it appeared—to his horror—that the queen might ask them to stay at the palace.

"My fear," Mayne continued, "was that the intruder might have regained access to my house, waiting for my family and me to emerge from the bedroom. With great unease, we finally took the risk. After we slid the bureau away and opened the door, I aimed the Enfield toward the corridor. The pounding downstairs increased, along with a man's voice shouting my name. The door to the closet in the corridor remained open. We hurried past it, and past my daughter's shattered door. I aimed the musket this way and that as we descended.

"When I called to the man beyond the front door, he identified himself as the constable who'd driven me home the previous night. I quickly unlocked the door, but even if two other constables had accompanied him, I wouldn't have felt safe. The window of the sitting room was shattered. The house was extremely cold, but no colder than I felt inside. After the constable used his clacker to summon other officers, they searched the entire house. They found marks where the intruder had indeed pried open the skylight."

"And your servant?" Ryan asked.

The commissioner shook his head. "While she slept, the intruder had . . ."

The group became silent.

"There was a note, of course," De Quincey finally said.

Mayne nodded. "The intruder dropped it into the sitting room after he shattered the window."

"And I assume that the note's message was 'Young England'?" De Quincey asked, fingering his laudanum bottle.

"Yes."

"Today there'll be another murder in a public place comparable to the church and the skating area—somewhere that a crowd would normally feel safe," De Quincey predicted.

"I recalled every constable who isn't already on duty," Commissioner Mayne said. "But given the increased protection at the palace and the various crime areas that need to be investigated, there aren't enough constables to watch everywhere."

"The storm may have helped us," Becker suggested. "Given the condition of the streets, there's less traffic. Not to mention, even before the newspapers appeared this morning, word of the killings spread rapidly. Some people are staying home out of fear."

"But because houses have been attacked in addition to public places, people won't feel safe behind their locked doors, either," Ryan said.

De Quincey looked up from his laudanum bottle. "Commissioner, please repeat what the intruder said about you, your wife, and your daughter."

"As he tried to smash down the bedroom door, he shouted, 'Your daughter will suffer the way my sisters did!' Then he yelled, 'Your wife and you will suffer the way my mother and father did!'"

"Does that mean anything to you, sir?" Ryan asked.

"Not in the slightest," Mayne replied. "It's impossible for me to imagine harming anyone's family."

"The killings include a prison administrator and a judge," De Quincey pointed out. "And now *you*, a police commissioner, nearly became a victim, along with your family. Clearly someone has a tiger's rage to avenge an injustice of the criminal system—or what the killer *perceives* to be an injustice."

"But that would include almost everyone who ever went to prison. They all claim they're innocent," Mayne said. "I've been a commissioner for twenty-six years. If we searched my records, how would we ever single out one family in all that time? Then we'd need to look at Lord Cosgrove's records and those of the judge, trying to find a common link. That could take months."

Ryan echoed what Commissioner Mayne had told them. *"Your daughter will suffer the way my sisters did."* He thought for a moment. *"Your wife and you will suffer the way my mother and father did."*

"That's what the intruder yelled," the commissioner agreed.

"Please help my mother and father and sisters," Ryan added.

"No, the intruder didn't say that."

"But I heard it." Ryan had a long-ago look.

"You're not making sense."

"In eighteen forty, when I arrested Edward Oxford after he shot at the queen, when it seemed at first that he was part of a revolutionary group, there was a theory that someone had staged a diversion to distract the queen's guards," Ryan explained.

"A diversion?"

"A boy," Ryan said. "A beggar."

The ragged urchin raced next to the queen's carriage.

"Queen! Please listen, Queen! My mother and father need help! My sisters need help!" His accent was Irish.

A mounted guard commanded, "Get out of Her Majesty's way, you vermin, before I run you down."

Breathing hard, the boy strained to keep up with the carriage.

"Please, Queen, help my parents! Help my sisters!"

"You Irish scum, move on!"

The horseman kicked the boy into the gutter.

Ignoring the blood on his face, the boy struggled to his feet and raced after the carriage, yelling, "Please, help my mother and father and sisters!"

"That's when Edward Oxford fired at the queen," Ryan said. "I told you how the surprise of the shot made the queen's driver halt and how that gave Oxford a second chance to fire. Before I could get to him, the crowd pounced. They'd have killed him if I hadn't got there and if other constables hadn't arrived.

"The crowd also attacked the boy," Ryan added. "I remember a man punched the boy and yelled, 'This Irish scum's part of it. Ran in front of the horse guards! Tried to distract them! Yelled at the queen! Tried to make the carriage stop!'

"The man held the boy by the back of his collar the way he would a struggling animal. 'He's part of it, I tell ya!'

" 'Help my mother and father and sisters!' the boy kept shouting.

"I had no idea if he was involved or not, but it was better to take him to the police station than leave him with the mob. 'Right, we'll arrest him, too,' I said.

"But when I reached for the boy, the man loosened his grip. The boy fell to the path and scrambled away through the legs of the crowd. The man who'd punched him gave chase, but the boy reached the railing of Green Park, grabbed two of the spikes on top, pulled himself up, and leapt over before the man could stop him. I remember seeing a spike gouge one of the boy's legs. The boy cried out and fell to the grass on the other side. But before the man could climb over, the boy lurched to his feet and managed to escape among the trees. He was limping, favouring his undamaged leg."

"Do you believe that the boy was part of a conspiracy against the queen?" Emily asked.

"None was ever established," Ryan answered. "When I went to Edward Oxford's lodgings and found the documents about Young England, naturally I wondered if the boy was part of a plot. I investigated as best I could, but then my sergeant told me that Young England had been proved to be only a delusion of Edward Oxford's deranged mind. I decided that the boy was no more than what he seemed—a child desperately trying to help his family. My curiosity remained, though, making me wonder why the boy's family needed help. Perhaps because he was Irish like me, I never stopped looking for him as I patrolled."

"Did you ever see him again?" Becker asked.

"Not once. Strange how memory works. I haven't thought about him in years. And now . . ." Ryan turned towards De Quincey. "I'm sure I know what you're going to say."

De Quincey nodded. "There's no such thing as forgetting. The inscriptions on our memories remain forever, just as the stars seem to withdraw during daylight but emerge when the darkness returns."

"Ryan, do you truly suspect that the boy grew up to be the man who attacked my family and me?" Commissioner Mayne asked.

"Your daughter will suffer the way my sisters did. Your wife and you will suffer the way my mother and father did," Ryan quoted again, then switched to what he'd heard the boy shout years earlier. *"My mother and father need help. My sisters need help. Please help my mother and father and sisters."* He shrugged. "Maybe it's just a coincidence, but the boy fifteen years ago and the man last night are both related to a threat against the queen."

"You mentioned that the boy had an Irish accent," Commissioner Mayne said. "So did the man who attacked my family and me."

The morning's streets were a mess. Sir Walter Cumberland cursed as he left his club and saw the grimy slop that he was forced to walk through to reach the cab that he'd instructed the porter to summon.

His head pounding from the considerable brandy he'd drunk the previous night to celebrate his engagement, he climbed into the cab and told the driver, "Half Moon Street in Mayfair. Traffic looks slight this morning. You shouldn't take long getting there."

"Slight indeed," the cab driver said. "People are keepin' off the streets because of the murders. Newsboys are shoutin' about 'em everywhere. You're only the second fare I had this mornin'."

"Just drive."

Half Moon Street was where Catherine Grantwood's parents lived, and after Sir Walter's victory yesterday, he was on his way to reinforce what he'd achieved. But to his dismay, he saw another cab at the kerb in front of his destination. He had no doubt who had hired it.

It's a good thing I decided to come back this soon, he thought. Furious, he jumped from the cab.

As he prepared to knock on the door, it opened and Trask came into view. Sir Walter refused to think of him by his military title, let alone as "Sir."

At least he isn't wearing his damned uniform, Sir Walter thought. *The way he tries to impress people with it is shameless.*

But what Trask did wear annoyed Sir Walter almost as much. The brushed fur on his top hat and the quality of his tailored overcoat were better than Sir Walter's, even though Sir Walter's were very fine indeed.

"I should have known that you weren't gentleman enough to accept the decision as final," Sir Walter told him, gesturing with his walking stick.

"It was Lord Grantwood's decision, not Catherine's," Trask replied.

"So you thought you'd appeal to him one more time? Do you think I don't know about the collapse of the bank in which Catherine's father had large deposits? Do you think I don't know that he lost almost everything?"

Trask closed the door, adjusted the sling on his arm, and glanced at people walking along the street. "If you don't lower your voice, the entire neighbourhood will know about it," he said.

"You took advantage of Lord Grantwood's financial crisis and persuaded him to sell you a railway easement through his country estate."

"I paid more than the easement was worth."

"Of course you did—because you wanted to buy more than the easement. Soon you found a strategy to meet Catherine while you supervised the railway construction."

"Her horse bolted. I rescued her."

"No doubt her horse bolted from the noise of the construction. Perhaps you timed an explosion so that it frightened the animal."

"Be careful, Sir Walter."

"Then you took advantage of your visits, supposedly on business, to strengthen your friendship with her."

"I did nothing that Catherine didn't welcome."

"When her family came to London, you followed them and continued your attentions to her. Lord and Lady Grantwood were so dependent on you that they couldn't object."

"Kindly lower your voice," Trask told him.

Sir Walter's headache from the brandy the night before was stronger than his patience.

"You gave orders in the army, but you can't give orders to me. For all your railways and steamships and money, you can never buy respectability. People who matter will always see remnants of sweat on your brow. There'll always be a residue of dirt beneath your fingernails. Even your language gives you away. Your embarrassing use of 'blasted' at the queen's dinner last night reminded everyone of your poor breeding."

Sir Walter's sarcasm about poor breeding referred to Trask's father, Jeremiah Trask, who'd built the first train link between Liverpool and Manchester in 1830, beginning the Railway Era. Trask senior was rumoured to have financed the start of his empire by selling stock in worthless African gold mines.

"Again, I caution you to be careful," Trask said.

"Step out of the way. I have personal matters to attend to."

"Indeed you do," Trask said. "You'll find that Catherine's father had second thoughts. The announcement of your engagement to Catherine was premature."

"What are you talking about?"

Trask didn't reply.

"What have you done?" Sir Walter demanded.

"I merely asked Lord Grantwood to reconsider his decision."

"Damn you!"

Shoving past him to pound on the door, Sir Walter knocked Trask off balance and toppled him into the slush.

Trask landed on his injured arm. Wincing but refusing to groan, he used his left hand to grip the railing and stand. His sling was now filthy. His hat lay in the ash-covered slush, its carefully brushed fur ruined. Half-melted snow slid from his overcoat.

Pedestrians halted and stared. Drivers leaned from their cabs in shock, never having expected to see such a scene on a Mayfair street.

Trask picked up his dripping hat. If he was angry, his impassive features concealed any sign of it.

But Sir Walter was overjoyed. "If you wish satisfaction, I'll meet you at Englefield Green."

"A duel? No. I saw enough killing in the war."

"How noble. Or maybe you're afraid that your injured arm will give me an advantage—which I would be happy to take. A manslaughter charge would be worth the price of never seeing you again."

The door suddenly opened.

Lord Grantwood's butler frowned at the commotion and at Trask's soiled hat and overcoat.

Storming inside, Sir Walter asked, "Is he in his study?"

Not waiting for a reply, he headed in that direction and found Catherine's father standing at the study's open doorway.

"Did you hear us?"

"The entire neighbourhood did," Lord Grantwood told him.

"Was Trask lying that you changed your mind about Catherine marrying me?"

"He did not lie."

"Where's Catherine?"

"Preparing to visit a sick cousin in the country."

"Tell her to come down. I wish to speak to her."

"That won't serve a useful purpose."

Sir Walter had never seen Catherine's father look so pale. "What on earth is the matter with you? What happened here this morning?"

"Colonel Trask and I had a discussion. He persuaded me that Catherine's affection for him mattered more than any other consideration."

"Why do your features look strained? Did he threaten you?"

"No."

"I remind you of our conversation yesterday afternoon. Your financial disasters are common knowledge."

Lord Grantwood's face looked tighter.

"As beautiful as Catherine is, no member of the peerage would offer to marry her," Sir Walter pointed out. "She can't bring any material advantages to a marriage, and she might even prove to be a drain if she asks her husband to take care of you and Lady Grantwood."

Catherine's father sank onto the chair behind his desk.

"Moreover, Trask's knighthood might qualify him to be called 'Sir,' but I shouldn't need to remind you that it impresses commoners more than it does the aristocracy. I also shouldn't need to remind you that the title of a knighthood can't be passed on to an heir. If, God forbid, you allow Catherine to marry him, any child from their union couldn't inherit his title. I, on the other hand, am a baronet. *My* title of 'Sir' is not only superior to Trask's, but it *can* be inherited. If you renege on your promise and allow Catherine to marry him, you doom your descendants to life without a title. Finally," Sir Walter said with emphasis, "my fifty thousand pounds per year might not be comparable to Trask's fortune, but it's far more than *you* now have. It would support Catherine in comfort while affording you some luxury as well."

Lord Grantwood stared at the glowing chunks of coal in the fireplace, his expression indicating that he received no warmth from them. "There's no need to remind me of yesterday's conversation."

"What the devil made you change your mind? How much money did Trask offer you? Enough to remove all your debts?"

"I won't allow you to insult me by suggesting that I'd be willing to sell my daughter."

"Then what did Trask say to make the difference?" Sir Walter stepped closer. "You're not telling me everything. I can see it in your eyes."

"He persuaded me that emotional considerations are finally what matter."

"*Emotional* considerations? What do *they* have to do with anything? A woman learns to love her husband—or at the very least to appreciate what he provides for her."

"I must ask you to leave."

"He threatened you. I'm right. I know it. Not physically, perhaps, but he threatened you all the same. With what? What are you hiding? What's your secret?"

Lord Grantwood continued to stare forlornly at the burning coals.

"I'll find him and make him tell me what he used against you," Sir Walter vowed.

"He'll tell you that he loves Catherine and that Catherine loves him."

Sir Walter tapped the knob of his walking stick against the palm of his hand. "When I finish with him, he'll tell me a great deal more than that."

★　　★　　★

"I'll have more of that Cream of the Valley," the banker's clerk told Thaddeus Mitchell as midday business in the Wheel of Fortune reached its peak. "Bring another glass for my friend."

Here in London's business district, talk of money usually flowed like the Wheel of Fortune's gin and beer. But today the only topics were the several murders and whether appointments should be cancelled so that everyone had a chance to hurry home before the sun went down, which would happen in three hours. The lingering question was whether they would be safe even in the sanctuary of their homes.

"It's the Russians doing this," a stockbroker insisted, setting down his glass of beer.

"Right. They're trying to distract us from the war," a telegraph executive emphasized.

"The Russians want to make us afraid to go anywhere," a commodities distributor complained, finishing his glass. "We'll soon be bowing to the tsar."

"If we're not murdered in our beds before then. Nobody's safe."

"Bring another glass of beer," the stockbroker called to Thaddeus Mitchell. "I can't believe how thirsty I am."

Thaddeus smiled at the exceptionally active Monday business. "Coming up!"

Someone else commented that the beer made *him* feel thirsty also. The man—a cotton importer—took another swallow, set down his glass, leaned sideways, and toppled off his chair, striking his head on the floor.

Three tables away, a property developer finished his Cream of the Valley, put a contract into his pocket, stood to return to his office, and crashed across the table.

Someone shouted.

Another man collapsed.

Thaddeus Mitchell's smile dissolved into an expression of

horror as the banker's clerk hurled a glass into his companion's face.

The telegraph executive removed a knife from a pork pie and drove it into a passing waiter's neck.

Then the violence truly began.

The sign consolidated english railway company was remarkably subdued for one of the richest privately owned enterprises in England. Even its address was inauspicious, located on Water Lane, off Lower Thames Street, away from the grandeur of the business district's famous landmarks, such as the palatial East India Company headquarters and the Bank of England colossus.

In one of his many shrewd business moves, Trask's father had used intermediaries to purchase all of one side of Water Lane, with no seller realizing Trask senior's plan and raising the price accordingly. He had broken through walls and added new corridors that unified the interiors of the row of anonymous buildings. He'd reduced the numerous entrances to three, one at each end of the block and one in the middle.

After creating the Liverpool and Manchester Railway in 1830, Trask senior had built numerous other lines, criss-crossing the country with noise, smoke, and cinders. Other businessmen understood the immense profits that could be made and built their own railways. In 1846 alone, 260 companies applied to Parliament for the right to build railways. But many of those companies weren't able to survive, and Trask's father purchased them at bargain prices, again using intermediary companies so that few realized the immense empire he was creating. By 1850 there were six thousand miles of railways in England, and Trask's father owned more than half. Telegraph lines ran next to railway tracks, and soon Trask's father built a second empire. But railways couldn't traverse oceans, and so Trask's father expanded his interests into steamship lines.

All this from selling stock in worthless African gold mines, Sir Walter thought. As he raged through the central entrance, he remembered his uncle telling him that Trask and his opportunistic father were examples of the new wealth that threatened to sweep away class distinctions. "Make no mistake—commoners with money will ruin this country. Soon it'll get to the point that we need to ask permission to hunt foxes on land we used to own."

"Your business, please?" a porter at the front desk asked.

"I want to see Trask."

The porter raised his eyebrows at the omission of "sir" or "colonel" or even "mister."

"Do you have an appointment?"

"Just tell him Sir Walter Cumberland wants to have words with him."

"I'm sorry, but if you're not on this list . . ."

Sir Walter felt his face turn red. "Tell him that if he doesn't see me, he'll definitely receive that invitation to settle our differences at Englefield Green."

The porter considered Sir Walter, frowned, and wrote something on a piece of paper. He handed it to a clerk. "Take this to Sir Anthony."

"I'll go with you," Sir Walter said, angered at the reference to Trask as "Sir."

"I can't allow you to do that." The porter stepped in front of him.

"Perhaps *you'd* like to meet me at Englefield Green also."

"What's going on here?" a voice demanded.

Sir Walter turned towards Trask, who stood halfway down a staircase, glaring at him.

"This gentleman insists on—" the porter began.

"Yes, I heard him insisting all the way up in my office," Trask said.

"I don't know how you threatened Catherine's father, but I won't let you get away with it!" Sir Walter told him.

"Lower your voice."

"Maybe you *did* buy Catherine from her father. I wouldn't put anything past you. How much did she cost?" Sir Walter made a threatening motion with his walking stick. "When I learn what you used to pressure him, I'll—"

By then, Trask had descended the stairs. With his uninjured left arm, he grabbed Sir Walter's walking stick, yanked it from his hands, and hurled it away. Then he struck Sir Walter so hard in the face that Sir Walter stumbled from the building and landed in the slush-filled gutter.

Trask emerged from the building and took a sideways position so that the sling on his injured right arm was protected.

"I accept your invitation to Englefield Green."

When Sir Walter tried to stand, Trask struck him again, using his left fist to knock him back into the slush.

"Unless you'd like to settle the matter right now," Trask said.

Before Sir Walter could express the fury that his bloodied face communicated, shouts filled the end of Water Lane.

"Help!" a man screamed.

Someone with a knife was chasing him.

Other shouts filled the neighbourhood. "Over at the Wheel of Fortune! They've all gone mad!"

Around the corner, a pistol sounded.

The man with the knife gained distance on his prey.

Trask stepped towards the attacker, tripped him as he went past, and stomped a boot down hard on the hand that held the knife, breaking fingers, forcing the man to release the knife. Trask then placed a boot on the back of the man's neck, applying his full weight.

"Stay down!" Trask warned.

The man squirmed and wailed like an animal.

"What the blazes is wrong with you?" Trask demanded.

The porter rushed forward to help, pinning the man to the cobblestone lane.

"The Wheel of Fortune!" someone shouted. "Hurry!"

Trask spun towards Sir Walter, who remained in the gutter, holding his bleeding mouth, astonished by what he'd just seen.

"For a change, make yourself useful," Trask told him. "Help my porter subdue this man."

Around the corner, the shouting persisted.

Cradling his right arm in its sling, Trask ran towards the commotion. As he turned left onto Lower Thames Street, he saw a man in the slush, moaning from a wound to his stomach.

Several men wrestled with someone who held a pistol.

Trask kicked the assailant's left knee. As the man screamed, Trask kicked his other knee, dropping him to the cobblestones. He prepared to kick the side of the man's head, but seeing that the captors now had the advantage, Trask hurried towards more intense shouting.

People scuffled in front of the Wheel of Fortune tavern. An actual wheel hung above the front door—not the fortune wheel depicted on tarot cards, with someone falling from the wheel's downward motion while someone else clung to the upward side. No, this was a wheel from a gambler's game of chance. From beneath it, a stool crashed through the front window, spraying glass over the crowd.

Constables struggled to subdue the fighting. Some were forced to use their truncheons when people in the mob attacked them.

A man stumbled through the chaos.

Trask recognized him as Thaddeus Mitchell, the tavern's owner. Blood dripped from his forehead, staining his white apron.

"Good God, what happened?" the colonel asked.

"Customers dropped over."

"What?"

"Others began screaming. Some had knives or pistols because of the murders. They pulled them out and—"

Around them, the screams persisted.

"Somebody even used blood to write on the counter."

"Wrote something in blood?" Trask tugged the owner towards the entrance, demanding, "What are you talking about? Show me."

Ryan and Becker hurried from a cab, avoiding shards from a broken window that protruded from the slush. Someone sagged against a wall, his head down, moaning. Somebody else was carried from the tavern.

A tall man with a military bearing approached them. Until now, Ryan had seen him only in uniform and might have taken longer to recognize him, if not for the sling on his right arm.

"Colonel Trask, thanks for sending your message."

"My offices aren't far from here—on Water Lane. When I heard the commotion, I came to learn what caused it. I quickly realized that you needed to be told."

A police sergeant finished questioning members of the crowd and walked towards them. The insignia on his brass buckle made clear that he belonged to the business district's police force, separate from the Metropolitan Police to which Ryan and Becker belonged.

"You understand that you're guests," the sergeant said.

"We're here to help, not try to take over," Ryan told him.

"Well, if you can make sense of this, you're welcome."

The sergeant led them inside.

The shadows of the Wheel of Fortune were pierced by daylight through the shattered windows. The place had a stale odour of beer and gin.

Ryan and Becker surveyed the damage. Tables had been broken, chairs destroyed, bottles, glasses, and a mirror smashed. Blood coloured the sand on the floor. Two police-men helped a groaning victim limp away.

In a corner, a man with an injured forehead stared at the scene, his hands pressed to the sides of his face in shock.

"That's the owner—Thaddeus Mitchell," the sergeant said. "He admits to hiring a drink doctor to dilute his beer and gin so they last longer."

"And the man he hired added more than the usual chemi-cals," Ryan concluded. "Something so powerful that people who drank it either passed out or suffered visions of monsters trying to attack them."

"How this happened I can understand," the sergeant said. "But the why of it doesn't come to me. What would possess someone to do this?"

"To keep people from feeling safe in places like this, where they normally feel relaxed," Becker answered. "The same as they no longer feel safe in churches or parks—or even in their homes."

Colonel Trask pointed towards the counter. "What I mentioned in my note is over there."

They spread out, studying what stretched before them. Someone had stuck his fingers in blood from one of the wounded and used it to write a name along the counter.

Ryan turned again towards the owner. "Mr. Mitchell, when did the drink doctor come here?"

Not accustomed to being addressed with a term of respect, the dazed man lowered his hands from his cheeks. He worked to focus his thoughts. "Last night. A little after midnight."

"Excuse us for a moment," Ryan told the owner.

He motioned for Becker, Colonel Trask, and the constable to step a distance away.

Keeping his voice low so that the owner couldn't hear, he asked Becker, "Do you understand?"

"A little after midnight. That's the same time Commissioner Mayne and his family were attacked," Becker answered.

"The commissioner and his family were attacked?" the colonel asked in alarm.

"At their house in Chester Square."

"But Chester Square is at least three miles from here. After yesterday's snowfall, it would have taken an hour to travel that distance," Colonel Trask said.

"Exactly. The man who attacked the commissioner and his family couldn't have been in this tavern at the same time. More than one person was involved. The same as with the murders yesterday."

Ryan gave Becker a warning look, hoping that he wouldn't say what both of them were obviously thinking. Young England was very real.

He turned towards Thaddeus Mitchell, who straightened after having leaned forward in an effort to hear what the group was saying.

Ryan pointed towards the words written in blood on the counter. "Mr. Mitchell, did you see who did this?"

"Yes. But what I saw is as crazy as everything else that happened."

"What do you mean?"

"Notice how thin the finger marks are. A beggar boy wrote that name."

"A beggar boy?"

"Before everything happened, the boy came in here, saying he needed to find his father. He looked around, but he didn't find his father. He told me that his father had said he'd be coming here. His mother was sick, and the boy needed to make his father go home to take care of her. Would I let him stay out of the way in a corner until his father showed up?

Well, the pitiful way he asked, I figured it would be all right as long as the father didn't take too long. So the boy stayed over there."

Thaddeus Mitchell pointed towards a corner near the counter.

"When people started falling down and screaming and attacking each other, the boy suddenly leapt onto the counter, rubbed his hand in blood on it, and wrote *that*."

Becker leaned over the counter, reading the name in the blood. "John William Bean Junior."

"Whoever *he* is," the owner grumbled. "I know all my customers, but I never heard of *him*."

"I have," Colonel Trask said. "That's why I sent my note."

Ryan nodded. "Six years ago, John William Bean Junior tried to shoot the queen."

9

Bedlam

"Good day, My Lord," De Quincey said.

Lord Palmerston frowned as he descended the staircase towards his front door.

"Why are you and your daughter waiting? No need to thank me for allowing you to continue staying here. I simply feared that your obvious poverty might have embarrassed the queen into offering a room. Now if you'll excuse me, my impending duties as prime minister ... Wait. Have I possibly misinterpreted? Can it be that you decided to travel back to Edinburgh after all, and that you're finally saying goodbye?"

"My Lord, I am here to do you a service."

"Then you *are* finally leaving," Lord Palmerston said with delight.

"In a manner of speaking. We wish to take a short journey to the place where you frequently threaten to send me."

"I don't understand."

"But to go there, I need a note of permission from you—and cab fare."

"To go *where?* For heaven's sake, stop confusing me."

"My Lord, I wish to go to the madhouse."

Bethlem Royal Hospital dated back to 1247, when it was originally a house for the poor. Its name—a contraction of Bethlehem—was often mispronounced as Bedlam, a word that people associated with deranged behaviour after the hospital became Britain's first institution devoted to the insane. In 1815, Bedlam acquired a new facility below the Thames, at St. George's Fields in Southwark. "Fields" was an accurate description, for to offset the building's gloom, a park stretched before it. Bleeding and purgatives were standard treatments, voiding the foul humours that were believed to cause insanity. Neighbours often complained about "the cryings, screechings, roarings, brawlings, shaking of chains, and swearings" that came from the building.

Bedlam's entrance was south of Westminster Bridge, near the intersection of Lambeth and Vauxhall Roads. Leaning from a cab as it entered the grounds, De Quincey ignored the slush-covered lawn and focused on the large building that he and Emily approached.

"It resembles Buckingham Palace," he commented.

"I'm glad that I'm the only one who heard you say that," Emily told him.

"But it does," De Quincey insisted as the cab drew closer. "It's nearly as tall and wide as the palace."

He raised his laudanum bottle to his lips.

"Give that to me," Emily instructed. "If a supervisor sees you drinking from it, he'll take it from you, fearing that you might offer it to a patient."

De Quincey reluctantly handed it to his daughter while he continued to stare out of the window towards the imposing structure.

"Finally Lord Palmerston gets his wish. Perhaps the madhouse is indeed where I belong."

The cab reached the end of a treed lane. The leafless branches were as dreary as the soot that darkened the slush.

Emily descended from the cab and paid the driver with coins that Lord Palmerston had grudgingly given her. Then she and De Quincey studied the steps that led up to the stone building's ominous entrance.

"After Edward Oxford shot at the queen in 1840, rumours

spread that his incarceration in Bedlam was not a punishment," De Quincey said. "Some newspapers claimed that he
enjoyed excellent food and wine. Some even maintained that
tutors instructed him in German and French. John Francis,
the next man who shot at Her Majesty, hoped that his arrest
would put him here also, relieving him of debt."

"Surely anyone who actually saw this gloomy place would
understand the truth," Emily said. "The third man who tried
to shoot Her Majesty—did *he* wish to come here also?"

"John William Bean Junior? His seventeen years were filled
with biblical affliction. He was a hunchbacked dwarf, and all
he wanted was to die."

"A hunchbacked dwarf?"

"His arms were spindles. His back was so crooked that he
needed to walk with his head down, his face peering at the
gutter. He couldn't earn a living. His brothers mocked him,
prompting him to run from home and sleep in fields. One
week, he somehow survived on only eight pennies that he
gained from begging. In desperation, he managed to obtain
an old pistol and gunpowder, but he couldn't afford bullets, so
he crammed clay pieces of a tobacco pipe into the barrel.
Only seven weeks after John Francis shot at the queen, he
waited for the queen's carriage to pass him on Constitution
Hill. Then he stepped forward and pulled the trigger."

"Good heavens," Emily said. "Was the queen injured?"

"Thankfully, no. Like so many things that went wrong in
Bean's life, the powder failed to ignite. He fled, but not before
witnesses saw what he'd attempted to do. In a grotesque spec-
tacle, the police searched all of London for hunchbacked
dwarves, arresting dozens before they finally located him."

Emily shook her head as if the idea of the police arresting
dozens of hunchbacked dwarves proved that the world was
indeed going mad.

"Lacking the courage to end his suffering by killing himself, he hoped that the government would end his life for him, hanging him or at least putting him in Bedlam, where he wouldn't need to worry about his next meal," De Quincey said.

"Did he get his wish?"

"No. Bean was sentenced to eighteen months of hard labour in prison."

"Hard labour? A hunchbacked dwarf?"

"The government wished to make people understand that there were severe consequences for attempting to shoot the queen. After Bean was released, his health declined until he attempted what he hadn't been brave enough to try earlier—to put an end to his wretched life."

"How?"

De Quincey shrugged. "It's of no matter."

"Father, the evasive look in your eyes makes me insist that you tell me how he tried to kill himself."

"With laudanum." De Quincey stared at the columns of the forbidding entrance. "We've postponed this long enough."

Bedlam had an administration area at the core of the building. Galleries stretched to the left and the right, extending for a considerable distance. Windows admitted sunlight, revealing numerous people along each gallery who were waiting to see patients.

Emily approached a man behind a desk. He had spectacles perched on the tip of his nose and peered over them towards the trousers that showed beneath her bloomer skirt.

"May I help you?" he asked doubtfully.

"My father and I have a note from Lord Palmerston."

The name had its usual effect. Sitting straighter, the clerk hurriedly reached for the note. After reading it, he told them, "You'll need to see Dr. Arbuthnot about this. Wait here."

He quickly crossed the entrance hall, knocked on a door, and entered.

To the left, in a distant region of the hospital, a woman wailed. Visitors stopped talking and frowned in the direction of the wails, their echo becoming shriller. Even after the anguished outburst stopped, everyone remained motionless.

The spectacled clerk returned. "Dr. Arbuthnot will see you."

He led them into a cramped office, where an elderly man stood to greet them. His scalp was as hairless as the half-dozen skulls on a shelf next to his desk. A large diagram of the human brain hung on a wall, its sections neatly labelled.

Emily noted that there were books with titles such as *On the Functions of the Cerebellum* and *A System of Phrenology*. She introduced herself and her father.

"De Quincey. The name sounds familiar," Dr. Arbuthnot said.

"I can't imagine why." Emily gave a warning look to her father, who turned his attention to the skulls on the shelf.

"The note giving you permission to speak to Edward Oxford is extremely unusual," Dr. Arbuthnot said. "The government has been very restrictive about who can see him. His mother was allowed to visit him only once a month, and only through a barred opening in a door, with her son sitting several feet away. Often she complained that she couldn't hear what he said. Apart from her, no one from outside has been authorized to see Edward Oxford since he was admitted in eighteen forty."

"No one in fifteen years? Not friends or newspaper reporters?" Emily asked.

"Especially not newspaper reporters."

"And the same conditions apply when we see him? A barred opening in a door? He must sit several feet away from us?"

"Those are my instructions. Mr. De Quincey, your face glistens with perspiration. Do you feel ill?"

He did indeed look ill, his features drawn, his face

resembling moisture-beaded, aged ivory. As in their coach ride to the queen's dinner, Emily had the unnerving sense that her father was in a half state between living and dying.

"I need my medication," he said.

"Perhaps our pharmacy can supply it for you."

"My father already has ample medication," Emily informed the doctor.

De Quincey's feet moved restlessly as he studied the numerous books on the shelves. "Dr. Arbuthnot, do you consider Edward Oxford to be a lunatic?"

"He has an indentation on the side of his forehead that indicates diminished capacity."

"So you believe in phrenology, as some of the titles on your shelves indicate," De Quincey said.

"It's the only way to make a science of studying the mind. Since we can't expose a living brain and examine it without injuring and perhaps killing the patient, the alternative is to measure the outside of a skull and then infer which portions of the brain are under- or overdeveloped, the negative and positive pressures causing the skull to assume its shape."

Dr. Arbuthnot took a skull from a shelf and pointed towards a protuberance at the back. "This is the result of an overdeveloped cerebellum, the source of uncontrolled emotions. On each of these other skulls, I can show depressions or protrusions that indicate similar abnormalities within a brain."

"But surely the mind is more than the shape of a skull," Emily proposed. "How do you account for ideas?"

"They're galvanic processes. One day we'll be able to measure them."

"Are you referring to electricity?"

"England's own Michael Faraday pioneered theories about electrolysis," Dr. Arbuthnot replied. "The brain functions because of it. When parts of the brain are under- or overdeveloped, the flow of electricity becomes uneven, causing unusual and sometimes dangerous behaviour."

"Fascinating," Emily said.

Dr. Arbuthnot looked pleased, distracted by Emily's blue eyes.

"How do you use these theories to treat your patients?" she asked.

"Because it's impossible to cure a physical defect in the brain, all we can do is try to keep our patients subdued. Sometimes restraints are the only method, but the current thinking is that hydrotherapy is effective."

"Soothing baths," Emily said.

"Essentially. A hot bath can be a useful relaxant. Sometimes the shock of a cold bath is required in order for a subsequent hot bath to do its work."

"And will this treatment produce a cure?" Emily asked.

Dr. Arbuthnot looked startled. "There is no such thing as a cure for mental illness. Perhaps one day we'll be able to perform surgery to correct a physical defect in the brain. Until that time, mental affliction is a lifelong curse."

"But don't you think that talking to patients might help them?"

"Talking to them? What possible use could *that* be?"

"My father has a theory about dreams."

Dr. Arbuthnot shook his head in confusion. "Dreams? I miss your point."

De Quincey used a handkerchief to wipe sweat from his brow.

"Are you certain that you're not ill?" the doctor asked.

De Quincey chewed a pill that he removed from a snuffbox. "There's a mountain in northern Germany called the Brocken."

The doctor looked more baffled. "I have not been to Germany."

"The peak has interesting rock formations, huge blocks of granite with names such as the Sorcerer's Chair. A spring is called the Magic Fountain."

"This sounds like a children's story."

"I assure you it's an actual place," De Quincey said. "On a June morning, if you hiked to the top and gazed across the valley towards a neighbouring peak, you would see the monstrous Spectre of the Brocken."

"Yes, a children's story. I'll take you to Edward Oxford."

"The spectre's threatening gyrations in the mountain mist have caused many a heart to beat faster." De Quincey chewed another pill. "An astute witness sometimes realizes what is happening. Occasionally a guide will relieve the anxiety of those who hired him by explaining what they see."

"And what is the explanation?"

"On June mornings, the sun rises behind the observers. Their shadows are cast upon the swirling mist. Magnified, the shadows reflect every motion of the observers, but in a grotesque, unnatural way that at first doesn't seem connected to the people whose shadows have been cast."

"So there you have it. A scientific explanation," Dr. Arbuthnot concluded.

"My father believes that dreams are like those shadows," Emily said.

"Dreams? Shadows?"

"Troubled people might fail to see how a nightmare is a reflection of their personalities," De Quincey explained. "But if the reflection is explained to them—or better yet, if they are encouraged to understand how their nightmares are distortions of the elements in their personalities that trouble them—then they might experience the first steps to being cured."

"Mr. De Quincey, I take it that you are not a physician. While your theories are amusing, they have no basis in science.

Dreams and nightmares are merely phantoms created by electricity."

"How foolish of me to think otherwise. Then let us forget about interpreting dreams. Consider that Edward Oxford was frequently beaten by his father and often saw his mother beaten. The shock of this persistent violence could explain why he was too unstable to hold jobs, why he frequently burst out into hysterical laughter, and why he enjoyed tormenting others."

"Surely you're not suggesting that because Oxford's father beat him and his mother, he felt compelled to inflict violence on others until at last he focused his anger by shooting at the queen."

"Doctor, you express the idea far better than I ever could," De Quincey said.

"The idea is nonsense. Are you seriously proposing that by being encouraged to discuss the violence inflicted upon him in his youth, Oxford would understand his motives for shooting at the queen and no longer wish to do it?"

"The theory is worth considering."

"Well, to repeat, you are not a doctor. If you wish to see Oxford, you'd better do so now. I have an appointment in a half hour."

When they emerged from the office, a woman again shrieked from the hospital's left wing. Once more, visitors stared towards the unseen source of the commotion. Dogs sleeping under benches raised their heads in distress.

"Our female patients are over there. Our male patients are in the opposite wing," Dr. Arbuthnot said, leading the way past visitors.

Sunlight streamed through windows, illuminating paintings that showed soothing streams and meadows. Birds chirped in cages.

"Emily, the birds . . ." De Quincey said.

". . . are not in your imagination," she told him.

"The cells are off a corridor through there," Dr. Arbuthnot said.

"Cells?" Emily asked.

"Because the patients are here at the order of the court, we acquired the habit of calling the rooms 'cells.'"

Another wail—this time from a man—echoed from somewhere deep in the building. They reached the end of the gallery and turned to the left, entering a different portion of the hospital.

"This is where our criminally insane male patients are kept," the doctor explained. Despite sunlight through windows, the area seemed to darken as they proceeded.

"Bring Edward Oxford to the visitors' area," Dr. Arbuthnot told a guard, who looked puzzled at the idea of Oxford having visitors.

The doctor told De Quincey and Emily, "Oxford is confined to a cell for much of the time, but during midday hours, he's permitted to exercise in a courtyard. We encourage him to be useful by pumping water into pails for the hospital to use. But mostly he paces, muttering that he doesn't deserve to be here."

They reached an alcove so far from sunlight that an overhead lamp was needed to dispel the shadows. A bench was positioned in front of a locked door, through which a small barred opening provided a view of the area beyond.

"Oxford will soon be visible through there," Dr. Arbuthnot noted.

De Quincey sat on the bench and studied the barred opening.

"Emily, please sit next to me. I would like Oxford to see the face of a healthy young woman. Perhaps it will raise his spirits."

Self-conscious, Emily did what her father requested.

Beyond the opening, several heavy footsteps approached. As they grew louder, shadows came into view. Then the shadows became two guards, escorting a man who wore loose grey clothes.

In the gloom, the guards set the man at a table that was perhaps ten feet from the opening through which De Quincey and Emily gazed.

"Dr. Arbuthnot, can't he be brought any closer?" De Quincey asked.

"Not according to my instructions."

"Do the guards need to stand next to him?"

"Yes."

"Edward Oxford, my name is Thomas De Quincey. This is my daughter, Emily."

Oxford had been eighteen when he shot at Queen Victoria: short and thin, with boyish features. Now he had put on weight, presumably from a fatty hospital diet. He was thirty-three, but his sagging cheeks made him look older. His long dark locks had been shorn, leaving tufts that had begun to turn grey.

"I don't know you," Oxford said nervously.

De Quincey and Emily leaned towards the barred opening in an effort to hear him.

"Lord Palmerston gave us permission to visit you," De Quincey informed him.

"Lord Palmerston? Bah."

"We wish to speak to you about Young England."

Oxford's gaze drifted towards Emily. "How can we speak about something that the police say didn't exist?"

"It's what *you* say that my daughter and I care about," De Quincey told him.

Oxford kept looking at Emily. "There were four hundred of us."

"Yes, that is what the documents in your locked box indicated," De Quincey said.

"The documents tell it all." Oxford laughed bitterly. "We invented names for ourselves. We worked in positions close to the rich, ready for the moment when Hanover would tell us to act."

"Are you referring to the ruler of the German state of Hanover?" De Quincey asked.

When Oxford didn't reply, De Quincey looked at Emily.

"Mr. Oxford, do you mean the queen's eldest uncle?" she asked.

"Thank you. No one ever calls me 'mister.' Yes. Hanover. The queen's uncle. You shouldn't need to ask. Has he disappeared from memory in fifteen years?"

"He died four years ago," De Quincey said.

Oxford ignored him, continuing to look only at Emily. "Died?"

"Yes."

"Ha. They said that he wished us to seize the government so he could become king in Victoria's place."

"They?" Emily asked.

"The other members."

"Of what?" Emily asked.

"Young England!"

Dr. Arbuthnot murmured, "You can see how delusional he is. If you upset him, I'll need to have him put back in restraints."

"Mr. Oxford, can you tell us if an Irish boy was part of Young England?" Emily asked.

"Irish boy?"

"When you shot at the queen . . ."

"Without bullets!" Oxford shook his fist, agitated.

"An Irish boy wearing rags rushed towards the queen's carriage, begging Her Majesty to save his mother and father and sisters," Emily explained. "He distracted the queen's mounted guards. Some people believe that he was part of your plan."

"Part of my plan?" Oxford sounded mystified.

"While the guards directed their attention towards the boy, you had an unrestricted field of fire."

"Without bullets! I know nothing about an Irish boy or about his mother and father and sisters! It was Young England, not Young *Ireland!*" Oxford pounded the table.

"I can't permit you to continue," Dr. Arbuthnot said. "Guards," he ordered through the barred opening, "return Oxford to his cell."

Oxford resisted, staring towards Emily. "Just another moment to look at you." When the guards tugged at him, he struggled, keeping his gaze on Emily through the bars.

"You're beautiful."

"Thank you," Emily said.

"All I did was what I was told, and look where it got me. Young England. Damn Young England."

Oxford's frantic gaze remained on Emily as the guards dragged him through a shadowy archway.

Another patient shrieked as they returned to the gallery. Birds stopped chirping in the cages that hung from the ceiling. Once more, dogs raised their heads from under benches. Visitors again froze.

But Dr. Arbuthnot paid no attention as he escorted De Quincey and Emily impatiently toward Bedlam's exit.

"I should not have allowed the conversation to continue," the doctor complained. "It may take Oxford weeks to regain the slight equilibrium he possessed. And what was accomplished? You learned nothing that hadn't already been established—Oxford is delusional."

"In some respects, his thoughts are perfectly clear," De Quincey noted.

"You made sense of that raving? Wait. Now it comes to me. De Quincey. Lord save me, are you the Opium-Eater? Those pills you've been munching ... They're opium! *Anything* would make sense to you, except logic."

"Thank you, Doctor. The experience was very informative."

He and Emily passed a guard and stepped outside. A cold breeze greeted them.

"Refreshing," De Quincey said, surveying the slush-covered lawn.

When he held out his hand, Emily gave him his laudanum bottle.

"Father, what did you learn?"

"That there are many kinds of treason."

"Catherine, I apologize if I embarrassed you," Colonel Trask said.

"Embarrassed me? Because of Sir Walter's outburst? *You* weren't to blame." Catherine's eyes flashed, their spirit making them more lustrous and lovely. "I heard him shouting all the way up in my room. For certain the neighbours and the cab drivers heard him. After you left, he directed his anger at my father."

They were in the drawing room of the Grantwood house, next to the warmth of the fireplace. Trask boldly reached for Catherine's hand. Although the door was open, the lack of a chaperone would have been unacceptable if her parents hadn't given permission for them to marry.

"I worried that you might be ashamed because Sir Walter shoved me down and I didn't fight back."

"What would *that* have accomplished? Only a greater scandal in front of the neighbours. Brawling at my doorstep? Anthony, I was proud of you for showing restraint."

"Even so, be prepared for gossip," Trask said. "I'm supposed to be a war hero. Now perhaps people will say that I'm actually a coward." He tried not to focus on her lips.

"Your right arm is in a sling. How could you have fought back?"

"In truth, I eventually did fight him."

"What?" Catherine sounded pleasantly surprised.

"After he argued with your father, he tried to force his way into my office on Water Lane. He said some things about your parents."

"What things?" Catherine demanded.

"That I'd purchased you from them, that they valued money more than they valued *you*."

Catherine's cheeks coloured, enhancing their lustre. "*Purchased* me? Like a horse?"

"Sir Walter and I fought outside my office."

"Well, at least it was on Water Lane, not here on Half Moon Street."

For a moment Catherine's expression was difficult for Trask to interpret. Perhaps her reference to the business district indicated contempt for the way he and his father had acquired their wealth.

Then she chuckled. The chuckle became an appealing laugh, making Trask laugh also. Soon their laughter was uncontrolled.

A frowning butler peered into the sitting room. They did their best to restrain themselves.

"This time around, I hope you knocked *him* down," Catherine said.

"I did."

"Good," Catherine said with delight.

"Twice, in fact."

"Better. And with only one arm." Catherine touched his handsome face. "I love you," she whispered.

Despite the barrier of her hooped dress, she stood on her tiptoes, leaning forward to kiss him.

Breathless, he held her close, their kiss lasting as long as they dared. The sound of footsteps in the corridor made the moment all the more exciting. They stepped back only an instant before another servant looked into the room.

"I can't wait for the church ceremony," Catherine said. "To be married in front of the entire world."

"With all my heart, I too look forward to when we can live together. It will happen soon," Trask assured her. "But for the next few days, things won't be easy."

"What do you mean?"

"Sir Walter won't give up gracefully. I'm afraid he'll return and cause another outburst. Perhaps he'll direct his fury at you instead of your father."

"At *me?* No matter what my father said to him, I never promised Sir Walter *anything*. I gave him no assurances whatsoever."

"Of course you didn't. But Sir Walter's an angry man, and anger doesn't see clearly. I can't be here this afternoon if he returns, Catherine. Your father and I agree that you should go through with your plan to visit your sick cousin in Watford."

"The coach will take me to the station in an hour," Catherine assured him.

"I'll join you tomorrow. But for God's sake, don't tell your cousin that I own the railway. When my father built it, her parents hated the engine noise so much that they made him route the tracks away from their estate."

"And now the village depends on your railway for its livelihood. Anthony, to the contrary, I intend to brag about you."

Trask looked towards the open door. No one was in view. No footsteps approached in the corridor.

He drew her towards him. This time when they kissed, their desire was so intense that they wouldn't have known if anyone discovered them.

★   ★   ★

De Quincey and Emily took shallow breaths as Ryan and Becker lifted a trapdoor, permitting them to climb into the musty attic of a police building in Whitehall.

Commissioner Mayne followed them up the ladder, explaining, "These are the arrest records for eighteen forty."

Dust hovered in the light from their lamps. Becker sneezed. Neatly arranged rows of boxes upon boxes stretched before them.

"So many," Emily said, amazed.

"The details of every crime committed in Greater London fifteen years ago," Mayne indicated. "They're arranged according to the type of crime and the month in which it occurred."

"Commissioner, this is brilliant," De Quincey said.

Mayne studied the rows of boxes with rarely displayed pride. "There's no criminal-record system as thorough anywhere in the world. Can I help in any other way?"

"Thank you, no. Sorting through these files is suitable work for Emily and me while the rest of you do what you're trained for. This is a good place for us—out of your way."

"The more people searching through these records, the better," Ryan said. "This is the best method I can think of to explain the motive behind the killings. Becker and I intend to stay."

As Commissioner Mayne descended from the attic, Becker sneezed again. "Sorry."

"We'll soon all be sneezing," Ryan said. "You can see from the thickness of the dust that many of these boxes haven't been opened since they were stored up here."

"June tenth, eighteen forty," De Quincey said. "The day when Edward Oxford shot at the queen and when the Irish boy tried to stop the queen's carriage."

"Help my mother and father and sisters," Ryan recalled. "But we have no idea if it was his mother or his father or his sisters who were arrested, and we don't know for what crime."

"Why don't we each choose a row of boxes and go backwards from June tenth, looking for Irish names?" Becker suggested.

Despite the glow of their lanterns, shadows hovered in the attic's corners.

Ryan opened a box, lifted out some files, and as predicted, he too sneezed.

"Because of poverty, a lot of Irish came to England and London in the thirties and forties," he said for the benefit of Emily and Becker, who were too young to know how bad it had been back then. "They were starving, willing to work for almost any wage. Most people were hostile to them, blaming them for taking jobs from English workers. As a boy, I learned to hide my accent and my red hair."

"William Hamilton was Irish," De Quincey said as he studied a faded document.

"William Hamilton?" Becker asked in confusion.

"The fourth of the men who shot at the queen," De Quincey answered. "He was raised in an orphanage in Ireland. During the potato famine he tried his luck here in England but couldn't find work and went to France in eighteen forty-eight. That was the Year of Revolution over there, with most of Europe in flames. When Hamilton returned to London, he brought back ideas about destroying the government. After months of living on food scraps from women who felt sorry for him, his rage so consumed him that he shot at the queen."

"If the pattern stays true, we'll soon find a victim who has a note with William Hamilton's name on it," Ryan said.

"Without doubt the killer is moving relentlessly towards the present," De Quincey agreed. He took out his laudanum bottle, stared at it, shook his head, and put the bottle back in his coat. "Perhaps a note left with a further victim will refer to Young Ireland instead of Young England."

"Young Ireland?" Emily asked.

"Hamilton belonged to a group called Young Ireland, which organized riots against the government."

"I suppose I shouldn't be surprised that I'm finding many Irish names in arrest records from that period," Ryan said. "Constables often paid extra attention to the Irish."

"I'm finding the same thing," Becker added, reading through files. "Too many Irish names to investigate in the limited time we have."

"Perhaps we're doing this the wrong way," Emily told them.

"What do you mean?"

"Since the boy was begging the queen to save his mother and father and sisters, it may be we need to look *beyond* June tenth, not before it," Emily suggested. "We need to search for something terrible that might have happened to an entire Irish family *after* that date, within the next couple of days or a week."

Colin's father normally had a healthy, ruddy complexion, but as he waited impatiently among the jostling, clamorous crowd outside Newgate Prison, his cheeks were pale.

"This is taking much longer than I hoped," his father said. "Emma and Ruth can't stay by themselves for many more days. Go back to them. Bring them here. Every day at eight, noon, and six, I'll look for you on this spot."

"But I don't want to leave you," Colin protested.

Sweat beaded on his father's forehead. "There's no choice. I can't concentrate on getting your mother out of prison if I also worry about what's happening to your sisters."

After Colin tearfully hugged his father, he hurried away, desperate to reach home. The sooner he could bring his sisters to London, the sooner he could be with his father again . . . the sooner they could free their mother . . . the sooner they could be a family once more.

But he felt light-headed as he raced through the choking air of London's congested streets. By the time he reached the outskirts, he was sweating more profusely than his exertion and the June heat could explain. When he finally arrived at St. John's Wood, he had the sensation that he was floating. He dizzily recalled that he and his father had used a water pump near the alley in which they slept. After drinking from it, they had soaked their hair and rinsed dirt from their faces. A few people in the neighbourhood had warned them not to use the pump because people who drank from it became sick. But other people insisted that bad air was what made people sick. In the end, there hadn't been a choice—it was the only water they could find.

At twilight Colin staggered when he reached the dusty lane to their half-completed village. His vision was so hazy that he arrived at their cottage without realizing it. He found out later that Emma and little Ruth saw him lurch past and ran to help him.

For three days, fever overpowered him. When he finally wakened and recognized the terrified faces of Emma and Ruth, all he could murmur was, "We need to go to Papa. He's waiting for us."

But Colin wasn't strong enough to travel for another day.

"You shivered so powerfully that we feared you were going to die," Emma said.

"Do the neighbours know what happened to Mother?"

"Yes."

"Did any of them bring you food?"

"No," little Ruth said.

"But what about the friend Mother made down the road? The one who said that Mother's knitting would find a market at Burbridge's shop?"

"She turns her back on us," Ruth said. The gap in her front teeth had formerly brightened her features, but now it made her look like the saddest child Colin had ever seen.

"Father." He managed to stand. "We need to go to him."

"Yes," Ruth said bravely. "We need to help Papa."

They gathered all the food that they could find: a few crusts of bread and a potato.

Colin's weakness prevented them from hurrying. Hour after hour, they plodded along the dusty road, slowly nearing the roar and the brown haze of London.

The light was dwindling when they finally reached the spot near Newgate Prison where their father had said he'd be waiting at eight, noon, and six. But the bells of St. Paul's Cathedral tolled that it was much later than six.

"He'll come in the morning," Colin said.

But their father didn't arrive at eight or at noon the next day, either.

Holding hands to keep from being separated in the chaos of the crowd, they set out in search of him.

Colin recognized a costermonger he'd seen on prior days. The weary man pushed his cart along the street, and although his smock was dirty from the day's efforts, his large silk neckerchief was spotless, a mark of pride among his kind.

"Please, sir, do you know where—"

"No beggin' here," the man complained, waving them from his cart. "I didn't haul these vegetables all the way from Covent Garden market, just to give 'em away to the Irish."

Colin approached a crossing sweeper. Sweepers knew everything that happened in a neighbourhood. This one— even with his ragged broom and his bare feet—had a cheery expression that went with the sunny colour of his tousled hair. He didn't seem much older than Colin, but despite their shared poverty, the sweeper's manner made clear that even he had better prospects.

"Do you remember seein' me and my father around here the past week?" Colin asked.

"I remember everythin'. Just a minute."

The sweeper ran ahead of a gentleman and a lady. Without being asked, he swept dirt and horse droppings from in front of the well-to-do couple as they made their way toward the Old Bailey courthouse.

The man tossed a penny onto the grimy paving stones.

"Thank you, sir!" the sweeper exclaimed, as if he'd been given a fortune.

He returned to Colin. "What do you want?"

"Do you remember what my father looks like?"

"I told you I remember everythin'. I been on this corner for five years, and nothin' gets past me."

"Have you seen him?"

"Maybe. What's it worth to you? Ah, never mind. You look worse off than me. Your father's down that alley."

It was the alley with the water pump that Colin and his father had used.

Colin, Emma, and Ruth rushed along it. Their father lay at the far end, unconscious and delirious. Soaked with sweat, he raged with fever. His boots had been stolen. So had his coat and his shirt.

"Papa!" little Ruth exclaimed. "What are we going to do?"

"Surely someone somewhere will help us," Colin said. His voice breaking, he fought against his despair. "Surely in this great city, with so many millions of people, someone will pity us."

10

Watford

Away from London's fog, the dark English countryside had a canopy of stars. In his private railway car, Colonel Trask watched shadowy meadows, streams, and thickets appear to speed past.

A clock on the wall indicated eight minutes past seven. Every other clock in England's railway network would display the equivalent time, because years ago when Jeremiah Trask had founded the British railway system, he'd established a universal railway time, the specifics of which were telegraphed each morning to every station in the country. In precisely one minute this train would reach the village of Watford, seventeen miles north-west of London's Euston Station.

As the locomotive reduced speed, Trask noted the irony that Catherine's cousin would soon need to accept him as a relation, even though the cousin belonged to one of the aristocratic families that had objected to Jeremiah Trask and the coming of the railway.

When the train hissed to a stop, lamps revealed a rustic building with a ticket office, a telegraph office, and a waiting room.

Trask slipped his left arm into his overcoat and draped the opposite sleeve over his sling. After putting on his top hat and leather gloves, he opened the door to his car and stepped onto the wooden platform. No other passenger departed. This wasn't a scheduled stop. He had made a sudden decision not to wait until tomorrow to visit Catherine at her cousin's.

A man in livery approached him. "Colonel Trask? Your telegram arrived. The carriage you requested is on the other side of the station."

"Do you know the way to the Clarendon estate?"

"Yes, sir." The driver picked up his bag. "Please follow me. I read about what you did in the war, Colonel. May I say that it's an honour to meet you?"

"Tell that to every soldier who returns from the Crimea. They're *all* worthy of honour."

A breeze carried the scent of the moisture from yesterday's snowfall and the nearby River Colne. As the train chugged out of the station, Trask listened to the crackling sound of horses' hooves breaking pockets of ice in the road. Laughter from a pub was the only other noise. After the roar and clatter of London, the silence reminded Trask uneasily of the quiet that had preceded Russian attacks in the war.

"Here are the gates, Colonel," the driver said ten minutes later.

Lamps glowed in the windows of a splendid manor. Dogs barked.

After the driver set down his bag, Trask gave him a sovereign, a generous payment.

"You're a gentleman, Colonel."

Sir Walter Cumberland and many others disagree, Trask thought. As he mounted the steps, he looked forward to Catherine's smile.

He knocked on the door, hearing the carriage clatter away. Dogs continued barking.

He knocked a second time.

A manservant opened the door and looked puzzled.

"I'm Colonel Anthony Trask, here to see my fiancée, Miss Catherine Grantwood."

"Catherine Grantwood, sir?"

"She expected me tomorrow, but I decided to come this evening."

"I don't understand, sir."

Blast it, the driver brought me to the wrong manor, Trask thought.

"Who is it, Henry?" a woman asked in the background.

"A Colonel Trask, My Lady. He says he's here to see Miss Grantwood."

A shadow approached, revealing a middle-aged woman with greying hair. She wore an elegant hooped dress.

She studied Trask, judging the quality of his tailoring. She frowned at the overnight bag next to him. "Colonel . . .?"

"Trask, My Lady." He removed his top hat and bowed slightly.

"Catherine isn't here."

Trask's mind swirled with confusion. "I don't understand."

"We expected to see her late this afternoon, but she never arrived. It's quite unlike her not to send a telegram if her plans changed. I hope nothing's wrong."

"Never arrived?" Trask felt stunned.

The woman stared past him towards the darkness, not seeing a carriage. "From where did you travel?"

"London."

"I'm afraid you made your journey for nothing."

Catherine never arrived? Trask thought. *My God, what happened? Did Sir Walter come back to the house? What did he do to stop her from leaving?*

In the distance, he heard the receding sound of the carriage. With a chilling premonition, he dropped his bag and rushed from the door. In the light of the moon, he saw the carriage's lantern wavering in the distance. Beyond the gates to the estate, the road curved to the left towards Watford.

If I race across this field, Trask thought desperately, *I might be able to reach the driver at the curve!*

"Stop!" he yelled.

He charged across frozen slush that reminded him of the Crimea.

"For God's sake, stop!" he yelled to the far-off carriage, running with a frenzy that exceeded anything he had known in the war.

"Stay here with Papa," Colin told his sisters. "Maybe no one will notice you in this alley. If anyone bothers you, tell him I went to find a constable."

It was actually a doctor he went to, but the doctor frowned at his dirty face and tattered clothes, telling him, "I have too many patients already. The ones I have can pay."

Colin found no better response at several hospitals. "Your father sounds too far gone to be saved."

He ran back to the Inns of Court and tried to beg solicitors and barristers for help, but their clerks relentlessly scratched the steel nibs of their pens across sheets of paper and, without looking at him, told him to go away.

The only suggestion came from an elderly gentleman who sat reading a newspaper while waiting to be admitted into an inner office. After listening to the boy implore a clerk about his mother and father and sisters, the man lowered his newspaper, saying, "If it's *that* bad, claim to be debtors. Petition the prison to let your two sisters stay in the cell with your mother. At least they'll have shelter and something to eat until your mother comes to trial. A shoplifter, eh? Not good."

Drenched with sweat at the end of the hot June day, dizzy from his lingering illness, Colin told a guard outside the prison, "My father's sick."

The guard showed no interest.

"My mother's inside." Colin pointed towards the gloomy, soot-covered entrance to the prison. "I don't know when she'll be sent to trial."

"For what?"

By now, he knew enough not to say "shoplifting." He quickly answered, "She borrowed money to buy food for my sisters and me, but now she can't pay the money back. We don't have any way to get food."

"Debtors, eh? And Irish to boot."

"A man at a barrister's office told me my sisters could stay in prison with my mother until our debts are settled and she can go to trial."

"The law allows it. Sisters, did you say? How old are they?"

"Five and thirteen."

"I'll speak to my sergeant. I can't promise anythin', but if I was you, I'd have 'em here in an hour."

Finally, someone would help!

Colin rushed back to the alley, where a man who stank of gin studied his father and particularly his sisters.

Colin straightened his back and walked past the man, trying to muster the authority of someone ten years older and a foot taller.

Emma's blue eyes looked weary. "Papa doesn't move. He only whispers Mother's name."

"I found a place for the two of you to stay."

"The two of us? But we can't leave Papa," Ruth said. Tears streaked the dirt on her cheeks.

"If you're in a safe place, I'll have more time to try to help Father and Mother. Please. You need to come with me. We have less than an hour."

"Come where?" Emma asked.

"To the prison. You'll stay with Mother. You'll have food and shelter. She'll be glad to see you and know you're safe."

They reached the prison just before the cathedral's bells rang and the hour would have elapsed.

"So these are your sisters?" the guard asked, a sergeant standing next to him.

"Yes, sir. Emma and Ruth."

"Well, we're here to help you, Emma and Ruth," the sergeant said. "Come inside. We'll take you to your mother."

"Thank you," Colin told him with relief.

"You're a small one to have so much responsibility," the sergeant said. "We'll make your burden lighter."

"Thank you," Colin repeated.

He stayed long enough to watch the guard and the sergeant escort his sisters into the prison. Emma held little Ruth's hand. Nervous about the clamour into which they entered, his sisters looked back and waved to him uncertainly. He waved in return, trying to assure them that this was the best way.

The moment they disappeared beyond the studded door, he ran to the alley where his father lay. After wiping his father's sweat-beaded brow, he soaked a rag in water from a different pump and squeezed it over his father's lips.

"I'm doin' everythin' I can think of," he promised, and raced away.

"Thank heaven you heard me!"

His overcoat flapping, Colonel Trask scrambled up a ditch onto the frozen road. The carriage's lantern revealed the frosted vapour of his frantic breathing.

"At first, I thought I was imagining a ghost," the driver said. "A labourer died in that field last summer when a cart struck him. At night, people claim they can still hear him scream for it to stop."

Rushing into the carriage, Trask barely heard what the driver said. "Return to the station! Hurry!"

"What happened back there, Colonel?"

"There's no time!"

As the driver urged the two horses onward, their iron shoes slipped on the ice.

"Any faster and the horses will fall," the driver said.

"The station! Just get me to the station!"

Despite the cold, Trask found that he was sweating. He'd lost his top hat in his race to intercept the carriage. Beneath his overcoat and suit, his undergarment stuck to his skin. *Never arrived,* he kept thinking. *Catherine. Sir Walter.*

The lamps of Watford gradually became brighter. Before the driver had a chance to stop at the station, Trask jumped down and rushed towards the ticket office.

But no one was there. The telegraph operator wasn't on duty, either.

The office door was locked. Trask used his gloved fist to smash the window. He stretched his arm through and grabbed a schedule that lay on a desk.

The driver approached, looking startled at the broken window. "What if a constable heard?"

"I own the damned railway," Trask muttered, searching through the schedule. "I can break every window if I choose."

In the glow of a lamp above the door, he ran a finger down a list.

"Blast it, there isn't a train into London tonight!"

"Not until eight o'clock tomorrow morning," the driver said. "That's when I bring travellers to the station."

"We're going to London."

"Pardon, Colonel?"

"Now." Trask tugged him towards the carriage.

"But London's seventeen miles in the dark! It'll take us at least three hours to get there. The horses won't bear it."

"I'll pay you fifty pounds."

That was a fortune. The driver probably took home only a pound a week after he fed and stabled his horses.

"But Colonel, if my horses get lamed, even fifty pounds—"

"A *hundred* pounds! I don't care *what* it costs!" With greater desperation, Trask yanked the driver towards the carriage. "Take me to London!"

*   *   *

"Caitlin O'Brien," Becker said, staring at a yellowed document in the Scotland Yard storage room.

"You found something, Joseph?" Emily asked.

"I'm afraid so."

"What's the matter?" Ryan asked.

"Caitlin O'Brien," Becker repeated, moving the document closer to his lantern. "She's described as thirty years old. Fair hair. Pleasing features. The word 'Irish' is underlined. Married. On the first of June, she was arrested for stealing a shirt from a linen shop in St. John's Wood."

"But we're looking for something that happened on or after the tenth of June, when the boy begged the queen to save his family," Emily reminded him.

"Yes," Becker said. "The last date on this document is the *eleventh* of June. It didn't take long."

"Didn't take long for what?" De Quincey asked.

Becker shook his head sadly and pointed at the faded document. "There's nothing here about her son, but the record indicates that she had two daughters: Ruth, who was five, and Emma, who was thirteen. Somehow they were admitted to the prison under the guise that their mother was arrested for debt rather than stealing. In that case, the law permits a mother and her children to stay together until arrangements are made to pay the debt."

"Joseph, you sound as if something happened," Emily said.

In the attic's gloom, they brought their lanterns and peered over his shoulder, reading.

"Oh," Emily said when she saw the item.

"*Save my mother and father and sisters,*" Ryan murmured, recalling what the ragged boy had begged the queen. "But he wasn't able to save them. The thirteen-year-old smothered her little sister. Then she did the same to her sick mother. Then she hanged herself."

The horses struggled to maintain a rapid pace on the frozen road. Perched in front, Trask held a lantern before him, augmenting the light from the one on the driver's side, revealing furrows of ice.

"But why the urgency?" the driver insisted. "What happened?"

"She should have been here."

"*She*, Colonel?"

"Why didn't she arrive? Faster! Does the road get any better?"

"When we reach the turnpike."

"Thank God. How far is the—?"

Abruptly the horse on the right slipped. With a panicked squeal, it dropped to its knees. The carriage tilted. Amid the animal's anguished wails an axle snapped.

The vehicle flipped, throwing Trask into the air. To avoid landing on his lantern, he hurled it away, hearing it crash above the ditch. He landed so hard that the breath was knocked out of him.

Coal oil gushed from the shattered lantern, the wick igniting it. In the sudden blaze, Trask gaped upward from the ditch as the carriage kept tilting and plunged towards him.

The horse on the left dropped to its knees also, the upending carriage dragging both animals. Their shrieks combined with those of the driver.

Trask felt that he was back in the war, that a cannon shell hurtled the carriage towards him. The vehicle crashed into the ditch, straddling it, stopping inches from his face.

As the struggling horses threatened to pull the carriage apart, Trask squirmed along the trough, his sling restricting his desperate movements. Emerging from beneath the wreckage, he followed the sound of the driver's groans.

The man lay under a wheel. His lantern had shattered also, and its flames were streaming towards him.

"Can you hear me?" Trask shouted.

"My leg's broken!"

The flames streamed closer.

"If I raise the wheel, can you crawl out?" Trask yelled. "I can't pull you and hold up the wheel at the same time!"

"Do it!" the driver groaned. "Hurry!"

Trask squirmed into the trough again. On his back, he braced his boots against the wheel above him and strained to thrust his legs up.

"It's rising!" the driver shouted. "Higher!"

Trask put all his strength into his legs, raising the wheel another inch.

"Try to crawl out!" he yelled.

As the flames flowed nearer, the driver clawed at the frozen earth. Screaming from pain, he moved.

"I can't hold it up much longer!" Trask shouted, his legs weakening.

"I'm out!"

The muscles in Trask's legs collapsed, the wheel crashing above him. He squirmed from the trough before the burning oil reached him. Using his unhindered arm, he grabbed the driver and tugged him along the ditch, away from the flames. Tears of pain streaked down the driver's face.

Trask hurried up to the road, staring at the fallen horses flailing in their traces. As he struggled to unbuckle one of the straps that confined them, a light streaked towards him. He feared he was hallucinating.

Then he realized that the light was from a carriage lantern.

"My God!" a man yelled.

The carriage stopped. The man jumped down.

"I'm Dr. Gilmore!" he shouted, helping to free the horse on the right. "One of my patients is a farmer down the road!"

"Thank heaven you came along!" Trask yelled.

"There's blood on your face!"

"It doesn't matter!" With his free hand, Trask unbuckled another strap. "The driver broke his leg! He was taking me to London!"

"At *this* hour?"

"Someone important to me needs my help."

Untangling the horse on the right, they jumped back as the terrified animal struggled to stand. Its iron shoes thundering, it galloped away into the darkness.

They hurried to the second horse.

"The colonel saved my life!" the driver groaned as the flames reached the wheel that had trapped him.

"I'll pay you more than the hundred pounds I promised!" Trask told him. "You'll never worry about money for the rest of your life! Doctor, hold the horse! Keep him steady."

They freed the final buckle.

As the frenzied animal surged upright, Trask straddled him.

"What the devil!" the doctor exclaimed.

Holding makeshift reins with his left hand, Trask kicked the horse's flanks. *Catherine!* he inwardly screamed. Urging the animal forward, he charged along the dark road to London.

Lord Palmerston stepped past the doorman at his house and frowned towards where De Quincey and Emily sat on the staircase, waiting for him. They quickly stood.

"Whenever I leave or return, I find you lurking."

"My Lord, may we speak to you?" De Quincey asked. "In confidence?"

"I expect visitors soon—members of the cabinet I'm forming."

"We wouldn't presume on your time if this wasn't urgent."

"As long as I don't see the laudanum bottle that you're reaching for in your coat."

They climbed the staircase and entered the library, where

lamplight reflected off mahogany shelves. Chairs were arranged for a meeting.

"My Lord, in eighteen forty, when Edward Oxford fired his two pistols at the queen, a young Irish boy distracted Her Majesty by running next to her carriage and begging her to help his mother, father, and sisters," De Quincey said. "Do you know anything about that?"

"I have no idea what you're talking about."

"The boy's last name was O'Brien. Perhaps that helps your memory."

"It does nothing of the sort. If that's all you need to speak to me about, kindly leave before my visitors arrive."

Emily stepped forward. "My Lord"—she fixed her blue eyes on him—"we believe that the young boy begged for help from many people who had influence with prisons and the law—Lord Cosgrove, the judge Sir Richard Hawkins, and Commissioner Mayne among them—but that he was unsuccessful. We further believe that the recent murders were committed by that boy—now grown—in retribution for the failure of those people to help his family. Do you possibly remember a young Irish boy begging for help from *you?*"

Lord Palmerston's tone became less impatient. He never failed to respond to an attractive woman. "The streets are filled with beggars. Surely you don't expect me to remember one of them from fifteen years ago."

"*Help my mother and father and sisters.* That is what he begged," Emily persisted.

"I served as foreign secretary in eighteen forty. Since I had nothing to do with police matters at that time, the boy would have had no reason to come to me."

"Perhaps he came to you after he exhausted other channels," Emily suggested.

"If so, I have no recollection. The person to speak to is Lord Normanby. He acted as home secretary that year."

"It's more than essential that we contact him," De Quincey said. "Lord Normanby might be one of the next victims."

"It'll take great effort for you to speak to him. He lives in Italy. He's our representative in Florence."

"That distance might save his life," De Quincey said. "Please send a telegram to him. Request any information he might have about a family called O'Brien. Warn him that his life might be in danger."

"You're serious about this?"

"Right now, Inspector Ryan is asking Commissioner Mayne if he has any recollection of the boy. We need to search the commissioner's records for references to anyone with the name of O'Brien between June the first and June the eleventh of that year. We also need to search the records that Lord Cosgrove and Sir Richard Hawkins kept. Meanwhile Sergeant Becker is investigating the records at Newgate Prison."

"June the eleventh?" Lord Palmerston asked. "Why would the search end on that date?"

"Because that's when the boy's mother and two sisters died in Newgate."

"All of them on the same day?" Lord Palmerston frowned.

"One sister hanged herself after smothering her younger sister and her sick mother."

His Lordship became still. "Newgate can indeed produce despair." He drew a breath. "What terrible crime did the woman commit?"

"She was accused of stealing a shirt from a linen shop," Emily answered.

"They all died because of a shirt?" Lord Palmerston lowered his head, looking suddenly weary. "Sometimes the law can be unduly harsh. The father? What happened to *him?*"

"We're trying to determine that. But given the killer's fury, we believe that the father met his own pathetic end," De Quincey said. "My Lord, there's another matter about which

I need to speak to you. Would you kindly leave us alone for a moment, Emily?"

"Alone?" Lord Palmerston asked, looking as surprised as Emily did.

"Yes, My Lord. The topic is delicate."

From below, voices sounded in the mansion's vestibule.

"My potential cabinet ministers have arrived. If this doesn't pertain to the threat against Her Majesty—"

"It relates to the *first* threat against her, My Lord," De Quincey said.

"But you already explained that the Irish boy is the suspect in the *current* crimes. The opium has addled your mind and made you confuse fifteen years ago with now."

"My Lord, I wish to discuss Edward Oxford and Young England."

"What could Edward Oxford possibly have to do with the current threat against Her Majesty?"

"I'm more concerned about Young England, My Lord. The true reality behind it."

"The true reality? As opposed to the false reality or opium reality?" Lord Palmerston's gaze intensified.

"There are *many* realities."

"You sound delusional."

"On the contrary, My Lord."

The tension between the two men made Emily look from one to the other in bewilderment.

"Father, what's going on?"

The voices on the lower floor became louder as more visitors arrived.

"The only reality I care about is that we're losing the war," Lord Palmerston emphasized. "Leave by that servants' door over there. I don't wish my cabinet members to know that I kept them waiting because I was sequestered with the notorious Opium-Eater."

"We can discuss this matter at another time, My Lord."

"When you visited Edward Oxford in the madhouse, I could have arranged for you to remain there. Remember that. Take care how you test me."

"I appreciate your indulgence, My Lord."

"Occupy your time to greater purpose. Speak to Lord Grantwood."

"Lord Grantwood?" Emily asked in confusion. "The gentleman we met at the queen's dinner last night?"

"His house is just around the corner on Half Moon Street. You were right about this conversation jogging my memory. It suddenly occurs to me that Lord Grantwood served as deputy home secretary in eighteen forty, under Lord Normanby. As the second-highest official in charge of law enforcement, maybe *he* heard something about the Irish boy."

"Deputy home secretary?" De Quincey's short legs hurried towards the servants' door. "Lord Grantwood's in danger also."

Continuing the Journal of Emily De Quincey

"Father, what's going on?" I again demanded while we descended a rear staircase.

A back corridor brought us to the mansion's front hall as the last of Lord Palmerston's important visitors reached the top of the staircase. None of them saw us leave the building.

A servant shut the door behind us. Another servant opened one of the driveway's gates.

I tightened my coat in the chill of a gathering fog. "Father, don't pretend you don't hear me. Tell me what you and Lord Palmerston were really arguing about."

"We need to warn Lord Grantwood that he's a target."

I couldn't tell whether Father was avoiding my question, but I didn't have time to find out. As we hurried to the left towards Half Moon Street, a horse's frantic approach startled me. Father and I froze as the animal and its rider thundered past.

The horse lacked a saddle. Its reins were those used for a carriage. Froth at the animal's mouth revealed how fatigued it was. But its desperate rider urged it onward. The rider's face was streaked with dried blood. His ragged overcoat was only partially secured, flapping, revealing an arm in a sling.

Abruptly, animal and rider disappeared into the fog, the clatter of horseshoes diminishing.

"Good heavens, that was Colonel Trask," I managed to say.

We ran after him. A short distance along Piccadilly, the sound of the horse moved to the left.

"Half Moon Street!" Father said as we hurried along it, following the clatter of the horse.

Midway up the street, we heard the horse stop. Boots hit the pavement and charged up steps.

Running, Father and I came to the horse, whose head hung low in exhaustion. We heard pounding on a door and rushed to the left, finding Colonel Trask, who shouted, "Catherine!"

A nearby gas lamp revealed that all the windows in the house were curtained. Not even the faintest illumination was visible, making this the darkest house on the street.

"Catherine!" Colonel Trask yelled, continuing to pound on the door.

He tried the latch and discovered that it wasn't locked. Thrusting the door open, he encountered an obstacle. "No!"

"Colonel Trask!" I called. "It's Emily De Quincey!" I remembered the gallantry that he'd shown to me at the queen's dinner. "Whatever is wrong, Father and I wish to help!"

But the colonel didn't seem to hear me as he charged farther into the house.

Father and I entered, finding the obstacle that had so dismayed the colonel.

"Emily, I don't have time to shield your gaze," Father said.

"Yes, there are more important things to do," I agreed.

Father located a candle and matches on a table beside the door. He lit the candle, revealing the body of a servant with his head crusted with blood.

I raised a hand to my mouth but refused to allow myself to weaken.

Colonel Trask rushed deeper into the house, shouting Catherine's name.

Father and I followed. Our candle illuminated the body of another servant. With growing dread, I couldn't help being reminded of what we had found at Lord Cosgrove's house.

The colonel rushed into a room on the right.

"Emily," Father said, "while I hold the candle, light as many lamps as you can find."

We went along the walls in the vestibule. Gradually the area became vivid with light.

Breathing hoarsely, Colonel Trask backed from a room and burst into an opposite room.

We reached the doorway he had just left, where I remained as Father stepped forward with his candle.

Lady Grantwood dangled from a wall. Her arms were wrapped in a net so that she would have been powerless to struggle while her neck weighed down against a loop in the net, choking her.

My vision wavered.

"Emily?" Father asked.

"I'm all right, Father."

I turned away.

"When the judge's wife was drowned in milk," Father said, "you correctly understood that it was a reference to the milk of human kindness that Shakespeare mentions in *Macbeth*.

What does Shakespeare have to say about what was done to this woman, about the law and a net, Emily?"

"Not now, Father!" I told him impatiently.

"Let the reality inside your mind protect you from the reality outside it. If you can't recall the quotation, let me help by giving you the title of the play."

"Don't condescend, Father. The play is *Pericles, Prince of Tyre*," I said angrily. Perhaps that was the reaction he intended to create in me. If so, he was more than successful.

"And the quotation, Emily?" Father challenged, making me angrier.

" 'Here's a fish hangs in the net, like a poor man's right in the law,' " I almost shouted at him. "Are you satisfied?"

"Yes."

"God help this woman."

"The killer's intention was the reverse—to send her to God's eternal judgement for what the law did to his family."

A sudden noise made me turn.

Colonel Trask now held a lamp as he backed from another room. Desperate, he peered around, shouted Catherine's name, and raced up the staircase.

Dreading what I might find but compelled to see the worst in the hope that nothing afterward could ever exceed it, I moved slowly towards the opposite chamber.

On the floor above me I heard Colonel Trask thrusting doors open, shouting for Catherine.

Father's candle wavered as he shifted past me and entered what I saw was a library, the arrangement comparable to the one in Lord Cosgrove's house.

Here again I saw a corpse. At first I thought there were two corpses, one atop the other in what was perhaps intended to be an imitation of a man and a woman in congress.

But Father's wavering candle revealed that the figure on top was not a human being. Rather it was a mannequin dressed to resemble Lady Justice, holding a pair of scales in one hand while the sword that she customarily held in the other hand had been thrust through Lord Grantwood's chest.

"Father," I said.

He turned a chair towards a wall and eased me into it.

"Do not tell me that this is fine art," I told him in a fury. "If I were a man, if I could find the person responsible for these horrors, I wouldn't care what grievances had been done to him. I would—"

Above us, Colonel Trask roared in anguish.

Father hurried towards the vestibule. Refusing to remain alone, I followed. Initially my legs were unsteady, but as my rage overcame my revulsion, my bloomer skirt allowed me to mount the steps two at a time.

Father was forced to move more slowly, shielding the candle's flame. Nonetheless he provided enough illumination for me to see blood on the staircase's carpet. Because there wasn't any blood below me, I concluded that someone had been attacked on the stairs and had fled upward.

Again we found the colonel backing from a room. The trail of blood led into it. The colonel moaned. His left hand—the one holding the lamp—trembled so alarmingly that I feared he would drop it and set the house afire.

I grabbed the lamp from him, shocked by the dried blood on his handsome face.

The hero who had survived apocalyptic battles, who had surely seen violent death in almost infinite variety, sank to his knees in anguish.

"Catherine," he murmured. "Catherine."

I knelt beside him, putting an arm around him, trying to comfort him. But in his grief he seemed oblivious to anything except what he saw beyond the open door.

Father approached the room. I tried not to look, but my

furious determination to endure this as if I were a man compelled me to turn in that direction, only to wish that I hadn't.

What had been done in that room was unspeakable.

"Catherine," the colonel murmured as I held him.

"Catherine," he repeated through his tears.

Then another name passed his lips.

"Sir Walter Cumberland. Sir Walter Cumberland."

11

A Darkness within a Darkness

"Sir Walter Cumberland," Inspector Ryan said. Brooding, he turned from the bedroom in which the remains of Catherine Grantwood lay.

The photographer whom Ryan had summoned to St. James's Church was again setting up his camera. The artist from the *Illustrated London News* was opening his sketchpad once more.

"This'll be the last time," the illustrator told Ryan. "I can't bear the nightmares."

Ryan didn't say anything about his own nightmares. "We're grateful for your help."

Passing the constables searching the house, Ryan descended to the entrance hall.

There, Colonel Trask slumped at the bottom of the staircase. Past the dried blood on his face, his eyes stared ahead, focused on infinity.

"Has anyone ever seen anything like this?" Ryan asked. "He's gone out of his mind."

"He's trapped *inside* it," De Quincey corrected him. "While he seems to stare outward towards nothing, he stares inward, paralyzed by the horrors that he found here."

"And what happened to him *before* he got here?" Becker asked.

The normally immaculate sling on the colonel's right arm was covered with dirt. The odour of smoke came off his torn overcoat.

"He has a gash on his forehead," Commissioner Mayne noted. "It stopped bleeding, so he must have been injured a while ago."

"The horse outside—do we know where it's from?" Ryan asked a constable.

"A tag on its bridle refers to a carriage service in Watford, Inspector."

"Watford? But that's miles from here. Sir Walter Cumberland?" Ryan turned towards De Quincey and Emily. "That was the last thing the colonel said? Someone named Sir Walter Cumberland?"

"Yes," De Quincey answered. "As it happens, we met Sir Walter at the queen's dinner yesterday evening."

That information made Ryan step closer.

"Whenever possible, Sir Walter expressed strong differences with Colonel Trask, seeming to regard him as a rival," De Quincey continued. "The tension was finally explained when Miss Grantwood's parents announced her engagement to Sir Walter. Emily and I were surprised. We assumed that it was Colonel Trask to whom Miss Grantwood would be engaged."

"So Colonel Trask might have been jealous of Sir Walter?" Ryan asked.

"That wasn't my impression," Emily answered, casting a sympathetic gaze towards the motionless colonel. "What I sensed was Sir Walter's vindictiveness towards him."

A constable entered, bringing with him a young, expensively dressed gentleman of perhaps twenty. His open overcoat revealed a gaudy yellow waistcoat, the sort of colour that a rake might wear when touring lower-class establishments. He had a sporty moustache. His eyes were red, perhaps from too much brandy.

"Inspector," the constable said, "this is Lord Jennings. He lives across the street with his parents, Earl and Countess

Westmorland. He just returned from his club and has information that might be helpful."

As the constable shut the door, numerous loud voices indicated that a crowd was gathering in the street.

"Please tell me what you told the constable," Ryan said.

"This morning, outside this house, Sir Walter Cumberland and Colonel Trask had an argument," the young gentleman explained. He enunciated carefully, perhaps trying to disguise the effects of alcohol, the odour of which hung about him.

"How serious was the argument?" Ryan asked.

"Enough for Sir Walter to shove the colonel down into the slush."

"You refer to Colonel Trask and Sir Walter as if you know them."

"I was invited to a reception at which the colonel was honoured. That wretched-looking man seated on the stairs, don't tell me that's . . .? What happened to him?"

"That's one of many things we're trying to learn," Ryan said. "What about Sir Walter? How do you come to know *him?*"

"Until six months ago, I didn't. But then I started seeing him at the same clubs I frequent. I have no idea of his origins before that. Mostly I met Sir Walter at card tables. He plays so badly that if not for his inheritance, he'd be in the streets."

"Inheritance?" Commissioner Mayne asked.

"Six months ago his uncle died, leaving no heirs except Sir Walter. Of course, he was just plain 'Walter' then. The inheritance included a baronetcy, along with fifty thousand pounds a year."

"I wonder what he and Colonel Trask were arguing about," Ryan said.

"Miss Grantwood."

"Are you telling me you heard the specifics?"

"The whole neighbourhood did. It was eleven o'clock in

the morning, and their voices were loud enough to waken me. I parted the curtains in my room and peered out. I noticed servants parting curtains across the street. You'll find plenty of people to tell you about the fight. At the clubs the night before, Sir Walter wouldn't stop bragging about his engagement to Catherine Grantwood."

"So Colonel Trask confronted Sir Walter because of jealousy," Commissioner Mayne concluded.

"No. The opposite. It was *Sir Walter* who confronted the colonel because of jealousy. What I heard Sir Walter yelling was that Colonel Trask had somehow persuaded Miss Grantwood's parents to change their minds. Now it was Colonel Trask who was engaged to Miss Grantwood. Sir Walter was so furious that he actually threatened to shoot Colonel Trask."

"Shoot him?" Ryan asked in amazement.

"At Englefield Green. In a duel. Sir Walter's exact words to the colonel were, 'A manslaughter charge would be worth the price of never seeing you again.' Is that how Colonel Trask was injured? Did Sir Walter shoot him?"

"No," Ryan answered. "But perhaps Sir Walter did something else."

They all looked at the colonel, whose stare remained vacant.

"God knows what Sir Walter intended to do when he came back here this afternoon," Lord Jennings continued.

"What? Sir Walter came back here?" Becker asked.

"At three o'clock. His shouting and pounding woke me again. Now he looked as if *he* were the one who'd been shoved into the slush. His clothes were dirty. His nose and mouth were bloodied. It only shows that simply because someone inherits a title, that is no assurance of good breeding."

"What was Sir Walter shouting?" Ryan persisted.

"He demanded to see Lord and Lady Grantwood. He yelled that he wouldn't be treated so shabbily, that he had loaned Lord Grantwood money and now he wanted it back, and if he didn't see Miss Grantwood—for everyone to hear, he actually called her 'Catherine,' as if she were no more than a servant—he would ruin them more than they already were. In the afternoon on Half Moon Street in Mayfair, mind you. Of course, the neighbourhood already knows that Lord and Lady Grantwood bankrupted themselves in a failed business venture. But that's no reason for Sir Walter to shout it to the rooftops. The man has absolutely no manners. He paced the street in front of the house for several hours."

"Didn't anyone summon a constable?"

"No one in Mayfair would ever summon a constable to arrest a baronet." Young Lord Jennings looked shocked. "Everyone hoped he would become tired and leave."

"And did he?"

"At six."

"Can you tell us if he returned later?" Commissioner Mayne asked.

"I left for an appointment at seven. I have no idea if he came back."

"I need to speak to him," Ryan said firmly. "Do you know where he lives?"

As the constable escorted the young gentleman from the house, the noise of the crowd outside was louder. Then the front door was closed again, and the only sounds came from constables searching rooms.

"The Fairmount Club on Pall Mall," Ryan said. "I know the place."

"While you look for Sir Walter, where should we take Colonel Trask?" Emily wanted to know.

Everyone turned towards the colonel, whose body remained rigid, his gaze blank.

"The burn marks on his clothes, the dried blood on his

face," Commissioner Mayne said. "This is probably how he looked after battles in the Crimea. I read in *The Times* that if any of his men were wounded, he never failed to risk sniper fire, rushing forward to carry comrades back to safety before the enemy could capture and probably kill them. Like most officers, he paid for his rank—two thousand pounds, I was told—but those other officers had no military character whatsoever and merely wanted to wear colourful uniforms that impressed the ladies. That's one reason we're losing the war. But the colonel truly wanted to fight for England, and fight he certainly did. After everything he endured in the Crimea, he had every right to feel safe here. But instead he came home to *this*."

"He can't be left here," Emily said. "He needs to lie down and rest."

"But where can we take him?" Becker asked. "We don't know where he lives."

"Wherever it is, it needs to be familiar to him," Emily replied. "Imagine his further shock if he regains his awareness but doesn't recognize where he is."

"When the colonel summoned Inspector Ryan and me to the outburst at the Wheel of Fortune tavern, he mentioned that his offices were in that area, on Water Lane," Becker recalled. "There might be a couch or even a private apartment."

Emily's blue eyes became resolute. "Then we shall take him there. We'll send for Dr. Snow. He helped us seven weeks ago. I have no doubt that he will help us again."

"Perhaps there's someone else who can help," De Quincey offered. "Someone acquainted with the hardships of the war."

"An army officer?" Commissioner Mayne asked.

"Actually, I was thinking of William Russell."

"The war correspondent?" The commissioner reacted with surprise.

"Russell wrote at length about Colonel Trask's heroism. He understands the stress that soldiers endure. Perhaps his familiar face will provide the assurance that Emily referred to."

"But William Russell is in the Crimea," the commissioner objected.

"No. An article in this morning's *Times* indicates that he returned to London with the colonel. My newspaper friends should be able to tell me where to locate him."

"Then we all have our tasks," Ryan said.

As Becker and Emily helped the colonel to stand, De Quincey drank from his laudanum bottle. "A moment, please."

The little man's troubled tone made the group pause.

"Inspector, were notes found on the bodies of Lord and Lady Grantwood? I saw none in obvious view, and I didn't want to risk your displeasure by touching anything before I had your permission."

"We found a note in Lady Grantwood's dress," Ryan answered. "It had the same black border we found earlier."

"And what was written on it?"

"The name of William Hamilton."

"Yes, the fourth man to shoot at the queen. As predicted, the killer's references are speeding closer to the present."

"We also found a black-bordered note in one of *Lord* Grantwood's pockets," Becker said. "Again, the words were 'Young England'—Edward Oxford's fictitious revolutionary group."

"Were there two additional words?" De Quincey asked, fingering his laudanum bottle. "'Young *Ireland*' perhaps? William Hamilton's very real insurrectionist group?"

Ryan studied him. "Your talent for prediction is such that you should have been a fortune-teller instead of a writer."

"Regrettably, there are many things here that I could *not* have predicted. The carefully established pattern was broken. As with the other murders, Lord and Lady Grantwood were killed in a symbolic way that expresses the killer's hatred of the law. But one of them should have been found in a public place, perhaps in front of the Old Bailey courthouse, to reinforce the fear that no one is safe anywhere. Why didn't that happen? Commissioner Mayne, at your home, the killer shouted that he wanted to kill you, your wife, and your daughter to avenge what happened to his father and mother and sisters. Presumably, he would then have arranged your bodies in a symbolic manner, including that of your daughter."

"I fear so."

"Then why wasn't *Miss Grantwood's* body arranged in a symbolic fashion?" De Quincey asked. "Her murder was not fine art at all. Why was the pattern changed?"

Ryan opened the door. "Sir Walter Cumberland may have the answers."

"You're cheating," Sir Walter said.

The young gentleman opposite him at the card table pretended not to hear.

"It's impossible to be as lucky as you are," Sir Walter persisted. He wore fresh evening clothes, but his nose and lips remained swollen. No one had shown bad form by commenting on the damage to his face.

"Whist is a game of skill, not luck," the young man replied, setting down his winning cards.

"Skill? Is that what you call cheating?"

"I think it's time for a brandy," one of the other gentlemen decided and walked from the room.

"I'll join you," another young man said, leaving.

"Really, Sir Walter," the remaining young man offered, "you should polish your manners. We're the only players you have. No one else will sit down with you."

At this late hour, they were the sole occupants of the card room. Each of the six green-baize-covered tables had an ornate brass lamp hanging above it, but theirs was the only lamp that was lit.

"If you don't have the means to pay your wager, I'm willing to take your marker," the young man said.

"Now you insult me in addition to cheating me," Sir Walter replied. "I caution you—take care."

"Never mind. To spare you further embarrassment, I forgive the debt." The young man stood. "But I wouldn't depend on your being able to persuade anyone in this club to play cards with you tomorrow evening. In fact, there's a petition afoot to rescind your membership." The young man smiled. "I happily signed it."

"I warned you!"

Sir Walter's walking stick was propped against the table. He grabbed it, lunged to his feet, and swung.

"Yes, Sir Walter Cumberland has lodgings here," a club attendant said.

"For how long?" Ryan asked, keeping his badge in view.

The attendant searched his memory. "Almost six months."

"After he came into his inheritance?" Ryan asked.

"Yes."

"Did you know his uncle?"

"The uncle was a member before Sir Walter was. That's how Sir Walter was accepted as a member—because of sympathy."

"Do you recall how his uncle died?"

"I can't forget how swift it was. The unfortunate man became sick to his stomach one day. The illness persisted. But he didn't have a fever, and his physician couldn't determine what was wrong. Finally Sir Walter's uncle blamed it on the miasma of London. He went to his country estate, but the change of air didn't treat him any better, and he died two weeks after becoming ill. Very sad, especially considering how pleasant and generous Sir Walter's uncle was."

"Unlike Sir Walter himself?" Ryan asked.

"I never speak untoward about our members, Inspector."

"As it should be. Do you know if Sir Walter is on the premises?"

"A while ago I saw him go into the card room above us. No, wait. There. I see him on the staircase."

Clutching his walking stick, Sir Walter backed away from the body on the floor.

Breathing quickly, he hurried out of the card room. From a balcony he peered down towards the marble floor of the lobby. At this late hour the only people he saw were a man in shapeless commoner's clothes speaking to an attendant.

Sir Walter decided to summon help and claim that what had happened was an accident. He could make a good case for that. His blow hadn't struck its target. The young man had reeled back as the knob on Sir Walter's cane hissed past him.

But the young man had lost his balance. He struck his head on a table. Blood streamed from his head, staining the carpet.

He wasn't moving.

Yes, get help, Sir Walter thought. If the young man died, there wouldn't be anyone to say that he hadn't merely stumbled and fallen.

Ryan approached the staircase.

Raising his badge so that Sir Walter couldn't fail to see it, he told him, "I'm a Scotland Yard detective inspector. I need to speak to you."

Abrupt movement at the top of the staircase made Ryan peer towards the second level. A man staggered from a doorway. He wavered on a balcony, gripping it for support. Blood streamed from the side of his head.

"Stop Sir Walter! He tried to kill me with his walking stick!"

Sir Walter's mouth opened in surprise. At the bottom of the staircase he looked at Ryan approaching him.

He looked at the bleeding man on the balcony.

He ran.

The police wagon's lantern probed the fog as it proceeded down Water Lane. The sounds of the unseen Thames—waves lapping against hulls and docks—felt disturbingly close.

Becker gazed from the wagon and was dimly able to distinguish a sign that read consolidated english railway company.

"Driver, stop."

Becker stepped down onto cobblestones and opened the back hatch. He and the driver helped Colonel Trask get out, a difficult task because the colonel remained motionless, staring blankly.

"Stay close to us, Emily," Becker cautioned as he pounded on the door.

A window showed a light growing in the darkness, someone approaching with a lamp. The person on the other side raised the light to peer out. In a rush the man unlocked the door.

"What happened to the colonel?"

"He isn't able to tell us," Becker answered.

"We didn't know where else to bring him," Emily added.

The man looked surprised that a strangely dressed but respectable-seeming woman was in the river area at such an hour. His surprise increased when Becker identified himself. "Detective Sergeant Becker. Is there a place where the colonel can rest?"

"He has a room behind his office."

The man guided them past a murky reception area and up a staircase. The lamp revealed pockmarks on his face.

"Are you a nightwatchman?" Becker asked.

"A porter. The colonel lets me keep a room here. I helped

him build railways. He's always been fair to me. If he'd asked me to go with him tonight, this wouldn't have happened."

"Where did he go?"

"He was taking the train to Watford."

So the horse did come from there, Becker thought.

"Why was he going to Watford?" he asked, feeling the colonel's weight as they carried him up the stairs.

"The colonel's fiancée has a cousin there."

The colonel's dead fiancée, Becker thought.

"Did Sir Walter Cumberland do this to him?" the porter asked.

Becker reacted to the name. "What makes you say that?"

"Sir Walter came here around noon and accused the colonel of buying Miss Grantwood from her parents. The colonel struck him several times and knocked him into the gutter."

They reached the top of the stairs, where a corridor of shadows faced them on each side. The echo of their boots resounded in a vast darkness.

"This is the colonel's office."

The porter searched among keys on a ring and unlocked it. Inside he lit a gas lamp on the wall, then opened a farther door and led Becker and the constable into a private room that was simply furnished with a wardrobe, a table, two wooden chairs, and a narrow bed tucked into a corner.

Becker felt uncomfortable about invading the colonel's privacy.

"It's a pleasant room—one that I'd be happy with." He helped the constable place the colonel on the bed. "But it's not what I expected of a wealthy man. I imagined him living in a fine hotel or the luxury of a Mayfair mansion."

"His father has a house in Mayfair, where the colonel often stays," the porter explained. "Mr. Trask senior is confined to his bed. Nearly worked himself to death. But the colonel makes certain that his father is cared for."

Through the open doors, Becker heard someone pounding on the entrance downstairs. "We're expecting a physician named Dr. Snow."

"Will he stop the colonel from being this way—not moving, not even blinking? If I didn't see his chest rising, I'd swear he was dead."

Sir Walter charged past a gentleman who came around a corner, the force of his passage knocking him against a wall.

"Watch where you're going!" the man exclaimed.

But Sir Walter paid no attention. Hurrying along a corridor, he reached the club's back door, thrust it open, and raced into an alley that tradesmen used for deliveries.

Still clutching his walking stick, he veered to the right. Without an overcoat, he immediately felt the night's cold. In spite of the fog he saw his urgent breath bursting from him in frosty gusts.

Shouts pursued him.

"Sir Walter, stop! I told you I'm a Scotland Yard inspector! I need to speak to you!"

The alley ended at the Haymarket. Sir Walter darted to the left, hoping to rush into one of the many theatres along the street and mingle with the audience when it departed. But the quantity of brandy he'd consumed caused him to misjudge how late the hour was. All the theatres were dark.

He reached an oyster house, but it was dark also. Ladies of the night beckoned him towards the glaring gaslights of a tavern, but when they saw the desperation on his face, they quickly retreated.

Behind him, the bootsteps pounded closer.

As he sped to the right onto a side street, the effect of the brandy made it difficult to keep his balance on the frozen slush. For a moment he considered stopping, but he feared that the brandy would also make it difficult for him to explain why the man at the club had accused him of trying to murder him.

What other things might I not be able to explain? he thought.

He rushed onto another street, the night's chill seeping into him.

"Sir Walter, I order you to stop!" the pursuing voice shouted.

At the shuttered food shops on Coventry Street, a constable's lantern startled him. He charged towards the opposite side, and now there were *two* shouting voices. The raucous noise of a police clacker filled the night. A second clacker answered.

He scurried into an alley and paused in the darkness, trying to catch his breath. Plodding forward, ready with his walking stick in case someone accosted him, he stumbled over something. When it groaned, he realized that it was a beggar on the verge of freezing to death. In horror, he again hurried forward.

More police clackers and shouting voices joined the pursuit.

I'll die like that beggar if I don't find a place that's warm, he thought.

At the next street, he was completely confused about his location. The number of police lanterns behind him increased, illuminating the fog.

"This way!" a voice yelled. "I hear him over here!"

A noise guided him: the stomping of hooves. He reached a wall on which a sign advertised aldridge's horse and carriage repository. The commotion had wakened the animals.

Can I climb the wall? he thought. *Can I hide among the hay bales?*

He shoved his walking stick under his waistcoat and jumped upward, but his numb fingers lost their grip on the top. He fell hard onto the cobblestones, stood with effort, withdrew his walking stick, and lurched onward. The street narrowed. The lamps became farther apart.

Then nothing made sense. In every direction, there was

only a jumble of decrepit lanes. Walls leaned, touching and supporting one another. Broken windows gaped. Doors hung askew. Boards dangled.

Amid a pile of debris, something made a scraping sound.

"Who's 'ere?" a feeble voice asked. "A bobby?"

"Naw. Don't have a uniform. This un's dressed like a gentleman."

"Don't have an overcoat, neither," a third voice said. "Maybe some'un took it afore *we* could. Kind sir, it's terrible cold. Can you spare us some pennies?"

"And your frock coat and your waistcoat?" a fourth voice asked.

The scraping sounds came closer, shadows surrounding him.

My God, Sir Walter thought in a panic, *I'm in the Seven Dials rookery.*

"Thank you for coming," Becker said as Dr. John Snow entered the dimly lit room behind Colonel Trask's office.

"Well, I can't complain about being wakened to treat a war hero."

The man who had identified a Soho water pump as the source of a cholera epidemic the previous year, Dr. Snow was in his early forties, with a slender face, a high, balding forehead, and dark sideburns that emphasized his narrow jaw. He carried a leather satchel.

He paused in surprise when he noticed Colonel Trask sitting motionless on the bed, staring in anguish towards a wall.

"We don't know how badly injured he is," Emily said.

"Bring hot water and clean rags," Dr. Snow told the porter. "Hurry."

"I'll help," Emily said, rushing away.

"We need to undress him," Dr. Snow told Becker, who knew how unusual it was for a physician to be willing to do this. Physicians rarely laid hands on their patients, leaving that crude job to surgeons, the lower members of the medical establishment.

They raised the colonel and removed his tattered overcoat.

"Look at the burn marks on it," Dr. Snow commented. "Easy with the sling. Good. Now help me with the rest of his clothes."

Although Trask's eyes were open, he showed no indication of being aware that the two men moved his legs and arms to undress him.

Already uneasy about having entered the colonel's private room, Becker felt more self-conscious as he helped Dr. Snow tug off the colonel's shirt and trousers. Beneath was a woollen undergarment that reached from his neck to his ankles, covering his arms to his wrists.

"I don't see any blood on his undergarment. No need to remove it," Snow decided.

Emily and the porter returned, the porter carrying a basin of steaming water while Emily held a stack of rags.

"Emily, you shouldn't be here," Becker said. "The colonel isn't in a decent state."

"Nonsense. I see nothing that I didn't see when I ministered to Sean as he recovered from his wounds. When I changed the dressing on Sean's abdomen, I saw more than his drawers, I assure you. If I'm to pursue a career as a nurse, I expect to see even more without being shocked."

It was Becker who exhibited shock.

"A career as a nurse?" he asked.

"Yes. Florence Nightingale's service in the Crimea shows that women are fit for more than being shopgirls or governesses. If not for her, many of our wounded soldiers would have died from lack of care."

"You never said anything about wanting to be a nurse," Becker continued in surprise.

"One sad day, I shall no longer need to attend to Father. I must consider what to do then."

Emily placed the stack of rags on the foot of the bed. She washed her hands in the basin of steaming water that the porter set on a table. Then she dipped a rag into the water and began cleaning the dried blood from the colonel's face.

For the sake of modesty, Becker put a blanket over him.

Dr. Snow opened his satchel and removed a metal canister, from which a tube and a mask extended. He took out a bottle and poured a clear liquid into the canister. A faint sweet odour drifted from it.

"What's *that?*" the porter asked.

"A chloroform inhaler."

"Is it safe?" the porter asked with suspicion.

"The queen herself asked me to make chloroform available when she gave birth to her most recent child."

The porter continued to look suspicious.

"Depending on the colonel's injuries, sleep might be the best treatment that I can give him," Dr. Snow said.

Emily finished cleaning the colonel's face. She swept grit from his hair and studied him. "The only wound I can find is the gash on the side of his forehead."

"It doesn't appear to need stitches," Dr. Snow decided.

He reached into his satchel and removed a bottle that was labelled white vitriol. He used a dropper to apply some of the mild sulphuric acid to the gash. Then he took out a recently developed device known as a stethoscope. After attaching tubes to both of his ears, he pressed the device's cup to Colonel Trask's chest.

He pulled out his pocket watch, opened it, and listened, moving his fingers as if counting.

When Dr. Snow finally looked up, even in the room's dim light, it was clear that his face was pale.

"What's wrong?" Emily asked.

"His heart is racing two hundred beats per minute—almost three times what is normal."

"*Three times?*"

"Motionless, he has no way to vent the energy inside him. I'm astonished that his heart hasn't failed. I need to administer the chloroform. Quickly. If the colonel doesn't manage to sleep, if his heartbeat doesn't decline, I fear he will die."

"He went in there!" a constable shouted.

Ryan hurried along the narrowing street and stopped where it converged with six other streets in a pattern that its long-ago designer had meant to look like a sundial.

But there was nothing sunny about this wasteland. Originally a respectable area, Seven Dials had descended into squalor as the construction of railways into London destroyed numerous buildings in which the lower class lived. Ambitious developments such as fashionable Regent Street and New Oxford Street had similarly destroyed cheap housing for the poor. In the same way that countless rooks built nests in a single tree, tens of thousands of London's underclass had sought shelter in those few affordable areas that remained and that eventually acquired the name "rookeries."

Most lodging houses here had six beds per room with three people sleeping in each bed, although many also slept on bare floors. More than a hundred unfortunates squeezed into each three-storey structure, the congestion stressing walls, stairways, and corridors until the crammed buildings were in danger of collapsing. Water pumps didn't exist. Alleys were urinals. Each privy served four hundred people, the overflowing waste spreading into cellars. Only the most hopeless lived in Seven Dials—the mudlarks who waded along the Thames, searching for chunks of coal that had fallen off barges, or the scavengers who sold dead cats and dogs to fertilizer makers and, if the dead animals were fresh, to cookshops as supplements to so-called pork pies.

As Ryan stared at the gloomy, rotting entrance, he felt the desperation of Seven Dials waft over him. The rookery was considered so dangerous that few strangers—usually only policemen—entered it, and only for an unavoidable reason.

Ryan was forced to admit that the recent murders and Sir Walter's possible link to them constituted a definite unavoidable reason.

"Constable, are you absolutely certain he went in there?" Ryan asked.

"No question about it, Inspector." The constable aimed his lantern towards the tangled shadows of the forbidding wilderness.

Bloody hell, Ryan thought, pressing a hand to the barely healed wounds on his abdomen.

From deep within the rookery, he heard a scream.

Two figures—one of them short and slight—climbed the dark stairs towards Colonel Trask's office, proceeding into the private room behind it.

"Father," Emily said.

De Quincey watched as Dr. Snow put the mask on the colonel's face and turned a valve on the chloroform canister. Then De Quincey gestured towards the stocky man next to him whose black, curly hair and matching beard gave him a dramatic appearance.

"Allow me to introduce the esteemed journalist William Russell." De Quincey was careful not to call Russell a "war correspondent," a term that Russell hated.

Becker, the porter, and the constable nodded in greeting, awed to be in the presence of the man whose writing had toppled the British government. They tactfully ignored that his shirt collar was open, his waistcoat unbuttoned. Above his beard, his cheeks were flushed, presumably from alcohol, although he gave no other indication that he'd been drinking.

Russell was thirty-four. His sad eyes communicated his weariness about the pain and death that he had witnessed. The previous year, the London *Times* had sent him to the Crimean War, the first time a journalist for a major newspaper had been dispatched to a combat area. He didn't bother to request permission from the war office, the foreign secretary, or even from military commanders. Instead he disguised himself in a uniform of his own design. Then he boarded a ship loaded with army personnel, all of whom thought that he belonged to someone else's unit. When he arrived on the Crimean Peninsula, an English officer described him disapprovingly as someone who "sings a good song, drinks anyone's brandy and water, and smokes as many cigars as a Jolly Good Fellow. He is just the sort of chap to get information, particularly out of youngsters."

Russell's irresistible personality did indeed prompt revealing conversations that allowed him to report about the wretched conditions in the war. Because of incompetent planning, ordinary soldiers were forced to endure fierce winter storms while wearing summer uniforms, the lack of tents further exposing them to the deadly weather. In contrast, officers enjoyed warm accommodations, one of their commanders, Lord Cardigan, sleeping comfortably on his steam-powered yacht. As British officers savoured wine, soldiers drank water from mud puddles. As officers feasted on cheese, hams, fruit, and chocolate, soldiers subsisted on salt pork and stale biscuits. Scurvy and cholera were rampant. More soldiers died from starvation, disease, and cold than did from wounds.

Russell seized on the disastrous Charge of the Light Brigade as the supreme example of incompetence. Lord Raglan ordered the Light Brigade, a cavalry unit, to attack a Russian artillery installation, but he neglected to specify which of many installations he had in mind. Other officers argued among themselves and failed to demand clarification, with the result that the Light Brigade attacked what turned out to be a heavily fortified Russian embankment. Caught in a devastating crossfire, 245 riders were killed or wounded, 60 taken prisoner, and 345 horses slaughtered.

Thanks to the telegraph, Russell's outrage-producing dispatches reached British readers with then-unimaginable speed and fuelled equally rapid consequences, his vivid turns of phrase adding to their immediacy. The Russians "dashed on towards that thin red streak tipped with a line of steel," he wrote, a description that became "the thin red line" as an enduring synonym for the determination of British soldiers.

Emily stepped forward to shake Russell's hand. "I'm honoured to meet you, sir. You've done a service to women and the wounded by describing Florence Nightingale's attempts to relieve suffering in the war."

"I fear that I haven't accomplished enough," Russell said, peering downward. "Perhaps the new government will be wise enough to pursue the war with greater organization and discipline. As things now stand, we cannot win. In a few days, I return to the Crimea. Perhaps if I write better, the effect of my words will be better."

"You write well enough, sir."

With a nod of thanks to her, Russell approached the bed.

Dr. Snow had finished administering the chloroform. Colonel Trask's eyes were now shut, but his body remained rigid.

"He looks as haunted as he did in the Crimea," Russell noted.

"With new horrors to torment him," Emily said.

"So your father explained. When the colonel discovered the bodies of his fiancée and her parents last night, he must have felt that he was still on the battlefield."

"Mr. Russell, during the war, did you see paralysis of this sort?" De Quincey asked.

"Frequently. The privations that our soldiers endure, the terror that grips them as they wait for yet another battle— these sometimes cause even the bravest of men to be paralyzed. But I never expected it from Colonel Trask. The other men considered him an example of what they ought to be."

Dr. Snow removed his stethoscope from the colonel's chest. "His heart continues to race."

"Perhaps laudanum will help," De Quincey offered.

"No, Father," Emily said.

"I agree with your daughter. Combined with the chloroform, laudanum might kill him. Keep someone with him at all times," Dr. Snow advised. "I'll return in the morning."

"Mr. Russell, your familiar face might be the reassurance that he needs. Until he wakens, would you kindly wait with me in the next room?" De Quincey asked.

"For a man such as the colonel, I can't refuse."

"And Joseph," Emily asked, "would you please stay so that I might ask you something?"

Becker looked surprised, both by the request and by Emily's use of his given name, which attracted the notice of everyone except Emily's father.

"Of course," he answered, uneasy.

"The screams come from *this* way!" Ryan yelled.

Accompanied by the wavering lights of numerous police lanterns, he hurried through the fog-shrouded maze of the Seven Dials rookery.

Sir Walter's screams became more desperate.

Ryan charged along a lane that was so narrow it scraped his shoulders. A drooping overhang forced him to lower his head. He squirmed over timbers that propped up listing walls, the entire district in danger of collapsing.

The screams stopped.

A nearby voice startled Ryan. "Never saw so many bobbies come in here in me life."

"But how many'll get out?" another voice wondered in the darkness. "This one over here looks like the peeler who arrested me last year."

"Warm-lookin' coat he has."

Ryan heard a faint scuffle.

"Here!" a constable shouted, pointing.

Ryan charged down steps and kicked at a door, the wood so decayed that it crumbled off its hinges. In shadows, what looked like dogs raged over a struggling figure.

But they weren't dogs.

Ryan waded into the chaos. As constables struck with their truncheons, he pulled away a ragged man, then another, a frantic boy, a snarling woman.

Police lanterns revealed Sir Walter trembling at the bottom of the pile. His boots, frock coat, and waistcoat were gone. His face had claw marks.

"There's more coming all the time!" a constable warned from the doorway. "This lane will get us out! But you'd better hurry!"

Sir Walter whimpered when Ryan reached for him, seeming to fear that Ryan was another attacker. His walking stick lay on the dirt floor, blood on its knob showing that he'd tried to defend himself.

"Stop Sir Walter! He tried to kill me with his walking stick!" the man at the top of the staircase had shouted.

What else *might he have done with it?* Ryan wondered.

He grabbed it and dragged Sir Walter from the building. He flinched when a rock struck a wall next to his head.

Something rumbled.

"They yanked away a timber support!" a constable shouted. "The wall collapsed! The lane's blocked!"

"Climb over!" Ryan ordered.

A rock hit his shoulder, but the pain of it didn't worry him as much as a different pain. The effort of chasing Sir Walter had strained the scar on his abdomen. He struggled over the collapsed wall, the frenzy of police lanterns guiding him.

"Faster!" Ryan yelled to Sir Walter, who shivered uncontrollably.

More rocks hurtled towards them.

"You can push us around outside, but in here, *we* do the pushin'!" another voice jeered. "This is *our* world!"

"Give us a shillin'!"

"Give us a pound!"

"Give us ever'thin' you have!"

Pulling Sir Walter with his left hand, Ryan used his other hand to keep a tight grip on the walking stick, although what he really wanted to do was press his fingers over the strain in his stomach.

With a startling *bang*, a board landed next to Ryan, so close that he felt a rush of air. The pursuers had climbed to the roofs and were hurling down whatever they could find. Bricks, roof tiles, and even dead rats cascaded into the alley.

Ryan saw the deeper shadows of a recessed doorway. Despite his throbbing abdomen, he raised a boot and kicked at the barrier, hearing a satisfying *pop* as the door's latch disintegrated.

"This way!" he yelled, pulling Sir Walter through the opening.

Constables followed, their lanterns revealing a cluster of faces so accustomed to permanent darkness that the lights agonized them, making them raise their arms to shield their eyes.

Ryan tugged Sir Walter along a cluttered hallway, managed to avoid a gaping hole, crashed against another door, and burst into a farther alley.

Amid cascading debris, the passage widened. As a rock struck Ryan's back, he hurried through an archway and entered a street, the rocks, bricks, and roof tiles now clattering behind him.

Sir Walter slumped against a wall. Ryan slumped next to him, holding Sir Walter's walking stick.

Constables struggled to catch their breath.

"Inspector, the front of your coat has blood on it," one of them said.

As De Quincey, Russell, and the porter left the bedroom, Emily adjusted the blanket over Colonel Trask. She dimmed the lamp and sat in a chair. Despite the reduced light, her blue eyes were intense.

Becker stayed in the room as Emily had requested. Self-conscious, he sat opposite her.

"Joseph, what I wish to ask you about is Newgate," she said.

"An unhappy subject."

"Indeed. After you searched Newgate's records, you reported to Sean, Commissioner Mayne, and my father about what you found. You told them why the boy's thirteen-year-old sister smothered her younger sister and her ill mother and then hanged herself. The expression on your face made clear that the motive was disturbing. Please tell me what you told the others."

Becker glanced down at his hands.

"I proved that I'm steady," Emily said. "Please don't isolate me."

Becker looked away.

"I wasn't aware that we had secrets," Emily said.

"It's better if you don't know. This isn't something for men and women to discuss."

"Joseph, do you wish to be my friend?"

"I *am* your friend," Becker said.

"Not if you treat me as something less."

"I think of you as something *more*. I'm a policeman so that others can have a pure life, even if mine is in the gutter."

"But I have the right to choose to be told," Emily said. "Why did the thirteen-year-old sister do these things, Joseph?"

"Don't make me answer you."

"For the sake of our friendship you *must*."

Becker took a long moment to respond. "Do you insist that the difference between men and women is not as great as society maintains?"

"Yes."

"You insist on never being sheltered?"

"Yes."

Becker breathed deeply. "Then in friendship, I shall tell you. Death in Newgate is common, but these three deaths were so unusual that they prompted an investigation."

"What did the investigation reveal?"

"A sergeant and one of the Newgate guards ..." Becker chose his words carefully. "... took advantage of female children who lived with their parents in the prison."

"Oh." Emily's voice sounded hollow.

"The mother was too deathly ill to defend her daughters. The older daughter fell into such shame and despair that she ..."

Emily didn't speak for a long moment. "Were the sergeant and the prison guard punished?"

"Yes, they were sentenced to the hulks."

Becker referred to decommissioned navy ships that served as prisons along the Thames, their congestion and filth so intense that cholera and typhus were constant threats.

"Until the horror that I saw at the Grantwood house tonight," Emily said, "I never wished to have the physical strength and coarseness of a man. But now, if I could personally punish the man responsible for those murders, if I could have caused pain to the sergeant and that prison guard, I . . ."

"That is why men wish to raise women above them. I'd hoped to shield you from these emotions. I'm sorry, Emily."

She stood and walked over to Colonel Trask, who murmured in his chloroform sleep. She rested a palm on his forehead. "He isn't feverish."

She returned to the chair. "Joseph, I have something else to ask you."

"It can't be more uncomfortable than the last question."

"Why were you surprised when I said that I considered becoming a nurse?"

"I was wrong," Becker said. "This is a different way of feeling uncomfortable."

Emily waited for an answer.

"I suppose I . . . It's so new an idea . . . I . . . May I ask *you* a question?"

"There are no barriers between us," Emily said.

"Have you not considered perhaps . . ."

"Joseph, please say what you're thinking."

". . . accepting a husband?" Becker spoke as if the subject had weighed on him for a long time.

Emily blushed. "Now *I* am surprised."

But in a way, she wasn't. For several weeks, she'd had the sense that this conversation was inevitable. Late at night, after descending to the ballroom of Lord Palmerston's mansion and compelling her restless father to go to bed, she had lain in her own bed and wondered what she would say if either of her cherished new friends—or even both—asked that question.

"Accept a husband? With Father as my responsibility, how can I assume another?"

"Being a nurse wouldn't be a responsibility?" Becker asked.

"It wouldn't require me to give up my independence." Emily suddenly realized how important that was to her.

"But marriage wouldn't need to take away your independence," Becker assured her.

No, this was certainly not how she'd imagined that a proposal would occur.

"Joseph, you know very well that in marriage, a wife surrenders everything. She no longer has control over her choices or even over the children she bears. She becomes her husband's property."

"That's the law," Becker acknowledged. "But a marriage doesn't need to follow the law. With the proper kind of husband, a wife could have all the independence that she desires."

"Including the choice of being both a wife and having a profession?" Emily asked.

"Again, with the right kind of husband."

"What you are saying is far beyond anything that I imagined a man would ever think," Emily said.

Now it was Becker who blushed.

"Joseph, there's something I need to tell you. Because you were honest with me about Newgate, I shall be honest with you about myself. I said earlier that I wasn't aware that we kept secrets from each other. In fact, I do keep a secret. It's something that anyone who feels close to me must eventually find out."

"I don't wish to pry," Becker said, puzzled.

"All my life, because of Father, I have fled debt collectors. Seven weeks ago, I told you how my mother and I and my brothers and sisters lived apart from Father because bailiffs constantly watched us. I sneaked out of back windows, squirmed through holes in walls, and climbed fences. I reached whatever building in which Father hid, bringing him food, ink, and paper. He gave me manuscripts to take to his publishers, who were also being watched by our creditors. Again, I sneaked through holes and over fences. I brought back money, a small portion of which Father kept, and took the remainder home to Mother.

"In Scotland, for a time Father took refuge in a compound that was like the sanctuary of churches in the Middle Ages. Debt collectors were forbidden to enter. On Sundays, the law permitted Father to leave the compound and visit us, as long as he returned there before sunset. But Father's sense of time is different from everyone else's, and each Sunday, as the sky darkened, he ran breathlessly from us, hurrying to return to his sanctuary while the debt collectors snapped at his heels. Once, when we lived near Edinburgh, he was forced to flee all the way across Scotland to Glasgow, where he took refuge in the observatory there. Often we fled cottages in the middle of the night because we didn't have the money to pay the landlord."

Emily went over to Colonel Trask, felt his forehead, and returned to the chair. She felt an ache in her eyes and hoped that she wouldn't weep.

"Two of my brothers escaped, one moving to South America, the other to India. Of my two older sisters, one married as soon as she could and moved to Ireland. The other is engaged to a military officer and will soon live in India also. The responsibility for taking care of Father is mine. Indeed, that responsibility has been mine for a long while. Without my presence, I fear that his opium use will soon kill him. At night, as he leans over a lamp, writing to try to pay our bills, I tell him, 'Father, you set fire to your hair again.' Thanking me, he swats at the embers in his hair and continues writing.

"It's not as if he hasn't tried repeatedly to banish opium from his life. I've been with him on several occasions when he managed to reduce his intake from one thousand drops of laudanum to one hundred and thirty and then eighty and sixty and then none at all. For a day and a week and some-times several weeks, he functioned without opium, and then suddenly he wailed, claiming that rats gnawed at his stomach and his brain. The torture that afflicted him was unbearable to witness. In the end, the anguish was too much for him, and he relapsed. People say that he is weak for not mustering the strength to overcome a habit. But I believe that it's more than a habit. I wonder if someday we might learn that it's possible for a drug to control someone's mind and body so completely that only death seems to offer a release from its domination.

"I can't walk away from anyone who endures that much anguish, Joseph. Yes, a caring husband would allow his wife to bring her father into his home, but as long as Father lived, he would be more important to me than my husband. I devote myself to Father not merely from duty, not merely because I love him with as full a heart as a daughter should have—but also because, heaven help me, despite his faults Father is truly the most fascinating man I have ever met. The remarkable thoughts he puts on paper, the incomparable words that he uses to express them—do those thoughts and words come from opium or does opium hinder them? Would they be even more brilliant without the drug? I don't know. But I do know *this*."

Emily looked plaintively at Becker.

"I'm exhausted. The day on which, to my everlasting grief, Father shall leave me for ever, I cannot imagine suddenly binding myself to yet another person. Do I truly want to go to nursing school? I have no idea. I've devoted myself to Father for so long that I haven't the faintest notion of what freedom is or of what I wish to do afterward. This much I can tell you. Father has so influenced me with his unique ideas that few men would tolerate my own unique ideas."

"I not only tolerate your ideas—I admire them," Becker said.

Emily thought for a moment. "I believe you do."

In the adjacent office, Becker heard the murmur of De Quincey speaking to Russell.

"As you note, you have a responsibility to your father, but sadly he will not always be with you. Perhaps one day, if I earn more as a detective and save much of what I earn, we can again have this conversation. Meanwhile"—Becker smiled—"if you choose to become a nurse, I'm confident that your service to others will be fulfilling."

Colonel Trask murmured in his sleep.

"Our voices disturb him," Emily said.

"I'd better go out and join your father," Becker told her.

"Thank you for being my friend, Joseph."

Emily kissed him.

In Colonel Trask's office, William Russell drank from a brandy flask and continued to tell De Quincey about the war.

"After the Battle of Inkerman, military commanders discovered that I was a reporter for *The Times*. They ordered their officers to stay away from me. Lord Raglan himself refused to allow me to use the military telegraph and also refused to allow military ships to take my dispatches to the civilian telegraph lines on the Turkish mainland. That's how I met Colonel Trask. One night he found me in a tent, where I was drinking brandy with some officers who despised Lord Raglan sufficiently to disobey him and speak to me. After I acquired the information I needed, the colonel discreetly led me away and indicated that he had heard about my difficulties in sending reports. He offered his own vessel to transfer my dispatches to the Turkish telegraph."

"His own vessel?" De Quincey asked.

"With his vast resources, the colonel sent it back and forth, repeatedly delivering my dispatches, then returning with the food, clothing, and tents that our soldiers desperately needed."

"A hero in many ways," De Quincey said.

"We met privately at numerous times. He told me about the accumulating Russian victories. He informed me about the increased incompetence of our English officers. Thanks to him, I learned that Lord Raglan still thinks he's fighting the Napoleonic Wars. He can't remember that the French are now our allies and keeps calling them the enemy."

"Your descriptions of the colonel's exploits were so detailed that you must have observed him in combat," De Quincey said.

"Many times. He expended all his ammunition and that of dead soldiers around him. He charged up a blood-drenched slope, with only the bayonet on his musket as a weapon. Other soldiers, spurred by his example, joined him, relentlessly fighting continuous onslaughts of the enemy, overcoming one after the other, winning the day for England. On another occasion, I saw him lead a desperate charge through mist and smoke, saving the queen's cousin when his unit was nearly overrun by the Russians. The fighting became so primitive that I saw the colonel hurling rocks at the enemy. In close combat, he kicked and even bit."

"You observed this at the risk of your own safety," De Quincey noted.

Russell gave a modest shrug. "Colonel Trask understood the importance of my dispatches and found places from which I could watch in relative safety. I emphasize 'relative.' I admit there was no place that was completely safe from Russian snipers and bombardment. Often I heard bullets zipping past me."

De Quincey peered down at his laudanum bottle. "There are many types of heroes."

"I am merely a reporter who seeks the truth."

"Sad truths and fearful ones," De Quincey said.

Becker emerged from the colonel's bedroom. "I'm going to find Inspector Ryan and see if he needs help."

"Perhaps it would be more useful if you rested," De Quincey told him. "Mr. Russell, you look fatigued also. It won't be comfortable, but possibly you could sleep with your head on Colonel Trask's desk."

"In the Crimea, I slept in the rain on cold, mud-covered slopes. By comparison this is luxurious. What about you? Don't *you* intend to sleep?"

"In my opium nightmares, all the regrets of my life haunt me. I struggle to avoid them by remaining awake as long as possible."

Continuing the Journal of Emily De Quincey

The colonel's body stayed rigid. His only movement was the agitated heaving of his chest, his chloroform sleep obviously troubled.

Sitting next to his bed, I recalled when I had first met him in the horror at St. James's Church. He had focused on me, frowning as if he'd seen me before but couldn't remember when. The next time I met him, at the queen's dinner, his expression had no longer indicated puzzlement. Instead he seemed pleased to see me again. At the table, he had shown me an unexpected kindness when he coughed to hide . . .

Movement interrupted that fond memory. Father's shadow entered the room. He sat next to me, his short legs not touching the floor. With tenderness, he put his hand on mine.

"I'm sorry, Emily."

"Why? What's wrong, Father?"

But despite my question, I had a suspicion about what he meant.

"In my Opium-Eater confessions, do you recall my description of how the drug made me able to hear the details of countless conversations all around me in crowded markets?"

Something in me sank, my premonition confirmed.

"You overheard what I told Joseph? I tried to keep my voice low, Father. I didn't mean to hurt you."

"You didn't hurt me."

"But . . ."

"Never apologize for speaking the truth, Emily. I know what I am. When I heard you say that you loved me in spite of everything, that you loved me with as full a heart as a daughter can have, my own heart broke. I can never thank you enough for watching over me. In many ways, you are the parent, and I am the child. I only wish that I had watched over you with as much devotion. I'm deeply sorry."

"Father, you often say that there's no such thing as forgetting."

"Layers of images and feelings fall upon our memories. Each succession seems to bury what came before. But in reality, no memory is ever extinguished."

"But sometimes it's worth at least *trying* to extinguish some of them," I said.

"Let us *both* try," Father told me, holding my hand with greater affection.

We sat in silence. The adjacent office became quiet, Joseph, William Russell, and the porter evidently having drifted off to sleep.

As the morning's light showed at the window, a sound made Father and me straighten: a murmur from the colonel, although I couldn't determine exactly what he said. Perhaps the effect of the chloroform was what made his voice strangely different.

For the first time in a long while, he moved his head from side to side. Then his body shifted, the effects of the anaesthetic becoming weaker.

With his eyes still closed, the colonel murmured again. "Cath . . ."

The movement of his head became abrupt.

"Catherine," he said more distinctly.

The anguish with which he spoke his dead fiancée's name was palpable. But his voice had a disturbingly unfamiliar tone.

A cold wave swept through me.

"Catherine!" he groaned

In shock, I raised a hand to my mouth. The colonel had an Irish accent.

As he squirmed on the bed, slowly regaining consciousness, Father approached him and removed his blanket, exposing his undergarment.

Self-conscious about the intimacy, I watched Father roll up the colonel's right sleeve. That arm—which usually had a sling—revealed no sign of the wound that the colonel had discussed with the queen's cousin before the dinner at the palace.

Next, Father pulled up the left leg of the colonel's undergarment. It revealed nothing remarkable. More self-conscious, I looked away from the colonel's bare skin.

But then Father pulled up the *right* leg of the colonel's undergarment. Unable to continue looking away, I peered down at that leg and saw an ancient scar. It projected inward where, long ago, something had speared him.

Abruptly, the colonel's eyes opened. He looked at me with incomprehension. Then the terror of the previous night flooded through him. With a scream, he sat upright in panic, staring around wildly.

He was in a bed, he realized. *Where?* Desperate to clear his thoughts, he saw that inexplicably Emily stood before him. So did her father.

Hearing his scream, Sergeant Becker, William Russell, and another man rushed into the room.

In a haze he recognized the other man as a porter in his building and understood that he was in the bedroom behind his office.

"Colonel, it will take you a while to recover from the shock of last night," Emily's father said.

Colonel?

Yes.

"Last night?" Bewildered, he looked around. "How did I get here? Why am I undressed? The last thing . . ."

At once, blood-drenched images rushed through his mind, making him want to cry out.

"Your memory will take a while to focus," Becker said. "The chloroform has a lingering effect."

"Chloroform?" He hid his panic. "I was given chloroform?"

"It was the only way to force you to rest."

What might I have said? he thought. Why were Emily's eyes filled with shock? Why did her father seem to look at him with new awareness?

"We're sorry about your fiancée's death," Becker said.

"Fiancée? No, no, no." He gestured with violent emphasis. "That's wrong. I didn't have a fiancée."

"Colonel, please try to concentrate. Catherine Grantwood was—"

"Not my fiancée." He could barely force out the words. "My wife."

"Your wife?"

Everyone became very still.

The horror of it seized him. He'd lost his wife and . . . His mind ached so much that he pressed his hands against his head.

"We married two months ago . . . before I went to the war . . . in case I didn't return."

"But Catherine's parents . . ."

A sob shuddered through him. "... would never have allowed someone with a history of dirt on his hands to enter their family." He was barely able to summon the voice to continue. "Catherine told her parents that she was going to visit a friend in the Lake District. Gretna Green is just across the border."

Everyone recognized the name. That village in southern Scotland had marriage laws that didn't require a waiting period or the posting of banns. Impatient couples often eloped there.

The pain in his mind intensified. "When Catherine's parents told Sir Walter he could marry her, we were forced to confess to them." He clutched his head tighter. "We couldn't have hidden our secret much longer anyhow."

"What do you mean?" Becker asked.

"Catherine ..." It was the most difficult thing he'd ever said. "My wife ... was with child."

The porter gasped.

"Although the child would have been born in wedlock, Catherine's parents were scandalized. They revoked their promise to Sir Walter, feeling so ashamed that they didn't give him an explanation. Insane with jealousy, he attacked me."

"What happened last night?" Becker asked.

Gripping his throbbing skull, he managed the strength to continue.

"Catherine was supposed to visit her cousin in Watford. Because I was worried about Sir Walter's rage, I encouraged her to go through with her plan. At the last minute, to provide further protection, I decided to join her, but ..." He shuddered. "When I arrived at her cousin's house, I learned that Catherine had never left the city. I was overcome with a premonition, and I used every means possible to hurry back."

Grief of a sort that he hadn't endured since he was ten years old welled up inside him. One part of him felt as if a powerful hand squeezed his heart to the point of crushing it. But another part warned that if he allowed anguish to overpower him, he might do something else that could betray him.

"God help me, I didn't reach her soon enough."

God help me? he thought. *God can't* possibly *help me.*

Mother.

Father.

Emma.

Ruth.

Catherine.

My unborn child.

"Sir Walter." Attempting to divert attention, he said, "Nobody knew a thing about him until six months ago. Where did he suddenly come from? He never talks about his past. He's hiding something."

"He is indeed hiding something," a voice intruded.

Everyone turned.

Braced against the doorjamb, Ryan pressed a hand to his stomach. He sounded in pain.

"We caught Sir Walter at the Seven Dials rookery. We took him to jail, where he confessed to poisoning his uncle. We have his walking stick. We're comparing its knob with the wounds on the heads of the servants at Lord Grantwood's house and the houses of the other victims." Ryan's words were quick, conveying even more pain. "We're trying to make Sir Walter admit that he murdered Catherine Grantwood and her parents and that he killed Lord and Lady Cosgrove and—"

"Sean, there's blood on your coat!" Emily exclaimed.

Ryan slumped to the floor.

As Emily and Becker hurried towards Ryan, De Quincey remained in the colonel's bedroom.

With a clatter, William Russell swept everything from the desk in the adjacent office. "Put him on this!"

"My wound reopened. I expected Dr. Snow to be here," Ryan murmured.

"I'll bring more hot water and clean rags," the porter said. The floor reverberated as he rushed towards the hallway.

"Joseph, help me get his coat off," Emily urged.

Alone in the bedroom, De Quincey and Colonel Trask looked at each other.

"I'll dress quickly," the colonel told him. "The inspector can have my bed."

De Quincey nodded but stayed where he was. "Your wife's murder was not fine art."

"Not fine art? What are you talking about?"

"It was clumsy. It lacked style."

"In my grief, you speak to me this way? Has laudanum made you insane?"

"The murders of your wife's parents were staged so that they related to the other killings and the threat against the queen. But your *wife's* murder was crass, as if the killers didn't expect her to be there. Colonel, while you were unconscious, I rolled up the right sleeve of your undergarment."

"You *what?*"

"That arm shows no sign of the wound that you discussed at the queen's dinner."

"My injury is a sprain. The Duke of Cambridge called it a wound. I chose not to correct him."

"You do have the mark of another wound, however," De Quincey persisted. "Your right calf has an ancient scar that projects inward, as if your leg had been spiked by something when you were young, the spike on top of a fence, perhaps."

"The scar is from an accident when I was helping my father to build railways."

"While you slept, you spoke your wife's name."

"I'm in grief. Of course I spoke my wife's name."

"Your voice sounded different."

"Everyone's voice sounds different in their nightmares. Kindly leave me to mourn my wife and my unborn child."

"You had an Irish accent."

Again, the two men assessed each other.

De Quincey suddenly was aware how small the bedroom was, how near to touching he and Trask were. It would take the colonel only an instant to close the distance and strike him dead.

But instead of retreating, De Quincey stepped forward. The prospect of dying this way was better than dying from opium. "You're the boy who ran next to the queen's carriage fifteen years ago, begging the queen to help your father, mother, and sisters."

"My father is Jeremiah Trask, who certainly isn't Irish. Ask *that* man." Trask pointed towards the porter, who peered into the bedroom, having returned with the hot water. "He worked with me when I helped my father build railways."

"It's true," the porter said. "Mr. Trask senior definitely isn't Irish."

"What possible need would I have had to beg the queen to help my father," Trask demanded. "Did you say 'fifteen years ago'?"

"The year of the first attempt against Her Majesty."

"In eighteen forty, my father had established much of his railway empire. He wouldn't have needed me to beg the queen for anything. Inspector Ryan needs this bed. Since you won't give me privacy . . ."

Trask stood and dropped his blanket. He started to unbutton his undergarment.

"I'll ignore your sensibilities as my comrades and I were forced to do in the war. The moment I finish dressing, the inspector can have this room."

Opening more buttons, he walked towards the wardrobe and removed a shirt from it.

De Quincey stepped from the bedroom.

As Colonel Trask shut the door behind him, De Quincey watched Emily wipe blood from Ryan's wound.

"Do you have a key to that door?" he asked the porter.

"On this ring."

"Lock it."

"Lock it?"

"While we send for constables."

"To arrest the colonel?" the porter asked in surprise.

"I may not be able to prove that he's the Irish boy who begged the queen for help fifteen years ago, but at least I can try to stop him from killing her."

"You don't know what you're saying," the porter told him.

"Lord Palmerston has often maintained as much. Please lock the door."

"Colonel Trask is my employer and my friend. I cannot do it."

A sound at the door made them look in that direction. Although cautiously done, it was the unmistakable scrape of a bolt being secured.

"Colonel Trask?" De Quincey approached the door. "Is everything all right?"

He didn't receive a reply.

"Colonel Trask?" De Quincey knocked.

Again, he didn't receive an answer. De Quincey knocked harder.

"Force it open," Ryan told them, trying to sit up.

"Sean, be still," Emily ordered.

Becker walked to the door and rammed his shoulder against it. But the door was made of thick oak; it barely moved.

"Leave him alone, if that's what he wants. He's not going anywhere," Becker decided.

"Perhaps he intends to harm himself," De Quincey said.

"Harm himself? Why would the colonel want to do that?" the porter asked.

"I heard your accusations," William Russell said. "From a journalist's viewpoint, your reasoning is based only on coincidence."

"Mr. Russell, have you ever seen paintings that show one thing when viewed from the right but show something else when viewed from the left?"

"At the Crystal Palace Exhibition. When I stood on one side, a woman was smiling, but when I stood on the opposite side, the painting showed a man who frowned."

"Which was the reality?" De Quincey asked.

"Both of them, depending on how you looked at the painting."

"Immanuel Kant would applaud your conclusion. Please consider the Crimean events that you described to me. The commander of the military discovered that you were sending war reports to *The Times*. He ordered his officers not to speak to you, and he refused to allow your dispatches to be taken to the Turkish mainland, where the telegraph could relay them to England."

"That was the case," Russell agreed.

"Colonel Trask sought you out, offered his own vessel to transport your dispatches, and further impressed you by ordering his crew to bring back food, clothing, and tents for our soldiers."

"He is generous."

"He then arranged for you to have a vivid vantage point from which to witness various battles in which he proved himself to be heroic."

"What are you implying?"

"I don't yet know how the Irish boy from fifteen years ago became the man in that room. But I do know how he managed to get close to the queen. As soon as he arrived in the Crimea, he sought you out. He made you his ally. He arranged for you to see him perform heroically, even to the point of rescuing the queen's cousin. Without you, no one in England would have known of his bravery. Without you, he never would have been knighted and have gained access to the queen. Without the information that he supplied to you, the British government would not have collapsed."

"You can't prove any of this!"

De Quincey turned towards Becker and Ryan, the latter watching in pain from the desk.

"At the church, the colonel's dramatic entrance provided the distraction that allowed Lady Cosgrove's body to be propped up in her pew without anyone noticing. Last night, the colonel provided another deception. Travelling to Watford to visit his wife, he hoped to ensure that no one, especially not her, would suspect that he was responsible for what happened at the same time—the slaughter of her parents by the members of the new Young England that he created. That's why Catherine's murder was so crude. The men he sent to commit the crime never expected to find her there. They didn't know how to react, except to stop her from being a witness. They chased her up the stairs, stabbing her repeatedly until she stopped screaming."

"Father," Emily said.

"My apologies, Emily. After what they did to Catherine, the men the colonel sent were too unnerved to make a proper display of her parents. The notes about Young England, Young Ireland, and William Hamilton—the fourth man to shoot at the queen—were hastily shoved into pockets instead of being dramatically positioned. It was a poor job, performed clumsily because the script had changed. Indeed, at that point, there *wasn't* a script, and the killers fled as soon as they could."

De Quincey turned towards the bedroom door.

"Colonel, did you have any true regard for Catherine Grantwood? Or did you marry her merely as another way to achieve revenge against her parents, to the point of conceiving a child with her so that you could show them how much you possessed her?"

On the opposite side of the door, the silence persisted.

"Perhaps he *did* harm himself. Is there an axe in this building?" De Quincey asked the porter. "Sergeant Becker, I suggest you break through the door."

Sweat glistened on Becker's face as he swung the axe, chunks of wood flying from the door jamb.

"It'll be easier to get around the hinges than to go through the door," he said.

The axe rang as it struck metal.

"There! I see a hinge!"

"Let *me* have a go," the porter said.

He inserted a ripping chisel into a gap and pried, a large section of wood cracking free around the hinge. He and Becker charged towards the door, crashing their full weight against it. Wood split. The door banged inward, taking Becker and the porter with it onto the floor.

"Careful!" Becker warned.

With the porter behind him, he scrambled to his feet and scanned the bedroom.

"What do you see?" De Quincey asked from the office.

"Nothing."

"What?"

"The room's deserted."

De Quincey squeezed past them. "But he couldn't have vanished."

Becker searched behind the table and two chairs. He looked under the bed.

De Quincey crossed the room and raised the window. His

short legs required him to stand on tiptoes in order to peer out the window. The cold morning air struck his face as he stared towards an alley that led to the Thames.

"It's a sheer drop. I don't see how he could have climbed down."

"Then where did he go?" Becker demanded. "Is there a trapdoor?"

He and the porter tugged up the carpet, but found no sign of a hatch. They tapped the walls, listening for hollow sounds, feeling for cracks in the wainscoting that might reveal a hidden door.

"What about the ceiling?" William Russell asked.

They stared upward.

"Even if the ceiling has a trapdoor, how could he have climbed to it?" the porter wondered.

"Maybe he used a chair to climb onto the wardrobe," Becker suggested.

"The wardrobe," De Quincey repeated.

"Yes!" Becker said.

With abrupt understanding, he pushed the wardrobe. It shifted, revealing a door. But when Becker tried the latch, he discovered it was locked.

Becker and the porter assaulted the new obstacle. After using the axe and the ripping chisel to weaken the door's hinges, the two men thrust their weight against it. With a thundering echo, it fell inward.

"Watch out, there's a drop!" Becker warned, grabbing the porter.

They peered down into darkness.

Russell brought a lamp and scanned a steep, shadowy stairwell.

"I had no idea that this was here," the porter said.

Slowly, they went down the steps, Becker taking the lead. As the wood creaked, the motion of the lamp made everything seem to waver.

Something snapped. Becker cried out, a step collapsing under him. The porter clutched his arm and pulled him back as the step dropped, clattering off walls, splashing into water far below.

"Lower your lamp towards the step," Becker told Russell with an unsteady voice. He crouched and pointed, the lamp revealing a clean mark where the step had been sawed partially through.

"Go down in single file. Stay close to the wall," Becker said. "Keep a tight grip on the person ahead of you in case one of us falls."

"I hear water dripping," Russell said.

"We're close to the Thames," the porter reminded him. "But I hear something else."

"Rats," De Quincey said. He felt that he descended dizzily through chasms and abysses, depths below depths as in an opium dream.

The staircase creaked and trembled.

"Stop," Becker said. "Even single file, there are too many of us."

"I'll go first," De Quincey told him.

"But the risk . . ."

"I weigh almost nothing. Even a board that's been partially sawed might hold me." The little man stooped, inspecting the next step. "And this board has indeed been sawed." He peered at something above him on the wall. "Mr. Russell, may I have your lamp, please? Yes. There. Does everyone notice?"

"Notice what?"

"This black mark above my head. And there ought to be . . . yes. Five steps down, there's a similar mark. That's how the colonel identifies the boards that he tampered with, preventing him from being caught in his own trap. He puts the marks above his head because the natural impulse for a potential victim is to look cautiously down the stairs, not warily above them. The odds are slim that anyone would notice."

"But *you* noticed," Russell said.

"Because I'm trying to enter the reality of a trap-setter."

De Quincey stretched a leg over the compromised step and continued descending. Raising the lamp, he pointed towards another small black mark.

"One more step to avoid."

The sound of dripping water became louder. De Quincey's boots splashed into a pool.

"I've reached the bottom!"

Looking under the staircase, he aimed the lamp towards a stack of wooden crates over which rats scurried.

As the men joined him, he turned in the opposite direction and revealed a dank tunnel whose moisture-slicked walls glistened in the light.

"A long time ago, smugglers might have used this," the porter said.

"Look. Someone carved a date in the stones." Russell pointed.

"It's just a bunch of *X*s and such," the porter said.

"No. They're Roman numerals," Russell told him. "Sixteen forty-nine. This tunnel's older than the Great Fire of London."

"And probably ready to collapse," Becker said.

They reached a rusted iron door. But the rust covered only a few sections, indicating that the door had been recently installed.

"Let's see if it's locked," the porter said.

He lifted the latch and pulled. "We're in luck. It's moving."

"Wait." De Quincey put a hand on his shoulder. "Would the colonel have left it unlocked?"

"He was running from us. Maybe he didn't want to take the time."

"But a locked door would have held us back and gained him *more* time."

"You think it's another trap?" Becker asked.

De Quincey raised the lamp towards the rocks that formed the ceiling. "I prefer to die another way."

"But if the colonel didn't go through here, how did he get out of the tunnel?" the porter demanded.

"There must be *another* tunnel," Russell answered.

"Where? We didn't see it."

"Because we weren't looking," Becker said. "Isn't that your point, Mr. De Quincey? To see, we first need to look. The crates underneath the stairs—the tunnel's behind them."

They hurried back in that direction. As De Quincey held the lamp, the three men dragged away the crates and revealed a second tunnel.

Cautious, they moved along wet cobblestones, reaching a second door.

This door was wooden.

It was locked.

"Which probably means it's safe," Becker said.

Frenzied minutes later, he finished chopping the lock from the door jamb and pulled the barrier open. Daylight made him squint.

A chill breeze cleared the tunnel's moldy odour. Stone steps led up to a dock that teemed with workers unloading crates from boats.

Slouched against a wall, an overweight man smoked a pipe and gave orders. He glanced towards the group hurrying up the steps.

"How long have you been here?" Becker asked.

"Since dawn, makin' certain this lot don't steal from me. What's goin' on with so many people comin' out that door?"

"You saw someone else come out?"

"A half hour ago, in a terrible hurry." The man aimed his pipe towards the dock. "He got on a steamer."

The Thames was busier than any of the streets in London,

with numerous steamboats acting as cabs, transporting groups of passengers up and down the river.

"Did you notice which way the steamer went?" Becker asked.

"The answer's obvious," De Quincey said before the man could answer. "He went upriver."

"That's right," the man told him in surprise. "How did you know?"

"Because Buckingham Palace is upriver."

12

From the Workhouse to the Graveyard

Aboard the steamer, amid the jostling waves produced by hundreds of boats on the river, Colin O'Brien ... Anthony Trask ... the revenger ... the hero ... whoever he was ... stared at the passing shore.

One of the buildings, a tavern perched above a wharf, attracted his attention, his bitter thoughts taking him back fifteen years. It was there that he had been a penny diver, he and other desperate, starving boys leaping into the foul Thames, fighting the current and the mud to find pennies that the tavern's drunken customers threw into the water. The men who tossed the pennies laughed at the frenzy with which the boys dived to retrieve the meagre coins. Sometimes he banged his head on submerged objects. Sometimes he and the other boys punched one another in an effort to reach the pennies first. Streaks of slime stuck to him, making the coin throwers laugh even harder.

It wasn't exactly the same tavern at which he had been a penny diver. That place had been rebuilt—because a few years later, he had returned and set it ablaze, almost destroying the entire district before firefighting boats arrived, their crews frantically pumping water onto the flames. The newspapers said that the fire could have destroyed much of the waterfront between Blackfriars Bridge and the Tower.

He wished that it had.

Smoke billowed from the steamer's engine, contributing to the pall above the river. As cold waves pounded the hull, he stared past roofs in the direction of the workhouse to which he had gone.

Workhouses were supposed to be where orphans and the hopelessly poor could find a bed and food in exchange for tasks that they were given. But politicians feared that the workhouses would be too comfortable and encourage sloth, so conditions were made appalling to the point that only the most desperate applied for admission. Families were separated, wives and daughters put in one section while husbands and sons were put in another, seldom having the chance to meet. Dormitories consisted of cramped rooms with a few holes for ventilation. Food was gruel and stale bread. From sunup to sundown, the occupants were given numbing, repetitive work, such as separating strands of rope, which would be soaked in tar and used as caulking for ships' hulls.

He endured the workhouse for two weeks before running away. He worked as a chimney sweep, thrusting a bag and a broom above him while his employer lit a fire under him to make him climb the inside of chimneys faster. When his cough became persistent and he realized that the dust would kill him, he took the advice of a fellow sweep and broke a tavern window, making certain that a constable saw him and grabbed him. A broken window was worth a month in jail, where he wouldn't freeze to death as winter loomed and where the food he received was slightly better than the gruel and stale bread in the workhouse. A week after he was released, he broke another window to earn another month's free food and lodging, as terrible as the conditions were. The third time he broke a window, the judge recognized him and refused to put him in jail another time. It was just as well, because he eventually learned that habitual window-breakers were sent to Newgate, and that was the last place he ever wanted to set foot in again.

★　　★　　★

A thumping sound jolted him from his hateful memories. As the cold breeze strengthened, he watched the steamer's crew tie mooring ropes to the dock at Blackfriars Bridge, three stops from Westminster Bridge and its proximity to Buckingham Palace. A snowflake drifted past.

Stepping onto the dock, he noticed a ragged boy who used chalk to draw trees on cobblestones as a form of begging. For the first time in many years, he deliberately revealed the Irish accent he had worked so obsessively to conceal.

"What's your name?" he asked.

"Eddie."

"You mean 'Edward.' If you wish people to respect you, always use your formal name."

"Around here, they'd laugh."

"They wouldn't laugh if you rose above a dockside life."

"What could I possibly rise to?"

"You see that clothing shop? I want you to buy some items for me."

"That shop ain't fancy enough for someone like you, even if you do sound Irish."

"I have some physical work that needs to be done."

"Physical work for a gentleman?"

He ignored the question. "Plain corduroy trousers and a warm coat are all I need, Edward, plus gloves and a cap."

"Why don't you buy them on your own?"

He pointed. "Your own clothes are ragged. Perhaps you could buy a new coat and trousers for yourself."

"Yeah, and perhaps a cow'll jump over the moon."

"Give this list to the clerk. I'll wait for you in that lane over there. Five gold sovereigns ought to be more than sufficient for your clothes and mine."

"Five gold sovereigns!" One sovereign was more than the boy could hope to acquire in three weeks of begging.

"Whatever coins the clerk gives you in return are yours,

Edward. And there will be three other sovereigns when you bring the clothes to me. The note includes an explanation that the coins haven't been stolen and that you're performing an errand for someone of means. The clerk might give you a look, but he won't bother you. I suggest that you also purchase new boots for yourself. Your toes are visible in the ones you have."

Not believing his luck, the boy ran excitedly into the shop.

This was how he had established the new Young England. In the world's largest city, desperation festered everywhere. He had sought out the hopeless, offering them a chance to rise above their misery. Five gold sovereigns—with regular payments thereafter—bought loyalty, especially because he had once shared their misery and knew how to appeal to them.

But money and respect weren't enough. He chose beggars who hated the rich and powerful as he did, who would keep secrets if they thought that their silence and loyalty would help them to achieve the revenge that he taught them was possible.

The new Young England.

He entered the lane, from where he scanned the chaotic dock to see if anyone had paid attention to him. The clouds darkened. Another snowflake drifted past.

Ten minutes later, the boy returned with the clothes.

"Thank you, Edward. The trousers and coat that you bought for yourself are good choices."

"You promised to give me three more sovereigns."

"And I shall. But first, I have one more task. Some people might come here, asking for anyone who looks like me."

"What kind of people?"

"The police."

He opened his hand, displaying not three but five extra sovereigns.

The boy's eyes fixed on them.

"Take your new clothes and your new wealth and go to Lambeth."

"That's a distance," the boy said.

"Precisely. Find a warm eating house there, Edward. You have enough money that the owner won't object if you stay a long time. Eat slowly. Enjoy a day without begging. Tonight, it won't matter if you return here. If the police ask about me, tell them the truth. By then, I'll no longer care."

"You'll be gone?"

"Yes," he said. "I'll be gone."

"I never tell the bobbies anythin' anyway. You can count on me."

"Perhaps your new wealth will allow you to see an opportunity for advancement. The trees that you drew on the cobblestones indicate that you have a talent. When I was your age, I started with much less than what you now have."

"But who'd pay me to draw?"

"With your new clothes, you might not be chased away if you draw on the pavement of a wealthy district. Someone of means might be impressed. Hurry along, Edward. Think about my advice."

He waited until the boy vanished into the crowd. Then he proceeded north, using randomly chosen lanes, looking behind him to determine whether he was being followed.

He came to a public privy, went inside, changed his clothes, and stepped outside. The workers who impatiently queued up behind him seemed not to notice that a gentleman had gone into the privy and a labourer had emerged. Nonetheless he kept his eyes down and averted his face. If there'd been time for him to get to it, he'd have worn the beard he frequently used to conceal his features.

The breeze became colder. More snowflakes fell. As he continued northward, he placed his gentleman's clothes at the entrance to an alley. They would be grabbed within seconds.

The expensive garments would be worth many blessed sovereigns to the starving wretch who found them and sold them to a second-hand shop.

The dome of St. Paul's Cathedral beckoned. Beyond it lay the bleak stone wall and the iron-studded door to Newgate Prison. Sombre families waited to visit loved ones. Even fifteen years later, he remembered standing outside with his father, and the oppressive feel of the dark interior when they were finally admitted.

He remembered when he had seen his mother in there for the last time and how sickly and despairing she had looked after only a few days. He remembered the last time he'd seen Emma and Ruth, his beloved sisters, peering back at him, hopeful and yet afraid, waving what they thought was a temporary goodbye as the guard and the sergeant led them into the prison and their doom.

He went to the nearby alley that he'd limped back to after begging the queen and had discovered that his father was dead, the body being placed on a morgue cart. He had never learned where his father and mother and sisters were buried, so he had made a random choice of graveyards and decided that they were in the paupers' section at St. Anne's Church in Soho, where his pilgrimage now took him.

The same as fifteen years earlier, he again saw gravediggers burying the bodies of the poor between layers of boards, stacking them as deeply as possible. So many bodies. There wasn't the slightest marker to identify who was deposited in the paupers' section.

Because his mother had always wanted a garden, he had decided that a spot near bushes next to a wall was where they rested. As a boy he had come here every day, standing where he imagined they'd been buried, telling them how much he loved them, promising how strong he intended to be, vowing that he would punish everyone who had put them there.

It gave him intense satisfaction to remember that, when his leg had finally healed, he went to the Inns of Court and waited for a solicitor who'd been particularly uncaring. He watched the arrogant man step from his chambers. He ran past the man and lunged, thrusting him under a speeding carriage. Hearing a thump and screams, he darted into an alley, squirmed over a fence, squeezed through a hole in a wall, and kept running, his escape route thoroughly practised.

He'd done the same to a heartless barrister. The thump and the screams were gratifying as he raced down another alley, but it wasn't enough merely to *hear* them die. He wanted to see fright. He wanted to see pain. Quick punishment didn't make up for what had been done to his mother and father and sisters, to dear Emma with her brilliant blue eyes and blessed Ruth with the endearing gap in her teeth.

Now, amid the falling snow, he bowed his head.

Tonight, at last, the four of you will rest in peace, he thought.

Abruptly he was racked with grief for two other loved ones.

"My wife. My unborn child."

Forget about them. They don't matter, a part of him thought.

"Catherine."

She was only one more way to punish her parents, a voice within him said.

"No."

You used her.

"No, I *loved* her."

You convinced yourself of that in order to make her believe you. Oh, the shock on their faces when they learned that she was married to you, a man they considered beneath them. Oh, the more satisfying shock when they learned how completely she was yours, that she was with child.

"My unborn . . ."

A vicar walked through the graveyard's archway and glanced towards him in surprise. "You're alone?"

Instead of answering, he wiped tears from his cheeks.

"I was certain I heard two voices," the vicar said.

"A storm's coming. I'd better be on my way."

"One of the voices was Irish. Are you certain no one else was here?" the vicar asked.

"No one."

"Young man, you look troubled. I hope you find peace."

Tonight, he thought, *peace will come.*

He headed westward.

No! That's the wrong way! a part of him shouted. *The palace is to the south, not the west! Where are you going?*

In the falling snow on Half Moon Street in Mayfair, he stood across from the Grantwood mansion, watching constables come and go.

His labourer's clothes prompted a constable to tell him, "Move along."

"I did some carpentry work for Lord and Lady Grantwood. This is a terrible thing."

"Yes, terrible," the constable said. "There's nothing to see here. Keep walking."

"The daughter was pleasant to me, for which I was grateful. Please give my respects to the family."

"There's no family left," the constable said.

"Do you know when the funeral is to be?"

"As soon as the bodies are released from Westminster Hospital."

"Hospital?" His breathing quickened. "You mean some of them are still alive?"

"The detectives ordered the wounds to be studied in the morgue there. Maybe there's a way to tell what sort of knives killed the daughter."

"Knives? There were *several?*"

"For the final time, I'm telling you to move along."

No, the palace is to the south! Why are you heading south-east?

As the snow strengthened, he took a wide route around the treed expanse of Green Park and St. James's Park. Because of their proximity to Buckingham Palace, police patrols would undoubtedly be watching for him in those places. Even disguised as a labourer, he might be stopped by an enterprising constable.

Westminster Hospital was behind Westminster Abbey, on a street called Broad Sanctuary. Centuries earlier, the area had acquired its name because that was where desperate people sought the church's protection from debt collectors and political enemies. But he had received no sanctuary for his father when he'd gone to Westminster Hospital to beg doctors to help him.

Inside the dour building, he brushed snow from his coat. He heard groans and smelled disease.

"Can I help you?" a man behind a counter asked.

"My brother's here. I came to visit him."

"What's his name?"

"Matthew O'Reilly."

"I don't remember an Irish patient," the clerk said in confusion.

"He was knocked unconscious by a horse. He wouldn't have been able to give his name."

"I'll check the records."

The man went into a back room as if determined to assure himself that he couldn't possibly have forgotten an Irish patient.

Stairs led downward. A sign said medical school, another word for "morgue."

He descended the stairs and reached a hallway of doors,

one of which was open. A clerk peered up from a desk. "Can I help you?"

"Inspector Ryan sent me with a message for the surgeons examining Catherine Grantwood."

The clerk nodded, seeming to recognize Ryan's name. "Third door on the left. But you'll need to wait. The surgeons haven't arrived yet."

"Thank you."

He went down the corridor and knocked on the door. When no one answered, he went inside.

The room had a tiled floor with a drain in the middle. It was cold because of ice along both sides of a metal object the shape of a shallow bathtub. The odour of death was familiar from the months he'd spent on battlefields. A sheet covered what was obviously a body.

With a trembling hand he pulled back the sheet. Despite the horrors of the Crimea, he wasn't prepared for what had been done to the most beautiful woman he had ever known.

To his wife.

To his unborn child.

"Catherine," he murmured, weeping.

He imagined her terror as she came down the stairs and heard what was happening to her parents. When the intruders looked up and saw her, panic must have made her heart pound so fast that she feared she would faint. Hearing frantic steps behind her, she raced in the only possible direction—upward—hoping to reach her bedroom and secure the door.

He flinched as he thought about the pain when the first knife struck her. But she kept running upward, and the men kept stabbing, trying to quiet her. Frenzy gave her the strength to reach her room, but she couldn't shut the door in time, and the men burst inside, striking with their knives, doing everything they could to stop her screams.

His tears fell on Catherine's face. He drew a trembling

finger along her once-glowing skin that now had the dullness of death. Dried blood covered breasts that he had previously seen only once—on his wedding night.

"This is *my* fault," he said. "*I'm* the one who did this. *I'm* the one who killed you."

No! a part of him insisted. *Her parents killed her!*

"I want to die," he said.

The queen *killed her! Lord Cosgrove and all the others did it! The shopkeeper Burbridge did it! The same as all of them killed our mother and father and Emma and Ruth!*

"I want to die," he repeated with greater determination.

Not before we kill the queen.

The door suddenly opened. A man wearing an expensive frock coat stepped in, only to pause in surprise and stare over his spectacles.

"Who the devil are *you?*"

"I was looking for my brother. A horse kicked his head and—"

"What are you doing with that woman's body?"

"I told you I'm looking for my brother. I raised the sheet to see if—"

"Quickly, someone bring a constable! There's an Irishman touching Miss Grantwood's body!"

"I'll get help!" a voice yelled from along the corridor.

"Please," he said. "No. This isn't what you think."

"Step away from the body!" The accuser raised his walking stick. "You vermin, you'll regret coming here."

"Don't call me 'vermin'!"

He twisted the walking stick from the man's hand and struck him across the forehead.

Before the body hit the ground, he reached the corridor and saw a snow-specked constable hurrying down the stairs, accompanied by the clerk he'd spoken to in the hallway.

"What are you doing there? Stop!" the constable demanded.

Aware that police helmets were reinforced, he struck the walking stick against the constable's chin, then swung and cracked the clerk's skull.

He charged up the stairs and reached the main floor, where the first man he'd spoken to was bringing a constable through the entrance. Snow gusted beyond the open door.

"There!" the man said. "That's the Irishman I told you about!"

"Put down the walking stick!" the constable ordered.

He knocked the policeman to the floor.

He knocked the other man to the floor, then raced outside, disappearing into the snowfall.

"That's where Colonel Trask lives." The porter gestured towards one of the adjoining houses on Bolton Street in Mayfair. "I sometimes come here to deliver business papers."

"Thank you," De Quincey said.

As the chill flurries thickened, De Quincey, Becker, and a constable stepped down from the police van. They approached the white stone building, where Becker knocked on the oak door.

A butler opened it, looking puzzled.

"I'm Detective Sergeant Becker. Is Colonel Trask here?"

The butler frowned at the badge that Becker showed, apparently unable to imagine why a policeman would come to this particular door—and surely the badge should belong to the uniformed constable, not to a man who was dressed in a commoner's clothes and had a scar on his chin.

"The colonel hasn't been here in several days," the butler replied.

"What about Mr. Trask senior? We need to see him."

"That isn't possible. He never receives visitors without appointments."

"Please tell him to make an exception. We're here on an urgent matter that concerns the queen."

"But this is his hour for manipulation."

"I don't care *what* he's manipulating. Tell him—"

De Quincey slipped past the butler and entered the house.

"Just a moment," the butler objected.

"We don't have a moment," Becker said.

He and the constable followed De Quincey.

"Where's Mr. Trask?"

"In his bedroom, but—"

As speedily as his short legs allowed, De Quincey scurried up the elegant staircase. The butler rushed after him. Becker and the constable quickly followed.

They reached the entrance to a huge dining room and continued climbing.

"You don't understand," the butler insisted. "Mr. Trask can't be disturbed."

"I wouldn't care to see Her Majesty's expression if she heard about his indifference to her," Becker said.

At the next level, they faced several doors.

"Which one?" Becker demanded.

The butler raised his hands in frustration. He opened a door, peered inside, and motioned for them to enter. "Now you'll realize what I've been trying to tell you."

De Quincey, Becker, and the constable entered a bedroom, and finally they did understand.

The manipulation to which the butler had referred wasn't anything that Jeremiah Trask was doing, but rather it was something that was being done to him. A thin, frail-looking man of perhaps sixty, he lay on a bed while an attendant moved his pajama-covered legs up and down, flexing and extending them. Another attendant raised his arms, lowered them, and shifted them from side to side.

The interruption made the attendants pause only briefly before resuming their task. The gauntness of Trask's arms and legs, not to mention their lack of resistance, suggested that Trask was incapable of moving them on his own.

"He's paralyzed?" Becker asked.

"For the past eight years," the servant answered. "Because of an accident."

Pitying him, Becker took a moment to adjust to what he was seeing. "Mr. Trask, I apologize for intruding. I'm a detective sergeant. We need to speak to you about an urgent matter concerning the queen."

"He can't reply," the servant explained. "The accident left him incapable of speech."

Becker sighed, as if he'd thought he'd seen every form of misery but now had encountered a new one. "Can he communicate at all? Perhaps he can use a pencil and paper."

"He can blink."

"Pardon me?"

"He can answer questions that require a yes or no by blinking—once for yes and twice for no."

"For the past eight years?" Becker shook his head forlornly. "God save us."

De Quincey approached the bed.

Although Trask's face was immobile, his eyes managed to shift in De Quincey's direction. Their grey matched the pallor of Trask's hair and his sunken cheeks, all of them the colour of despair.

"Mr. Trask, my name is Thomas De Quincey. Many years ago, I wrote a book called *Confessions of an English Opium-Eater.*"

As if to prove his assertion, De Quincey withdrew his laudanum bottle and drank from it.

"I also wrote a series of essays about the fine art of murder and one about *Macbeth* and another about the English mail coaches that travelled our great land before your railways put an end to that adventurous means of transportation. At night, I used to enjoy sitting atop those coaches, feeling the speed of the mighty horses, watching the different shades of darkness we passed."

Trask kept staring at him.

"I was a friend of Coleridge and Wordsworth, and even wrote essays that helped establish their reputations before the latter—a snob—turned against me for marrying what he called a milkmaid. The quantity of my opium ingestion is such that crocodiles and sphinxes threaten me in my nightmares. The only things more persistent are the infinite bill collectors who pursue me. A landlord once kept me a prisoner for a year, forcing me to write my way out of the debt I owed him."

Trask's eyes communicated no hint of confusion or annoyance or amusement. His gaze was as impassive as the sphinxes to which De Quincey had referred.

Noting that saliva leaked from a corner of Trask's mouth, De Quincey took out a handkerchief and dabbed it away.

"All that is by way of introduction. As a stranger who imposes himself upon you, I hope that this helps to remove any barrier between us, for I have a question that I must ask, and its personal nature is such that I beg your indulgence. Are we sufficiently acquainted? Do I have your permission to ask the question?"

Trask studied him with motionless features. He closed his eyelids for an instant longer than a normal blink would require.

"I take that as a yes. Thank you. Forgive my bluntness. Is Anthony Trask your son?"

A moment passed. Then another. And another.

Trask closed his eyes once. Then again.

It seemed to De Quincey that the effort Trask made to scrunch his eyelids shut was the equivalent of screaming.

No!

*   *   *

From the prison of his withered, unfeeling body, Jeremiah Trask peered up at the strange man whose clothing suggested that he'd just come from a funeral. This tiny visitor, the tall man with him, and the constable were the only unfamiliar people he had seen in . . . had the servant said "eight years"? The force of so much lost time assaulted Trask's mind, making the room seem to spin. Could he possibly have lain immobile on this bed for *eight years?* With each day the same, with no way to measure the passage of weeks and months, he felt trapped in a constantly repeating hell. The only variation occurred when the man who called himself Anthony Trask brought bankers and lawyers, claiming to have carefully explained the details of various business ventures to him.

"Isn't that right, Father?" the man who called himself Anthony Trask would say. "Last night, I read the documents to you. I told you my analysis of their implications. You agree that we should move forward with these projects and that I represent you when I sign the contracts."

In front of witnesses, Jeremiah Trask had always closed his eyes once to indicate yes, afraid of the scissors or the acid that his supposed son had vowed to inflict on his eyes if he failed to obey. He couldn't bear the thought of being trapped not only in his withered body but also in the blind darkness of his mind. His mind was already dark, tortured by the countless times he'd imagined how his life would have been different if he hadn't gone to Covent Garden market that morning fifteen years earlier and seen the ragged boy desperately begging vegetable sellers for food.

Now, for the first time in eight years, he was alone with strangers. Two of them were police officers. This might be his only chance.

"We think that the man who calls himself Anthony Trask actually has the last name of O'Brien. Is that true?" the Opium-Eater asked.

Trask scrunched his eyes shut once.

"Do you know his *first* name?" the Opium-Eater continued.

Again Trask scrunched his eyes shut once.

"If you have the strength, let us assign a number to each letter in the alphabet. In that way, you can spell his name."

Trask lowered his eyelids three times.

"The letter *C*," the Opium-Eater said.

Trask calculated which number would correspond with the letter *O*. Exhausted, he pressed his eyes shut fifteen times.

Then he closed his eyes twelve times.

"*L*," the Opium-Eater said.

And nine times.

"*I*," the Opium-Eater said. "Is the next letter *N*? Is his first name Colin?"

Yes! Protect me from him! Trask inwardly screamed.

13

A Bottomless Inner World

Horseshoes thundering, the police wagon sped down Constitution Hill, passed Green Park, and stopped at the main gate to Buckingham Palace. Snow kept falling.

De Quincey and Becker jumped down among the many guards at the entrance. Officers shouted directions to soldiers. Constables took positions along the walls that bordered the palace's gardens.

As Becker showed his badge to the guards at the gate, another police wagon arrived. Commissioner Mayne hurried to join them.

"A man who matches the colonel's description was seen at the morgue in Westminster Hospital," Mayne reported. "A surgeon found him holding up the sheet that covered Catherine Grantwood's body. After attacking the surgeon, two constables, and two clerks, he escaped. He's wearing brown corduroy trousers and a matching labourer's coat. Every patrolling officer is looking for him."

"But dressed that way, he can hide among millions of labourers," Becker said, "or else he can change his appearance again."

Commissioner Mayne nodded tensely. "The palace is more heavily guarded than ever. Unless he shows himself again, I don't know what else can be done."

"Has Her Majesty been informed?"

"That's why I'm here. She's in conference with Lord Palmerston. It's better to explain everything to both of them at once."

With Mayne giving orders to constables, they gained speedy access to the palace. An escort hurried them along spectacular hallways and up the Grand Staircase.

Again they were taken to the Throne Room.

"I don't understand why Her Majesty chose so vast an area to meet with her prime minister," Mayne said.

The explanation became obvious when they were permitted to enter.

This was Lord Palmerston's first official day in office. Prime ministers weren't sworn in during a public ceremony. Instead they received their power in a symbolic private conference with Her Majesty. Queen Victoria sat on her throne. Prince Albert stood conspicuously next to her. She wore a regal tiara as she peered down from the high dais towards Lord Palmerston, who seemed uncharacteristically small—which was evidently how she and Prince Albert wanted him to view their relationship. The chill of the immense room perhaps emphasized their attitude towards him, also.

They turned, confused by the interruption.

De Quincey, Mayne, and Becker swiftly approached and bowed.

"Your Majesty, at your dinner on Sunday, do you recall our discussion about Thomas Griffiths Wainewright?" De Quincey asked.

"The murderer?" Queen Victoria nodded, continuing to look confused about the interruption. "Albert remarked that murderers must inevitably reveal their guilt by their behaviour, but you maintained that some murderers are so callous, they manage to conceal what they are. You used the example of Wainewright, with whom you shared a meal without having any suspicion of his homicidal character."

"On Sunday evening, at least one of your guests no doubt followed the conversation with great interest, Your Majesty. When Edward Oxford discharged two pistols at you fifteen years ago, do you recall a young Irish boy who ran next to your carriage, begging you to help his mother and father and sisters?" De Quincey asked.

"I have no recollection. The gunshots are all that I remember."

"No one else paid attention to him, either," De Quincey said. "The boy's mother and sisters died in Newgate. I suspect that the father suffered his own harsh fate. Since that time, the boy has plotted to avenge himself on everyone whom he begged for help."

"An Irish boy? But no one who is Irish attended Sunday's dinner," Lord Palmerston objected.

"Colonel Trask did, My Lord."

"Colonel Trask? Why do you mention him? He isn't Irish."

De Quincey merely looked at Lord Palmerston.

"You're telling me that Colonel Trask is Irish? How can that be, when his father isn't Irish? How is it possible that the father of a beggar could have become as wealthy as Jeremiah Trask?"

"We don't yet know those answers, but our thoughts often create a false reality, My Lord."

"I haven't the faintest idea what you're talking about."

"Just because everyone says that Jeremiah Trask is the colonel's father, that doesn't make it true." De Quincey turned towards Queen Victoria. "Your Majesty, Colonel Trask is the man responsible for the recent murders and the threats against you."

"A war hero who saved my cousin's life? A knight of the realm? One of the wealthiest men in the empire? No."

"His real name is Colin O'Brien, Your Majesty," Becker said, "and please believe us, with all his might, he intends to harm you."

"Colonel Trask ... Sir Anthony ... I didn't recognize you in—"

"These work clothes? I decided that I've come too far from the days when I helped my father build railways. It's a lesson to see how people react to me when I'm dressed as a labourer."

"I meant no offence, Sir Anthony."

"None taken. But I find myself short of funds and need to make a withdrawal."

"Of course. What amount do you require?"

"I wish to transfer five thousand pounds to a man who operates a carriage service in Watford."

"Five thousand pounds?" the banker asked in surprise. It was a huge sum, given that a carriage driver might earn no more than a pound or two each week.

"In service to me, his business was destroyed. I wish to repay him. I don't know his name, but he recently broke a leg, and a Doctor Gilmore in Watford can identify him. Kindly make the arrangements at once."

"Yes, Sir Anthony," the banker replied, not approving of such munificence.

"Also I require five thousand pounds in notes."

Now the banker was truly perplexed. "Are you taking a long journey?"

"Indeed."

At the end of the meeting, he put some of the banknotes in his pockets and the majority in a leather pouch.

Outside the bank, he entered a clothing shop. Knowing that the police would be searching for a man in corduroy clothes, he bought woollen ones to replace them, changing their brown to grey, a colour that would soon blend with the night and the worsening weather. He kept his workman's cap but stuffed it into his overcoat pocket and replaced it with a gentleman's top hat.

He entered a cutlery shop and bought a knife in a sheath.

By then the streets were almost deserted, only a few people shifting past him, eager to take shelter from the snow and the murderer whom newsboys were warning about. A few cabs and coaches braved the accumulation on the slippery cobblestones, but they would soon be gone.

Constables lingered, however, watching from alcoves, alert for anyone who matched the description of the man who'd fled from Westminster Hospital. But his top hat and gentleman's overcoat automatically excluded him from being the criminal they watched for. Within five minutes he passed three constables, and each time he said, "Thanks for keeping the rest of us safe."

"Just doin' my job, sir."

He entered a chophouse, which was almost empty. He crossed the red and black tiles that checkered the floor and sat at a cloth-covered table next to shimmering coals in a glowing iron-lined hearth. He hoped to absorb the heat, knowing that it might be a long time before he could get warm again—or possibly never.

"Sorry, sir, the kitchen's closed," the proprietor said, wiping his hands on an apron stretched over his large chest. "Because of the weather."

"For a sovereign, can you give me bread, butter, strawberry jam, and hot tea?"

The gold coin he set on the table was far more than anyone usually paid for those items.

"Right away, sir."

Bread, butter, strawberry jam, and hot tea had been what Jeremiah Trask offered him fifteen years earlier.

Jeremiah Trask, he thought bitterly. *You were punished, too.*

The sequence of his many victims streamed through his seething memory. He thought of the Newgate guards whose abuse had prompted Emma to strangle her mother and young Ruth and then hang herself. After ten years the guards had been released from their punishment in the nightmarish hulks. But that punishment wasn't sufficient. By then he was in a position to receive reports about them. Discovering their shabby lodgings, he'd arranged for a tavern owner to promise to bring children to them. When they eagerly responded to a knock on the door, they discovered that it was he who visited them.

He'd located the St. John's Wood constable who'd callously delivered the news about his mother's arrest. After following the constable to his lodging house, he had waited for him to go to sleep, then hurled three lanterns through his basement bedroom window, flooding the room with fiery coal oil, listening to the constable's screams as he burned to death.

He'd returned to the half-completed village in which he and his parents and sisters had lived. Because the people there had failed to offer food to his helpless sisters while he and his father struggled through the labyrinth of London's legal system, he had poisoned the village well. A month later, it had given him satisfaction to find the village abandoned, the graveyard filled with many new occupants.

The law clerks who'd scorned his father and him ... the governor of Newgate Prison who'd failed to supervise the guards ... the sergeant at the St. John's Wood police station who'd sent his mother to Newgate ... Year by year he'd advanced through his list, constantly adding to it, postponing and yet relentlessly approaching the culmination of his revenge: the destruction of those who most deserved to be punished.

"Here's your bread, butter, jam, and hot tea, sir."

In the Crimea, he would have given anything for a simple meal like this before he went into battle. He needed his strength. There was much to do.

Mother.

Father.

Emma.

Ruth.

Something switched in his mind, other victims joining the litany of those for whom he grieved.

My wife.

My unborn child.

I want to die.

"Surely if we remain in the palace, he can't reach us," Prince Albert said.

"Indeed, you're surrounded by constables and soldiers, Your Highness," Commissioner Mayne confirmed.

"But how long can the palace be guarded this way? Weeks? Months?" Prince Albert persisted.

"If necessary, Your Highness."

"Longer than that?"

The commissioner glanced down. "We're searching for him, Your Highness. He needs shelter and food. He can't escape us forever."

"But he has such immense resources. He's been channelling his rage for fifteen years. His patience is infinite," Prince Albert said.

"No," Queen Victoria interrupted. "I refuse to allow it."

"Your Majesty?" Commissioner Mayne asked in surprise.

"With so many soldiers outside the palace day after day, possibly for weeks and months, the people on the street will wonder why we feel the need for so much additional protection. The people might even think we fear that the Russians are about to invade."

"We could go to Windsor Castle," Prince Albert proposed. "The increased guards would be less conspicuous there."

Becker walked to a curtain and pulled it open, revealing snow that streaked past a tall window. Shadows thickened.

"You wouldn't be able to travel until tomorrow at the earliest, Your Highness. How many coaches would you need for yourselves, your children, and your staff?"

"Too many to avoid attracting attention," a voice said.

They turned towards the interruption.

Ryan entered the room, leaning against Emily. Becker ran to him.

"Inspector Ryan," Queen Victoria said, "you have blood on your coat."

"I reopened the wound I received seven weeks ago, Your Majesty." As Ryan reached a chair near the dais, Emily and Becker helped him ease onto it. "Dr. Snow has bandaged me securely." Ryan winced. "Perhaps *too* securely."

"You shouldn't be here." Showing her fondness for Ryan, the queen descended from the dais and walked towards him. "You need to rest."

"When this is over, Your Majesty. All the time I was at Dr. Snow's office, I kept thinking that the palace is exactly where I needed to be, protecting you as I did fifteen years ago."

"Your loyalty touches me."

"I would die for you," Ryan said. "I heard you consider shifting locations to Windsor Castle. Your Majesty, you'd need so many coaches that you couldn't possibly do it in secret."

"Perhaps if we prepared *several* groups of coaches and sent them to different places," Lord Palmerston offered. "The colonel couldn't know which of them to follow."

"But what would the newspapers make of numerous coaches leaving all at once and in all directions?" Queen Victoria objected. Although her voice was high pitched, it carried remarkable authority. "The result would be the same. With so much confusion, the people on the street would decide that we're in a state of panic, presumably because of a Russian threat. Our enemy would take heart while our soldiers lost morale. No. While the storm persists, assign as many guards to protect the palace as you can. But when the weather clears . . ."

"Your Majesty, to make sure that I understand,"

Commissioner Mayne said, "are you truly suggesting that tomorrow, to project confidence to your subjects, you wish the guards to be reduced to their usual number?"

His direction took him past the gentlemen's clubs on Pall Mall.

Despite his respectable appearance, a constable stopped him.

"If you don't mind me asking, sir, what's your business?"

"I'm on a personal errand to deliver a large amount of money to a lord whose identity I'm not permitted to reveal."

"Large amount of money?"

"Five thousand pounds in banknotes."

He opened the leather pouch and invited the constable to aim his lantern at it. The constable had never seen that much money in his life. He inhaled sharply.

"Best be on your way and finish your business in a hurry, sir. There's a bad man on the streets."

Two other constables stopped him as he made his way towards Green Park. By now the snow was so thick and the light so dim that they definitely needed their lanterns.

"You're not safe out here with that much money. Hurry to your destination, sir."

When he reached Green Park, he grabbed the spikes on the metal railing and vaulted the barrier, landing and rolling in the snow.

He remembered vaulting the railing fifteen years earlier, fleeing a mob that accused him of taking part in Edward Oxford's attempt against the queen. He re-experienced the agony when a spike pierced one of his legs and he limped painfully away, bleeding. Back then, after his family died, he had spent so many weeks in Green Park, finding refuge in it, even sleeping there, that he felt at home.

Now, as snowflakes stung his cheeks, he threw away his top

hat and replaced it with his worker's cap. He also threw away the pouch of money. It was too bulky to keep with him, and he had no further use for it. Eventually, a poor soul would find the money and thank God for it.

Proceeding through the cover of the storm, he reached the section of the railing across from the palace. He was only a few feet from where he had begged the queen to help his family and where Edward Oxford had shot at her.

In the gloom he pressed against a tree, his grey clothes blending with it. A lantern moved along the opposite side of the fence. Abruptly, another lantern came from the opposite direction.

"See anythin'?" a murky shape asked.

"All quiet. As much as I hate this weather, at least we'll see footprints if anybody crosses towards the palace."

"Unless this blasted snow falls harder and fills them."

"No chance. I counted how long it takes me to walk my section. Forty seconds from end to end. Even a blizzard wouldn't fill tracks *that* fast."

"I hear the man we're lookin' for was in the Crimea. He's used to runnin' and bein' in the cold."

"After we catch him, he'll be sorry he didn't stay in the Crimea."

The figures parted. Their lanterns going in opposite directions, the men faded into the falling snow.

He moved farther along and reached a gate. From the protection of another tree, he watched one of the silhouettes walk past.

He quietly opened the gate and followed. Approaching close enough to see a constable's uniform, he thrust a gloved hand over the man's nose and mouth. With his other gloved hand he grabbed the constable's throat while tugging him backward.

As the man struggled, he gripped tighter, suffocating the

constable while at the same time breaking his larynx. He pulled the dying man through the open gate and into the park, leaving deliberately obvious marks in the snow. All the while, he counted.

Forty seconds from end to end. That was how much time the constable had said it took him to walk his section.

Thirty-three, thirty-four, thirty-five.

The constable went limp.

He dropped him in the snow and hurried backwards along the tracks he'd made. He leapt for a tree branch and pulled himself up, climbing to the opposite side of the tree, his grey clothes again blending with it.

"Help! He's got me! Hurry! He's *killing* me!" he shouted, directing his voice towards the ground.

The other constable would have become suspicious by now, expecting to see his counterpart again before they turned and retraced their steps along the railing.

"Help!" he repeated.

Boots hurried through the snow, coming from the left. He heard someone else charging from the right.

Two shadows raced through the open gate.

"Tracks! Someone was dragged!"

"The blighter's in the park!"

He heard other steps, this time from across the street. Vaguely visible in the darkness and falling snow, two more constables raced through the open gate.

After they had rushed below him, he dropped, landing on their path. He walked backwards in the tracks that came from the opposite side of the street.

"That's Harry!" a man yelled from the park. "The bastard killed him!"

"But where'd he go? I see *our* tracks but nobody else's!"

He reached the gloom on the other side of Constitution Hill. Having scouted this location many times, he knew that a tree stood across from the park gate he had used. It was next to the wall that protected the palace gardens. The nearest branch was so high that only a man of his height could reach it, provided that he jumped up with sufficient force. Remaining in the tracks that one of the constables had made, he leapt.

"Go back the way we came!" a man shouted from the park.

Dangling, he flexed his arms and pulled himself up.

"Search the other side of the street!" someone ordered.

He straddled the branch and squirmed along it. Although he couldn't avoid dislodging snow from it, he hoped that the constables would pay more attention to the top of the wall, where the snow was undisturbed. The growing wind tossed the tree's branches, shaking snow from all of them, so perhaps it wouldn't seem unusual that this particular branch was barer than the others.

He heard the frenzied breathing of constables as they ran from the park.

"Search everywhere!"

"But we made so many tracks, how will we know which are *his?*"

The opposite side of the wall was lined with evergreen shrubs separated by areas where flowers presumably grew in the spring. He swung down and dropped between bushes.

A lantern approached. This time, the guard was a soldier. Wearing a greatcoat, the man passed the bushes, his head down, searching for tracks.

The revenger lunged, again pressing a gloved hand over his target's mouth and nose while using the other hand to clutch the throat. He pulled the struggling man behind the bushes and kept choking until arms and legs shuddered and the body lay still.

In a rush he removed the soldier's greatcoat and put it on. He shoved his worker's cap into a pocket and grabbed the soldier's helmet.

A voice called an indistinct name. Able to secure only two buttons on the coat, he picked up the lantern and stepped onto the path that the soldier had made. He proceeded in the voice's direction.

A figure came near. "Corporal?" a voice asked.

The insignia on the newcomer's uniform indicated that the man was a sergeant, who relaxed when he recognized an army coat and the outline of the helmet.

"What were you doin'?" The sergeant shielded his eyes from the light. "Relievin' yourself in the queen's shrubbery?"

He struck a fist to the sergeant's throat, shattering his voice box. He pressed a gloved hand over the sergeant's mouth so that the man's frantic wheezing couldn't be heard. He dragged him behind the bushes.

Two other sentries needed to be killed before he saw the back of the palace through the blowing snow.

"Your Highness, at one time was your dining room located next to the area in which your guests assembled on Sunday evening?" De Quincey asked. "It would have been reached through a door that now leads to a servants' area."

"What sort of question . . .?" Lord Palmerston muttered.

Prince Albert answered, "Yes. Recently we moved the dining room to a new location. How did you know?"

"On Sunday evening, before we went in to dinner, Emily and I spoke with Colonel Trask and the Duke of Cambridge. The colonel gestured towards a door and seemed to think that the dining room was on the other side. The duke explained his error."

"A simple mistake," Lord Palmerston said. "Anyone could have made it."

"But it was *Colonel Trask* who made it," De Quincey noted. "The Irish boy who begged Her Majesty to save his mother and father and sisters."

"I don't see how Colonel Trask could possibly have known where the dining room used to be located," Prince Albert said.

"Eight years ago you renovated the palace, is that correct, Your Highness?"

"Yes. To create the east wing. But the work didn't involve the dining room, which, as I said, remained in its former location until recently."

"Apart from you and your architect, who else supervised the work eight years ago, Your Highness?"

"The Cubitt brothers. Their firm is quite respectable. They built many homes in Bloomsbury and Belgravia."

"No one else, Your Highness?" De Quincey asked. "The task must have been enormous."

"Naturally they employed various contractors who had large numbers of labourers," Prince Albert said.

"And one particular man had an abundance of labourers," De Quincey said.

Prince Albert looked confused, then suddenly understood. "Heaven help me, I remember. One of the contractors was Jeremiah Trask. The colonel would have had access to the architectural plans for the palace."

As the implication struck them, everyone became silent, the only sound the howling of the storm outside.

A door opened, its sharp echo startling them.

"Your Majesty," a servant announced, "there's a police sergeant with an urgent message for Commissioner Mayne."

Covered with melting snow, the sergeant hurried into the immense room. When he discovered that he was in the presence of Queen Victoria and Prince Albert, he looked flustered and bowed.

"Commissioner, may I speak to you in private?"

"You may deliver your message to everyone."

After an uncertain look at the queen, the sergeant obeyed. "Sir, a constable was killed in Green Park."

"What?"

"And we found three dead soldiers in the palace gardens. The killer stole one of their greatcoats."

"Which means he can now pose as a guard," Becker said.

The light in the Throne Room suddenly changed. All along the wall, the gas lamps dimmed. Their flames sputtered, going out. The only illumination came from the flickering coals in the fireplaces, emphasizing the shadows.

"He's inside the palace," Ryan said.

Continuing the Journal of Emily De Quincey

Although I could no longer see the remote corners and door-ways of the Throne Room, the vast, dark area seemed to grow larger rather than shrink. I imagined infinite threats accumulating in now-mysterious recesses.

"Bring lanterns and candles!" Prince Albert told the suddenly invisible servant at the door.

"Put a constable in every hallway!" Commissioner Mayne ordered the sergeant who'd delivered the alarming news. "Warn the soldiers that the killer is dressed like one of them!"

Despite the urgent commands, the men couldn't rush to obey. They were trapped in the darkness, just as we ourselves were. Only when the servant lit a candle were they able to hurry along the corridor outside, their diminishing shadows ghostly.

I heard Commissioner Mayne take something from his pocket. A scraping sound on a box was followed by the igni-tion of a lucifer match.

In the faint light Sean said, "There's a candle on the table next to me."

The commissioner quickly lit the wick and then saw another, lighting it also.

"If the colonel's attempting to toy with us, he hasn't

accomplished much," Prince Albert said, showing a brave face. "In my youth, all I had was candlelight."

"Your Majesty, how many of your children are in residence?" Lord Palmerston asked.

"Seven. Our oldest son, Edward, is at Windsor Castle."

"We need to place constables outside their rooms."

"No, bring the children together," Sean murmured in pain. "Here. Bring them all here. They'll be easier to protect if they're all in one place."

"Or perhaps easier to reach," Father said.

Sean's voice tightened. "Indeed, the colonel has us in a position where every choice can be wrong."

"I hear something," I told the group.

"The snow blowing against the windows," Queen Victoria said.

"No, something else, Your Majesty. A hiss."

I moved along the wall.

"The lamp up here," I said. "The gas is flowing again."

"I smell it!" Commissioner Mayne said.

He lit another match and ignited the gas lamp.

Lord Palmerston rushed to other lamps and did the same. There were many. By the time they reached the ones on the opposite wall, the gas had accumulated sufficiently that there was a tiny blast of flame when a match was applied.

"Prince Albert, how many gas lamps does the palace contain?" Ryan asked.

"I don't have a precise number. Four hundred. Perhaps more."

"At this moment, most of those several hundred lamps are spewing gas," Ryan said. "Will Colonel Trask have made it impossible to turn off the gas once more? If so, how long will it take the servants to relight every lamp? Will they locate all of them? Are there lamps in the basement or the attic or in various rooms that will continue to release gas until it reaches sufficient volume to cause an explosion? Quickly—we need to gather your children and get everyone out of the palace."

Movement caught my attention. I turned towards the dais and the throne. The rest of the group did the same.

Wearing an army greatcoat, the grey colour of steel, Colonel Trask emerged from the pink curtains that hung behind the throne. Like decorations for a stage play, they revealed a door that Her Majesty presumably used for special entrances.

The colonel's sudden appearance wasn't as shocking as what he carried.

"Leopold," Queen Victoria said in alarm.

The delicate-looking, frightened boy appeared to be two years of age. His forehead was bandaged, reminding me of something Her Majesty had mentioned during Sunday's dinner.

"Has Prince Leopold recovered from his injury?" the Duke of Cambridge had asked.

The queen had responded, *"Thank you, yes. The cut on his forehead finally stopped bleeding. Even Dr. Snow is at a loss to explain why the slightest of falls can cause Leopold to bleed so profusely."*

This was Her Majesty's youngest son.

Colonel Trask no longer presented himself with the control, discipline, and military bearing that he had displayed when I first saw him at St. James's Church. Now his movements were abrupt and impatient. His once-noble, handsome features were distorted by rage. He sat on the throne and placed the child roughly on his left knee, positioning him the way I had once seen an entertainer place a puppet in order to project his voice through it.

With one hand, the colonel gripped the back of the child's neck. With the other, he held the point of a knife against the boy's cheek.

"Lord Palmerston, call out to the servants that Her Majesty doesn't wish to be disturbed. Then close the doors," Colonel Trask ordered. His Irish accent was far stronger than it had been when I heard him say Catherine's name in his restless sleep the previous night. "If a slight fall causes the boy to bleed uncontrollably, imagine what a nick from my knife can do."

The boy's eyes were wide with terror.

"Lord Palmerston, do what I tell you. Don't test my resolve," the colonel warned.

His Lordship went to a doorway and leaned out, telling a servant, "We are in conference with Her Majesty. She doesn't wish to be interrupted."

He shut the door.

"Good. Now, everyone, step closer," the colonel told us from the throne as the boy squirmed on his knee.

We obeyed.

"I'm certain that Dr. Snow is gifted at determining that a cholera epidemic can be caused by a cesspit-contaminated water pump in Soho," Trask said. "But he is ignorant in many other matters, such as why your son bleeds."

The colonel's anger made his usually handsome features cling to his facial bones, emphasizing his skull.

My stomach felt cold.

"Evidently I'm more curious than you, Victoria," the colonel said.

It was shocking to hear the queen's name without her title.

"Months ago, when I learned about your son's condition, I sent men around the world—to the greatest universities and hospitals—to find out if anyone could explain the disease. Can you believe that in the American city of Philadelphia, of all places, a Dr. John Otto conducted an early study of the so-called bleeding disease? But it is Dr. Friedrich Hopff at the University of Zurich who has thoroughly explained the disorder. He calls it 'haemophilia,' which Mr. De Quincey, with his knowledge of Greek, can no doubt translate for us."

"Blood love," Father said.

Colonel Trask nodded. "A disease of the blood produced by love, by mating. Only boys contract the ailment, Victoria. Their mothers carry it and pass it along without showing symptoms."

"No," Queen Victoria said.

"Your child lacks an element in his blood that would normally cause it to thicken when he's injured. He's doomed to be a bleeder because of you. The disease lurks within you. It waited to be released when you married your close cousin and mingled bloodlines that should have stayed apart. If your daughters weren't going to die tonight, if they had the chance to marry and give birth, they too could pass the disease to male children and contaminate the royal houses of Europe. It's a sign of your rottenness, Victoria."

"Damn you," Prince Albert said.

"Albert, we are all damned," Colonel Trask said. Again it was a shock to hear the prince's given name used nakedly.

The colonel looked at me with the same odd expression that he'd shown the first time we met.

"Em—" he stuttered. "Emily, I want you to leave. You don't belong here."

"I'm staying with Father."

"Then your father can leave also. I don't want you here. Take your chance and go. Inspector Ryan and Sergeant Becker can leave as well. I have nothing against them. I applaud their skill."

Holding his abdomen, Sean grimaced and managed to stand. "I'll remain with Her Majesty."

"I'm staying with Her Majesty, too," Joseph said.

"Do whatever you foolishly want. But Victoria, Albert, Commissioner Mayne, and Lord Palmerston remain."

"For how long?" Lord Palmerston demanded.

"Until the palace explodes and kills us, of course. If any of you attempt to leave, I'll nick the little boy's face, and he'll bleed to death. It's an interesting dilemma. Victoria and Albert, you can run and save yourselves, at the expense of your son's life. Or you can stay and hope that I'll show mercy, that you and your son can somehow escape before a servant lights a match and ignites a lamp that's near a pocket of gas. I assure you that the room containing the main gas valve is no longer accessible and that the basement and the attic are now filled with fumes. What do you suppose would win you and your son a reprieve? Let us think. Do you suppose begging me would help? Try saying to me, 'Please let my son live.' "

The colonel's voice suddenly changed. His Irish accent now belonged to a little boy.

I shivered.

"Please help my mother and father and sisters," he said.

At the same time, he tilted Prince Leopold's head up and down, as if moving a puppet. He made it seem that the Irish voice came from the child.

"Stop!" Prince Albert demanded.

Colonel Trask pressed the tip of the knife harder against the boy's cheek, making an impression in the skin.

"Instead of giving orders, you ought to beg as desperately as *I* begged. *'Please help my mother and father and sisters,'* " he said in that Irish accent that seemed to come from the child on his knee. "Now beg *me!* Get down on your knees and say, 'Please save my son.' "

Father surprised me, stepping forward.

"Colonel Trask, having lost a child of your own, you understand how agonizing a parent's grief is. I'm surprised that you're willing to put anyone's child in jeopardy."

"What are you talking about?"

"The murder of your unborn child, Colonel Trask, a murder for which you are responsible," Father said.

"My name is Colin! I had no unborn child!"

"But Colonel Trask did, and he was also responsible for the murder of his wife."

Suddenly the colonel's bearing changed, no longer compacted in rigid fury but instead assuming a military posture. Similarly, the Irish accent was gone, and the London voice I knew as Colonel Trask's exclaimed, "It was a mistake!"

"Did you love Catherine, or was your marriage to her only a further means to punish her parents?" Father asked.

The Irish voice returned, seeming to come through the frightened child. Fury again shrank his features, making his face like a skull. "They all deserved to die for what happened to my family!"

"Yes, we learned that your mother and your two sisters perished horribly in prison," Father said.

"Emma with her wondrous blue eyes. Ruth with the gap in her smile where a tooth had fallen out, but her smile continued to be radiant."

Those words shocked me. A mystery that had troubled me for days was solved. Now I understood why he wanted me in particular to leave.

I stepped forward.

"Colin, what happened to your father?" I asked.

"He died in the filth of an alley, consumed with a raging fever. No doctor would help him."

Father's voice broke as he quoted from one of his essays. " 'The horrors that madden the grief that gnaws at the heart.' "

"Take your daughter and go!"

"Colin, look at me," I said.

He turned. His gaze was filled with an intensity that chilled me.

"I won't leave you," I told him.

"Go!" he pleaded, sobbing.

"Colonel Trask, why was your mother arrested for shop-lifting?" Father asked.

"My name is *Colin!* We were newly arrived from Ireland." He spoke swiftly, unable to contain his outrage. "We lived in a half-built village four miles outside St. John's Wood. Father did carpentry work to help complete the village. Mother tried to make friends with the neighbours, who were suspicious of our origins. One of them was more open than the others. When she saw that my mother had a skill for knitting, she suggested that Mother take some of it to a shop in St. John's Wood to earn money. The shop was owned by a man named Burbridge."

"The merchant who accused your mother of stealing," Father said.

"No matter how hungry we were, my mother would never have dreamed of stealing! Each night she read the Bible to my father and my sisters. That's how she taught my sisters and me to read."

"And yet Burbridge accused her," Father said.

"I couldn't understand it. Only after I grew older did I have the strength to force him to explain why he did it. The neighbour whom my mother tried to befriend was Burbridge's sister. One day when he visited our village, he noticed my mother and was taken by her beauty. He told his sister to suggest to my mother that she bring her knitting to his shop."

"But why did he accuse her of stealing?"

"It was his intention . . . I cannot speak of this in front of Em—" again he seemed to stutter—"Emily."

I became more certain of why he looked at me the way he did.

"I believe I understand," I told him, stepping even closer. "It might be easier if I say it for you. Burbridge wished to extract private favors from your mother in exchange for withdrawing his accusation. Because your mother was Irish, she was at his mercy."

Tears trickled down his cheeks.

"The law moved too fast," he said. "She was transferred to Newgate before Burbridge had a chance to speak to my mother at the local jail and try to make his bargain. Then my father confronted Burbridge in his shop. Burbridge decided that the situation was out of control. He remained silent."

"The law will punish him," Commissioner Mayne vowed.

"For bringing false charges against an Irishwoman? Ha. The punishment would be only a few months in prison. No need. Burbridge received his punishment long ago. I forced him to eat strands of yarn until he choked and died."

Someone gasped.

The colonel looked at Queen Victoria with contempt while pressing the knife to her son's cheek.

"I could have shot you easily in one of your many public outings. But that would not have been sufficient. Four years ago, at the Crystal Palace Exhibition, I stood among the audience at the opening ceremonies. A Chinaman wearing a colourful costume stepped from the crowd and approached you. I was astonished. With all the guards positioned in the Crystal Palace, not one of them tried to stop the Chinaman from reaching you. Because of his costume, almost everyone assumed that he was the Chinese ambassador, but he could have been anyone. He was introduced to you, to Albert, and even to your children. He walked with you as you proceeded through the many displays at the exhibition. You gave him your confidence when in reality he turned out to be no more than a local merchant who wanted publicity for a museum of curiosities that he maintained on a junk on the river.

"From that day, I devoted myself to becoming a version of that Chinaman. How could I trick you into welcoming me?

How could I become a friend? My wealth wouldn't be sufficient, because the dirt from building railways never washed off me. I needed an advantage, and when the war occurred, I found it. I paid for an officer's commission that placed me near your cousin's unit. I made the acquaintance of William Russell and arranged for him to see me in battle. Russell depicted me as a hero fighting for England, but the truth is, with each enemy soldier I killed, I imagined I was killing *you*. And you and you and you." He pointed towards Prince Albert, Commissioner Mayne, and Lord Palmerston. "But most of all *you*, Victoria. When I saved the life of your cousin, my plan was secured. It gave me satisfaction that you would never expect death from someone you had knighted, someone who sat with you at dinner, someone you had invited into your life."

"But then you caused the death of your wife and your unborn child," Father said.

"I had no wife or unborn child," the Irish voice insisted.

"But Colonel Trask did. There is no such thing as forgetting."

"I recall my mother and father and Emma and Ruth very clearly." The Irish voice deepened in anger.

"But not your wife and your unborn child? I cannot tell if Colin is an alien creature living within Colonel Trask or if Colonel Trask is an alien creature living within Colin. But at the moment, I wish to speak to Colonel Trask."

As the man on the queen's throne pressed the knife against the boy's cheek, more tears leaked from his eyes.

"Answer me, Colonel," Father demanded. "Did you love Catherine, or did you marry her and conceive a child as a way of achieving revenge against her parents?"

"The shock on their faces was perfect," the Irish voice said.

"My wife," another voice said. It belonged to Colonel Trask. "My unborn child."

"Tell me about Jeremiah Trask."

The sudden hate in his eyes was blinding. I had never seen such utter rage.

Abruptly, a fist pounded on one of the doors. From outside a man shouted, "Your Majesty!"

"Order him to go away," the Irish voice demanded as he gripped the child's neck tighter.

Before anyone could respond, a constable charged in.

"Your Majesty, we need to evacuate the—!"

The policeman's voice froze when he saw what was happening.

The knife caused blood to drip from Prince Leopold's cheek.

"Colin," I said, no longer able to postpone what I needed to do.

Something shifted in his expression.

I moved towards the steps. "Look at my blue eyes, Colin. The first time you saw them, you recognized me. What is my name?"

"Emily."

I climbed the steps to the dais. "Emma. Emily. Emma. Emily."

"Emma," Colin said.

"Yes! Emma! I'm ashamed of you!"

"What?" the Irish voice asked in shock.

"You never bullied Ruth and me! Now look what you did to this boy! Only a monster would make a child bleed!"

"Monster?"

"Give me that knife!"

In my frenzy I was able to pull the knife from his grasp. I dropped it onto the dais and pried his fingers from the back of the boy's neck.

"Leave the child alone!"

I tugged the boy away and lowered him to Prince

Albert. The previous night, seeing the brutality that had been inflicted upon Catherine and her parents, I had wished for the strength of a man to punish whoever was responsible.

Now I spun. With all my strength, I slapped him across the face.

The next time I struck him, I used my fist, knocking him against the back of the throne. This way and that, with one fist and then another, I struck and struck and struck, ignoring the pain in my knuckles. The fury that I'd felt for days became stronger and stronger.

"You didn't deserve Emma and Ruth!" I screamed. "You didn't deserve Catherine! You didn't deserve to be a brother! You didn't deserve to be a husband or a father! For threatening a helpless child, this is what you deserve!"

I kept striking him, suddenly aware that my hands were smeared with blood, both mine and his.

A roar of emotion filled my ears. Through it, I heard shouts and someone charging up the steps to the dais. I was suddenly aware of Joseph running towards us. Colin hurled me into him, then picked up the knife and threw it.

In a blur I saw the knife speed towards the queen. In another blur I saw a man step before her.

Joseph and I crashed to the dais.

When I looked up, the curtains behind the throne billowed as the colonel disappeared through the hidden door.

Becker swept the curtains aside and rushed through the door. He entered a waiting area that the queen presumably used before emerging dramatically into the Throne Room for state functions. Dim illumination from the Throne Room behind him allowed him to see an open door that led to a dark corridor.

The odour of gas made him cough. He turned off the gas

jet on a wall lamp. Then he cautiously entered the corridor, where he heard a man racing down shadowy stairs to the left.

Becker did his best to hurry after him, but he was forced to slow his pace when he bumped into a landing. Turning, he groped along a banister into deeper darkness.

Below him, the hurried steps became fainter. Hearing the hiss of gas, Becker stopped just long enough to feel along a wall and turn off the valve on another lamp. Descending, he closed the valve on yet another.

The air got colder. He felt a stone floor and realized that he had reached the bottom level. Warily opening a door, he saw grey light from barred windows along another corridor.

In a rush, Becker opened all of the windows, dispelling the gas. As cold wind streamed in, he closed the valve on every lamp he found.

He reached an unbolted door. Snow lay before it, evidently having been blown in when the door was opened. Becker pulled up his right trouser leg, withdrew the knife strapped above his ankle, and pushed it open.

Dim tracks in the snow led away from the palace. As he ran after them, gusts made it difficult for him to see. Having left his coat, gloves, and cap in the palace, he felt numbed.

As much as Becker could tell in the gloom, he was racing across the queen's gardens. *Trask might circle around and come at me from behind,* he thought. *Or will he take his chance to escape and attack the queen another time?*

He saw the army greatcoat where it had been abandoned in the snow. Now he couldn't tell the soldiers and the constables what Trask was wearing.

The tracks led to a wall. Next to it was a tree. In the shadows Becker saw that a branch above him was bare of snow. Had Trask leapt to it and crawled along it towards the—?

He sensed quick motion behind him. As something streaked

towards his head, intense pain made him sink to his knees. His vision blurred.

The pain struck again and sent him sprawling.

"Got 'im!" a voice yelled. "The sod's down! This 'un won't be threatenin' the queen again!"

Lord Palmerston gripped his arm, where the knife meant for the queen had struck him.

"You rushed in front of me," Queen Victoria said in disbelief.

"I vowed to be your loyal prime minister," Lord Palmerston told her as blood dripped from his sleeve. Pain made his features pale against his brown-dyed sideburns. "I know your low opinion of me, Your Majesty, but in ways that you can never imagine, I devoted my life to you. I would do *anything* to ensure your safety. Right now, however, all that matters is your son."

Prince Albert continued to hold the terrified child. From a drop on the boy's cheek, the blood had become a relentless stream that pooled on the floor.

"When he last bled this severely, he nearly died," Prince Albert said.

Emily tore a strip from her bloomer skirt and applied it to the cut. Quickly, the cloth became soaked.

"You need to take him to Dr. Snow," Queen Victoria urged.

"There's no time," Emily managed to say, "but we do need snow. Seven weeks ago, ice kept Sean from bleeding to death. Maybe snow will work the same way."

De Quincey and Commissioner Mayne ran to one of the room's tall windows, pushed it open, and hurried back with handfuls of snow.

Prince Albert set the boy on the floor and held his hand.

"Leopold, we're here with you," Queen Victoria said. "Don't be afraid."

The boy nodded, although his eyes communicated how much he was indeed frightened.

Emily turned Leopold on his side and pressed the snow to his cheek. *So small a cut and so much blood,* she thought.

The snow became crimson.

As Emily ripped another piece from her skirt, De Quincey and Commissioner Mayne hurried to bring more snow.

Emily compacted it and covered the boy's cheek with it, placing the new strip of cloth over it so that the heat from her hands wouldn't melt the snow.

Again the cloth turned crimson—but less quickly.

Looking paler, Lord Palmerston swayed as he clutched his wounded arm.

"Commissioner Mayne, please tie a cravat around His Lordship's arm," Emily said.

"You need more cloths," Prince Albert said. "Take my handkerchief."

"And mine," Commissioner Mayne said.

Emily pressed more snow against Leopold's cheek. "His cheek should be numb, tightening his blood vessels, slowing the flow. Good. I think it's stopping. I think he's—"

The lamps sputtered. Once more the room plunged into blackness. Footsteps rushed through a doorway.

"It's Colonel Trask!" Queen Victoria said in alarm.

"No, a police sergeant, Your Majesty," a voice said. "*We're* the ones who shut off the gas this time. The intruder jammed the lock on the control room. It took us a long while to force our way in and close the valve. We're opening every window. Until the danger's eliminated, you need to leave the palace."

"But Colonel Trask is still out there," Prince Albert said.

Using a key that he kept hidden behind a loose brick at the back of the house, he entered the kitchen on Bolton Street.

It was deserted. He followed voices and the odour of recently fried lamb chops, stopping in the doorway to the room where the servants ate their meals.

The four of them looked up, astonished by the blood on his face.

"Good heavens, sir," the maid said, "you startled me."

"If you knocked at the front door, I didn't hear," the doorman said. "Your face . . . What happened to you, Colonel?"

"It doesn't matter."

"The police came here earlier, looking for you. They insisted on seeing your father, but I'm afraid his mind has failed."

"What makes you say that?"

"In the limited way he has of communicating, he claimed that you weren't his son and that you were actually an Irishman named Colin O'Brien. What nonsense. The constable stayed with him, waiting to speak with you."

"Colin O'Brien?"

"You sound as if you know someone with that name, Colonel."

"Indeed," Colin said.

They gasped when he revealed his Irish accent.

"Who has the key to this door?" Colin asked.

"I . . . I do," the housekeeper managed to reply.

"Give it to me."

Colin set down two hundred pounds in banknotes that he'd taken from the pouch before abandoning it. "This should tide you over until you find new employment. Thank you for your service."

"But . . ."

Colin locked the door.

With the snow falling outside, the house felt muffled as he climbed to the entrance level and walked to an umbrella stand near the front door. In addition to umbrellas, the stand contained a silver-knobbed walking stick, hidden in open view.

Holding it, he climbed to the next level and the level after that, his footsteps soft on the carpet.

When he opened the door to Jeremiah Trask's bedroom, a man's voice asked, "Come to get the dishes, have you? I never tasted better lamb chops."

Entering, Colin found a constable seated at a small table with lamb bones on a dish in front of him.

The constable gaped. Rising in alarm, groping for his truncheon, he accidentally upended the table. Colin struck the walking stick across his head and knocked him onto the floor.

Jeremiah Trask lay motionless beneath the covers of his bed—motionless except for his eyes, whose pupils grew larger as Colin approached. The eyes moved desperately from Colin's blood-covered face to the blood on the knob of the walking stick he clutched.

"I understand that you answered questions for people you shouldn't have," Colin said.

Jeremiah Trask's eyes projected as much panic as a scream would have.

"Tonight I failed to punish the queen," Colin said. "I had the opportunity to destroy her—and I failed. But *someone's* going to be punished."

Tears leaked from Jeremiah Trask's eyes. How different his withered body was from the strong, able man he'd been fifteen years earlier when he'd visited Covent Garden market and seen the desperate Irish boy begging for food.

Damn me, why didn't I walk away? he thought. *Why did I let my weakness destroy me?*

At first glance there'd been nothing different about the boy compared to the others who roamed the teeming market and begged for food. His cheeks were as gaunt, his hair as scruffy, his clothes as filthy.

But there was something about the boy's determination.

Keeping a distance, Trask had followed him through the chaos of the market.

He watched as the boy reached for an apple and a stall owner struck his hand.

In another aisle, the boy reached for a potato. This time the stall owner struck the side of his head.

"Pay or I'll summon a constable."

"I don't have any money. I'll work for food."

"Bother someone else."

The boy picked crushed cabbage leaves from the flagstones, hardly making a face as his teeth no doubt crunched on grit that was mixed with the leaves.

The next day Jeremiah Trask returned and saw the boy approaching the same stall owners.

And the day after that.

"You again! Don't you get tired?"

"Give me food, and I'll work harder than anybody ever worked for you."

"Take this apple, and don't come back."

"I'll take it only if I work for it."

The stall owner sighed. "Make a pile of those empty sacks and put 'em in the back."

Afterwards, the man tossed the boy the apple. "Yeah, you're hungry all right. I never saw anybody eat an apple so fast. Even the core."

"Maybe you have another job for me."

"Oh? What makes you think so?"

"The way you're shiftin' your weight from boot to boot. You look like you need to use the necessary."

"The what?"

"That's what my mother called the privy." The boy's voice trembled when he mentioned his mother. "You don't have anybody to watch the stall when you use the necessary."

"My wife's usually here. She's sick."

"When you go to the necessary, I bet people steal from you."

"It can't be avoided."

"Today it can. Have you got a stick? Give it to me. Nobody's goin' to steal from you while you're gone."

"God help me, I need to go so bad I'm leavin' a shoeless boy to watch my stall."

As the man hurried away, two beggars approached.

The boy cracked one of them across the head and bared his teeth at the other. "I work for the man who owns this stall! If you want more of this stick, step closer!"

"Hey," a constable demanded. "What's this about?"

"These beggars tried to steal from here."

"And *you* didn't try to steal also, I suppose?" the constable demanded.

"I work here."

"Certainly you do. You're comin' with *me*."

"Hey, what's the trouble?" the returning stall owner asked.

"This Irish beggar claims he works for you. He struck this one here and looked like he was about to do the same to the other."

"Oh, did he now?" The stall owner smiled and tossed the boy another apple.

Chomping on it, the boy looked in Trask's direction and noticed him watching. With a chuckle, Trask turned away.

The stall owner's wife died the next day. The day after that, the man sold his business, and the new owner told the boy to go away, summoning a constable to emphasize the point.

But the boy refused to be discouraged. Not only was he determined; he also had imagination. Seeing that many farmers couldn't get their carts close to the stalls, the boy told one of them, "I'll watch your cart for a penny while you deliver your baskets and sacks."

"Steal from me is what you'll do."

"I worked for Ned, the stall owner, until his wife died. *He'll* tell you I can keep the beggars away."

The farmer frowned at the gathering crowd. "Stealin's always a problem."

"For a penny, it ain't a problem any longer. Just give me your horse whip."

"A horse whip, eh? You're a tough 'un, are you?"

"As tough as I need to be. Deliver your baskets and sacks. No one'll steal from you."

"If you trick me, I'll find you and give you a whippin'."

"What you'll give me is a penny."

When the farmer returned, he saw the beggars keeping their distance.

"Looks like you didn't have any trouble." The farmer picked up another basket.

"Well, we did for a moment, but everythin's fine now."

One of the beggars held a blood-streaked chin.

"Hey, did you say a penny to guarantee nobody steals from my cart?" another farmer asked.

When the last of them drove away, the boy held five pennies.

He looked up warily as Jeremiah Trask approached, offering his hand.

"What's your name, boy?"

"Who wants to know?"

Trask laughed. "You're right to be suspicious of everyone. But perhaps I can help you. My name is Jeremiah Trask. And yours is . . ."

The boy hesitated.

"What harm can there be if you say your name to someone who offers help?"

". . . Colin O'Brien."

"Irish."

The boy bristled. "Does that bother you?"

"Performance matters, not origins. I'm pleased that you

gave your formal name and not a nickname. If you expect to rise in the world, you must make people respect you. Do you wish to be respected, Colin? Would you like to rise in the world?"

"That's what I'm tryin' to do."

"Yes, I've been watching."

"Not just today. I saw you watchin' me a lot."

"Colin, you're not only smart—you're observant. I come to Covent Garden market often because I have numerous business dealings that require me to feed large numbers of workers. I buy food here in bulk to keep my costs down."

"If you have numerous business dealings, as you call 'em, why don't you hire someone to come here for you?"

"But would that person make as clever a bargain? Never give people responsibility unless you're confident that they can do the job better than *you* can."

"I do everythin' myself."

"So I noticed. Would you like to work for me, Colin?"

"Doin' what?"

The boy was distracted by a man trudging past with a basket of strange-looking objects.

"What in blazes are *those?*"

"Pineapples. They come via ship from a faraway place called the Caribbean. Expensive restaurants pay a premium to have pineapples brought to London for their best customers."

Trask impressed Colin by paying a sovereign for one. "Here. Be careful. It's prickly."

The weight of the pineapple surprised Colin. He almost dropped it. "But how do I eat it?"

"Use a knife to cut off the sharp leaves and remove the core. Then slice what remains. The juice is especially sweet. Perhaps you can share it with your mother."

The seemingly offhanded remark was deliberate. Trask

needed to know whether his suspicion about Colin's mother was correct.

The boy looked down. "My mother's dead."

"I'm sorry to hear that. And your father?"

"Dead." Colin's voice was filled with anger as much as sorrow. "You still haven't told me what work you want me to do."

"It's difficult to explain in all this noise. May I buy you some bread, butter, strawberry jam, and hot tea at the eating house around the corner? Save the pineapple for later. By the way, it was one of my ships and one of my railways that brought the pineapple to London."

"If you're so rich, how come you need *me?*"

"Before I answer . . ." Trask guided him to the pillars at the back of a nearby church. "This once had a convent next to it. The convent had a garden. Over the centuries the name was shortened from 'convent' to 'covent.' Do you find history interesting?"

"The past is all I think about."

"I want to hire you to pretend to be my son."

Jeremiah Trask's nightmarish memory of regret ended abruptly as Colin leaned over the bed. A tear fell from Colin's face and landed next to the tears that Trask himself wept.

"Did you ever consider how many people might still be alive if you hadn't approached me that morning in Covent Garden market?" Colin asked. "I might have died from disease or starvation. Or else I might have been so exhausted earning pennies that I wouldn't have had the strength to pursue my revenge."

In the darkest of the night, in his blackest thoughts, Jeremiah Trask had indeed deluded himself that he could muster the willpower to reverse time, to go back to the past and make it different.

If only. If only.

At Covent Garden market, he had told the boy, "I'm going to spend a week at the estate of a business competitor while he and I negotiate a merger. He has a boy about your age. It would help my negotiations if you come with me, pretending to be my son. I'll explain that your mother lived apart from me in Italy, that she died recently, and that I decided to accept responsibility for you. That will make me seem a person of character. If you become friends with his son, it might encourage a friendship between his father and me, helping the negotiations."

Promising Colin twenty pounds, Trask had taken him to a country house, where servants bathed him and cut his hair and provided him with clothes of a quality Colin had never dreamed of. He was given food of a variety and abundance unimaginable to him, and in such quantity that for a brief time it made him ill. An actor arrived to teach him how to disguise his Irish accent. He was given details about his supposed life in Italy with Trask's supposed wife.

All of it had been a lie. Jeremiah Trask had no such wife. The business rival was actually one of Trask's friends, and the other boy had been the friend's companion, not his son. During the week at the estate, it was too much to expect that Colin wouldn't sometimes lapse into his Irish accent. Even so, he made a commendable effort, and when he failed, he had the wit to explain that his supposed mother had employed an Irish servant whose accent was contagious. No, the accent wasn't the point. That could be corrected. The point was to determine whether Colin could stay with the story about Trask's wife having died in Italy and about Trask having accepted responsibility for his son.

Colin was so amazingly believable that Trask rewarded him by taking him to Paris and showing him the opulence that Trask could provide. One night, after encouraging Colin to drink two glasses of wine, Trask entered the darkness of his bedroom and crawled into his bed.

"I had a terrible choice to make," Colin had explained to him years later, after Trask was paralyzed. "If I protested and screamed, you'd simply have told anyone who knocked on the door that your son had suffered a nightmare. Then you would have abandoned me in the worst of Paris's streets. With revulsion tearing at my stomach, I agreed to do what you wanted. All the time I kept thinking of my mother and father and sisters. I told myself that if your wealth could be the means by which I achieved my revenge, then I would pay the cost. I would suffer anything for my family, just as *they* suffered."

And suffering there was. Night after night. With Jeremiah Trask's business associates and his servants actually believing that Colin was Trask's son—how else could Trask cohabit with a boy and not fear being hanged?—Trask had imposed the discipline he expected a son of his to tolerate. Colin had the best tutors so that his conversation wouldn't embarrass Trask in front of his associates. Colin worked on Trask's railways, helping to dig the channels and lay down the tracks until calluses grew so thick on his hands that he knew he would never be rid of them. "If you're my son, you'll show everyone you're a man!" Trask had said, so that no one would suspect what Trask did to him each night.

In an anguish of remembering, Jeremiah Trask peered up through his tears. If only he had never gone to Covent Garden market that day. If only he hadn't seen the desperate Irish boy.

His mind leapt forward to the summer seven years later when he'd told Colin that he'd grown too old to be of interest. "I'm sending you on a tour of Europe. You'll have enough money to establish a new identity. In a few months I'll tell everyone that, like my supposed wife, you sadly died from fever in Italy."

Trask   relived   his   shock   as   Colin—amazingly

strong—roared and threw him from the private car of the moving train. He remembered the panic that replaced his shock . . . then the pain that replaced his panic . . . and then the absence of pain as he lay paralyzed across a rail on the opposite set of tracks, blinking at the cinder-filled smoke that the train's departing engine spewed.

Trask wept for all his sins. *Yes, if only. God help me, if only.*

Colin leaned over him. "Father, Mother, Emma, Ruth, Catherine, and the child I didn't have a chance to name." Abruptly the Irish accent dropped away. "Tonight, a woman whose likeness and blue eyes remind me of my dead sister—even their names, Emma and Emily, are similar—said that she was ashamed to know me. She called me a monster for threatening a two-year-old child. She said that I didn't deserve Catherine and that I didn't deserve to be a brother, a husband, or a father."

More tears dripped from the tormented, blood-covered face hovering above Trask.

"Many times over the years, I could have killed the queen whenever her carriage left the palace and proceeded up Constitution Hill. It wouldn't have been difficult. The only requirements are planning and the will to do it. But I kept postponing it, finding others to punish first. Did I fail to kill the queen tonight because I couldn't bear for my hatred to end? Did I put myself in a position to fail so that I could try to kill the queen again and again and again? If I finally succeeded in punishing her, what then? Only *you* would have remained. And after you, who else could I have found to hate?"

Colin O'Brien, or Anthony Trask, or whoever this man was, looked around in search of something. "Do you recall what I told you I would do if you answered questions from strangers when I wasn't here? I vowed to imprison you even more in your body by blinding you."

Trask felt terror growing within him. *Is he reaching for scissors or acid?*

Instead, the hand that came into view held a bottle of lauda-num, one of the medications on the table next to the bed.

"Who would I finally have found to hate and punish? The person who killed my beloved wife and my unborn child."

The anguished man pointed at himself.

"My punishment can never be severe enough. Long ago I vowed that one day I would allow myself the ultimate satisfac-tion of lancing your eyes and your eardrums. Blind, deaf, unable to feel, you'd be entombed in the darkness and silence of your paralyzed body, with nothing to do except to bemoan the cesspit that you are."

Colin trembled and opened the laudanum bottle.

"As the start of my punishment, I refuse to do that. Instead I shall do something that every part of me screams for me *not* to do. To give myself pain, I'll perform a kindness to you and put an end to your suffering. Are you weary of being impris-oned in your body? Would you like me to end your penance and pour this opium down your throat? You'll drift quickly off to sleep, and perhaps your final dreams will be about some-thing other than your sins. Would you allow me to begin *my* punishment by ending *your* punishment?"

Squeezing away his tears, Jeremiah Trask shut his eyes once. His voice would have broken with gratitude if he'd been able to speak.

Yes!

For a second time, De Quincey stepped down from a police wagon in front of the mansion on Bolton Street. As snow blew past, an overhead lamp allowed him to study the front door.

"There aren't any tracks leading up to it," Commissioner Mayne noted.

"All the same, I'm certain that he came here," De Quincey said. "At the palace, when I asked him to explain about Jeremiah Trask, the look of hate on his face was so profound that I can't imagine him not returning here to deal with that hate before he runs."

Accompanied by three constables, they approached the door and knocked. No one answered. When De Quincey tried the door, he found it unsecured. "The same as at the homes of his other victims."

De Quincey pushed the door open and felt relieved that he didn't discover the corpse of a servant lying on the floor.

"What do I hear?" Commissioner Mayne asked.

Muffled shouts and pounding led them downstairs to the servants' area.

A key protruded from a locked door next to the kitchen. The door rumbled with the frenzy of the assault on the inside.

When a constable unlocked it, four desperate servants hurried out, blurting what had happened.

De Quincey cautiously led the way to the upper levels. The door to the bedroom was open. In response to a groan, one of the constables entered first, then motioned for everyone else to follow him.

Holding his bleeding head, a policeman rose from the floor. A servant hurried to him.

De Quincey and Commissioner Mayne approached the motionless figure on the bed. There was a difference between the immobility of paralysis and the immobility of death. After eight years of having been imprisoned within his body, Jeremiah Trask finally wore a peaceful expression. His eyes were closed. An empty laudanum bottle lay next to him.

De Quincey withdrew his own bottle and swallowed from it.

"This is where opium will lead you," the commissioner warned.

De Quincey shrugged. "But now whatever memories afflicted him have finally been extinguished, and he suffers no regrets."

A constable entered the bedroom. "Commissioner, footprints in the snow approach and leave through the kitchen's back door. I followed them, but they merged with other footprints on a nearby street. There's no way to tell where he went."

"So he's still out there, waiting for another chance to kill the queen," Mayne said.

"Or perhaps he's finished," De Quincey offered. "Whatever his reason for hating this man, something in him changed. Notice the peaceful expression on Jeremiah Trask's face. He wasn't afraid of what was being done to him. This death wasn't an act of hate. It was a blessing."

"Good evening, My Lord," De Quincey said, rising as a servant opened the door and Lord Palmerston entered. Outside, a coach departed from the curved driveway, disappearing into the darkness and the snowfall.

Only a few days earlier, De Quincey had stood on this spot, greeting Lord Palmerston for what he had assumed would be his final hours in London. An eternity of terror had happened in the meantime, somehow making him feel alive, but now despair again settled over him, and given what he was about to do, he believed that this occasion would truly mark his final hours in London.

"Once more, I find you lurking on my staircase," Lord Palmerston said. His bandaged left arm was in a sling.

"I trust that Dr. Snow treated your wound with his usual skill," De Quincey told him.

"He recommends rest, which I'm about to enjoy before tomorrow's cabinet meeting about a new war offensive. If you'll kindly step aside . . ."

"My Lord, I'd like to discuss the confidential matter that I alluded to yesterday evening."

"Confidential matter?"

"Edward Oxford and Young England, My Lord."

Lord Palmerston gave him a warning look. "Are you really determined to do this?"

"I consider it essential, My Lord."

With a stern gaze, Lord Palmerston mounted the staircase. De Quincey followed him into the ballroom, where His Lordship closed the door, then walked across the vast area towards a table and two chairs arranged along the back wall.

"This will be sufficient to prevent us from being overheard."

"My Lord, when I visited Edward Oxford in Bedlam, he spoke as if he believed that Young England was real. He was mystified by the evidence that the group didn't exist."

"Of course," Lord Palmerston said. "An inability to distinguish reality from fantasy is the reason Oxford resides in the madhouse."

"He was also mystified that his two pistols didn't contain bullets."

"Because he can't separate what he actually did from what he imagined he did."

"But depending on one's perceptions, there are many realities, My Lord."

"I don't have time for your ravings."

"My Lord, in eighteen thirty-seven, when Her Majesty ascended the throne, she was cheered. People welcomed her after the excess and immorality of her recent predecessors. Young, smiling, and full of life, she astonished her subjects by appearing in public every day. Her smiles brought joy, the sense of a new beginning."

"Yes, yes, what is your point?"

"Only three years later, Her Majesty was despised. Her marriage to Prince Albert was greeted with alarm. People feared that he would bankrupt the nation by channelling its funds to his poor German state and indeed that he would transform England into a German colony. Meanwhile the queen interfered in politics, expressing strong approval of one party over another. People were afraid that she would abolish any party with which she disagreed and return the nation to the tyranny of earlier times. There was talk about doing away with the monarchy."

"But Her Majesty was still learning," Lord Palmerston protested. "Yes, she shouldn't have cared which party happened to enjoy power at any particular time. The pendulum always swings from one side to the other. A queen is supposed to be above the vagaries of government. She needs to be steady, representing the constancy of the nation. But Her Majesty learned and became a great monarch. All she required was the time to adapt."

"Which you provided for her," De Quincey said.

The most powerful politician in England narrowed his eyes. "Perhaps I don't understand you."

"It must have taken your operatives a long while to locate exactly the right person—someone who had difficulty finding employment, who was poor and aggrieved, and who displayed eccentric behaviour such as staring at walls and suddenly bursting into laughter."

"Be careful."

"Your operatives pretended to be part of a group of rebels called Young England. They claimed to take orders from Her Majesty's uncle, who supposedly plotted the takeover of England from the German state he ruled."

"Truly, I caution you."

"I assume that there were meetings in which Oxford was introduced to some of the supposed members of Young England, who were actually your operatives. They elected him secretary of the group. He was told the names of the supposed members and dutifully recorded them, along with details of its meetings. With the assurance that he would begin a bold new day for England, he was persuaded to shoot at Her Majesty."

"Do you realize what I can do to prevent you from speaking this way?"

"At the least, you can put me in Bedlam the way you disposed of Edward Oxford. If he'd been executed, he might have become a martyr, but someone in a madhouse is merely pathetic, babbling about an imaginary organization. He truly believed that Young England existed. He truly believed that the pistols he fired were loaded. But of course, when your operatives provided him with the weapons, they made certain that the barrels contained only gunpowder and wadding so that Her Majesty couldn't be injured. She knew nothing about the plot, but her reaction to being shot at fitted the scenario perfectly. She ordered her driver to proceed calmly onward. She completed her announced carriage outing to Hyde Park and even went to visit her mother in Belgravia. What a brave monarch, the people decided, strong and steady. Then came the glorious news, a secret that your operatives spread among the excited crowds, that Her Majesty was with child, that an heir was on the way. Prince Albert was no longer an unwelcome foreigner. He was the father of a possible future ruler. 'God save the queen!' people yelled everywhere."

"The proof that you're insane is that you say these things to my face. I could have you removed to Van Diemen's Land— or worse."

"I realize that, My Lord."

"Then why on earth did you disregard your safety by forcing this conversation upon me?"

"My intent is to help you exercise your new responsibilities as prime minister, My Lord."

"I can't imagine how."

"Because of your actions fifteen years ago, the queen was nearly killed tonight."

"What?" Lord Palmerston said.

"In a crossing of destinies that you couldn't possibly have

foreseen, the desperate Irish boy happened to occupy the same space that Edward Oxford and Queen Victoria did. Would Colin O'Brien have been as consumed with the need for revenge if he hadn't been there when Edward Oxford fired his two pistols? Was that the moment when his anger acquired a focus? Would he have killed Lord and Lady Cosgrove, Lord and Lady Grantwood, and how many other victims we don't know about if Edward Oxford hadn't provided the example? But Oxford didn't inspire only Colin O'Brien. He also inspired John Francis, John William Bean Junior, and William Hamilton, all of whom said that they were prompted to shoot at Her Majesty because of the example Oxford provided."

Lord Palmerston shifted in his chair.

"My Lord, to preserve the monarchy and to give Her Majesty the time to learn to be a queen, fifteen years ago you unwittingly set forces in motion that almost led to her death many times since then, and especially tonight. My purpose in coming here is to remind you that, with the immense power that you now possess, you have an even greater obligation to imagine consequences."

"If I accepted your logic, I wouldn't do anything."

"Yes, absolute power creates an absolute burden." De Quincey stood. "My Lord, I shall never speak a word about this conversation to anyone. Think of me as the rarest person you know."

"Rarest? I don't understand."

De Quincey drank from his laudanum bottle. "I'm the only person you ever met who cares so little about himself that he will tell you the absolute truth."

Her knuckles swollen, Emily sat between Becker and Ryan. The two men rested on beds in a small servants' room in the attic of Lord Palmerston's mansion.

Becker's head was heavily bandaged. Ryan kept still, trying not to aggravate the restitched wound in his abdomen.

"It seems that we haven't come far from where we were seven weeks ago," Emily said.

"If anything"—Becker winced from his headache—"we've taken a step backwards."

Seated next to Emily, De Quincey offered his laudanum bottle. "A sip of this will remove your pain."

"No, Father," Emily told him.

"At least our injuries have one benefit," Ryan said. "Thanks to Dr. Snow's suggestion, you and your father decided to remain in London a while longer to help us get back on our feet."

Emily suppressed a smile.

"The thanks should go to Lord Palmerston for extending his hospitality," De Quincey suggested.

Emily shook her head. "He's not being generous. His motive is to keep us close. He always seems to worry that we know something we shouldn't."

"I have no idea what that would be," De Quincey said.

A tall, slender figure appeared in the doorway.

"Your Highness!" Emily exclaimed, standing, curtsying quickly.

With Lord Palmerston behind him, Prince Albert nodded. "Inspector Ryan, please don't try to raise yourself. Nor you, Detective Sergeant Becker. Lord Palmerston suggested that you come downstairs to meet me, but I decided that your injuries would make that difficult, so I came to you."

"We're deeply honoured, Your Highness," Ryan said.

The prince looked around with curiosity, no doubt unaccustomed to the austerity of servants' quarters. "Are you comfortable in this small area? I could arrange for you to be transferred to the palace."

"Your Highness, these accommodations are only temporary," Lord Palmerston assured him. "My staff is preparing larger rooms for them. And for Miss De Quincey and her father," he added quickly. "They are welcome here."

"Her Majesty will be pleased to hear it. I came personally to invite all of you to a dinner at the palace as soon as your injuries permit."

"Dinner at the palace," Becker marvelled. "If only my parents were alive to hear about this."

"We also intend to bestow a suitable honour upon all of you, but as Lord Palmerston points out, at this critical time of the war, we can't acknowledge that an attempt was made on Her Majesty's life, lest it imply that she is vulnerable. It might encourage other threats. We'll find another way of rewarding you."

"A reward isn't necessary, Your Highness," Ryan said. "The safety of you, Her Majesty, and your family is reward enough."

"Inspector Ryan, you could be a politician." Prince Albert chuckled.

That prompted Ryan to chuckle also, then wince and again hold his freshly repaired wound.

"As for Miss De Quincey, no reward could measure our gratitude for saving our son's life."

"I merely combined my intuition with what Dr. Snow trained me to do, Your Highness."

"Your quick thinking prompted me to appreciate the practicality of your bloomer skirt. If you'd been wearing a hoop, you wouldn't have had the mobility to attend to my son. In gratitude, I brought you this." He handed Emily an envelope.

When Emily opened it and read its message, her confusion changed to surprise.

"Dr. Snow informed us that you considered applying to Florence Nightingale to be trained as a nurse," Prince Albert said.

"Be trained as a nurse?" Ryan asked.

"Oh, yes," Becker told him. "Emily and I had a long discussion about it."

"When did you have time to talk about *this?* While I was risking my life in the Seven Dials rookery?"

"Miss De Quincey, Her Majesty and I decided that if you want freedom of choice for women, then you should have this opportunity," Prince Albert continued. "We're aware of your limited means. If you decide to learn to become a nurse, we wish to provide you with a stipend, books, clothing, and a place to live in the palace. I should also mention food. I think that we're sufficiently acquainted for me to say that I heard your stomach rumbling during dinner the other night."

"I'm speechless, Your Majesty."

"As rare for her as it is for her father," Lord Palmerston murmured.

"Take as much time as you need to decide whether you wish to do this," Prince Albert said. "Of course, it would be challenging."

"As Sean and Joseph and my father know, I welcome challenges." Despite her raw knuckles, Emily held Sean's hand and Joseph's. When she smiled at her father, tears stung her eyes. "At the moment, however, I can't imagine being separated from the three people who are the most important to me in the world."

"What is your name?"

"Jonathan."

"Good. Not Jon or Johnnie."

The newsboy came to attention. "Yes, I've been told that if I want people to respect me, I should use my formal name. Is it you, sir? Your voice is familiar, but I didn't recognize you without your beard."

"We're supposed to have a meeting tonight."

"Yes, on Old Gravel Lane in Wapping."

"Tell the others I won't be there. I won't be at any of our meetings again."

"But what about Young England, sir? What's to become of us? You promised that we could bring the rich down to our level!"

"Or rise to theirs. Perhaps this money will help you to rise. Take it to the group. Divide it equally. It will serve you for a long time."

"But Young England . . ."

". . . is no more."

A Letter from William Russell

9 March 1855

Dear Mr. De Quincey:

Not having your address, I'm sending this letter to Detective Sergeant Becker, whom I met on a February night that I'm certain you remember. I suspect that the cleverness of Scotland Yard will enable him to locate you. For reasons of military security, I'm unable to tell you precisely where I am. Suffice to say, I'm back in the Crimea, in the thick of the new Allied offensive. The earlier details are in my dispatches to *The Times.* I won't repeat them here. The purpose of my letter is personal, although again for security reasons, I shall continue to be vague. With the passage of years, I hope that one day I'll be at liberty to write the tragic story that I learned on that terrible February night.

An odd thing has happened, as if I have seen a ghost. Although I have no basis for believing that the man whom I cannot name is dead, the chill is the same. A week ago, when the offensive began, I made my way as close to the fighting as I dared. One particular figure caught my attention. He fought with an astonishing frenzy, using all his ammunition, picking up the muskets of dead soldiers, using *their* ammunition, constantly lunging forward across muddy slopes, thrusting his bayonet, killing, killing. His ferocity was amazing. In my nearly a year in the Crimea, I have seen only one other man who demonstrated that relentless determination. I might almost call it savagery. You know to whom I refer. As I observed this soldier a week ago, and on the next day, and on the day after that, the similarities became more manifest, until I began to wonder if they were possibly the same person.

I observed him only from a distance. He has a beard, while the other man was clean-shaven, so it's difficult to be certain. Their height and weight are the same, as is the inexorable way they move. I questioned officers, but none could identify him or tell me to which unit he belongs. Perhaps he is all alone. During the battles, I did my best to keep him in sight and to move as close to him as I could, although the enemy's bullets and cannon bombardment are discouraging.

Yesterday, however, I managed to come close enough that he noticed me. Not merely noticed me, but reacted to me, and that is why I believe it is the same man. He stepped back in surprise and indeed alarm. Even from a hundred feet away, I could see his eyes widen with recognition. At once, he turned and made himself disappear among the welter of the gun smoke and the other soldiers.

Perhaps this is only my imagination. Nonetheless, as you are fond of saying, there are many realities. Fearing that I might distract him and make him careless in combat, I have backed away and again observe him only from a distance. But it is he. I am now certain. As I watch his frenzy, I cannot tell whether it is the enemy whom he attacks, or whether in his fantasies he again destroys the people who refused to help his mother and father and sisters, or whether his hatred is actually toward himself. Whatever the cause, a fierce emotion consumes him, and surely he can't persist in this way, constantly exposing himself to Russian fire in order to achieve his vengeance. But perhaps exposing himself is exactly the point. Perhaps his goal is for the enemy to silence the rage within him. If so, fate or the Almighty refuses to grant his desperate wish, and he ruthlessly presses forward, doomed to be in torment, never to find peace.

Through a field telescope, I observed a cannonball strike a slope next to him, hurling him into the air as dirt, rocks, and fragments of the projectile spewed in all directions. Certain that he was dead, I watched with stunned surprise as he squirmed among soldiers who had indeed been killed. He rose unsteadily, picked up his musket, and staggered onward. His right arm, which he had formerly pretended was injured, streamed blood. Bullets tore chunks from the sleeves and sides of his greatcoat, reducing them to tatters. The next time the shock wave of a nearby cannonball knocked him down, he was able to rise only to his hands and knees, clawing for his musket, forcing himself onward, finally collapsing. Stretcher-bearers managed to carry him off the battlefield.

After dark I went to the large tent that serves as a make-shift shelter for the wounded. The care they receive is minimal. Mostly they wait to see who will die or else be shipped to the large military hospital that Florence Nightingale manages on the Turkish mainland near Constantinople. I hoped to speak to him, to satisfy my curiosity. But no matter how intently I went from one horrid cot to another, I couldn't find him. I described him to a surgeon, who remembered him well and said that when the man regained consciousness, he insisted that other wounded men deserved treatment more than he did. After waiting impatiently while his arm was bandaged, he hurried away, having learned that volunteers were needed for a night attack.

I left the tent, peered up at the stars, and prayed for him.

More Adventures with the Opium-Eater

> De Quincey lives on in memory like a character in fiction,
> rather than a reality.
>
> —Jorge Luis Borges

At the end of my previous novel *Murder as a Fine Art*, I explained that a 2009 film, *Creation*—about Charles Darwin's nervous breakdown—prompted my interest in Thomas De Quincey. Darwin's favourite daughter died while he was preparing *On the Origin of Species*. Meanwhile, Darwin's wife, a devout Christian, wanted him to abandon the project because she believed that his theory of evolution promoted atheism. Grieving, he was also guilt-ridden, fearing that God might have killed his daughter as a warning for him to stop.

Darwin's breakdown took the form of persistent headaches, stomach problems, heart palpitations, weakness, and insomnia. In a pre-psychoanalytic world, his doctors were baffled, unable to link all these symptoms to any disease with which they were familiar. At the pivotal moment in the film, a friend suggests the true problem, saying, "You know, Charles, there are people such as Thomas De Quincey who maintain that we can be controlled by thoughts and emotions that we don't know we have."

This sounded like Freud, but *Creation* is set in the mid-1850s, and Freud didn't develop his ideas until the 1890s. Was the reference an anachronism, I wondered, or did De Quincey actually anticipate Freud?

The rest of the film was a blur to me. I couldn't wait for it to end so that I could hurry to my old college textbooks and learn more about De Quincey, whom my nineteenth-century English literature professors had relegated to the status of a footnote because of their prejudice against his notorious 1821 memoir, *Confessions of an English Opium-Eater.*

That book was the first literary work to deal with drug dependency, but I discovered that it was far from De Quincey's only "first." He invented the term "subconscious" and did indeed anticipate Freud's psychoanalytic theories by many decades. In addition, he created what he called psychological literary criticism in his famous essay "On the Knocking at the Gate in *Macbeth.*" His fascination with the Ratcliffe Highway murders of 1811—the first publicized mass killings in English history—prompted him to write "Postscript (On Murder Considered as One of the Fine Arts)," in which he dramatized those murders with such vividness that he created the true-crime genre. He wrote amazingly intimate essays about his friends Wordsworth and Coleridge and helped to establish their reputations. He influenced Edgar Allan Poe, who in turn inspired Sir Arthur Conan Doyle to create Sherlock Holmes.

I became so fascinated that I tumbled down a Victorian rabbit hole. Until then, my novels had mostly been about contemporary American subjects. To cross an ocean and go back more than a century and a half required research equivalent to earning a doctorate about London in the 1850s. For several years, the only books I read were related to that city and that period. Those fogbound streets (a large map of 1850s London hangs in my office) often felt more real than what was happening around me.

One of my goals was to see how closely fact could be combined with fiction. For example, the two snowstorms depicted here are based on newspaper reports about unusually severe winter weather that struck London during early

February of 1855, allowing me to substitute snow for the notorious London fogs, known as "particulars," that I described in *Murder as a Fine Art*.

William Russell's shocking dispatches from the Crimea did cause the British government to collapse on Tuesday, 30 January 1855. On Sunday, 4 February, Queen Victoria did reluctantly ask Lord Palmerston to become prime minister, and on Tuesday, 6 February, he assumed his duties, as I indicate here.

Birds in cages indeed decorated the galleries of Bedlam. Jay's Mourning Warehouse existed. The ice-skating accident in St. James's Park is based on an 1853 magazine account. So too is the account of the starving boy who earned pennies at Covent Garden market by keeping thieves away from carts while farmers delivered their vegetables. The menu at Queen Victoria's dinner is taken from *Mrs. Beeton's Book of Household Management,* a contemporary social-etiquette manual with such influence that even the queen's kitchen staff would have consulted it. Tavern owners hired doctors of drink to adulterate gin and beer, using the recipes I provide. Rat poison was an ingredient in the green dye of clothing. Seating in churches was based on the box-pew system that I describe. Members of the congregation rented the pews and gained access via keys that pew-openers carried. Wealthy churchgoers sometimes equipped their pews with canopies and curtains.

Lord Palmerston's mansion, directly across from Green Park, still exists. Once known as Cambridge House (because it was owned by the Duke of Cambridge), today it's the only property on Piccadilly that's set back from the street and has a semicircular driveway. A Naval and Military Club purchased it after Lord Palmerston's death in 1865 and attached In and Out signs at the gates to direct arriving and departing vehicles, with the result that the building acquired the nickname the In and Out Club. Deserted since the 1990s, it fell into disrepair. In 2011, two wealthy brothers announced their intention to renovate it for £214 million and make it the most expensive residential property in London, but by early 2014 repairs had not yet begun, and the ghost of Lord Palmerston seemed to haunt it.

Similarly, Commissioner Mayne did live in the Chester Square area of Belgravia. That exclusive London district isn't named after a European country in an operetta. Rather, its name derives from the aristocratic Belgrave family, who developed the area. Its adjacent white-stuccoed mansions rivalled those of Mayfair, with the added luxury that the streets were wider. These days, many of its buildings function as embassies.

St. James's Church still exists, despite massive damage during World War Two. If you visit this simple, wondrous church at the south-eastern corner of Mayfair, you'll feel transported back in time. Light streaming through the tall windows indicates why Sir Christopher Wren favoured this church more than any other that he designed, including St. Paul's Cathedral.

The graveyard at St. Anne's Church in Soho still exists also. This is where Colin O'Brien imagines that his family was buried. The yard is elevated above the street, the result of soil having been frequently added during the Victorian period as more and more bodies were buried on top of one another. Sometimes gravediggers jumped up and down on the previous remains in order to make room for new occupants. If you'd like to see photographs of many of the locations in this novel, please go to the *Inspector of the Dead* section of my website, www.davidmorrell.net, or else www.mulholland-books.com.

As a further example of how I tried to link fact with fiction, the only Thomas De Quincey detail that I invented is his presence in London in 1855. He was actually in Edinburgh at that time. Otherwise, every biographical reference to him is factual. His dead sisters, the Edinburgh sanctuary where he hid from debt collectors, the Glasgow observatory where he also hid from debt collectors, his failed friendship with Wordsworth, his opium dreams about sphinxes and crocodiles, the landlord who held him captive for a year, his chance meeting with King George III and his lie that his family had a noble lineage dating back to the Norman Conquest, his habit of setting fire to his hair when he leaned over candles and wrote—the list could go on and on. Also, I incorporated numerous passages from De Quincey's work into his dialogue. My fascination with him is so great that after several rereadings of his thousands of pages, I started to feel that I was channelling his spirit.

Form should match content. *Inspector of the Dead* incorporates many literary elements from the Victorian era. While modern novels almost never use the third-person omniscient viewpoint, novels of the nineteenth century favoured it (the beginnings of Dickens's *A Tale of Two Cities* and *Bleak House*, for example), allowing an objective narrator to step forward and provide information. That device is helpful in explaining elements of Victorian life that modern readers would otherwise find baffling. I ignored another modern convention by mixing the third-person viewpoint with a first-person journal and a first-person letter. This combination is seldom used today but was common in Victorian novels. Employing nineteenth-century techniques to dramatize nineteenth-century London felt liberating, old devices suddenly feeling new.

Inspector of the Dead is my version of a specific type of Victorian novel. The thriller as we know it was invented during the mid-1800s in what disapproving critics of the period called the sensation novel. Previous thrillers tended to take place in remote locations and distant times, involving clanking chains and draughty castles, but sensation novelists brought immediacy to their thrills, postulating that very real terrors occurred in the very immediate present in very familiar London locations that readers walked past every day.

Another previous thriller tradition, known as the Newgate novel, portrayed the exploits of thieves and murderers among the lower class, the best-known example of which is again by Dickens: *Oliver Twist*. But sensation novelists postulated that vicious crimes occurred not only in slums but in the supposedly respectable houses of the middle and upper classes, a concept that provoked outrage among highbrowed critics, who maintained that wealth, education, and good breeding were antidotes against evil impulses.

The first famous sensation novel was Wilkie Collins's *The Woman in White* (1859–60), the female-in-jeopardy chills of which set off a merchandising extravaganza involving items such as *Woman in White* stationery, perfume, clothing, and sheet music. People named their pets and their children after characters in that novel. Two other novels reinforced the power of this new genre: Mrs. Henry Wood's *East Lynne* (1861) and Mary Elizabeth Braddon's *Lady Audley's Secret* (1862). Although Collins and Mrs. Wood became less popular after the 1860s, Braddon (my favorite of the three) enjoyed a successful career until the end of the century.

Sensation novels favoured topics such as insanity, arson, bigamy, adultery, abortion, poisonings, forced imprisonment, madhouses, stolen identities, drug abuse, and violent alcoholism. De Quincey's *Confessions of an English Opium-Eater* is an early example of sensation literature. Also, his "Postscript (On Murder Considered as One of the Fine Arts)" illustrates the start of the genre, as do his suspense-filled novellas "The Household Wreck" and "The Avenger," elements of which I incorporated here. In one of the first detective novels, *The Moonstone* (1868), Wilkie Collins acknowledged his literary debt to De Quincey by using *Confessions of an English Opium-Eater* to solve the mystery. Because of the regard Collins felt for De Quincey, I couldn't resist borrowing a location from *The Moonstone:* the Wheel of Fortune tavern, on Shore Lane, just off Lower Thames Road, where a major incident occurs in this novel.

The numerous attempts against Queen Victoria aren't fiction. After Edward Oxford, John Francis, John William Bean Jr., William Hamilton, and Robert Francis Pate attacked the queen, there was indeed a sixth would-be assassin, although he didn't make his attempt in 1855, as I imagine, but rather in 1872. A seventh man attacked the queen in 1882, firing at her carriage as she departed from the Windsor train station.

But even though Victoria amazingly survived so much violence, her life had effectively ended two decades earlier. In November of 1861, Prince Albert became ill with what at first seemed to be influenza. As his chills and fever worsened, he was diagnosed with typhoid fever. After several weeks of suffering, surrounded by his family and friends, he died at Windsor Castle on 14 December. His popularity had waxed and waned during the twenty-one years that he was married to Queen Victoria. As if to compensate for the periods of low esteem, the nation entered a marathon of grief that lasted not merely the traditional year but an entire decade, during which countless communities erected monuments to him.

Queen Victoria's grief lasted not a year or a decade but the next forty years. Seldom seen in public except when a new statue was dedicated to Albert, she secluded herself in Windsor Castle. Always wearing black, she frequented the prince's death chamber, taking care that everything was preserved as he had left it, to the point that its linen was changed daily and hot water for shaving was delivered each morning. In contrast with her youthful intentions, she became as remote from her subjects as her predecessors had been.

There's no evidence that Edward Oxford was a pawn in a

conspiracy, but when I read various accounts about his attack on the queen, I realized that the events could be interpreted two ways. Whatever the truth behind his actions, after twenty-seven years of his incarceration, first in Bedlam and then in the Broadmoor Criminal Lunatic Asylum, his physicians convinced the government that he was sane. They pointed out that he had made productive use of his time, learning Greek, Latin, Spanish, Italian, German, and French. In addition, he had learned to play chess and had developed skill as a painter, earning £60 for his efforts.

Perhaps Queen Victoria agreed to the government's recommendation for clemency because Oxford's new home at the Broadmoor asylum wasn't far from Windsor Castle. It may be that she imagined him escaping and sneaking through the woods to attack her again. The condition of Oxford's release was that he would leave England and never return. In 1867, more than two and a half decades after he shot at the queen, he sailed to Australia, where he settled in Melbourne, in the state of Victoria, names that are doubly ironic because Melbourne was serving as prime minister when Oxford shot at Victoria. Using the allegorical alias John Freeman, he married and became a journalist. Nobody, not even his wife, knew his infamous background. He died in 1900, at the age of seventy-eight. Victoria died one year later, at the age of eighty-one, her remarkable sixty-four-year reign having defined an era.

Acknowledgments

I'm indebted to De Quincey biographers Grevel Lindop (*The Opium-Eater: A Life of Thomas De Quincey*) and Robert Morrison (*The English Opium-Eater: A Biography of Thomas De Quincey*). The quality of their scholarship is matched by their generosity in answering my questions and guiding me through De Quincey's world.

In Grevel Lindop's case, he literally became a guide, escorting me through De Quincey locations in Manchester, England (where De Quincey was born), and Grasmere in the Lake District (where De Quincey lived in Dove Cottage after Wordsworth moved out). Meanwhile Robert Morrison sent me numerous pieces by and about De Quincey that I hadn't been able to locate and that were invaluable to my research. Sometimes we exchanged e-mails several times a day.

Historian Judith Flanders graciously answered my questions and offered advice. Her books about Victorian culture—especially *The Victorian House*, *The Victorian City*, and *The Invention of Murder (How the Victorians Revelled in Death and Detection and Created Modern Crime)*—are central to my understanding of London in the 1850s. In addition to being a consummate scholar, Judith is also a novelist (*Writer's Block*) and has a rare sense of humour.

For more information about Queen Victoria's attackers, read Paul Thomas Murphy's *Shooting Victoria: Madness, Mayhem, and the Rebirth of the British Monarchy*.

The go-to volume for information about the Crimean War is Orlando Figes's *The Crimean War: A History*.

About Queen Victoria and Prince Albert, read Gillian Gill's *We Two: Victoria and Albert, Rulers, Partners, Rivals*.

The following books were very helpful also: Peter Ackroyd's *London: A Biography*, Richard D. Altick's *Victorian People and Ideas*, Anne-Marie Beller's *Mary Elizabeth Braddon: A Companion to the Mystery Fiction*, Alfred Rosling Bennett's *London and Londoners in the 1850s and 1860s* (a memoir), Ian Bondeson's *Queen Victoria's Stalker: The Strange Case of the Boy Jones*, Mark Bostridge's *Florence Nightingale*, David Brown's *Palmerston: A Biography*, Jennifer Carnell's *The Literary Lives of Mary Elizabeth Braddon*, Belton Cobb's *The First Detectives and the Early Career of Richard Mayne, Police Commissioner*, Tim Pat Coogan's *The Famine Plot: England's Role in Ireland's Greatest Tragedy*, Heather Creaton's *Victorian Diaries: The Daily Lives of Victorian Men and Women*, Judith Flanders's *Consuming Passions: Leisure and Pleasure in Victorian Britain*, Alison Gernsheim's *Victorian and Edwardian Fashion: A Photographic Survey*, Ruth Goodman's *How to Be a Victorian*, Winifred Hughes's *The Maniac in the Cellar: Sensation Novels of the 1860s*, Steven Johnson's *The Ghost Map: The Story of London's Most Terrifying Epidemic*, Petrus de Jon's *De Quincey's Loved Ones*, Henry Mayhew's *London Labour and the London Poor* (a contemporary account published in 1861–62), Sally Mitchell's *Daily Life in Victorian England*, Chris Payne's *The Chieftain: Victorian True Crime through the Eyes of a Scotland Yard Detective*, Liza Picard's *Victorian London*, Catherine Peters's *The King of Inventors: A Life of Wilkie Collins*, Daniel Pool's *What Jane Austen Ate and Charles Dickens Knew*, Charles Manby Smith's *Curiosities of London* (an 1853 account), Lytton Strachey's *Eminent Victorians* and his *Queen Victoria*, Judith Summers's *Soho: A History of London's Most Colourful Neighborhood*, Kate Summerscale's *The Suspicions of Mr.*

Whicher (A Shocking Murder and the Undoing of a Great Victorian Detective) and her *Mrs. Robinson's Disgrace: The Private Diary of a Victorian Lady,* F. M. L. Thompson's *The Rise of Respectable Society (A Social History of Victorian Britain 1830–1900),* J. J. Tobias's *Crime and Police in England 1700–1900,* and Yvonne M. Ward's *Censoring Queen Victoria: How Two Gentlemen Edited a Queen and Created an Icon.*

The complete *Works of Thomas De Quincey* are available in twenty-one volumes, for which Grevel Lindop acted as general editor. Robert Morrison edited two compact collections, *Confessions of an English Opium-Eater* and *Thomas De Quincey: On Murder.* David Wright's edition of *Thomas De Quincey: Recollections of the Lakes and the Lake Poets* features De Quincey's candid reminiscences about Coleridge and Wordsworth.

I'm grateful for the friendship and guidance of Jane Dystel and Miriam Goderich along with the other good folks at Dystel & Goderich Literary Management, especially Lauren E. Abramo, Mike Hoogland, Sharon Pelletier, and Rachel Stout.

I'm also indebted to the splendid team at Mulholland Books/Little, Brown/Hachette, particularly (in alphabetical order) Reagan Arthur, Pamela Brown, Judith Clain, Josh Kendall, Wes Miller, Miriam Parker, Amelia Possanza, Michael Pietsch, and Ruth Tross (in the UK).

My wife, Donna, gave her usual excellent advice. It takes a special personality to be married to a writer. I thank her for her decades of patience and understanding when each day for many hours I become a hermit.

About the Author

David Morrell was born in Kitchener, Ontario, Canada. As a teenager, he became a fan of the classic television series *Route 66*, about two young men in a Corvette convertible driving across the country in search of themselves. The scripts by Stirling Silliphant so impressed Morrell that he decided to become a writer.

The work of another writer (Hemingway scholar Philip Young) prompted Morrell to move to the United States, where he studied with Young at the Pennsylvania State University and received his M.A. and Ph.D. There, he also met the esteemed science fiction author William Tenn (real name Philip Klass), who taught Morrell the basics of fiction writing. The result was *First Blood,*a groundbreaking novel about a returned Vietnam veteran suffering from post-traumatic stress disorder who comes into conflict with a small-town police chief and fights his own version of the Vietnam War.

That "father" of modern action novels was published in 1972 while Morrell was a professor in the English department at the University of Iowa. He taught there from 1970 to 1986, simultaneously writing other novels, many of them international bestsellers, including the classic spy trilogy *The Brotherhood of the Rose* (the basis for the only television mini-series to be broadcast after a Super Bowl), *The Fraternity of the Stone,*and *The League of Night and Fog.*

Eventually wearying of two professions, Morrell gave up his academic tenure in order to write full time. Shortly afterwards, his fifteen-year-old son Matthew was diagnosed with a rare form of bone cancer and died in 1987, a loss that haunts not only Morrell's life but his work, as in his memoir about Matthew, *Fireflies,* and his novel *Desperate Measures,*whose main character lost a son.

"The mild-mannered professor with the bloody-minded visions," as one reviewer called him, Morrell is the author of more than thirty books, including *Murder as a Fine Art, Creepers,* and*Extreme Denial* (set in Santa Fe, New Mexico, where he lives). An Edgar, Nero, Anthony, and Macavity nominee, Morrell is a three-time recipient of the distinguished Bram Stoker Award from the Horror Writers Association. The International Thriller Writers organization gave him its prestigious Thriller Master Award.

With eighteen million copies of his work in print, his work has been translated into thirty languages. His writing book, *The Successful Novelist,*analyzes what he learned during his more than four decades as an author. Please visit him at www. davidmorrell.net, where you can also see images of Thomas De Quincey, his daughter Emily, and the fascinating Victorian locations featured in *Inspector of the Dead.*